WHISPERED EULOGY

_BY_

LUJANE OUD

CO-WRITER: CHRIS E. CALLEN

TABLE OF CONTENTS

CHAPTER ONE
THE OUTCAST

The older man drove. His seat was adjusted back, way back, and his long spindly legs still seemed to have not-quite-enough room. He controlled the car with a single hand, his arm swinging out widely in front of his reclining body. The other hand held a cup of steaming hot gas-station coffee, balancing it on the dash as if daring it to spill. The car was a 1990 Buick Rivera, bucking the trends towards more fuel-efficient compacts, taking the turns too fast, no seat belt, tires just short of screening through the curves.

Elijah Riley eyed him from the passenger's seat. It all fit what he'd learned so far about Detective Aaron Grayson: his new boss. A new friend? Maybe, but it was hard to say for sure. He could already tell that they didn't exactly see eye to eye. Not in terms of explicit disagreements as general worldviews. They were just very different people. Grayson was old school. Not only was he unapologetic about it, he radiated it. He dressed like a cowboy, drank whiskey straight, chain-smoked, drove a gas-guzzler, and was always quick to volunteer distaste for modern ways and "new-fangled" things. He proudly called himself a "throwback," suggesting he was one of the last examples of a previous, superior, specimen of manhood. A missing link to some kind of better model of masculinity than the bleeding hearts that were taking over.

Elijah's main question: how much of it was an act?

"You okay over there?" Grayson asked, squinting over at his companion. His voice had roughened into a near growl from years of heavy smoking. "You look a little green?"

"Excuse me?"

"Green around the gills," Grayson said. "Like you're thinking about losing your breakfast on my leather seats."

"I'm fine," Elijah said. Initially, he'd thought "green" was in reference to his relative lack of experience. It wouldn't have been the first time his boss had questioned his credentials. Grayson was a thirty-year veteran and Elijah was in his second deployment, only a few years from the academy. "You do take these turns pretty fast."

"I know this road like the back of my hand," Grayson said. The hand in question, gripping the wheel, bore wrinkles, a rough life sketched in their grizzled lines; he looked older than his fifty-five years. "I hate to waste time. Do you want me to slow down?" Grayson cocked an eyebrow. It felt like a test, as did so much of their interactions. Answer carefully, the raised brow seemed to imply. Your answer will determine whether you meet my standards. Whether you can be trusted.

Elijah just shrugged. No big deal. That seemed to satisfy Detective Grayson; he turned his minimal attention back to the road. That morning he'd picked up Elijah from his house along the river at a little after seven. Dora, his two-year old, was still asleep in the next room. Without even thinking about it, Elijah stepped lightly, spoke in whispers, lest they disturb her too-fragile sleep. As he light-stepped around the living room he could hear a hint of Dora's breathing, gentle, calm, and regular, through the open door to the nursery. The sound of her exhalations was a balm to Elijah, a soothing reminder that there was innocence in the universe. That there was hope.

His wife, Helen, had prepared him a travel mug of coffee and gave him a kiss on the cheek. "Have fun," she'd whispered. At the time, Elijah hadn't been sure whether the hint of irony he detected in the statement was in reference to the fact that he was going to investigate a murder or that he'd be spending the whole day with his grumpy and anachronistic partner. She'd heard more than an earful about Aaron Grayson since he'd started the job. Elijah had naturally vented when he first met the man he'd been partnered with and, yes, perhaps he'd called him a "caveman" or something along those lines. That morning, Elijah had hurried to get out of the house, predicting very confidently that if he tarried too long, Grayson would lean on the horn and wake up poor little Dora. When he'd climbed into the passenger's seat, Grayson's hand had been suspended above the horn.

"About time," he'd said.

Now, tearing around a curve in the two-lane mountain road, the coffee was still warm. Elijah took a sip.

"So, what's the story?" he asked. "You didn't give me any details over the phone."

"Murder," Grayson said, his words clipped but delivered in a country drawl. "But I guess I told you that much. Woman, fifty-five. Eleanor Pomeroy."

"Did you know her?"

"No. But everyone around here did," Grayson said. "Mount Hugh is a small town, remember? This isn't Philadelphia." Detective Grayson never missed a chance to remind Elijah that he was an outsider, from a big city. "And Eleanor had been the wife of the mayor, so the locals knew her. If not personally, then by sight. They'd seen her standing beside her husband at podiums and at fundraisers."

"You said she 'had been' the mayor's wife?"

"Yeah. Ex-wife. Word is they split up about six months ago. Happened very quickly. Anyway, they found her this morning. The murder was brutal. Head completely severed." Grayson looked over as he said this last bit, as if to see whether or not Elijah would react. Grayson had him pegged as weak: a big city liberal. Elijah wouldn't give him the satisfaction of reaction. And besides, he was a professional. He kept his expression neutral and merely nodded.

"So, what's your theory?" Elijah asked. "If you don't mind sharing."

"My theory?" Grayson said. "At this point? Well, more often than not, the most likely suspect turns out to be the guilty party. Same with the motive. Not always, but that's where I start. Who was likely to do it? Who had a reason to want this lady dead? Her ex-husband."

"Did he?" Elijah asked. "For what reason?"

"They got divorced, didn't they?" The comment sounded personal. Grayson himself was divorced. It had happened a long time ago, but it still seemed raw when he brought it up. Elijah chose to give Grayson the benefit of the doubt and not assume that he wanted his ex dead. "And the motive? Well, that's simple. Maybe he wasn't ready to man up and move on."

It felt like more bait. Elijah didn't know what the proper response was.

"Hm," he said. "Could be."

They'd only been partners a week. This was their first big case. First homicide. They were still feeling each other out. There might come a time where Elijah would have to tell his partner off, but today was not the day. The road took another turn, up over a rise and skirting along the foothills.

"That's a nice suit," said Grayson.

Elijah looked down at what he was wearing. It was a simple suit. Dark brown. Nothing fancy, nothing designer, if that's what his old-fashioned partner was getting at. Detective Grayson wore simple khakis and a white oxford, but his look was defined by the long black trench coat he wore. It made him look like a refugee from a Western movie, like one of the Earp brothers from Tombstone.

"My wife made it, actually," Elijah eventually said.

"She made it?" Grayson seemed sincerely surprised. "In this day and age, that's surprising. A woman that backs up her man. Takes care of him. That's a rare quality, a girl that knows that her place is in the home. It's commendable. My mom used to make our clothes. Of course, she came up during the depression, so she'd learned austerity the hard way. Women, generally speaking, were made of sterner stock back then."

Elijah found this tangent irksome, more than anything his partner had said to him this morning. He was trying to define Elijah's relationship with his wife in his own outdated terms. Helen wasn't a mere extension of him according to that 1950s model that Grayson was hinting at. They both had ambitions. His wife was a middle-school teacher, with a long-term goal of being an administrator. While caring for their young child, she was back in school, taking correspondence courses towards her master's in educational administration. She was spending more time in the home right now, but that was a temporary situation and part of the life plans they had made together. Step one: move away from Philadelphia. Get Dora out of the city. Let her grow up in the mountains, surrounded by nature and fresh air. Although Elijah felt defensive about his hometown, he didn't think it was the ideal place to raise a daughter. It was with that in mind that Elijah had searched for and found the job with the county police. When Dora was four months, Helen would move into a job in the local school system. No, she wasn't blindly following him. Together, they were a team, and their life was lived according to a strategy. Their objective: happy lives.

Elijah didn't suspect that Grayson would understand that. So, he kept it simple.

"We're very close," Elijah said. "And we back each other up."

"Oh?" Grayson said. "Well, don't let that one get away. She's doing you right. Those ones are rare."

Elijah smiled noncommittally. Grayson seemed determined to filter everything through his personal lens. His old-fashioned view of the world. His bitter attitude towards marriage.

The road took another turn, this one the memorable two-hundred-and-seventy-degree switchback that heralded proximity to the town of Mount Hugh. The road flattened and levelled out and the town laid itself out in front of them, the titular mountain rising in the distance. The sharp granite peaks brushed against low lying wisps of cloud, patches of snow visible towards its top. The rockface dropped off steeply halfway down into sheer cliffs, and towards the base it was lightly forested and peppered with patches of scrubby grass. It was an impressive view and Elijah wondered how growing up with that immensity dominating your horizon would influence your worldview. What would that do to your psychology? In the Philly neighbourhoods where he had been raised, he was surrounded by the verticality of the buildings but at a much smaller scale. He grew up used to cramped conditions. Never felt claustrophobic. To the contrary, it had been the open skies and distant horizons that had taken getting used to. When he first arrived in Colorado, he felt like he'd been transplanted onto an alien planet, one built on a different scale in terms of distance and size.

In the foreground, the town itself had seen better days. A hardware store looked close to collapsing in on itself. The roof dipped down in the middle, tarpaper shingles bunching up. Multiple storefronts were boarded over. A video store lay abandoned, its windows broken out. It was the same story all over the place in America. Small towns were slowly dying as industry moved elsewhere. Their reasons for living severed, these places declined for decades, barely existing. Businesses closed to briefly reopen as second-hand stores on their way to eventual oblivion.

"The town is looking pretty rough, isn't it? Seen better days, I guess," Elijah said, attempting to make conversation. "Not much money coming in."

Grayson grumbled his response. "It might seem that way," he said. "And I know what you're thinking. The town seems barely alive, right? Stumbling along like a zombie? Dead, but doesn't know it yet?" Elijah had to admit, Grayson's guess was pretty close to his thoughts. "But let me tell you, the heart and soul of the small town is its people. It's true here and it's true in every other little mountain town in our jurisdiction. Even once the mills and factories have packed up, it's the people keep the town alive. Marrying and having kids and living and dying. Families. A community. Generations of people living in these mountains. And one thing to keep in mind: our current case it going to rock this community to its core. The locals are not used to this level of violence. This hostility. It's going to feel like an invasion from outside, an assault on the values of these good people. It will attack the very soul of the community."

For a moment, Elijah was stunned quiet. The passion in Grayson's words was unmistakable. Maybe he wasn't all bluster after all. Sure, there were a lot of assumptions and prejudices wrapped up in what he'd said; his lecture about the sense of community in small towns wrongly implied that it was something that it didn't exist in urban areas, and his talk of violence being new to the residents of Mount Hugh suggested that it would be taken for granted in a city. None of that was true. Although he'd grown up in poor cramped neighbourhoods, Elijah had been certainly raised with a sense of security and among a community of values. Probably not all that different from the old-school values Grayson had been raised with, to be honest. Elijah's mom had been a churchgoer, a Catholic, and although he was not as religious as his forebears, just like Grayson, Elijah's value system had been formed in the forge of religion. Wrong-headed assumptions aside, Elijah was impressed at the passion with which Grayson spoke of the townsfolk. Maybe the old goat did stand for something after all. The moment was ruined seconds later, when Grayson said, "And that's why they're lucky to have the best detective around on the case. To give them assurance."

It was all Elijah could do not to roll his eyes.

Detective Grayson pulled the car over haphazardly, scraping the rims on the curb. There was plenty of free parking at this time of morning. Plenty of meters at only a nickel for thirty minutes. Grayson didn't bother contributing; presumably the meter maids knew him and would let it slide. Without saying a word, he got out. Elijah followed suit, feeling like he was a step behind, both literally and figuratively. Grayson started walking down the sidewalk and Elijah followed. Where were they going?

"I thought they found her at her home. In her bedroom," Elijah said.

"They did," Grayson said. "But that's not our first stop. We have a team gathering physical evidence as we speak. That's the 'how.' We'll get access to that in due time. I stopped by the scene at five this morning. Saw what I needed to see. If anything, useful comes up, I'll hear about it. But today, I'm more interested in working on the 'why' than the 'how.' "

"Okay," said Elijah. "A little unorthodox, but okay. So where exactly is our first stop."

Grayson lifted his hand, indicating a hanging sign on a poorly maintained brick building right beside them: The Watering Hole.

"A bar?" Elijah asked. "Seriously?" He wondered: was it possible that Detective Grayson was planning on starting the day, at eight-thirty in the morning, with a stiff drink? He knew Grayson was a drinker. He was one of those proud whiskey drinkers who managed to make reference to it a little more than was strictly necessary, as if he were trying to subtly boast about the fact that he drank too much poison and liked it straight, no chaser, burning his throat on his way to mental oblivion.

"Yes, a bar. Bars are where rumors are spread. Where secrets are whispered. Where indiscretions happen." It sounded good. Also sounded rehearsed. He'd clearly delivered those lines before. Part of the Aaron Grayson routine, the carefully curated hard ass he presented to the world. "I'm not a local here myself, but I've stopped by The Watering Hole a few times. I know a few people here who might have heard something."

Elijah shook his head. "But we don't have a lead. What are the chances someone in this bar knows anything?"

"Listen," Grayson said. "Mount Hugh is a small town. They've got exactly two bars. There's The Filling Station out on country route twelve. You familiar with it?"

"No," said Elijah, thinking: Of course, I'm not. Had his partner not been paying attention? He had a six-month old daughter. He was a family man. The only alcohol that had passed his lips in the past ten years had been during communion. Acquainting himself with the local drinking options in this small town hadn't been his top priority.

"Well that one's just out of town. Gets the farmhands and the guys from the lumbermill. Working class guys. Roughnecks. But The Watering Hole caters to the people here in town. The local politicians drink here. The doctors and lawyers, at least the ones who imbibe, do it here. And Eleanor was a drinker. I could see that at the crime scene. Private bar in the living room. And especially as the marriage fell apart, she'd be hitting the bar. Trying to meet people. Maybe drink her troubles away? I made a few calls this morning. She was a regular here."

Elijah nodded, grudgingly conceding the point. Okay, so they'd know her. And regulars in bars did have a tendency to talk. Maybe…

"Also," Detective Grayson said with a sly grin. "They serve breakfast."

The door was made of heavy wood, painted green, long since faded and flaking. Its opening triggered a hanging bell and a little ding announced their presence. There wasn't much going on at this hour of morning. A balding man in a classic rock t-shirt wiped down the bar with a stained rag as he chatted with a patron seated on one of the circular rotating seats, a woman who, on first glance, seemed overdressed.

"Where are you from, anyway?" Grayson asked Elijah in a seeming non-sequitur.

"Excuse me?" he asked in confusion. Was Grayson's memory failing him? They'd talked about this on more than one occasion. "Philadelphia," he said. "Born and raised."

"Nah," Grayson said, waving away the explanation "Where do your people hail from?"

"I mean, we've been in the Philadelphia area for generations…"

Grayson shook his head, talking slower as if trying to reach a slow pupil. "I'm talking about your forebears, Elijah. What stock are you from?" Elijah looked at him blankly. "You're not all-the-way white, are you?"

Elijah supressed an outward reaction. He couldn't believe he was asking this. Offensive on so many levels, from the general presumption to his choice of words. Stock. Like he was talking about cattle rather than a human being. Elijah imagined that the white slaveowners had used similar terminology before the Civil War.

Grayson was indeed a throwback.

"Because you look a little ethnically…" Grayson paused, wiggling his fingers as if trying to snag the proper word out of mid-air. "Ambiguous, I guess would be the best way to put it? I mean, 'Riley' is Irish, but you don't look completely Irish…" he trailed off in apparent hope that Elijah would solve this little mystery for him.

Elijah let out a slow breath, fighting through the discomfort he was feeling. "My mother is Mexican."

Grayson smiled, as if this somehow proved a point he'd been trying to make. "I knew it. I thought I was seeing something there."

"Is this relevant to what we're doing here?" Elijah asked, trying to make the question as flat as possible.

"Oh no," Grayson said. "It's only that some of the locals may not be as tolerant as I am. You know, if they see you, a stranger, a city-type, coming in here asking a bunch of questions. And, well, you don't look the same as what they're used to."

"Uh-huh," Elijah said, flatly.

"But don't worry. You're with me. You'll be fine."

Maybe the day for a confrontation was coming sooner than he'd anticipated. It was astounding, ridiculous, that Grayson would bring this up as they launched their investigation and represent it as somehow helpful. Right. He was the tolerant one.

But now was not the time. They were on the job. Regardless of his partner's bull-in-a-China-shop ways, Elijah was, first and foremost, a professional. He wasn't going to call out his partner in public, not as they were out on their first intel gathering operation. If they needed to have a conversation, it could happen later, in an office back at the county police headquarters.

If Grayson noticed the awkwardness, he didn't acknowledge it. He led the way to a small two-person table near the bar. The table was wooden, a dark brown that suggested a combination of varnish and spilled beer. Visually, the place had a strong "dive bar" vibe but it was moderated by the early hour and the morning sunlight slanting in through the front window, blinds open, casting dark slanting lines over the breakfast crowd.

"At night it's a dive," said Grayson, as if reading his thoughts. "But they mop the floor and air it out for breakfast. Run it like a diner."

Several tables were occupied by middle-aged residents, some dressed for work and others looking like they just stumbled out of bed. But the customer that particularly interested Elijah was the woman seated at the bar, the one who had seemed, on first glance, overdressed. From this angle he could see her more clearly and he could confirm she absolutely didn't fit in at this divey main street bar in a dried-up Colorado town. She was dressed stylishly, in a way that would distinguish her as inordinately classy even in a high-end Philadelphia restaurant. In Mount Hugh, the effect was even more shocking. She had long curly hair and sunkissed skin that seemed to radiate a glow. Gorgeous in that way that models and actresses were; sure, you knew they were attractive from the movies and magazines, but when you saw them in person it took your breath away, stopped your heart in its chest, and their fame made perfect sense.

Who was she? Why was she here? Elijah filed away the question. Likely of no import to their investigation, but an interesting area of inquiry nonetheless. She'd been chatting with the bartender, but Elijah couldn't hear what she was saying over the chatter in the establishment. He found it hard to tear his eyes away but, as he began to feel guilty, thoughts of his wife and child intruding, he forced himself to. The bartender came around from behind the bar and over to their table.

"What'll you have, gentlemen?" the bartender asked.

"Coffee, Ted," Grayson said.

"We've got espressos," the bartender said, turning towards Elijah. "Lattes."

Grayson frowned. "I don't need any of those fancy European drinks. None of that espresso crap." Elijah and the bartender made eye contact, sharing wordless disbelief Grayson's insistent fustiness. "Just the good old American coffee. Like I usually get."

"Right," said the barkeep with the merest hint of a patronizing smile. "A Café Americano?"

"You said it," Grayson said with a grin. Elijah stifled a laugh. "All American. You want anything to eat, Riley?"

"I'm good," he said. "Had a bowl of oatmeal this morning."

Grayson frowned at this. "Oatmeal? You need some protein. Get this boy a special. Eggs and bacon."

The bartender looked at Elijah, arcing an inquiring eyebrow. Elijah shrugged. He wasn't crazy about the condescension of his partner ordering for him, but he was a little hungry and figured he should take advantage of the chance to sample a local special. And besides, he was pretty sure Grayson was buying.

"Same for me," Grayson said, almost as an afterthought, as the man was walking away.

"I'll tell the kitchen," the bartender said.

"So," said Elijah, lowering his voice lest other diners might overhear. "Let's assume, for a second, that the ex-husband is the main suspect."

"Right," said Detective Grayson. "Mayor Lark. Married to Eleanor Lark for twenty-five, divorced six months ago. That's when she went back to being Eleanor Pomeroy. Six months. A man isn't really over a divorce, not when it wasn't his idea, in six months."

Elijah could tell that he was getting more of Grayson's autobiographical information here but chose to ignore the implications. "Okay. Let's go with that for a second. Do we know who initiated the divorce? What the issues were?"

"I don't," Grayson said. "But we'll look into that."

"Fair enough," said Elijah. "This all speaks to motive, which is part of your argument, right? Her ex might have a motive. Maybe he was mad. She left him. She cheated on him. Maybe there was a selfish motive. He didn't want to be paying her alimony for the rest of his life. Or she was threatening to clean him out. Going for the big settlement. Any of this could be possible, given what we know now. Which isn't much."

Grayson nodded. "With you so far."

"Great," Elijah said. "Now, I find that all fairly compelling. I mean, the ex-husband is the only culprit we're currently talking about, but in terms of motive, he seems to fit the bill. Right? Easy to think of a reason. And regardless of what went down in the marriage, it's easy to imagine a convincing reason. It works."

"I think so too," Grayson said.

"That's not to say that there might not be someone else who had an equally compelling reason, but taking your first assumption at face value—it's usually the most obvious person and the most obvious reason—then it works. But I have a reason to think that, in this case, it might not be the most obvious person."

Grayson grinned confidently. "Let me have it," he said. Elijah assumed that Grayson was anticipating an argument he might easily shoot down, looking forward to demonstrating his prowess, proving once again that he was the "best detective around," as he'd put it earlier.

"Okay, this argument isn't about motive. It's not about opportunity. It's really not about the means of the murder either. It's about the procedure."

"The procedure?"

"Yes," Elijah said. "The procedure by which she was killed. Let's take one of the examples we came up with: reasons an ex might want to murder his former spouse. Let's say she cheated. And he's going to use the knife. Or other sharp implement."

"Right…" Grayson, for once, looked thrown off. He had no idea where this was going.

"How would he go about it? Actually, committing the murder? With the knife."

"Well, he'd stab her," Grayson said, visibly uncomfortable. Elijah knew he shouldn't, but couldn't help feeling glee at throwing the overconfident grump off his game.

"Right," Elijah said. "He might be mad, right? Might stab her over and over."

"Right, I suppose," Grayson said, his face becoming visibly puzzled.

"Or, let's say he's doing it for the money. She's going to bleed him dry. Then what? Over and over? Or maybe just get the job done. In and out."

"Right," said Grayson with a revelation gradually dawning over his features.

"But that's not what happened, is it?"

"No," Grayson said. "He removed her head. It was clean. Almost surgical."

"Doesn't fit the motive."

Grayson nodded slowly. "I've got to say, Riley, you do have a point. So, I guess you're thinking serial killer, right? Some kind of nut job."

It was all Elijah could do to avoid breaking into a grin as he nodded his affirmation. He was very familiar with this phenomenon. He'd experienced it with his dad, a hard-ass military man, and his algebra teacher in high school. Praise meant the most from the hardest to please. Elijah almost resented how pleased he was with himself.

"But we've only got one body," Grayson countered. "That doesn't point to a serial killer."

"One body so far," Elijah corrected. "These cases have to start somewhere. And it does fit the profile."

The eggs and bacon came, and they lapsed into silence for a moment as they were delivered.

"Well, what about this?" said Grayson. "What if the ex-husband is just a very detached killer? Or what if he has his motive but also just so happened to have this psycho compulsion? Does the method of murder discount the motive? Or maybe he decided to make it look like a psycho-job to throw us off his trail."

"Maybe," said Elijah, but to his ears this speculation sounded desperate. Like a man trying to cook the books in support of an argument that had already been effectively shot down.

"Hey Daniel," Grayson said, calling their server back over. Daniel was an overly polite middle-aged man with greying red hair.

"What is it, chief?" Daniel asked.

"What do you know about Eleanor Pomeroy? Used to be Lark. Married to the mayor. You know her?"

"I've met her," Daniel said.

"A regular, wasn't she?"

"At nights. At the bar. But I don't work nights. I'd only occasionally see her here for breakfast. Nursing a hangover, usually."

"Any idea what happened in that marriage? To the mayor?"

Daniel leaned in closer. "Rumor has it, cheating."

"Him or her?" Grayson asked.

"Not sure," Daniel said.

Grayson leaned back in his seat and smiled. "Thanks, Daniel. And get me a refill on that coffee." Grayson looked over at Elijah, proud of himself, as if this tidbit proved his theory. It didn't prove anything of course. If the method didn't disprove the motive, the converse certainly wasn't true. They were no closer to knowing what happened. But Elijah didn't say anything.

Let him have his victory, he thought. We've got a lot more digging to do.

At that moment, Elijah happened to glance over at the lady at the bar. He'd been, with great effort, not looking her way. She was so stunning, it made him feel guilty, as if even in glancing at her he was being untrue to his wife. But when he looked over now, he noticed, quite clearly, that she had been eavesdropping on their conversation. He could see it in the way she turned away, too directly, with telegraphed casualness that felt fake. She'd been listening in and tried to play it off when he'd looked her way.

They settled in on a plan as they finished their breakfasts. Regardless of their theories and whose ultimately proved right, a natural first step would be to question the mayor. Even if he didn't pan out as a suspect, he'd naturally have valuable information to share. And as they currently didn't know who, if anyone, Eleanor Pomeroy had been currently romantically involved with, he'd make sense as their first point of contact. The two men reached a rare consensus on this plan of action. Grayson seemed uncharacteristically pleased, and Elijah was pleased to discover that he was, indeed, covering the bill. As they were at the register, paying up, Elijah caught movement from the corner of his eye, outside the large picture window of The Watering Hole: the mysterious woman, in a brand new, cherry red, Corvette. She was wearing sunglasses, but Elijah could have sworn that as she passed, she looked right at him, an expression of confusion and concern playing over her movie-star face.

Who was she?

Chapter Two
Lost In Translation

Aaron Grayson led the way back to the car. He was pleased.

It was a win-win.

His gut still told him it was the mayor. His new partner had brought up some decent points, but you could overthink this shit. Why tie yourself up in knots looking for a reason to disbelieve what was as obvious as the nose on your face? You see weasel leaving the henhouse, you see a bunch of busted eggs, a bunch of dead chickens, you don't start coming up with a list of long-shot suspects. The weasel did it. The obvious answer was obvious for a reason. It was likely. That spoke to probability. Why pursue longshots when you had a good bet? People killed each other when they had reasons to. Nobody had more reason than folks that had gotten divorced. Love throws you off. It resets your levels. Your highs are higher, and your lows are lower. And when love turns on you, changes into hate, well, then the lows are even lower because your baseline is fucked up. Aaron knew. He'd been there. He'd been in the delusional bubble of love, where everything is sunshine and light, and then felt the bottomless pit that opened up when it turned to its opposite.

Hate never runs as deep as it does in the afterglow of love.

Aaron wasn't sure he completely believed the sentiment, but he liked the sound of it. He could imagine himself delivering the line at a press conference. Sure, it was a bit of a soundbite, but there was something to it. He'd seen divorced people do crazy shit. He'd seen a dad destroy his kids' passports to get back at his ex. He'd seen a woman burn up her own stables, killing her own beloved horses, trying to pin it on her cheating husband. He'd seen an eighty-year-old man beat his wife half to death with a fire extinguisher because she asked to separate. He'd seen it in his own life, in the pain and anguish he still felt every time he heard Angie's name.

Yes. It was the mayor.

But what if it wasn't? That's where the win-win came in.

Even if Elijah's clever but overthought theory turned out to be true—even if it wasn't a crime of passion but instead the product of some sick compulsion—Aaron still would come out on top. He'd be the one clearing the mayor of the allegation. Nobody would blame Aaron for looking into the mayor. It being the obvious answer, it would also be the first one that occurred to anyone else. If he didn't look at the mayor, that would be suspicious If he left the mayor alone, people would accuse him of being in the pockets of politicians. But if it turned out the mayor was no good for it, Aaron could spin it so that he came out on top as the one leading the charge at his vindication. In either case, he was the hero.

He smiled, his lips working the toothpick, tucked into a corner of his mouth, that he'd picked up inside the Watering Hole. He unlocked the car.

"What are you grinning about?" Elijah asked him.

"It's a great day to be alive, partner," he said. Elijah looked at him blankly, confused. Good, he thought. Let him wonder. "We're heading over to the mayor's house," he said, glancing over as he pulled out onto the main street of Mount Hugh. "In case you were wondering."

Elijah could be off base, but he was sharp. Had some good ideas. The more Aaron thought about it, the more he liked the serial killer idea.

Aaron had risen through the ranks in a different era. In the seventies there'd been real crimes, real criminals. They were real villains, over the top and up to evil. Like something out of horror movies. It had started when the hippies had shaken up the world, getting the kids into drugs and craziness. In the early seventies, the country's big hangover from the summer of love, all of the idealism and free love transformed. Hippies turned into junkies, cultist, and killers. Maybe it started with Manson, but for a while there it kept going. The Night Stalker. Ted Bundy. Jeffrey Dahmer. Bad guys that the press and the public could sink their teeth into. And for men like himself, the lawmen sniffing out the murderers, it was a chance to fashion yourself into a hero. That was the world he'd come into out of the police academy. He'd worked high-profile homicides, first as a detective in Boulder and then on their major crimes task force.

That had all changed. In recent years it seemed like crime had lost its pizazz. He craved a big case but never seemed to pull one. It was all low-end amateur stuff. Theft. Burglary. And when there was a murder, it was the first person you'd expect. People were killing for the expected mundane reasons. Greed. Lust. Revenge. No killers with personality. No superstars.

Aaron had moved out of the city when he was still riding high, working on headline crimes, planning on building a life with Angie out in the mountains, the perfect place they could raise a family. But those dreams were dust. Now, a decade from retirement, it was all gone leaving him nothing but joints that ached in the wintertime and regrets, assigned to a post way the hell out in the middle of nowhere, floundering, desperate to catch a good case.

So, maybe it was a serial killer. Elijah had some good points. If you were pissed off at your ex, you might stab her a bunch of times, but you didn't cleanly sever her head like it was something for the trophy case. It was a good point, as far as it went, but why couldn't the mayor be the serial killer. That's where Elijah's thinking was wrong. Where did it say that a married man couldn't also have those sick feelings? Where did it say he couldn't also have a motive, and decide that his ex, the one who broke his fucking heart, deserved to be the target for his sicko urges? Maybe the urges were always there but it was whatever bullshit she'd put him through that had finally set him off.

Yes. Aaron liked that solution a lot. But in any case: there was no bad outcome. In any case, there would be press. Headlines. Cameras.

He'd be in the spotlight.

A win-win. All he had to do was catch the killer. He looked over at Elijah; he was tapping away at the squad car's computer terminal.

"Whatcha doing over there?" he asked.

"I requested any file information we had on the mayor," Elijah said. "Just came through."

"Bless your heart, kid," Aaron said. "You're reading my mind. What's it say?"

"Well, first off, his legal name isn't Lark," said Elijah.

Aaron narrowed his eyes, his imagination running wild with theories. "Are you telling me it's an alias?"

"Not exactly," said Elijah. "He legally changed it. Around twenty years ago. From William Lark to Abdoullah Khaled."

"What?" Aaron said, red flags shooting up his mental flagpoles. "What kind of name is that?"

"I don't know for sure," Elijah said. "Not by nationality. But it sounds Middle Eastern."

"Middle Eastern," Aaron said, the words sounding sinister to his ears even as he said them. A tidal wave of preconceptions flooded his mind. "Are we talking Muslim?"

Elijah shrugged uncertainly. "Possibly?"

Muslims. The first image that popped into his mind was the leering visage of the Ayatollah Khomeni, head wrapped up in a scarf, with his Satanic eyebrows and wizard's beard, enemy of America, prophet of his primitive religion. They cut off your hands, right? If you stole a loaf of bread?

Aaron wasn't sure where he'd heard it, but it sounded right.

"This could be important," Aaron said. "Might play into the case."

Elijah shrugged. "I guess so," he said.

"These people," Aaron said. "These Muslims, they have a medieval attitude towards morality."

"Do they?" Elijah said. "That sounds like quite a generalization."

"It's true," Aaron said, finding momentum in his words as they spilled out of his mouth. "They wrap up their women, you know. If this woman cheated, who's to say she didn't get killed to restore his honor. As some kind of ritual cleansing, maybe."

"Have you ever met a Muslim?" Elijah asked.

Aaron felt like he must have at some point but was having trouble conjuring up specifics.

"Because I have. A Muslim family ran a grocery store in my neighborhood back in Philly. Hard working people. Moral people. Just like you and me."

"Well," Aaron said, a little testy at his partner's bleeding-heart sympathies. "Good for them for assimilating into the big old melting pot. But we're not looking at that family from your old neighborhood for this murder."

That shut him up, Aaron thought smugly as Elijah's face collapsed into a frown.

"Wait a minute," Aaron said. "Who changes their name from Bill to Abdoullah? Wouldn't you naturally go in the other direction?"

"I don't know," Elijah said. "People have a lot of reasons for doing things."

Aaron paused, taking a long look at his partner. He suspected that was a dig, aimed at his philosophy: the obvious was the most likely. He decided to let it go.

"And another thing," he said. "He doesn't look Middle Eastern to me."

"Well, what's he supposed to look like?" Elijah asked. "Is he supposed to be wearing a turban?" Elijah said it like it was a joke, but Aaron realized that he had, indeed, been picturing a turban. "Maybe he's of mixed heritage."

Aaron shook his head. "I don't know," he said. "I think they mostly stick to their own kind." Of course, if the mayor was a Muslim, he hadn't stuck to his own kind, had he? It was puzzling.

Elijah exhaled, a puff of breath that sounded suspiciously close to a sigh, before returning his attention to the computer console. For a moment, they drove in silence, the car bouncing through muddy potholes on the poorly maintained rural road, Aaron's brain still scanning through its mental catalogue of Middle Eastern tropes. Hijackers. Sheiks. Terrorists.

"Hey," Elijah said after a minute. "Did you notice that woman? At breakfast."

"What woman?" Aaron said.

"The one sitting at the bar."

Aaron squinted as he tried to call up the memory. He remembered that a woman had been sitting there, but the details escaped him. "I had no reason to really take notice," he said eventually. "Why?"

"I don't know," he said. "She just stood out. Like she didn't belong here."

"Why do you say that?" Aaron said, at a complete loss as to where his partner was going with this. Mentally, he was still on high alert for suspicious Muslims. Those were the ones who didn't belong.

"She was overdressed," Elijah said. "Those clothes she had on were from top designers."

"Designers?" Aaron said. "I don't know anything like that."

"She dressed like a big shot," Elijah said. Aaron wasn't sure whether to be grateful or insulted by the way he dumbed down his observation. "Like someone from a big city. New York or Los Angeles. One of the movers and the shakers."

"Okay," Aaron said. "So, what?"

"Well, first I noticed she looked out of place. Then I noticed driving away. Peeled out of her spot and headed down main street. Looking worried."

Aaron a little impressed in spite of himself. He didn't know shit about clothes. He'd be the first to admit that. He didn't necessarily think it befitting a man to be carrying around a bunch of trivia about women's dresses. But he did appreciate that his partner was looking at the details and drawing conclusions. That was detective-work.

Still, he didn't see the relevance.

"Okay," said Aaron. "Maybe she was passing through? Maybe she was late for an appointment?" He shrugged. "Maybe she was up to something. But we're investigating a specific crime."

"But what if she heard us talking? What if she was nervous because we were cops?"

"What if she was late for a date? What if she was having her period? We can't go chasing down every woman in nice clothes who's having a bad day."

Elijah frowned, taking his point. Aaron had to admit it; he took a little satisfaction in deflecting the theory. His partner had potential, but dammit, the kid tried too hard. He was so invested in finding unlikely patterns, he'd invent them if he had to. Wanted to prove how clever he was.

Aaron, on the other hand, wanted to clear cases.

"We're here," Aaron said, pulling up in front of a modest house. It didn't fit Aaron's idea of what a mayor's house would look like. He didn't know all of the ins and outs of local Mount Hugh politics, but in his experience the type of people who ran for local offices tended to be those who had some money: men who came from money and had the expectation of being in charge, or those who had made a boatload of cash in business and were looking for new worlds to conquer. This just looked like a standard two-story home. A place to raise the kids. It looked like it could belong to a bank teller or a high school chemistry teacher.

He was a little disappointed that the press hadn't shown up, realizing he'd been anticipating fielding questions as he stepped from the car, mentally rehearsing the gruff down-to-business delivery as he gently pushed away the microphones aiming for his face.

I'm not going to make any guesses at this point.

It's really too early to say.

At this point, we're just gathering information.

I'm going to need you to stand back; this is an active crime scene.

But there was no press. Not yet. The street was quiet. First shift folks had already made it to work. Second shift were getting ready. Nothing was apparent to clue an observer in to the fact that he was standing in front of the house of a murder suspect. News usually travelled fast in small towns, but he didn't know Mount Hugh as well as some of the other towns under his jurisdiction. Maybe the gossips hadn't picked it up yet. He considered placing a call to one of the local TV stations. Anonymous tip. They'd get on the story eventually anyway. Wouldn't it be better if he had some say in the timing? It'd be good to get out in front of the narrative before the reporters invented their own version. In front of the cameras, he could let the public know what exactly they needed to know. No more, no less.

And, most importantly, he'd let them know that Detective Aaron Grayson was on the case.

"Listen," he said to Elijah as the two got out of the car. "Follow my lead. We're looking for any holes in his story. Weak points. Unverifiable alibis. Suspicious behavior. Things like that. If things seem to be going that way, I'll make a move."

"Arrest him?" Elijah asked.

"It depends," Aaron said. "Yes, if there's sufficient reason. If not, well, if there are holes in the story, we'll try to at least invite him downtown to continue the discussion. Once he's on our turf, we're more likely to get a confession."

Elijah raised an eyebrow as if he wasn't sure what Aaron was getting at. Well, he wasn't about to tell him. Aaron learned long ago not to put all of his cards on the table, not even for his partner. A wise man keeps an ace or two up his sleeve. Aaron noticed that the closest neighbor was about two-hundred yards away. This might make establishing an alibi challenging.

Aaron felt it. The anticipation. The thrill of the hunt. He was practically salivating.

"Come on, kid," he said to Elijah. "Let's do this." Then he marched right up to the door, not pausing, just lifting his hand and knocking. Confidently, aggressively. A few moments later, the door swung back revealing a short Caucasian man dressed in a t-shirt and track suit pants. Probably in his fifties. He looked harmless, gentle.

Like the imaginary high school chemistry teacher Aaron had conjured up when first seeing the home.

Who was this guy?

A gardener, maybe? Aaron's mental conception of the mayor had changed a lot since that morning. Originally, it had been a white guy in a business suit. Big fake smile. The typical upwardly mobile local politician type. He'd met so many over the years. But then, once his partner had uncovered the business of the legal name change, the picture in his head had changed. Yes, maybe still in a snazzy business suit, but darker skinned. Probably bearded. In his mind's eye, the beard was sinister, devilish. And the eyebrows, arched, like a villain from a cartoon.

Like the Ayatollah.

"Excuse me, sir," Aaron said, scrambling to cover his dismay, trying to deliver the question with the confidence with which he'd knocked. "I'm here to speak to William Lark."

"That's me," the guy said with what seemed like sincere friendliness. Not a care in the world. No suspicion of cops showing up at his door. "Why don't you step inside?"

Aaron felt his guard go up. The case had already surprised him more than once. This was the mayor? This was Abdoullah Khaled? This white guy? This milquetoast who looked like he actually belonged in this nondescript suburban home?

Aaron liked homerun cases. Open and shut. Slap on the cuffs and smile for the camera. He didn't like being surprised.

A few minutes later, Aaron and Elijah were seated in the mayor's living room on a big cushy couch with a floral pattern that was so soft it was hard to sit up straight. He'd brewed them cups of tea. Lemon Ginger. It wasn't Aaron's speed —he avoided hot drinks that didn't have caffeine —but it was tasty enough. Aaron had grudgingly consented to the gesture, reminding himself that he didn't know the man was guilty, and that against all appearances, this man apparently had some political power on the local level. It wouldn't do to be rude.

Still, he needed to get down to business.

"First of all, Mister Mayor, you have our condolences," said Aaron, playing it diplomatic.

"Thank you for saying that," he said. "And you can call me William. Or Bill, if you prefer."

"Sure, Bill," Aaron said. He stood up. It wasn't a conscious choice; it just felt right. The mayor had derailed their protocol with the hot tea business. Putting them on a cushy flowery couch was particularly emasculating. Like cutting their balls off. But now he was standing, looking down at his suspect. In a subtle way, he'd shifted the power back to himself. "When was the last time you saw your ex-wife."

"Yesterday," Lark said. "And I'll admit, we had a fight."

"A big one?" Aaron said. He didn't need to say anything else. The implication was clear. He took a sip of the tea, still warm but cooling in the cup.

"Yes," Lark said. "Loud and nasty. I'm afraid, and we both said and did things we regretted." Aaron had to admit, Lark didn't look like a violent man. He looked like the closest thing to violence he'd be capable of was swinging a tennis racket. Still, his gut told him that Lark was being evasive and vague. When he said he "did things we regretted," could mean a lot of different things. Did he call her a dirty whore or decapitate her?

"Mmm-hmm," said Aaron. When someone volunteered something like a nasty argument, it was because they knew that it was going to come out anyway. If nobody had heard the argument, would Lark be telling him this? "Were there any witnesses to this argument?"

"Yes," he said. "My son. Peter."

Here we go, thought Aaron, proud of his instincts. I knew it.

"And what were you and Eleanor arguing about?" Aaron asked.

"The usual stuff. Logistics. We've only been split up for six months or so. It's all very fresh. But we still have to co-parent. We have to negotiate our time with Peter."

"How old is Peter?"

"He's twenty-one," Lark said.

"Ah," Aaron said. "I was imagining a little guy. Is there really that much to negotiate now that he's grown up."

"Peter's a sensitive kid," Lark said. "The divorce hurt him. We're both trying to keep him happy."

"So, this argument…" Aaron prompted.

"Yes," Lark said. "I don't know if you've ever been through a divorce, but in the aftermath, there's a lot of emotions. Right under the surface." Of course, Aaron did know, first-hand, about the emotional whirlpool that followed the breakup of a marriage, but he did not let his expression show it. He revealed nothing, keeping his expression neutral, giving no indication whether or not he even believed the story he was hearing. Why give anything away? Keep those cards close to the vest. "Every argument you've ever had. Every resentment you've swallowed. It's all there. And when you get into it, all of that stuff comes out. It started as a discussion of our schedule, but quickly turned into a mutual accusation session. Basically, a second take of the argument that ended our marriage."

And why did that marriage end? Aaron had his questions. He'd heard the rumor, back at breakfast, of her being the one who had cheated. He was tempted to ask about that but decided to wait. He didn't want to put Lark on the defensive this early. Have him clam up or ask for a lawyer. No, let him talk. If he was guilty, let him play out enough rope to hang himself. If he didn't volunteer the cheating story, maybe they could get it from the son. Instead, he simply asked: "And why did the marriage end? I apologize if that's a personal question."

"No, that's perfectly okay," Lark said. "The marriage started falling apart when I decided to run for mayor. She didn't support me in that, didn't want me changing our lives. It was important to me, an ambition, but it was one she didn't share. She stuck with me through the campaign and through to the inauguration, but her resentment grew. The damage was done, the whole foundation of the marriage was corrupted. By the time I moved into my new office, we couldn't even have a civil conversation. And then she filed the papers."

How neat and tidy, Aaron thought, wondering what the real story was. Yes, he'd have to dig deeper with the son, with other people who had known Eleanor, as to what really happened. This could be it. The hole in the story. The loose thread that could be pulled at until the whole thing unravelled. Aaron reminded himself to be patient. It was like fishing. When you got that first nibble, it was tempting to yank back and try to set the hook, but you had to wait. Give that fish a chance to get its mouth around the bait. If you yanked too soon the fish would get wise and swim away.

"Excuse me," Elijah said, still sitting on the overly cushy sofa. "I have a question."

Aaron had almost forgotten his partner was there. He narrowed his brows, worrying that Elijah was planning on bringing up the cheating rumors. Definitely the wrong time for that; bring it up too soon and they'd scare off a suspect who was volunteering his story without counsel.

"Yes?" Lark said. "Let's hear it."

"Is your family Muslim?"

The mayor looked a little surprised at this. It was the first time since they'd started that he'd seemed so.

"The family? No."

"Because I noticed that you'd named your son 'Peter,' a traditional Christian name." Lark opened his mouth as if to speak, but Elijah continued, effectively cutting him off. "But we also noticed, in your files, that several years ago you legally changed your named to Abdoullah Khaled. About five years ago, to be exact."

Aaron had to give his partner credit. It was the perfect play. It threw their suspect off his game, but not in a way that shut him down or sent him running to a lawyer. He kept talking, but he seemed slightly disoriented. As if he was in danger of losing control of the version of his story that he'd chosen to tell.

"Yes, I did convert to Islam," he said. "But I don't force it on my family."

"Did this play a part in the divorce?" Aaron asked. Intuitively, it seemed like it must have. He'd married Eleanor, they'd raised a child together, but then, a decade or more into their marriage, he'd decided to turn his back on Christianity? It seemed plausible that the religious conversion had been a factor.

"No," Lark said. "I told you; it was all about my political ambitions. Eleanor and I were perfectly happy to keep to our differing beliefs. When our marriage worked, it wasn't about our respective faiths."

"But you chose to run as William Lark," Elijah said. "Why is that? After going through it all. The legal process of changing your name. Why not embrace it?"

"Well, you know as well as I do," Lark said. "This is a small town. The locals sometimes distrust that which they don't understand. Basically, I wanted to get elected." He shrugged and gave a self-effacing chuckle.

"So," Elijah continued. "Did you have a family background in Islam? How did you find your way to the faith?"

Aaron felt irritation swelling up in him as his partner tried to steer the conversation. His instructions had been clear. Hang back. Follow his lead. He was definitely not doing that, trying to turn this session into a seminar on comparative religion. Annoyed, Aaron glanced outside the house's windows. He could see the wind turbines on the hillside above. They didn't have them in town but here in the outskirts, they dotted the hillsides. Uncertain where he was going with it but following his instincts, like a hound dog on the trail of a raccoon, he asked, "So, do those turbines power your house?"

"The turbines?" Lark said, simultaneously seeming thrown by this seeming non-sequitur but also, perhaps, relieved at the change of subject. "Yes. These were a massive investment for Mount Hugh. They power the town during the winter months during fuel shortages. They represent an infrastructure investment that has been a boon for the town."

Lark was cooking now. Going off like he was giving a campaign speech.

Let him talk, Aaron thought. More rope.

"That's great," Aaron said. "Did you get these put in as mayor."

"No," Aaron said. "These are the reason I was elected mayor. Me and a business partner pioneered the technology in the area. It solved a long-term problem for the city."

"You must be very proud," said Aaron, trying to stroke his ego. "That's quite an accomplishment. Who was this business partner?"

"Leonard Maximoff," Lark said. Aaron made a mental note. Business interests. An ex-business partner. Money. Greed. Motive. Aaron wanted the case to be open and shut. Angry ex-husband chopping off the old lady's head. Maybe there was more to it. Money could drive a man to all kind of things. Still, none of this had clear ties to the crime. He'd have to redirect. Get it back to the wife.

At that moment a man burst through the front door. It swung back and banged against the frame. On the couch, Elijah jumped, spilling his tea on his lap. The man looked to be in his mid-fifties, like Lark or Aaron himself. He was slender and had a bad dye job: hair jet black and a beard shot through with gray. The stranger was panting. He looked frightened. He opened his mouth as if about to say something. Something dramatic, probably. Damning, maybe?

But then he noticed that Lark wasn't alone, noticed Aaron standing by the couch, teacup in his hand, and Elijah half-standing, drying his pants with a napkin. The man quickly composed himself, supressing whatever emotion he'd come in radiating. But it was too late. He'd been seen. Aaron noticed a glance pass between the newcomer and Lark. A twitch of the eyebrows indicating: don't say it.

Whatever "it" was.

Aaron smiled, loving the chaos. Threads were already loosening. The fabric would soon pull apart. And he'd be right there, leading the charge. Finding the answers. Facing the cameras and laying it all out.

CHAPTER THREE
NOSTALGIA

The dirty fan overhead twirled noisily as Dahlia dropped her purchase on the counter. A skinny man with eye bags and a tag that read Fred glared at her with red sleepy eyes. She flashed him a smile which made his scowl deepen.

It was pretty much still early in the morning. Not even yet six. When she had pulled up in front of the gas station, it was closed. Just as she was about pulling off, a woman with a bonnet had waved to her from a shack next to the station. Minutes later, Fred had staggered out, shooting her glares as he opened the convenience store and gas station.

It was a tiny store, with a window overlooking the gas station. The shelves were piled up with supplies, covered with dust as it went higher. It had the basic supplies she needed, a pack of water, chewing gum and some snacks she could munch on. And of course, the gas. She had overestimated that her tank would take her the three and a half hours drive from the city.

She spotted three signal bars on her cellular phone screen. She had lost signal for over two hours. She dialed Naomi's number, and it went straight to voicemail. She had been sleeping when Dahlia tossed her bags into the trunk and driven off while it was still dark.

"Good morning. Didn't want to wake you up. Network is pretty shitty here, but I should be in Mount Hugh in…" She glanced at her Rolex. "Thirty minutes. I am not sure how the signal is over there, but I will give you a call once I am settled in. Talk to you later… Love you."

"That's thirty-five dollars with the gas," Fred grumbled.

She left him a five-dollar tip. He grumbled a thank you, and as she got out of the store, she saw him put up the closed sign.

Her black Audi was a lone car in the small vacant park. She had barely seen a vehicle since she was on the road. It was still early she reminded herself, and small towns folks didn't have much going to be up early.

She got into the driver's seat, dumping the bag of supplies on the passenger's seat. She loved the quiet of the morning, especially so far away from the chaos of the city.

She grabbed her tape recorder from the dashboard. She opened a small bag, filled with new tapes. With a blue marker, she wrote the date on the tape, then slid it into the recorder.

"April sixteenth, nineteen ninety-six," she began in a firm voice. "This is Dahlia Crane. I am at…" She read the faded sign of the gas station. "Nolan's gas. It is just outside Mount Hugh, about thirty minutes' drive. Mount High is going to be my host community for my dissertation paper on sustainability of low-income areas in the Industrial Age."

Dahlia was heading to Mount Hugh for research work for her PhD dissertation. For the past three years, this had been her routine. Embed herself in small communities to understand them better, and tell their stories and rich culture, even though most of them had been forgotten by the developing world. Her journey to tell unique stories and to harmonize the strengths of these dwindling communities had taken her around the world to West Africa, the Himalayas, and across several states in the United States. Her papers were termed remarkable and were a locus standi in the Global Health field and beyond. However, this time around, it was personal. Mount Hugh was home. She had lived there until she was five years old and had quite the memories. She had always wanted to return, but it hadn't been at the top of her priorities. Now, with her PhD program coming to an end, it was time to wrap things up, and Mount High seemed like a great finale.

Thirty minutes later, Dahlia pulled up by the side of the road. She stepped out with her camera and stared at the amazing morning view of the town below her. From the vantage point she stood, Mount High was marvelous, a small steeping community surrounded by mountains, it presented a picturesque view found on postcards.

Her heart raced in excitement as she drove past a faded sign that read Mount Hugh. She had faint memories of waving the signpost goodbye as her mom's truck left town over twenty years ago. Whenever she told people she recalled a lot from that young of age, they thought she was bluffing. Naomi said it was because that year had made quite an impact on her life, so she held on to those memories.

Mount Hugh hadn't changed much since she left, she realized with a hint of disappointment. Her gaze lingered on a building with chipped paint and dipped roof, which was plastered in the middle with tarpaper shingles. She had gone a couple of times to that hardware store with her mother. Several storefronts had been boarded up, their porches now overgrown with grass and mildew. Her favourite store, the only ice-cream, store had its windows completely gone.

They had left town at the onset of the economy dwindle. She recalled that the stores used to bustle with clientele. As she headed to school in the mornings, the shops were usually open, and her mom would grab breakfast for her. Now, all of it was gone, leaving behind an empty shell.

She sighed. She hadn't expected much, but there had been a glimpse of hope that it wouldn't be that bad.

Her car screeched to a halt as she spotted a building on the other side of the street. The Watering Hole hadn't been around when she was still in Mount High. She reversed into a park, next to a couple of vehicles.

She pulled down her mirror staring right into dark eyes. She ran a finger through her black curly hair, patting it down. She needed to get another sunscreen, she thought as she pressed white cream from the tube, slashing it all over her brown face. It was probably the only makeup she used on her porcelain complexion. It was a habit she had picked up in high school, after watching a documentary about how UV rays were a cause of skin cancer amongst multiracial people.

A heavy wooden with chipped green paint creaked as she pushed it open, a bell ringing above her head.

The Watering Hole was far from decent. It was a dive bar, struggling to stay afloat, with its scarred wooden surfaces and faded cushion. The blinds were open, ushering in the morning rays. There was a bar to the left of the room, with a couple of circular chairs. The other side was occupied by chairs and tables which were occupied by the early crowd having breakfast.

Her entrance hushed conversation. She was a stranger, sticking out like a sore thumb in her olive-green denim pants, matching shirt, and black boots. A tall, curvy, brown-skinned woman, with long, thick black curly hair, with almond-shaped eyes and high cheek bones which she had gotten from her Korean roots. She was a clash of two diverse worlds, as Naomi had said in their early days.

She felt curious eyes on her, conversation picking up as she headed to the bar. The wall was covered was devoted to picture frames of the locals. Every town had one of these places. It could be a bar, a store, the church, but there was one place they found solace in. And from the look of things this was it.

"Welcome to the Watering Hole, name's Daniel," a bald man, wearing a faded T-shirt introduced.

"Dahlia," she answered.

"Passing through?" he asked, sliding a plain typed menu to her. It didn't have a lot of options.

"Spending a couple of days in Mount Hugh," she supplied, as she searched for signal on her phone. Three days actually, but if she didn't get the information she needed, she would have to be around longer.

"Trying to call your husband?" Daniel asked, nodding at her phone.

"My partner," she said.

"Signal is pretty shitty in the mornings. You are going to have wait till around noon before you can get something. Coffee?" he asked as he put in a fresh cup of coffee. She nodded. "Breakfast is being prepped out back. Go with the bacon," he said. Without waiting for her response, he called out back, "Jake, we need bacon and toast in five!"

"We don't get many strangers around these parts. In winter, a couple of folks come around to ski and all that, but there are no resorts or lodges, so they head back into the city. Milk? Sugar?" Daniel continued.

"Just sugar," Dahlia said. She was picky when it came to dairy products, as she tended to have an upset stomach if she consumed the wrong one.

"You got business here?" he asked as he poured the coffee into a white teacup, placing it in front of her.

"I am here for work," Dahlia said, taking a sip of the coffee. She nodded impressed, it was pretty strong. Just how she liked her morning coffee.

"Journalist?" he asked, staring at her intensely.

"Well… sort of, but not really," Dahlia said. Journalism was her mode of reporting, but most people's idea of a reporter was someone in front of the cameras or whose names appeared on the tabloid. "I am in my PhD program, and I have a paper I am working on that involves Mount Hugh," she said.

He seemed disappointed. "Oh. Thought you were here to investigate the murder."

Her eyes widened at the news. "Murder? Here in Mount Hugh?" She had certainly not been expecting this. He didn't seem like he was joking.

He nodded. "Sad thing. Eleanor was found this morning in her home. Mayor's ex-wife."

"Was it a break-in?" Dahlia asked. There was usually some sense of morality in small towns like Mount Hugh, which led to a low crime rate. Everyone basically knew each other and respected the sanity. However, with the harsh economic clime, there were those who resorted to crime to be able to sustain themselves and their families.

"I don't know. The news out there is that she was decapitated," Daniel whispered with a shudder. "Jake, my cook, his sister is a ranger. She was at the scene. Said there was blood everywhere."

Dahlia pulled out her notebook and scribbled on it. Murder. Mayor's ex-wife. Decapitated.

"Do you know if anyone has been arrested? Or if are there suspects?" she asked. The husband was usually the first suspect. And how crazy such a headline would be, Mayor kills Ex-wife. That was bound to stir the sleeping community.

"Hugh Slaughter," he leaned in with a dramatic whisper. He was clearly loving this, his eyes darting back and forth, his nose flared as he gave her information. She waited for him to expatiate. "Something like this happened twenty-five years ago. Woman's body was found around the mountain. Guess how she died?"

He waited for a dramatic silence before continuing. "Her head was also cut off! We called him Hugh Slaughter back then when the body was found. The cops didn't find out who did it, but he's back I tell you. He's back. It is a cycle, and he will be back in the next thirty years. Glad I wouldn't be around then. Too bad he went after poor Eleanor. She was a nice one. Sweet and kind." He cast a look at one of the portraits on the wall. It was of a family of three, an older man wearing a broad smile, a woman whom she supposed was Eleanor, and a teenager in the middle. They looked really happy as they celebrated the kid's graduation.

"Their kid, Peter is one of the smart ones. Properly brought up. Straight A's all through school and was on the football team. He got an all-covered scholarship to study medicine at Colorado School of

Medicine. You don't see that happen in these parts. Most kids graduate from high school and start popping kids or getting into trouble. He's got a good head on his shoulders. Polite and respectful. He works hard. Doesn't matter that his folks got money."

"Order ready Daniel!" a voice rang out from the back room.

Daniel scurried to the back as Dahlia made more notes. Every journalist had their method of reporting, but she preferred specialization. Focus on an area of global health and research on it. She hadn't decided what angle she was focusing on with Mount Hugh. Healthcare? Access to education? Social welfare for victims of domestic violence? She had deliberated over several angles over the past weeks leading up to her road trip. It was an unfortunate circumstance, but the answer had come to her on her arrival. The effect of grief on a small community was a good dissertation topic. It wasn't one she had covered before in the past, but exploring this new angle already had her excited. Community sweetheart. Ideal family respected and admired by the town. It made not only memorable storytelling, but there would be enough material she would have sufficient to work with.

A steamy white plate of bacon and toast was placed in front of her with cutlery. The brown bacon sizzled as she pierced her fork through it. Daniel watched her expectantly as she took a bite. It was surprisingly yummy, with an avalanche of spices in the right proportion. He relaxed as she took more hungry bites.

"He's seeing the Maximoff's girl."

She looked up, noticing the displeasure in his voice. "You don't approve?"

"He can definitely do better. Fawn was trouble in high school. A couple of folks said she has changed, but she used to be a troubled kid. Hung out with the wrong crowd. And her family," Daniel rolled his eyes. "Let me not even get started. She has a record, and her mother, she's nosy and in everyone's business. He could have gone with one of the Beckham's girls. Or with Claire. They dated in high school."

"Poor kid is staying over at the Maximoff's place with the entire family," a voice said, clearly not pleased with this. The voice belonged to a chubby man with a gruff of a beard, wearing a pinafore. She had been too absorbed in the conversation she didn't hear him come in.

"Morning Collins!" Daniel said as he poured some coffee into a cup, sliding it over to Collin. "This is Dahlia. She's a journalist," Daniel introduced.

Collins' eyes raked over her with suspicion. It was one of the reasons she didn't introduce herself as a journalist. Small towns folks were usually suspicious of journalists. More often, they were painted by the media and West in a negative light. Their weaknesses were used as sore topics, to belittle the people who tended to hold their guards up to newcomers. But she was here for a different purpose. One of her aims for her dissertation was to acknowledge that despite these areas lacked the development of urban areas, their sense of community, morality and contentment made them strong as a community.

"The Hugh Slaughter did it. Not his first time. And hopefully his last," Collins said. "Really sad news. Eleanor was one of us. Brought me a basket of food every day for a week when I broke my back. Tell Jake I want more butter today," he threw at Daniel as he headed for the tables.

"Jake! More butter for Collins!" Daniel yelled to the back, as the bell rang, ushering in two men. Like her, they seemed out of place. The older one wore a black trench coat, and the younger one a suit that didn't fit him properly. She wondered for a moment if they were journalists, but a murder out in Mount Hugh didn't warrant journalists coming over so quickly. It would probably take a couple of days before it was reported. With the way Daniel hurried over to them with familiarity, she figured they were no strangers, at least the older one who looked around with some sense of confidence. The younger one however, looked around with curiosity.

She turned her attention back to her notes. She had a story here, and just needed to draw up a plan. First, she had to talk to the cops, and then the family of the murdered woman. There were going to be a lot of interviews with the folks in town.

"Let's say she cheated… And he's going to use the knife. Or other sharp implement."

Her ears flared up at this. The younger man from earlier was speaking. It took her a milli-second to realize what they were talking about. The Mayor and his ex-wife. Above the chatter of the other customers, she strained to listen, catching bits of their conversation. The younger man had a point. Crimes of passion were usually personal. A knife stab, with multiple wounds. A gunshot. But decapitation? This was certainly of a brutal nature, and didn't fit the motive of a scorned husband.

She rolled her eyes as the older man began to speak. He was stubborn, and so full of himself, as he tried to weaken his colleague's argument and have the last word in. She pegged him for the investigating detective, and the younger guy had to be new to the job with his enthusiasm and attempt at hiding his irritation of the other man.

"Hey Daniel," she called to him when he returned to the bar. "Where do the Maximoff stay?"

"Northfield lane. It is around the town's square. Hey Jake! We need more eggs!" Daniel called out to the back.

Dahlia headed out after paying for her breakfast. She resisted the urge to talk to the police. If there was one thing she knew universally about cops, they didn't like to speak to journalists, especially when a case was ongoing. She needed to be steps ahead, to gather relevant information for her dissertation.

The streets were empty as she drove towards the park. Perhaps it was from shock of the murder. Such a crime had the impact of ripping through a small town, making them realize that evil could exist in their little bubble. Or perhaps it was just what Mount Hugh had been reduced to, silence followed by faded buildings, overgrown lawns, potholes in the road and an air of desolation.

The traffic lights had even stopped working, she noticed with a sigh as she stopped at the town's square which was made remarkable by a water fountain. It used to function back then, and she had memories of laughing and playing around the sprouting water, with other kids, while her mom called out to her not to get her clothes wet. The water had dried up, now replaced with flowers and grasses which were well-kept. Still, she preferred the water.

She slowed down next to a teenager walking a dog. "Hi, I am looking for Northfield lane," she said.

"Take the right turn," he pointed to a turn next to a bakery shop. "It is where the turbines are."

She followed his directions, taking the turn next to the library. It was a short drive, as she pulling into an enclosed dead-end with a couple of houses, surrounded by wind turbines which were currently off. Since she got into Mount Hugh, these were the most maintained houses. It seemed a recent paint job had been done, the gutters cleared with the lawns neatly mowed. She parked her Audi next to a truck and grabbed her bag.

There were about six houses in the close, and she had no idea where to start from. One of these houses belonged to the Maximoffs and…

"Hello!" A woman waved to her from the porch of one of the homes. She waved back at her. The woman met her halfway, her curious eyes studying Dahlia, just as Dahlia did the same. Middle-aged, pretty with a simple sense of style. "I haven't seen you in Mount High before, and I know everyone."

"I am Dahlia. I am looking for the Mayor's son. I was told he lives with the Maximoff's. Do you know—"

"Why do you want to talk to him?" the woman asked.

"I am a PhD student working on a dissertation report that will assist give a positive perspective on small communities. I would like to talk to him about his mother's death as she was an integral member of this community."

"Bless her soul, but Eleanor was the very heart of this town," the woman said with familiarity.

"Just a couple of minutes, and I would happy to compensate with a small fee."

"Welcome to Mount Hugh, Dahlia. Name's Malinda Maximoff," the woman said, putting an arm around Dahlia as she led her towards her building. "I have been close friends with William and Eleanor. Our families are tight, and you have no idea how disheartening Eleanor's death is for all of us."

"Maximoff?" Dahlia lifted a brow.

Malinda smiled. "Yes, my daughter Fawn is Peter's partner."

The Maximoffs lived in a modest home, with a vintage-theme, and a burst of colors. There was a floral and fruity smell that Dahlia instantly liked. It was overwhelmed with memorabilia. Pictures from when Malinda was a teenager, her first job, when she got married, Fawn's first birthday. It was quite a lot… And there was some bit of luxury like the china Malinda served her tea with, despite her turning down the offer.

"It wouldn't be heard that Malinda wasn't hospitable," Malinda said with a smile.

"My condolences on your loss," Dahlia said.

"It is unbelievable. I feel like someone is going to pinch me and I will wake up from this bad dream. I can't believe Eleanor is gone," Malinda said with teary eyes.

"And to think something like that happened here in Mount Hugh? Right in our community? Oh my! There he is."

Peter Lark was a good-looking young man. A bit burly, with brown hair like his father. His face was puffy, and his eyes red, and she guessed he had been crying. Picture Malinda twenty years younger, and that was Fawn. Her splitting image with a bit more of curves and steel. Behind those dark eyes, there were something Dahlia couldn't pinpoint that made her different from her mother. She had an arm around Peter, who leaned to her for support.

"This is Dahlia, she's a journalist and wants to talk to you about your mother's death for her PhD, right?" Malinda asked.

Fawn's eyes flashed in displeasure and Dahlia quickly said, "My condolences on your loss Peter. I am sorry for intruding at such a time. I could come around some other time, but I am here for a couple of days. Writing about grief wasn't my intention, I am not here to investigate her murder, but since I got here everyone has been talking about how loved your mother was, and I would like to write about how you feel. I believe this could help with dealing with your loss."

"My mom is… was amazing… Always supportive of me. She was always at my matches in school. Made sure I had everything I wanted… I just can't believe she's gone." He burst into tears, covering his face with his hand as his body jerked in tears. Fawn hugged him, comforting him with quiet words.

Her heart ached seeing Peter in such pain. Death was cruel, leaving behind heartache and a feeling of vulnerability.

"She was the happiest person when Peter got into medical school two years ago. The proudest mom in all of Mount High," Malinda said with a smile, as she relived her friend's happiness.

"And how has school been? Medical school must be crazy," Dahlia said, trying to ease his mind.

"Umm… yeah it is going well. But I don't know if I really want to be a doctor after losing my mom," Peter said.

"Don't say that! It is not what Eleanor would have wanted. You have to follow through and make her proud. You can't quit now, not after transferring back to Dent," Malinda scolded.

"Oh, I had no idea you had transferred to Dent University," Dahlia said. Dent was about an hour's drive from Mount Hugh; it was a much bigger town with a thriving economy mostly attributed to the university established there.

"Dent College of Surgeons," Fawn corrected.

"You moved closer to home," Dahlia pointed out.

Peter nodded. "Colorado was too far away. From my family. From Fawn," he smiled as he turned to her, and she smiled back at him tenderly. To be young and in love, Dahlia thought amused. "I moved… Transferred four months ago…"

"Three months ago," Fawn said.

"Yeah, three months ago. This way I get to see my family every weekend."

"And how has school been?" Dahlia asked. Despite being in a small town, Dent university was a top university amongst these parts.

"Great! The lecturers are helpful, and the library is pretty good. A lot of materials there," Peter said.

"Yeah, great textbooks over there," Fawn added.

Dahlia retained a plain gaze, but there was something off, she couldn't pinpoint just yet. "Did your mom ever visit you on campus?" she asked.

"Peter is always busy with his studies, or spending time with me, or our friends. And Eleanor is always busy, besides he comes home every weekend," Fawn answered for him.

"I would like us to pick up on this tomorrow. Give you some time to come up with memories of your mom, and also work more on my questions, since this is quite impromptu for me to be honest," Dahlia admitted. She had a list of questions in her notebook to fit different scenarios, but none were tailored towards grief.

"That would be great! To have you back here. That way you get to meet Leonard my husband. He went over to see poor William," Malinda said.

"Thanks a lot for your time. Is ten tomorrow okay?" Dahlia asked.

Malinda nodded. "That's awesome!"

She spared Peter one last look as he leaned onto Fawn's bosom. As she walked out of the house, she ran into the two men from the diner.

"Good morning gentlemen," she said politely.

"You are not from around here. Got a bit of color in you and squinted eyes," Aaron said.

For a moment she was stunned silent. Had he just said that? "No, I am not from around here."

"You friends with the Maximoffs?" he enquired.

"No, I dropped by for an interview with the Mayor's son," she said, flashing a polite smile.

Aaron frowned, clearly upset by her response. "You can't do that! You need to talk to me first. I am in charge of this investigation. I have to first give you clearance and share with you what you should know. Now I am a very busy man so you have to come around to the station for that interview."

"My questions are no obstacles to your investigation. Let it also be clear that the interviews I conducted were consented to," Dahlia said, holding Aaron's gaze as his nose flared at her rebuttal.

"You are going to get into trouble if you keep interviewing my suspects," Aaron said.

"Ms...?"

"Crane," Dahlia offered.

"What my colleague Aaron is saying is that—"

"Cut it out boy, I can handle myself. Stay off my case woman. You want to know about the investigation, come around to the station and fix a meeting with me."

"See you around constable," Dahlia smiled broadly as his nose flared at the jab. She heard him whine to Elijah as she walked towards her car. The nerve of him! If he thought she was actually going to go down to the station and sit with him, he was certainly wrong. Dahlia didn't like to judge people by her first encounter with them, but she was sure that Aaron was a self-absorbed prick who liked the sound of his voice.

There was some network signal on her phone and she called Naomi. She answered on the first ring.

"How's my adventurous journalist doing?" Naomi asked.

Dahlia smiled as she reclined on the seat. That was Naomi's nickname for her. Adventurous journalist because she was ready to take on anything. It didn't matter if she climbed up the Everest, or went into the deep forests of the Amazon, she would tell a passionate story about communities.

"How does it feel to be back in Mount Hugh?"

"There's a bit of nostalgia, and sadness I suppose. The town is a few steps from being a ghost town. Done with class?"

Naomi was a lecturer at a small private college in Colorado, where she taught Theoretical mathematics and Computer coding.

"Yeah, heading out for breakfast, before going for my afternoon class. Decided on what angle to go with for your paper?" Naomi asked.

"Well… A murder happened this morning, the mayor's former wife," Dahlia smiled as she sensed Noami's excitement on the other end.

"Dahlia Crane, you have a way of finding yourself in interesting situations," Naomi teased.

Dahlia chuckled. "I think I am going to explore the grief angle. It is new for me, but there is a lot of potential. By the way, how robust is Dent medical school?"

"We are talking about the Dent close to Mount High?"

"The very same one," Dahlia confirmed.

"They don't have a medical school. There are three colleges, biomedical, biotechnology and… let me ask my assistant…" There was a bit of silence and then Naomi was back. "Bioinformatics."

Dahlia frowned at this. "Are you sure about this?"

"As sure as I can be. Dent was one of the collages I got an offer from before deciding on Crimson. It used to be medical and nursing school, but this was until… 1963… yeah, then the medical school closed down, I think they had an issue with accreditation, or it was moved. But Dent right now just has those three colleges I mentioned. Is there a problem?"

"No…No Problem at all…"

Dahlia's thoughts trailed off. Why then had Peter and Fawn lied to her?

CHAPTER FOUR
CURTAIN CALL

Elijah felt like he was watching a play. A bad one. Maybe an audition or something from a beginner's drama class. Bad improv.

The man who had bustled in had been about to say something, to launch into a certain conversation, but as soon as he saw the police officers his demeanor changed, and he seemed to switch scripts.

"Leonard," the mayor said.

"Oh, Abdoullah," the man said, putting on a show of the emotion he was feeling. "I'm so sorry for your loss."

"Thank you, Leonard," Abdoullah, said. "It's such a shock." He seemed to be naturally matching the newcomer's emotion.

"Leonard," the mayor said. "I was just talking to these men, police officers, about her. Gentlemen, this is Leonard Maximoff."

Something was off. For one thing, the phrase, "sorry for your loss," while pretty common on greeting cards, didn't feel specific enough for the situation, given that the men had been long-time business partners. It was delivered with *apparent* emotion, but Elijah wasn't really feeling it, and he prided himself on his intuition when it came to sincerity. He had seen enough bad theatre in his day. These guys were performing for their benefit. *Something* wasn't being said, Elijah was certain of that. It would have been a very different conversation has there been no police presence.

"The business partner, right?" Grayson said, standing and extending a hand. Maximoff shook it, his expression neutral. "You guys put in the turbines?"

"That's right," said Maximoff with a nervous smile.

"Are you two still working together?" Elijah asked. He'd noticed that before their surprise visitor, Lark had only referred to their partnership in the past tense. It had seemed a subconscious choice, but perhaps a telling on.

"Yes," said Abdoullah. "We parted ways in business. It's natural, you know. People's interests change and they have their own things they want to pursue. But we go way back in spite of that."

Leonard nodded. "We do. Our families were very close. I've known Abdoullah and Eleanor for years. If anything, this tragedy will bring us closer. I am *here* for you, buddy."

Elijah kept his face neutral, but his B.S. detector was going off. More amateur theatre? Part of his issue was that Abdoullah was exhibiting a greater degree of grief now that Maximoff had arrived. Almost as if he were reading his ex-partner's take on the scene and trying to match him. He seemed sadder, more aggrieved, now than he had been when he'd given his initial interview. He was behaving almost as a grieving husband, not a grieving ex-husband who had a contentious relationship with the deceased. To Elijah, this made him seem more, rather than less, suspicious. Initially, when he'd seemed thoughtful but not particularly emotional, it had read as sincere. The thing that threw him was, *this* seemed sincere too. His manner had changed significantly, but his grief didn't seem obviously fake. Was this subterfuge or could it simply be a sincere reaction that came out when he was around his long-time friend? Grief was tricky and took a while to sink in. And people naturally reacted differently depending on context.

Maybe he wasn't guilty, but Elijah suspected that he too might be holding something back.

And Maximoff? His performance was even worse. He'd been so clearly taken aback when he saw the two detectives, he almost did a double take, then awkwardly shifted his demeanour into one more appropriate for the situation. Everything about Maximoff read as fake to Elijah, even his concern and condolences. At this point, Elijah knew little about him except that he was some sort of businessman. A developer or industrialist. He wondered if he was that certain breed of near-sociopathic capitalist that he had observed on occasions; men who would do anything necessary to get to the top and remain there, men for whom lying was just as natural as breathing.

"Listen, gentlemen," Abdoullah said. "Do you have enough information to get started? I haven't seen Leonard for some time and would like the chance to catch up. Particularly given the circumstances."

"Oh, sure," said Grayson. "You fellas have yourselves a nice conversation there. Call me at this number if anything comes up that you think would be useful for the investigation." He handed him a card.

"I absolutely will," Abdoullah said, taking the card, his delivery indicating such a complete willingness to cooperate that Elijah wasn't sure he bought it.

"And hey Bill, William or Abdul, or whatever you prefer," Aaron began brusquely. Elijah winced at the insensitivity and knew that it wasn't mere obliviousness; his partner knew what he was doing, knew when he was being insulting. "Where can we find this boy of yours. Peter, right?"

Abdoullah frowned. "Do you have to bring him into this?" he asked.

"Sensitive, right?" Grayson said. "You mentioned that he was sensitive. Well, I'd sure hate to upset him but, seeing as how he's the one who found the body, I thought he might have something of relevance to share." Grayson said this with a deadpan expression, but there was an obvious hostility boiling right beneath the surface.

"Oh, of course," Abdoullah said. "What was I thinking. He's been staying at Leonard's house."

"Yes," put in Maximoff. "He's there with my wife Malinda and our daughter, Fawn."

"Yes," Abdoullah said. "He and Fawn are dating."

From the way he said it, Elijah couldn't tell if he thought that was a good thing or a bad one. Maximoff's expression was similarly opaque. Abdoullah gave them an address and the men stepped out.

"So, what did you think of that?" Elijah asked, once they were outside.

"That?" Grayson said. "*That* was bullshit. Especially once Maximoff showed up I could tell we weren't going to get anything useful. I figure, let's go poke around elsewhere and see what we can turn up and then maybe circle back and talk to each one of those two separately. See if we can get them to contradict each other. Catch them in a lie."

Elijah nodded, pleased that, in this one case at least, they were in sync.

"So, where to now?" Elijah said from the passenger's seat. It was really just a conversation-starter since he presumed he knew the answer: to the Maximoff residence.

"How about we grab some lunch?" Grayson said.

Elijah bit down on an annoyed reaction. Really? Another meal? Do you think greasy food is an integral part of detective-work?

Instead, he said, "Isn't it a little early?"

Grayson shrugged. "I need protein. Helps me think." Elijah didn't even know what to do with that one. He wasn't a doctor, but he'd never heard about a connection between protein intake and problem-solving. "I know a good greasy spoon out in the county. They've got great biscuits and gravy."

Twenty minutes later, they were seated at a diner off the interstate named Molly's. Grayson had his biscuits and gravy, and Elijah had a fish sandwich. Grayson had argued for the biscuits, but Elijah put his foot down this time. He couldn't keep up with Grayson's culinary habits without unnecessarily increasing his risk of heart disease. And besides, he didn't like letting the old man order for him. It felt like a tactic, a way of asserting dominance, like the top dog in the pack. Elijah wasn't sure what he had been expecting, but he was pretty sure the fish was definitively *not* freshly caught or locally sources. He was fairly certain that the patty slapped into the bun in a bath of mayo was one he could have bought in the freezer aisle at the local supermarket.

Elijah took a disappointed bite of his sandwich and Grayson shook his head.

"You got to eat the specials, Riley," he said. "These local dives can only get a couple of things right."

Elijah shrugged, annoyed that his choice hadn't panned out. "I'm not really hungry, anyway," he said, putting down the sandwich and taking a sip of his iced tea. "So, what do you think?"

"Well, like I said, all of that stunk to high heaven," Grayson said. "Those fellows are lying. Or hiding something."

"I'm inclined to agree with that assessment," Elijah said.

"It's bringing me back to my original theory. The ex-husband."

"Well, I agree that they're keeping something hidden," Elijah said. "But how do you figure him for guilty? Are they in it together? That doesn't really fit your theory about an angry ex."

"Maybe not that version," Grayson said. "But a divorce is a full court press. Screws you up on a number of levels. Hits you in the emotions. Feel like you're losing control of your life. *And* there's the financial aspect, right? You get divorced, you stand to lose money. This Maximoff is a business partner. Maybe there's an angle."

"But this divorce is long ago litigated. Those emotions have to be going cold. I don't see how the financial angle explains a murder."

"I don't know. Maybe he finally got fed up paying alimony?" Grayson frowned, as if noticing that he was talking out of his ass, then said, "Anyway, I'm still working on it. But trust me, that mayor is up to something. Everything about the guy is fishy. A secret Muslim passing himself off as a regular American to get elected?"

Elijah groaned inwardly. He took issue with the presumption behind the phrase "regular American" but decided it wasn't worth getting into. Half of his partner's wrong-headedness was there to prove a point or get a reaction. Best ignored.

"I think the mayor is deep into it. Whatever it is. Maybe the murder. Could be something else, I guess. But he's in it."

"He might be hiding something, but I don't know if we can assume it's necessarily relevant to the investigation. He's not obligated to reveal irrelevant secrets."

"Nah. It's relevant. The mayor's smooth. Used to lying. The other guy? Maximoff? That one's jumpy. He's the one we should lean on."

"Maybe," Elijah said.

"What?" Grayson asked. "You aint buying his B.S., are you?"

"I don't disagree about Maximoff," Elijah said. "I saw his mask slip. He didn't expect anyone to be there, and his demeanour completely changed. Abdoullah, though? I think he might just be overwhelmed with the situation and doing the best he can." Grayson frowned, like he'd tasted something that disagreed with him. The dismissiveness was getting to Elijah. "You know," he said. "I'm pretty good at reading people." He had a hard time imagining that Grayson, insensitive bull in a China shop that he was, could say the same.

"Sure, partner," said Grayson. "You've built up some instincts in your years on the force. But I've been doing this for decades and I'm telling you those guys are liars. Both of them."

For a moment, Elijah just looked down at his fish sandwich, as if fascinated by the sesame seeds on the bun. Grayson loved pushing buttons, and he'd stumbled upon a big one. The older man seemed to have an unreasonable and unrelenting confidence. He believed, with certainty, every passing thought that originated in his head. Conversely, he completely disregarded all of Elijah's suggestions. It wasn't just that he disagreed, it was that he didn't consider them even worth considering. Elijah was still dealing with the fallout of having been raised by a similarly minded egotist: his father.

Growing up on the streets of Philly, Elijah's dad had been similarly old-school. An Irish Catholic who had, himself, been brought up with the most traditional of American values. One would think that Elijah, now a police officer, would have passed muster and met his father's standards for masculinity, but no: the old man's rubric had been too severe. He had seemed to resent Elijah for a number of things: his education, his open-mindedness, his willingness to acknowledge shades of gray in morality. But the worst offense he had committed was that he didn't choose to serve in the military. His father had been a military officer, a proud Marine, serving both in Korea and Vietnam. For him, it had been a foregone conclusion that his only male child would follow him in this tradition.

But there were signs, early on, that he was on a different path. As a child he had spent most of his time with his nose buried in a book. It wasn't something that his father exactly discouraged this—it was hard to justify pushing back against childhood literacy—but he'd regularly advocate for, as he called it, "balance." *You should spend more time outside. When I was a kid, I was more rough and tumble...* His father seemed to view Elijah as a failure.

So, as Elijah approached adulthood, military service had crystallized as *the* issue, the one that stood in for a lifetime of failing to meet up to his dad's expectations of masculinity. They got into heated arguments about it.

What's the point? During peacetime?

I can be of more service to my country in other ways.

I don't need the GI Bill. I have scholarships...

Ultimately, Elijah had followed his own path. He'd *had* to. His dad was an overbearing figure, and it was easy to just concede. But in this one thing he'd stood firm. If he let his dad push him into a career in the military, then he'd have given up his autonomy forever. He'd have let himself become his dad's proxy, just another enlisted man following his orders. The path he found for himself led to college, first a liberal arts degree which over time morphed into criminal justice. By the time he found himself enlisting in the police academy, part of his brain wondered: was all of it a sort of concession to his father's worldview? Had his subconscious led him into law enforcement as a way to prove his masculine worth to his dad?

He tended to reject such armchair psychology. The fact was, he'd never satisfied his dad, but he felt comfortable in his own masculinity. Masculinity as *he* saw it. The fifties were a long time ago...

All of this came back as he sat across the table, counting sesame seeds, considering his response to his dismissive partner, a product of similar upbringing and endowed with a similarly bull-headed psychology as his father.

"Well," Elijah said. "I don't know if it's wise to jump to any conclusions at this point."

Grayson shrugged. "The man just rubs me the wrong way."

"That's exactly what I'm talking about. It would be crazy to ignore all other possibilities because someone rubs you the wrong way."

"But that's what I was talking about. It's what my gut is telling me."

"Then let me ask you this: how many people rub you the wrong way? On a daily basis? From the time you get up to the time you go to bed? Hell, *I* rub you the wrong way and you know it. And how many of those people are murderers?"

Grayson laughed. "Well, I don't peg you for a suspect, Riley," Grayson said. "I figure your alibi's good."

There it was. The dismissive tone. You could never win an argument against a person with this kind of personality because he ultimately didn't respect the rules of engagement. Logic and rhetoric meant nothing. It was all about instinct, about will. About certainty. And if Elijah made a good point, all Grayson had to do was blow it off. Make a joke. Belittle.

Just like dad.

Elijah was annoyed at Grayson but also annoyed at his own reaction. It seemed so predictable. A son who had never received affirmation from his father reliving the patterns of resentment and praise-seeking with the first older mentor to come along. Almost embarrassingly simplistic in terms of psychology.

"Why is it so important to you?" Elijah asked. "Why does it have to be the simple solution? Why does it have to come from your gut? What does that prove?"

"I'm not trying to *prove* anything," Grayson said. "I'm just going with what I know works. You should try it."

Elijah shook his head. "I worry that you're becoming obsessed with the case. It's something they warn you about, you know? If you become obsessed, then you start to try to force your prime suspects into their roles as the guilty rather than approaching evidence with an open mind. Maybe you need to take a step back before you go into some kind of spiral."

Grayson just laughed at this like it was the funniest thing he'd ever heard.

"You playing head-shrinker now, Riley?" he asked, digging his fork into the biscuits and gravy. "Trust me, I'm fine."

Elijah wasn't so sure. His dad had been the same way. Presenting his front of confidence, of arrogance, to the world, like he hadn't needed anyone or anything, when the truth had been much more complicated.

By the time they were pulling up outside the Maximoff's, Elijah's stomach was rebelling. He'd mostly finished the unimpressive sandwich and was regretting it. As much as he hated to admit it, maybe Grayson was right and sticking to the specialties was the best approach to small-town diners. His mind was preoccupied with his intestinal situation as they moved up the walkway and he had been shocked to look up and see the woman from that morning at the Watering Hole. The sophisticated, almost glamorous woman who had so stood out, every visual cue sending the message that she wasn't from around here.

Their encounter with her was brief and, in its aftermath, the woman remained as mysterious to Elijah as ever aside from one tidbit of information, her name: Dahlia Crane. She was apparently conducting her own investigation which, predictably ruffled Grayson's feathers. She passed by them like a whirlwind, leaving Elijah a bit stunned and Grayson furious. As she moved past them, he turned towards Elijah, furious.

"What the hell was that?" he asked.

"What was what?"

"Your whole, 'what my partner is trying to say,' routine?" Grayson's eyes were narrowed to slits. "Listen, kid, I know you think I'm going off the rails, but I don't need you following me around apologizing for me or providing translations or whatever the hell that was supposed to be. Okay? You're overstepping. It borders on insubordination."

That word, insubordination, triggered a response in Elijah. Rage. It had been the same word his father had used every time Elijah had expressed disagreement: undoubtedly something he had brought with him from his military career. He felt an urge to lash back and tell Grayson what he really thought of him, that he needed to stop letting his desire to prove himself the alpha-male in every situation impede his investigation, but he forced himself to take a breath before speaking. Elijah hated to lose control, hated to let his emotions drive his actions, and he knew that if he did so now his angry retort would be fuelled by decades of unsatisfied frustration with his own father. Instead, he looked at it from Grayson's perspective. This woman *was* horning in on their investigation. Maybe he was justified in his snippiness? And maybe Elijah, in stepping in to try to modify his superior's response, had come off as condescending?

Maybe.

"Don't ever interrupt when I'm talking to someone, okay?" Grayson added, hotly. "I know what I'm doing. I don't need you stepping in and mucking things up."

Elijah, having considered the matter, simply nodded. "Got it," he said. "Won't happen again."

Grayson looked almost surprised, as if he had been relishing the prospect of an argument. "Well, good," he said and the two continued down the walk towards the front door of the Maximoff house.

"Do you know who that woman was?" Elijah asked.

"No clue," Grayson responded. "All I know is she better watch herself or she'd going to end out in jail for obstruction of justice."

"She was the girl from this morning. At the Watering Hole."

"Hmmm," Grayson said. "You don't say? Well, maybe you were onto something with her." Grayson knocked at the front door. A moment later a pleasant looking woman answered.

"Hi there," Grayson said. "We're police officers. We'd like to talk to you about Eleanor Pomeroy."

"Certainly," she said. "Come in."

The home was solidly middle-class, leaning toward "upper," and had a number of colourful flourishes that seemed to reflect the personality of the woman who identified herself as Malinda. Glancing around, Elijah noticed a display cabinet full of photos. Inside were pictures, some were school photos or ones commemorating professional accomplishments, such as the dedication of the turbines, but many pictured the two linked families: the Maximoff's and the Larks. In some of them, they were younger, still childless: two couples partying, double-dating, taking beach vacations together. In later ones, their children were also present, a boy and girl that looked to be approximately the same age, often hand-in-hand, seeming to foreshadow their current relationship.

Elijah focused on a few pictures in particular that showed the younger Malinda, Eleanor, and a third young woman, an attractive brunette, who did not look familiar to him. In the photos they were smiling for the camera. The body language seemed to imply to Elijah that the third woman was closer to Eleanor. In the photos, this unknown woman seemed to lean in towards Eleanor, and Eleanor always seemed to occupy the middle spot between the other girls. Elijah wondered if this might be one of those cases where one friend acted as a sort of bridge between other friends, brokering connections between acquaintances who didn't really yet know each other. In one photo, Eleanor was giving the young woman a hug while handed her a beautiful necklace, a line of exquisite pearls leading to a central pendant of white gold with embedded pearls in the shape of the letter "C." From the context clues of the decorations in the background, of the photograph, Elijah assumed it was the mystery woman's birthday. He wondered who she was and if the letter "C" might be a hint as to her identity. He made a mental note. Perhaps it would bear looking into…

"It's just so awful," Malinda said as she led them towards the kitchen table to sit. "I am just in shock. Who could think to do such a thing to such a wonderful woman."

She sounded sincere enough, but Elijah couldn't help noticing subtle cues that might suggest otherwise. She was wearing a floral dress, her hair immaculately styled, and wearing makeup: presenting as a woman perhaps about to go on a date, not one mourning the loss of a close friend. Upbeat jazz music played in the background, further confusing the picture she presented.

They sat at the kitchen table and Malinda served them coffee and cupcakes that she said she'd made that morning. Before she found out her good friend was beheaded? Elijah found himself wondering.

"So, who was that lady that we passed on the way in?" Grayson asked.

"She said she was a student. A journalist. Working on a PhD," Malinda said.

"A PhD?" Grayson asked. "On what subject?"

"I wasn't clear, exactly," Ms. Maximoff said. "She said it was about small towns thought. A positive perspective."

Grayson's frown clearly indicated what he thought of that. Elijah could almost hear the response coming: hogwash! But Grayson, apparently sometimes capable of exercising self-control, responded more diplomatically. "Well, you need to be careful. Journalists aren't always trustworthy. They'll twist things to make a good story and sometimes the positive perspective is the first thing to go out the window. I don't guess she showed you any credentials, did she?"

"No," Malinda said. "I didn't think to ask."

"Of course, she didn't. But you noticed, we showed you badges as soon as we stepped in, right? Because we have a legitimate reason to ask you questions. I'd suggest not talking to anyone else about the case without checking in with us first. You don't want to accidentally reveal something to a reporter that'd going to hamper our investigation."

"Oh, definitely not," Malinda said. "I loved Eleanor so much. It's very important to me that whoever is behind this be brought to justice."

Grayson nodded. "Of course, you do," he said. "So, can you tell me a little bit about your relationship with the deceased?"

She began to recall in detail the friendship that had existed between her and her husband, Leonard, and the Larks. The men had been business partners and the women had been best friends and the children had been playmates. It all sounded wonderful, the perfect friendship between families. But Elijah noticed that she too referred to their friendship in the past tense, just as the mayor had done when discussing his and Maximoff's business partnership. He wondered the degree and nature of the falling out that had occurred. As Grayson asked follow-up questions, Elijah found his attention wandering to what sounded like an intense conversation happening elsewhere in the house, seemingly resonating down through the floorboards from upstairs. He had first become aware of it in the lull between two songs and since he'd been able to focus on it, filtering out some of the noise in his head. It sounded like two young adults, one male and one female. Occasionally, he'd hear an occasional recognizable phrase when a voice was raised for emphasis. He picked up, "what should we do," and "what are we going to say." He wondered if the purpose of the bed of jazz music had been to mask this conversation.

He glanced over at Grayson to see if he had picked up on this, but he seemed completely immersed in his conversation. He probably didn't have the best hearing anyway: too much time on the gun range and the natural winnowing that happened with age doing their damage.

"We all went to college together," Malinda was saying. "Bill and Leonard were inseparable. They looked after each other like brothers. Kindred spirits, the two of them. They went off to school together but were both determined to return home to Mount Hugh and make a difference. And they did."

"Right," said Grayson. "The windmills."

"The turbines," she corrected. Elijah had no doubt that by this point, Grayson knew that the word was turbines and not windmills. It was all part of his gruff act, his constant button pushing. Sending out the message to the world that he was a gruff and backwards. What was the point of that act? To feed his own ego? Telling himself that he, as a throwback, was better than the watered-down men of the modern age? Could it all be a tactic? To throw suspects off balance? "Yes. They were a tremendous boon, providing reliable and affordable power and heat, especially during the winters which had always been unpredictable around here. They saw a problem and they solved it."

"Made a pretty penny doing it too, didn't they?" Grayson asked with a wicked grin. "And Bill, he got himself into local politics. Changing the world pays off if you do it right."

Malinda frowned, clearly displeased that he was poking holes in the narrative she'd chosen to present.

"So, what happened?" Grayson asked. "Why did they stop being chummy? I get the sense they had some kind of falling out."

"Well, they drifted apart over the years," she said. "It happens."

"I know that," Grayson said. "But what, specifically, caused them to drift apart?"

"Me and Leonard, we're pretty traditional. We grew up here in a small American town and those are our values."

"Right," Grayson said. "And you didn't like it when he jumped ship. Left the church. Decided he was a Muslim. Changed his name."

"Right," she said. "That's part of it. But it's not just the religious part. Like I said, we're regular folks. Leonard works hard and likes to cut loose on the weekends. He and Bill always had that in common. But once Bill had his conversion, he changed. Now he doesn't drink. Doesn't go to parties. Doesn't gamble. All of a sudden, he started disapproving of everything they'd used to have in common."

"Sounds like a wet blanket," Grayson said with a chuckle.

"That's one way to put it," she said. "But that's the gist of it. There's no bad blood between them. They just don't click anymore as friends."

There was another pause between songs in the jazz which emanated, unseen, from somewhere in the house and Elijah could hear, as clear as day, the female voice in the ongoing discussion say, "Just do what I asked you to do!" He couldn't know the context, only picking up a line here and there, but she sounded irate.

"So, this journalist lady, what was she asking you about?" Grayson said, apparently still oblivious to the argument upstairs. "What did she want to talk about?"

"She was interested in how people grieve in a small town," she said. "She heard about Eleanor and, I guess, saw an opportunity to get some research for her paper. She wanted to talk to Peter."

"He's around?" Grayson asked. "I might like to talk to him too."

Malinda stepped to the stairwell and called up.

While she was out of the room, Grayson turned towards Elijah. "You're being a bit quiet there, pal. Everything okay?"

"Everything's fine," Elijah said. "I'm just following orders."

"What orders?"

"You told me to keep my mouth shut, didn't you?" Elijah asked.

"Oh, Jesus," Grayson said. "You don't have to get all dramatic about it, okay? I just said don't interrupt me. Why don't you interview the kid."

"You sure?"

"Yeah, I'm sure," Grayson said. "Besides, I already have my suspect. All I need is evidence."

Elijah frowned. Grayson was *certain* the mayor had done it. He'd tried to warn his older partner about the danger of pre-emptive certainty and how it could derail an investigation, but of course, it had made no impact. Like everything else, it had gone in one ear and out the other. It galled him that Grayson was just treating the investigation like a series of obligatory boxes to be checked off as he narrowed in on his chosen suspect.

Malinda returned with Peter, accompanied by a young woman, her daughter: Fawn Maximoff. Malinda handled the introductions. Peter was a good-looking guy, built like a quarterback, and Fawn was a dark eyed beauty. But there was trouble in paradise. Peter's eyes were red-rimmed. Clearly, he had been crying. Elijah might have assumed they were, naturally, tears of grief. His mother had just been murdered, after all. But the overheard snatches of conversation that had drifted down from upstairs suggested that there might be something more complicated going on. Clearly the two had argued. Fawn had been trying to compel Peter to do… something.

But what?

"How can we help you?" Fawn asked, almost as if she was acting like Peter's representative. His lawyer. The two sat down at the table while Malinda went over to the counter to brew another cup of coffee.

"Pleased to meet you," Grayson said. "We're just here to ask *Peter* here a couple of questions."

Peter looked nervously to Fawn. Elijah wondered what was going on in that relationship. It certainly seemed like Fawn had him under her thumb.

"Detective Riley," Grayson said. "Why don't you handle this interview. Peter, my associate is going to ask you a few questions. I know you've had a rough day, but this should only take a few minutes."

Elijah nodded and prepared to begin. There was a logical series of questions to ask. About his relationship with his mother. When did he last see her. Had she expressed any concern for her safety recently? Did she have any enemies?

But Elijah felt compelled to throw that script out the window. He felt compelled to impress Grayson. Yes, he knew it was partially the desire to receive approval from his latest hard-to-please father figure, but that was only part of it. He also felt that he needed to shock Grayson out of his certainty. He needed to show him that there was more going on than he perceived. More than his gut told him. That the world was not all about the comfort of simple answers, that nuance existed.

He had to do the unexpected.

"Of course," Peter said. "What do you want to know?"

But instead of addressing Peter, Elijah instead looked at Fawn. He locked eyes with her, gazing so intently that she turned away.

"Ms. Maximoff," he said. "Fawn. Earlier, while my partner was interviewing your mother, I could hear you two upstairs." Elijah knew that it was a bold move but felt it was called for.

"Yes," she said. "We were having a conversation."

"Conversation?" he said. "It sounded more like an argument. And I distinctly heard you say the phrase, 'just do what I asked you to do.' I could hear it so clearly because you pretty much yelled it. You sounded mad. Frustrated. So, what I'd like to know is what were you two discussing upstairs? What had you asked Peter that was so important that you felt compelled you yell at him like that a couple of hours after he found out his mother had been murdered."

The room spiralled into a tightly wound tension. Peter's eyes widened; he looked like he was about to have a panic attack. Fawn looked desperately towards her mother, as if seeking a lifeline. Malinda just looked shocked; Elijah couldn't tell if she was in on whatever was going on or if she was utterly confused. And Aaron Grayson, for once, looked shocked as well. Elijah couldn't remember ever seeing him so thrown off his game. For a moment, everyone was silent, unmoving, like a theatrical tableau.

And Elijah revelled in it. He had pulled a pin and tossed a grenade, taking confident and decisive action that was sure to shake loose some answers when the dust cleared. And yes, part of his brain was aware that he was repeating the same tired pattern, trying to prove his value, his masculinity, to Grayson, but another part didn't care.

For that part, it was worth it simply to see the look on Grayson's face.

Chapter Five
Unscheduled Surgery

What the hell?

Aaron Grayson couldn't believe what he was hearing. He'd just told Elijah to watch himself. Not to go stepping on his toes and mucking up the investigation. The kid even made a big show, acting like a drama queen, telling him he was keeping his mouth shut because he'd been told to do so. But now? He jumped in accusing an interviewee. Of what exactly? What point was he trying to make?

But then, he saw the reaction. Saw little Miss Fawn start to stammer. He could see it in her eyes. Grayson supressed a grin. I'll be damned, he thought. He's onto something…

Fawn, who clearly wore the pants in the relationship, was the first to respond. "Well, you must have misheard," she said. "We were talking. Peter is naturally upset. I mean, his mother just died."

"Uh-huh," Aaron said and then, turning to Peter. "So, Pete, why don't you tell me, in your own words, what exactly my partner misheard. What do you think you guys were talking about when your girlfriend told you that you just needed to do what she'd asked you to do?" Peter looked over to Fawn as if seeking guidance. "Hey," Aaron said forcefully, annoyed at this weak-willed pantywaist, following his girl around like she was his commanding officer. "I'm talking to you. Look at me, not her. She doesn't get to help you."

"We were talking about college," he said. "I can't see myself finishing up. It's all too much. Mom… I was talking about how I wanted to drop out."

"And your girlfriend doesn't want you to?" Peter just nodded. Grayson wasn't sure if that was the truth or if Peter had just decided to agree with the suggestion. In any case, Fawn looked like the kind of princess who'd want to make sure her boyfriend had plenty in his bank account.

"He's been talking about it since this morning," Malinda said, jumping in. Grayson had almost forgotten she was in the room. "He's adamant that he's going to drop out of medical school."

Medical school. Aaron's mind started racing. This was significant. For one thing, it explained the Fawn situation. A girl might be willing to put up with a weak-willed man if he was going to be bringing in those doctor dollars. But more importantly: Peter suddenly looked good for it. Not only might he have the kind of surgical skills, maybe even the medical tools, to cleanly remove the victim's head from her body, but he was also the one who found the body. Well, that was his story. He'd called it in. But who knew what happened before the call came in? Maybe when he'd found her, she'd still been alive. Maybe he only called the cops after he'd done his sick business, killing his own mother and then taking off her head. Grayson couldn't even begin to guess what was beneath it all, but Elijah's theory about a serial killer mentality made a lot of sense. Weren't a lot of these guys momma's boys? Like Norman Bates, screwed in the head by overbearing mothers. Only instead of taking it out on girlfriends or hookers, maybe Peter had skipped the middleman and gone straight to the source of his problems.

For a moment, he tried to square it away with everything else he knew. The born-again Muslim mayor was definitely shady and, if anything, his business partner was even worse. The two had definitely been conspiring. But it only took a second's thought to realize that maybe the conspiracy had been to cover up for Peter.

You didn't have to bend over backwards to make sense of it. When Maximoff had burst into the room, he'd been showing up for a strategy session. Circling their wagons. If Peter had killed Eleanor, both men had an interest in getting him off the hook. Bill Lark, or whatever his name is, wasn't in love with his ex anymore. Maybe he was glad she was gone. And Maximoff? He was protecting his daughter's boyfriend. Admittedly, maybe you wouldn't want a surgical psychopath as a son-in-law—sure, there were still details to work out —but by and large, the story checked out.

There was a lot there. A good story for the cameras. Frustrated child, a repressed head-case kills his mom. Performs surgery on her head. It had everything: patricide, a cover up, shock value. The reporters would have a field day with that: a real headline grabber. And it would be Detective Aaron Grayson appearing on the nightly news in soundbites that would be picked up nationally, explaining exactly how he had caught the bastard.

"So, tell me about…" Elijah began to speak but Aaron cut him off. Now that he saw Peter as a person of interest, he no longer felt inclined to pass the ball to his young partner. Elijah might fumble and besides, Grayson wanted to be in the driver's seat. It would be his face on the camera after all.

"So, medical school," Grayson said. "What are we talking here? Surgery?"

"Yes," Malinda said with an almost parental pride. "Peter is studying at Dent College."

"That's right," Peter said. "I studied for a year outside the state and now I'm back in the area, going to Dent."

Aaron had a mixed reaction to this revelation. On the one hand, he was pleased to hear Peter admit to surgical training because it fit the narrative forming in Grayson's head regarding the murder. On the other: there was a problem.

"That's strange," Grayson said. "Because Dent College doesn't have a medical school."

"But I…" Peter stammered. "It does. You must be mistaken."

But Aaron knew he wasn't. These folks might have never gotten out of Mount Hugh but he did. Regularly. He knew the lay of the land on the local scene. If Dent College was giving out medical degrees, he'd have known it. It was the kind of deception that might have only worked on a woman like Malinda whose whole life revolved around her social status. He wondered if Fawn was in on the lie, but soon got his answer.

"You should check your facts, detective," she said with a slightly pushy tone. "He does study medicine at Dent."

So, she was in on it. He'd heard the exaggerated defensiveness from liars enough over the years to recognize it. They overplay outrage like that's going to get them off the hook, but what they're really doing is tipping their hands. She was acting all huffy because she was lying.

"Maybe you're confusing Dent with another college?" she suggested.

"Listen, Fawn," Aaron said. "I've lived in this state nearly my whole life. I know the score."

"Well, if he's attending there," Elijah suggested hesitantly, looking towards Aaron as if seeking permission to speak. "Then the medical school should be able to provide a departmental reference and confirm his attendance."

"Great idea," he said, grinning. "Why don't you get us one of those letters? Back up your story."

"Absolutely," Peter said. "I can ask for that. It might take a few days for them to get back to me. You know how these schools are with their bureaucratic red tape."

"Sure," Aaron said with a laugh, recognizing an excuse when he heard one. "The wheels grind slowly. But in a case like this, I'm sure they can expedite the process. This is a murder investigation, after all. Why don't you just give us the name of your department head and an email or office number, and we can take care of it."

"I know it's a murder investigation," Peter said, seeming to grow pale. "But what does that have to do with it? You don't think I did it, do you?"

"I'm not saying that," Aaron said. "I just want to check out your story since there seems to be some disagreement."

Malinda looked confused. "I really don't see what all of this has to do with anything," she said. "What difference does it make what classes Peter has?"

"Just being thorough," Grayson said, as if that explained everything, knowing that it didn't. But in his head, it was important. Means, motive, and opportunity. Nail all three down and you've found your killer. Opportunity was easy. He was there. No alibi. Yes, he called the police, but that didn't mean anything. Means. That was what the surgical training might help establish and was a big part of the reason for the tangent over Peter's school credentials.

And then there was motive. Aaron turned this over in his mind, mapping out some theories. It could be an inheritance issue. During his years on the force, he'd seen money motivate murder so many times. Probably more than any other motive. But maybe that didn't fit, because of the sick nature of the crime, the condition of the body? Maybe it was a long seething resentment, something from childhood, an unresolved mother/son feud? Grayson had to admit he liked that better. He needed to work a few things out, but if there was some deep psychological issue between Peter and the deceased, maybe it could have pushed him over the edge into that serial killer methodology that Elijah was so fond of discussing. As he'd pointed out before, so somebody gets a kick out of severing heads: doesn't mean he doesn't have a reason. Why do all serial killer victims have to be randomly chosen?

One thing he wasn't sure about is what the point was of lying about the college. He'd play along with the letter of confirmation, but he knew with a certainty that Dent College was not turning out surgeons. So, why lie? Did it speak to an alibi? Was Peter somehow trying to use college enrolment to account for himself? Didn't seem likely considering he'd placed himself at the scene. Or maybe it was the source of disagreement between him and Eleanor. Had they argued about his choice of career? His status as a student? It was possible. It could fit the theory that she'd been an overbearing smothering type and he'd been a Norman Bates in the making.

Peter looked like he was growing pale. His skin looked damp. Malinda was looking at him in concern.

"You have to take it easy on him," she said.

Aaron looked at the boy and what he felt was disgust. This weak-willed momma's boy. Probably a psycho to boot. "He'll be okay," Grayson said.

Suddenly the woman's features hardened into a defiant entitlement. The consummate all-American hostess, all polite and sweet, disappeared and Grayson could see the hard ass who now revealed herself was the real Malinda Maximoff. "No, he won't," she said her voice as hard as steel. "He's just a boy. And his mother just died. Can you see the toll it's taking on him?"

Grayson glanced over. The boy looked bad, but he wasn't sold on the reason. Was it grief? Or guilt? Or anxiety over lies called out? Who knew. All Grayson knew for sure was that he didn't like the way this lady was talking to him.

"First off, stop calling him a boy. He might act like one, but he's out in the world. Going to college. Unless he got confused about that part. But he's all grown up. No reason to keep coddling him like he can't handle himself."

Malinda started to say something, probably the bit about how sensitive he way, but he cut her off.

"Second," he said loudly, talking over her. "This is a criminal investigation. I'm a cop. You're out of your lane, lady. Stick to the cupcakes and coffee."

He could see her eyes widen, her lips tighten, in outrage. The expression was familiar and was usually followed up with, "how dare you?" or "do you know who you're speaking to?" but to circumvent those predictable reactions, Grayson gave her his nastiest glare, brows arched and lips drawn into a grim smile, sending the message: I dare you. Try it. See what happens.

Wisely, she backed down and made herself busy, wiping down a perfectly clean countertop with a dishrag.

"Okay, Pete," Aaron said, turning back towards his interviewee. "So, when did you find the body?"

Peter took a deep breath, closing his eyes for a second before responding. "It was around five-thirty."

"Were you up that early? Still up?"

"No, I'd been asleep. My mother had left to meet with dad at around ten and I'd gone to bed a little after that. In the middle of the night, I woke up."

"What woke you up?" Aaron asked.

"Weird noises. There was some kind of loud thump. But also, it seemed like all of the dogs in the neighbourhood were barking. And crows were cawing."

"Crows?" Elijah asked. "Do crows caw in the middle of the night?"

"Not usually," said Grayson. What the hell is this? he wondered. Some kind of fairy tale? "They're usually asleep. They're not nocturnal or anything."

"It was weird," Peter said. "Freaky."

"And did you get up?" Elijah asked.

"No. I was too tired. And I guess I thought I might have been dreaming. I rolled over and went back to sleep."

"What time was this?" Grayson asked.

"Around three. I glanced at the clock. Anyway, as soon as I closed my eyes, I felt panicked."

"Because of the noises?" Aaron said, adding dismissively, "The dogs and birds going nuts?"

"I don't know. Not really. I just felt, deep inside, a sense of danger. You know, like fight or flight? I felt like something was coming. A threat. My heart was racing. Adrenalin pumping. I was overwhelmed." Overwhelmed? Grayson supressed a scowl. This kid was so weak he couldn't handle anything. Scared of the dark like a child. "I must have fallen asleep again because when I opened my eyes, the clock said five-thirty. Outside, I could see the sun coming up behind the turbines on the hillside," Peter looked down at his hands thoughtfully, pausing for a moment. Grayson noted that his eyes were moist around the edges. Grief, a guilty conscience, or maybe just his weakness showing through. Was he overwhelmed now? "Usually by then my mom is up and ready for her morning run. I thought I'd join her. Felt like it would do me good. Kind of shake out the cobwebs, you know? I was still feeling freaked out."

At this point, a long pause extending for an uncomfortable duration. It was Elijah that broke the silence.

"And then?"

As Peter continued, his eyes widened in horror, as if it were replaying in his head, and his voice took on a quaver. The moisture at the edge of his eyes welled up and tears dripped down his cheeks.

"As I crossed the hallway, I could feel a cool breeze through her doorway. Air coming in through her window. That was odd. Even before I looked inside, I knew something was wrong. The door was only cracked, almost closed. So, I knocked. And then...." A shudder ran through Peter, like it had overtaken his whole body: head to toe. "That's when I found her. Her body. Lying across the bed, in a pool of blood. And the..." his voice choked as the word came out, rough, as if torn. "... her head. Sitting on the sill of the open window. Eyes closed."

Aaron Grayson was not impressed. Sure, the kids gave a good performance, turning on the waterworks and shuddering on cue, but that wasn't uncommon. Liars always put on a good show. What you had to think about was their reasons. Grayson had asked him what had happened. Simple question. He hadn't asked about his feelings. Yet, in telling his tale, the details he focused on had all about his feelings. When Grayson asked himself why Peter might approach the story that way, the answer was obvious and twofold. For one thing, it helped his case to establish he was upset. This was textbook guilty party playacting. You play up the shock and grief to put everyone off your tail. But in Peter's case, it also served his narrative about how weak he was. You even heard other people saying it: he was sensitive. And he continually showed it, in his relationship with Fawn, in his every reaction: this guy was weak. Paper thin. He had everyone believing it. So, how might that impression benefit him? Again, the answer was clear. If he was weak and sensitive, it became harder to believe that, in the middle of the night, he'd simply gone across the hall, sliced up his mom. Maybe after, he'd gone back to bed. Caught up on his sleep.

In Grayson's mind, that version of the story became more and more convincing. It all added up. Peter had the surgical background. He clearly had a history of lying because of his college fib. He was right across the hall from his mom and had 'found' her. No alibi. And this weird story about the dogs and crows. Maybe that made sense in his diseased mind, but to Grayson it was just more proof that this kid was unhinged.

Aaron glanced over at Elijah, who had dutifully been taking notes in a small legal pad during the interview. "Okay," he said. "Let's wrap it up. We have what we need here." Elijah raised an eyebrow as if he wasn't sure he agreed. Grayson ignored him. "Listen kids," he said, addressing Fawn and Peter. "I want you to get me that letter confirming Pete's classes by tonight."

"Tonight?" Fawn asked. "I don't know if we can do that."

"You've got all day," Grayson said. "Try it."

"Listen," Elijah said. "It might be easier if we just request it ourselves. They'll turn it over quickly if they know it will help an investigation." Grayson nodded approvingly at the suggestion, pleased that his partner knew his way around the college bureaucrats. Aaron, for his part, hadn't attended college. Maybe you'd pick up a thing or two that would be useful, a job skill here or there, but their bread and butter seemed to be filling people's heads with weird ideas.

"I'd rather you didn't call up my school telling them it's part of a murder investigation," Peter said.

"They'll think he's a suspect," Fawn added.

Who says he isn't? Aaron thought smugly. But he wasn't ready to tell them that. Not yet.

"We'll figure it out," Malinda said. "We'll get it to you today."

"Swell," Aaron said. "Well, you folks have a lovely day. Let's get out of here."

"A lovely day?" Elijah asked as they were walking back to the car.

"What's wrong with that?" Grayson asked.

"Well, they just lost somebody," Elijah responded. "It seems insensitive."

"Ahhh," Grayson waved away the complaint. "The hell with sensitive. I'm not here to coddle people's feelings. I'm here to catch a killer."

Elijah looked like disagreed but kept his mouth shut. "So, where are we going now?" he asked as they got in the car.

"I don't know," said Aaron. "Still early for dinner. Want to get a cup of coffee?"

"What is it with you and diners," Elijah asked. "Shouldn't we be doing more interviews?"

"We'll get to it," Grayson said. "But I need time to collect my thoughts. Chew things over. Diners are good for that."

"Okay," Elijah said. "Your call, I guess. Any thoughts on Peter?"

"Well," Aaron said, working it out in his head as he spoke the words. "The boy is very suspicious. I can very easily imagine him doing it. And I think he and Fawn might be involved in some sort of cover up."

"The college thing?"

"Yeah. Whatever that turns out to be. They definitely lied about that."

"Then why bother with the letter?"

"That lets me see what kind of lies they come up with," Grayson said with a smile. "Rope to hang themselves with."

"I thought you liked the mayor for the murder."

"I do. That's what's annoying me about all of this. You know my theory, right? Go straight to the most likely suspect?"

"Sure," Elijah said. "I don't necessarily agree with it, but I know your theory."

Aaron chuckled. "Anyway, here's the problem. Bill Lark? Obvious suspect. Fishy as hell. Leonard Maximoff? Even fishier. Clearly up to something. Peter and Fawn? Same deal. We've got too many liars. Too much bullshit to sort through. No obvious answer."

Elijah shrugged. "Then I guess all that's left is to do our jobs."

"Okay, smartass," Aaron said, grinning in spite of himself. "Watch it." The kid was right of course. They'd just have to sort through all of it. It was annoying that so many of his potential suspects were up to something. Hiding secrets. Some of it might relate to the case and some would inevitably be irrelevant bullshit. Less than a day in and he was already swimming in it.

And there was this woman, the journalist or college student, or whatever. Nosing around. Was she hiding something too? More likely, she was just trying to make a name for herself. He began to imagine her detailing the case, writing an article in one of those fancy academic journals about him, the detective who solved this complex crime penetrating and sorting layers of confusion to arrive at the truth. He'd be in the headlines, on the magazines, and they'd even be studying him in those same colleges that he'd always been so dismissive of.

Maybe this Dahlia would be useful after all. Maybe. If he could steer her in the right direction.

"What's on your mind?" Elijah asked.

"Hm?"

"You were miles away," Elijah said. "Chewing things over?"

"What's your opinion on that Crane woman?" Aaron asked.

"Well, I don't really see the problem," Elijah said. "It seems like she's writing about the emotional toll of grief on a small town. I doubt she'll step on our toes or impact our investigation."

"I disagree," Aaron said. "She's going to be nosing around asking questions of the same people we're talking to. To me, that feels like interfering. How do I know her questions aren't going to change their thinking about what happened?"

"I suppose," Elijah said, seeming unconvinced.

"And it's not just that. What if she changes their thinking on us. She's sniffing around our suspects and our investigation. How do I know she's not going to do another one of these law-enforcement hit pieces?"

"That seems paranoid," Elijah said.

"Does it? Don't you watch the news? The message is out there. You can't trust the police. Or the government in general. You see it all the time. Ow do I know she's not going to send that message out there with my name all over it."

"Well, there are reasons," Elijah said. "There's a lot of corruption out there. And hypocrisy. Police that bend the rules, or don't apply them equally."

"That's bullshit," Aaron said. Of course, Elijah, bleeding-heart-liberal that he clearly was, would feel that way. "That's what's wrong with the world these days. That kind of thinking. That disrespect for law and order. People want to nitpick everything we do instead of respecting our authority."

"Questioning corruption isn't nitpicking."

"So, what? There are dishonest cops? That's true in any profession. There are crooked shop owners and schoolteachers.

That's not a problem with cops, it's human nature. If anything, it's the reason we need cops that can get the job done. But all of the weak-kneed pansies out there want to whine and complain about rights violations."

Elijah didn't say anything in response, but Aaron noticed that his teeth were tightly clenched. As he were about to go off, or maybe repressing a reaction.

Grayson didn't care. "So don't let yourself get swayed by all the nonsense in the press. You're a cop. A law officer. Your job is important, and you deserve respect." This was the downside to Dahlia's continued involvement in their case. It was very easy to imagine this big city know-it-all coming in and representing the police as crooked or, even worse, incompetent. For a moment, Aaron felt horrified, imagining his name dragged through the mud. Press could cut either way: making you a hero or a laughingstock.

No, she would have to be controlled, that much was clear. He relished the idea of running into her again so he could lay down some ground rules.

"So, how about Peter's story?" Elijah said. "It was wild. Like something out of a horror movie. He was so focused on the fear he was feeling."

"Yeah," Grayson responded. "I noticed that too. He's an imaginative sort of kid."

"It's all so odd. The weird sounds in the middle of the night. Do you think he maybe… I don't know… sensed that his mom was in danger?"

"I don't think we can start considering angles like that," Grayson said. "It's just as possible that he's got a screw loose and imagined all of that. Or made it up. I say we take him in for questioning. Put on a little pressure. See if he cracks."

Elijah looked thoughtful for a moment and Aaron was anticipating some objection, but instead Elijah said, "Sounds like a good idea." He was quiet for a moment and then asked. "Do you believe in ghosts, Aaron?"

"I am a man of God. I believe in his word. In the good book. You'd do well to do the same."

"I was raised in the church," Elijah said. Aaron could tell from the way that he said it that there was more to the story.

"Right," he said. "So, what? You left the church?"

"I did," he said. "I got away from home. From my father. And I learned about the world."

"I figured," Grayson said. "You went off to school and they filled your head with a bunch of nonsense. Think they have all the answers. That science can show you the way. Hogwash! It seems ironic to me. The world's usually a pretty simply place but at college they convince you otherwise. Higher learning? Hah! The colleges just make people dumb."

"Uh-huh," Elijah said. "Or maybe you're sticking to the easy answers because its more comforting to see the world in black and white."

"Do your folks know that you're an atheist? You're mom, she's Mexican, right? Catholic. And Riley's Irish. So, I'm betting you're a double Catholic. How can you not be practicing?"

"Well, my mother passed away when I was a teenager," Elijah said.

This wasn't what Grayson was expecting and for a moment, he was quiet, uncertain how to proceed. Eventually he said, "But your dad. He's a Christian, right?"

Elijah was quiet a moment before answering. "Yes," he said. "He was." The simple phrase seemed charged with negativity. Aaron, uncertain of the ground under his feet in this conversation, decided to let the matter slide. He had clearly hit on a sore spot. Maybe that was his partner's problem: a lack of loving parents. Perhaps that's why he went so overboard with the bleeding-heart nonsense. He compensated for the lack of a loving home by overdoing the empathy. Some kids, lacking a loving family, lash out at the world and some spend their lives looking for surrogate parents. Maybe Elijah was in the second category. Aaron figured he'd throw the kid a bone.

"Well anyway, you handled yourself well in there," Aaron said. "Initially, I didn't know where you were going when you told Fawn what you heard, but it worked. You rattled them and I think we learned something." He could see Elijah brighten a bit. "So, job well done. How about I treat you to dinner as your reward?"

"I thought you said it was too early for dinner?"

Grayson looked at the clock on the car's dashboard. "Ah, screw it. I'm hungry. Let's go. How about we hit up the Watering Hole again? I want to try their meatloaf."

He didn't tell him, but he had another reason for wanting to return to the local dive.

On the way over, they got a call from headquarters. The dispatch informed them that a massive snowstorm was heading their way. They said it wouldn't be safe to go over the mountain roads towards the state police substation and their homes. The department was offering to put them up in the Mount Hugh Inn for the night, a hundred-year-old hotel that dated from the area's early days as a small mining town and the only hotel within fifteen miles.

"Helen's going to be disappointed," Elijah said, glumly. "She spends all day chasing Dora around and looks forward to the break."

Aaron was still feeling uncharacteristically sympathetic to his young partner, certain he'd correctly psychoanalyzed him as suffering from a lack of proper parenting. He resisted the urge to berate him as weak-willed and too worried about currying favor with his wife and instead just said, "She's a cop's wife. She'll understand."

They decided to get their dinner before settling in at the inn. As they walked through the door, Aaron saw her, just as he'd hoped. Dahlia. Trying to hook up some kind of phone cord to her computer.

"There she is," Grayson said.

"Hoping to run into her?" Elijah asked.

Grayson cast him a glance. He's observant. I'll give him that, he thought. "I've been wanting to talk to this lady. I think we need to lay some ground rules."

"That doesn't sound like a good idea," said Elijah.

"Why not? We can't have her making us look like idiots."

"If she does, it's her constitutional right to do so," Elijah said. Grayson just glared at him, unmoved. "Bill of rights? Freedom of the press? And of this ring a bell?"

"Why don't you just let me do the talking," Aaron said. Elijah's only answer was an annoyed sigh.

Grayson boldly walked across the dining area, much busier in the evening, and strode up to Dahlia. He stopped less than a foot from her, so she'd have to crane her neck up to see him. Basic intimidation tactics that any veteran cop would know. "What're you working on there?" he asked gruffly."

"Hooking up an ethernet cable so I can get online." Dahlia seemed completely nonplussed at his presence.

Grayson nodded although he really didn't get what she was talking about. At least a couple of the words were totally meaningless to him. "Swell," he said. "So, are you working for any particular news organization?"

"Listen," she said. "I don't have to disclose that, and I'm not interested in doing so."

"Well, I have a right to look into people nosing around my investigations."

"Really?" she said. "Do you? What gives you that right?"

Aaron couldn't think of a particular ordinance of the top of his head. Growing frustrated, he said. "Well, if you interfere, I can bring you in for obstruction."

"I haven't interfered and don't plan to," she said with a smug smile that pissed him off. "How about this: you don't interfere with my work, and I don't interfere with yours? Besides, my work is protected under the first amendment."

Grayson could see Elijah grinning from the corner of his eye.

"Just tell me who you're working for," he said. "I know you don't want trouble."

"Are you trying to intimidate me?" she asked.

"Nah," he said. "I'm just saying, if you find me annoying now, wait'll you see me after you refuse to answer my questions. This is nothing."

"Fine," she said, exasperated. "I'm here researching for my dissertation, but I have a job offer at a new agency once I finish it. That's it. Nothing for you to worry about."

Aaron wasn't sure. Anything she dug up could easily find its way into her reporting for this news organization. "How about I make you a little deal?" he said. "I'll let you keep doing what you're doing. Researching. I'll get off your back. All you have to do is keep me in the loop and let me give my input."

"First of all," she said. "You don't get to let me do anything. I'm well within my rights. Second: why should I include you in my research? What business is it of yours?"

"Fine," Aaron said, his voice gaining volume. "You want to play it that way? Listen: your presence here is causing interference. You're running around talking to my suspects. Doing that is affecting my work. You might be putting ideas in their heads. So, lay off."

"Listen," Elijah said in a placating tone. "I'm sure we can discuss this reasonably…"

"I'm done being reasonable," Aaron said. "I tried that, and princess wouldn't have it. So, let me lay it out for you. If I catch you nosing around my suspects, you're going to find yourself locked up."

"Listen," she said. "It's not my fault if you can't do your job. If you think you know who did it, why haven't you already brought them in instead of hassling random grad students."

"I have someone lined up," Aaron said. "I'm building a case. That's how this works. You just watch your back." As he turned, Dahlia blurted out.

"So, what, you've got your scapegoat? Is it going to be the same as last time."

Aaron wheeled on her. "What the hell are you talking about?" he asked.

"You ever heard of Hugh Slaughter?" she said. Aaron had heard it mentioned but didn't know the details. Just one of these fairytales the locals talked about. Like Bigfoot or Jack the Ripper.

"Yeah," he said. "So what?"

"I just think it's interesting. This crime is linked to another murder that happened twenty-five years ago. Same method. Female victim. There wasn't really much of an investigation. It seems like the cops back then just brushed it under the rug. Like maybe they were warned away. Or bought off." At this point, she pulled out a copy of a black-and-white photo. Aaron and Elijah leaned in to look at it. In the picture, a gruesome headless body lay discarded along a trail running through a valley. Trees lined mountainsides receded in the background. In the picture, several policemen stood around the body.

Aaron fumed at this attack. Another self-righteous liberal trying to paint cops as corrupt or evil. But, for a moment, he was still struck silent by the revelation.

This was an angle he hadn't seen coming.

"This isn't over," he said, and was only through the exercise of self-control that he didn't finish the sentence with the word "bitch."

Aaron led the way across the space to another seat, well across the room and out of earshot. He'd be damned if that nosy girl was going to eavesdrop on them.

"If she wants to butt heads, then so be it," he said. "She can just find out the hard way." Elijah didn't respond and Grayson, looking over, saw something surprising in his expression. "You okay?" he asked. "You look like you just saw a ghost."

"Maybe I did," he said. "Sort of."

"What are you talking about?" Grayson asked.

"That picture," Elijah said. "Wherever she got it… newspaper archives? I don't know. But in the photo, there was a small detail that stood out to me. A necklace lying on the ground beside the body."

"Oh yeah?" Grayson asked. "Didn't notice that myself. So, what?"

"I'd seen that same necklace once before. Earlier today." Grayson leaned forward, having no idea where this was going. "It was in a photograph at Malinda Maximoff's house. In the picture, Maximoff was giving the necklace to a woman I'd never seen before."

"What?" Grayson was struck, shocked at the revelation. "You mean…?"

"Yes," Elijah said. "I think the Maximoff's knew the victim from twenty-five years ago!"

CHAPTER SIX
CURIOSITY KILLS THE CAT

Phone to her ear, Naomi stared blankly. At the little cul de sac, the modest but pleasant little houses, the huge wind turbines on the hillside, slowly turning like gigantic pieces of clockwork. Her eyes took this in neutrally; they were just the backdrop. Inside, her mind was racing, trying to piece together a new puzzle.

Why had Peter and Fawn lied to her about Peter's program? Naomi had clarified the situation: Dent had no medical school. Hadn't for decades. So, why were the two lying?

It would be easy, she supposed, to assume they were hiding something related to the murder. To speculate involvement. But Dahlia was not prone to rash or exaggerated reactions, and she couldn't see the angle. How did falsifying a medical school relate to murder? It wouldn't supply an alibi: quite the opposite. As anyone with even a passing familiarity with mystery novels or cop shows knew, the first thing investigating officers would do would be to check alibis. A simple call to the school in question would clarify the issue. No, making up a school as an attempted alibi would only ascertain the failure of the alibi. So, what? Dahlia vaguely imagined some domestic drama behind it. Perhaps some pressure regarding parental expectations? She didn't know. She didn't know how this piece fit into the larger puzzle, but it was significant.

"Honey?" Naomi said. "Is something wrong?"

In her distracted state, Dahlia had forgotten that her girlfriend was still on the line.

"It's fine," Dahlia said.

"They told you he was there for *medical* school? Is it possible you misunderstood?"

"Sure, maybe that's it. Maybe I misheard. Or they misspoke." Even as she said it, Dahlia knew it wasn't true. As she reviewed the conversation in her head, she could remember the way they'd spoken, the way they'd underlined the school's location. They'd made a point of it. It was something she needed to mull further, but nothing she needed to worry Naomi about. "In any case, it's not really important to my dissertation. That's where I've got to put my energy."

"You're damned right!" Naomi said with a laugh. "I know you, baby. I know how you love going down those rabbit holes. But you're going to need to monitor your own tangents since I'm not there to rein you in."

Dahlia smiled. Naomi *did* know her. She knew her well. Dahlia had a free-associating mind. She went into a situation with the outlines of a plan, but an openness to being led in a surprising direction. When she indulged these impulses unchecked, she ran the risk of losing track of her original goals. It boiled down to personality types. She was a creative thinker. It was partially from this approach that Naomi had coined the term "adventurous journalist." She'd seen Dahlia reading a book on the "adventure journalism" movement of the nineteenth century, a movement in which intrepid reporters brought back travel stories from some of the most far flung, remote, and dangerous corners of the world: naturally appealing to Dahlia's sensibilities. Naomi had jokingly modified the term to "adventurous journalism" to cover Dahlia's wide-open approach to any story or investigation.

To her life itself, really.

Although they loved each other, they were very different. Naomi wanted to control her world, while Dahlia wanted to be swept away in experiences that were not necessarily under her control. Dahlia's ways had bewildered, and at times frustrated, Naomi with her mathematical mind and systematic ways. Naomi was a total left-brainer but had, over time, learned to find Dahlia's more creative approach endearing. At least that's what she said. They were very different but, having chosen to honor those differences, their union seemed to be working. For the time being, anyway.

"When are you coming home?" Naomi asked.

"For now, I need to stay," Dahlia said. "There's a massive snowstorm rolling in and I'm going to have to wait it out. The roads aren't going to be safe."

"Where are you going to spend the night?"

"The Mount Hugh Inn, of course," Dahlia said in a mocking tone. "Not a lot of five-star hotels out this way. I've got it booked for two days."

"Two days?" Naomi said. "I was hoping to see you sooner."

"I know," Dahlia said. "I'm playing it safe. The roads get crazy out here and I'm not sure what my tire treads can handle. I don't want to end out stuck out on an unplowed road waiting for someone to dig me out. Besides, if I can do a little investigating in the meantime, I may not have to make a follow-up visit."

"Uh-huh," Naomi said in a sulking tone.

"I'll call you every morning and every night. I promise," she said. "This *should* appeal to your rational mind, right? If I can get my work done on this visit, I won't have to come back. It'll be a net gain for our time together. Do your cost benefit analysis. It holds up."

Naomi laughed. "Okay, okay," she said. "You convinced me. Well, why don't you let me use my rigorous mind and organized approach to help you get your act together."

"Okay," Dahlia said, uncertain where she was going with this.

"Tell me your plan for the day. Your itinerary for your next steps. You know, that plan you go in with and subsequently throw out the window when you get a whim or see a shiny object?"

Dahlia laughed, well-used to the ribbing. "Okay. Yes. My plan. My itinerary," she said and then, after a pause, "I don't know. I don't know where to start. I feel like this project is pulling me in a lot of different directions. My mind keeps wandering."

"Looking for a rabbit to chase down a hole?"

"Maybe," Dahlia said. "Or maybe it's the journalist in me. Trying to figure out *what* the story is."

"That would drive me crazy," Naomi said. "How can you work on something when you don't even know what problem you're trying to solve?"

"That's why I'm the journalist and you're the math professor."

"Well, you *do* seem especially scattered with this one," Naomi said. "Is it possible that your memories, your baggage or whatever, are making it harder for you to stay on target? Are you feeling homesick? Or regretful?"

"I don't know," she said. "Maybe I *am* processing something. I was *very* young when I left. Only three. Not a lot of time to get attached. But still, I remember things. Since I've been here, I keep having these moments when I'll turn a corner and see something that I'd never have remembered otherwise but feels totally familiar. It's like discovering memories you didn't know you had."

"And is this making it hard for you to figure out what the story is?"

"Maybe. Maybe it's confusing the issue. I'm getting so wrapped up in my barely remembered childhood, I don't know if I'm coming or going. I don't know what the questions are I should be asking."

"Hm. Well, if I was writing a dissertation, I'd start at the library. Do they have one there?"

For Dahlia, it was one of those light-bulb moments. She needed the big picture of the town and its history. She needed to take a step back, to zoom out. Sometimes, when you were too close to a picture, you couldn't perceive the pattern. For her, her own memories have been skewing her perspective.

"That's perfect," she said.

"The library?" Naomi asked.

"Not exactly," she said. "But there's a bookstore here. They keep an archive of local content. The local paper, local writers. Anything relating to Mount Hugh. It's the perfect place to start."

"See?" Naomi said. "You have a plan after all."

"I do," Dahlia said. "A one-item itinerary."

"Hey, it's a start," Naomi said. "At least it'll keep you going until you find a rabbit to chase."

The bookstore looked vintage, built with the same dusty looking bricks from which the oldest buildings in town had been built. Although Dahlia didn't specifically remember it from her

Mount High toddlerhood, she knew it must have been there for at least a half a century. The faded sign out front read, "The Story Shelf," hanging over a tattered green awning. Inside, it was the best kind of chaos, perfectly appealing to Dahlia's creative mind. The shelves overflowed with books, sometimes stacked in oppositional directions, sometimes spilling over into piles on the floor. There were signs hanging above certain shelves, Sharpie on printer paper: *Mystery. Biography. History. Fiction. Children's.* But the system didn't seem sufficient to explicate the chaos. No, in this kind of bookstore, you needed a guide.

"Hi there," she asked the owner.

He was an old man, balding and stick-skinny, and peered at her suspiciously over a pair of bifocals secured with a chain that threaded behind his neck. His white hair had receded and stuck up in tufts around his ears like a neglected lawn.

"You need something?" he asked coldly.

Dahlia recognized the attitude. He saw the same people every day, as he had for years, and the appearance of a stranger threw his whole world out of kilter. Maybe he was used to outsiders talking down to him or annoying him with rude questions. Dahlia put on her "regular folks" smile. She had quite an arsenal and prided herself on knowing which smile to use on which occasion. There was a smile of polite professionalism that was often hands and another of shared intellectual superiority that she trotted out for dinners with professors and the other doctoral students her cohort. The wrong smile at the wrong time could make your audience feel condescended to or insulted.

"Morning," she said. She considered following it up by telling him what she loved about local bookstores. It was true. She loved the chaos of a room filled with books. She loved the fact that you could go in with no idea what you were looking for and come out with exactly what you needed. It appealed to her creative brain and its non-linear random-access processes. But she thought better of it. Trying to explain her love of run-down disorganized bookstores felt like it ran the risk of coming off as an unintentional insult. A rhetorical bear trap she was in danger of stepping into. Instead, she simply said, "I'm new in town."

"Uh-huh," the old man cocked a weedy eyebrow, white and overgrown with skewed darker hairs, as if this confirmed his suspicions. She was an outsider.

"Well, not really new, exactly. I was born here. Haven't been back since I was a kid. You know, I left when I was only three and I *still* remember things. I keep seeing stuff I recognize." All true, all sincere. But the sincerity was, in a sense, the ploy. She was opening herself up to him and giving him a chance to accept her as, at least, an honorary local.

"Three, huh?" he said, marginally warming up. "Do you remember this place? Been here for forty years."

"I do!" she said with excitement. That part was a lie. She didn't remember the store at all. "I love that nothing's changed." That, too, was not entirely true. There was a comfort in seeing things she remembered but, at the same time, the feeling that time stood still in Mount Hugh sort of depressed her. The biggest change since her childhood were the massive windmills on the hillside, all the more prominent in that they seemed to be the *only* change. They stood out like a sore thumb. A small town, stuck in an earlier decade, an idyllic Mayberry of a town, with these wild-looking modern devices, like something out of a sci-fi model, shoehorned into the landscape.

In any case, that seemed to do it; the old man's face fully thawed into a smile.

"And how can I help you?" he said.

"I'm here writing my dissertation about my hometown." Again, she was playing to the audience. Keeping it simple and appealing to his apparent biases. Did it even make sense that you would write a dissertation on "your hometown"? Of course not. You'd be laughed out of academia. But explaining dissertational premise and what it had to say about small communities. Yes, it was looking to present a positive perspective, but there were lots of complicated issues to untangle that she'd rather not get into in the case the man had follow-up questions. And she certainly wasn't going to mention the murder. That would flag her as a nosy outsider, stirring up problems. No, better to let the man imagine that her paper was going to be about how wonderful the town was. Like an elementary school essay. Fifty words on why you love your town. "I heard you had some kind of archive."

"That we do," said the old man, beaming with pride. He was not merely the clerk of *The Story Shelf,* but it's owner, that much was clear. She would tell from the way he puffed himself up, his slumpy posture suddenly correcting, that the archive was a personal project and one in which he took a lot of unapologetic satisfaction. "Come with me."

"Wonderful," she said. "I'd love to see what you have regarding the history of Mount Hugh and anything related to local fairs or celebrations."

"Come with me, young lady," he said. Stepping from behind the counter.

Oooh, young lady, she thought. *I'm in.* A clear term of endearment, polite with a bundled-in compliment. Probably what he called his teenage nieces Following him to a dusty bookshelf in the back, Dahlia smiled to herself. She was good at reading people, at knowing the right approach to take. She didn't think of it as dishonestly, more like a kind of social intelligence. Everyone had to adjust their personalities situationally. You didn't talk to your grandma the same way you'd talk to your children or your lover. It was natural. Dahlia was just more self-aware when it came to these adjustments.

"I'll be up front if you need anything," the old man said, transformed by her social acuity from curmudgeon to grandfatherly sweetheart.

The archive consisted of a single bookshelf. There were four shelves, wide and tall, and they were packed with leatherbound newspapers and other supplemental materials, including self-published novels by local authors as well as various histories of the town written decades apart by members of the Mount Hugh historical society. The collection reflected the passion of a guiding hand, probably the man she'd just met, but the layer of dust spoke to its relative disuse. Another reason, perhaps, that the man had warmed up to her. His beloved archive apparently didn't get many visitors.

Uncertain where to start, Dahlia began in the nineteen-sixties and started working her way forward. A lot of it was what you'd expect from a small-town paper. Local papers served an almost opposite function from their national counterparts. While, often, national papers sought to titillate readers into buying a copy, through shocking headlines or controversial editorials, the mission statement of local papers was often regarded as "building consensus" or "reinforcing a sense of community." Local papers tended to underline the things the community members have in common. And while this was conceptually interesting in the abstract, in practice it was often dreadfully boring as local editors avoided controversy like the plague in favor of puff pieces about high school events and church functions. Sometimes you had to read between the lines of a small-town paper to figure out what was really going on.

Dahlia pulled out the older volumes and sat down at a small wooden table parked in the corner apparently for that purpose. She sorted through a lot of bland consensus-building stories. Every year they'd do stories on the Harvest Festival. Coverage on the preparations and a photospread from the day itself. She had dim memories of the festival from childhood. At that age, festivals and parades and the like can feel almost magical, so she wasn't surprised that those memories were ones that had managed to stick. Occasionally, something big would stick out. The installation of the wind turbines got a lot of coverage, all of it overwhelmingly positive. She had to imagine there had been disagreements. Any major change to public utilities, especially one that permanently altered the local landscape, cluttering it with equipment, was sure to have had some opponents. She imagined local town council meetings where outraged residents had complained that they turbines would spoil the view or lower their property value. But these stories, if they had indeed happened, went unreported by the local paper and only definitively existed in Dahlia's mind as speculation. As far as the papers were concerned, it had been a triumph and the credit was squarely laid at the feet of Mayor Abdoullah and his business partner Leonard Maximoff. The two had apparently been big talkers with big plans and the paper, and presumably the local populace, had very much bought into their vision for an exciting view for Mount Hugh. The two seemed to have an almost messianic approval in the Mount Hugh Courier, and among the letters from the locals, at least the ones they'd seen fit to print, they were lauded as heroes. Consensus achieved, apparently.

In January of nineteen-seventy-one, Dahlia found one of the things she'd been looking for. The earlier murder. After countless pages of 4H functions and parent-teacher-club meetings, the stark headline and grisly picture stuck out like a sore thumb. The headline was simple, "Body Found," but it packed a punch, especially when taken in the context of what had preceded it. It was a shocker worthy of a big city paper. She questioned the judgement of the editor who had chosen to run the crime scene photo. Yes, the private parts had been blurred out in deference, no doubt, to the moral norms of the town, but it *still* had presented a headless body, naked except for a necklace. Dahlia leaned close, straining her eyes to see detail in the decades-old newsprint, faded and probably not crystal-clear when it was hot off the presses. The necklace was a simple chain with a jewelled letter "C" dangling from it. Although the head had been severed, the necklace looked almost carefully placed.

As shocking as this article was, the biggest revelation was the pattern that revealed itself in subsequent editions. Nothing. Unbelievably, there was no follow up. The editor had seen fit to run the attention-grabbing headline and then had apparently steered completely clear of the topic. This was out of sync with what she'd seen up to this point. When something noteworthy had happened, say a bus crash in nineteen sixty-three, or school vandalism in sixty-nine, there would be an initial headline, then in weeks following, information about the investigation, arrests if any, and plenty of commentary and editorializing about what it meant for Mount Hugh when tragedy struck.

But when the headless body of a murdered woman had been found? Nothing.

Dahlia struggled to understand it. Had the public outcry at the graphic photo been so severe that the editor had decided to permanently pull the plug on the story, pretending it had never happened? Dropping the subject and ignoring any letters to the editor on the subject? Or had it been a cover up? If so, at whose behest? Or was it something else entirely? The silence had a weird, almost uncanny feel. Had the town, in toto, supressed the unpleasant memory? Like a form of group hysteria? Had the town all simply emerged from the shock as if from a dream? This implied a different kind of consensus building…

More questions than answers, but they were interesting questions. As Naomi had predicted, Dahlia felt herself getting pulled down another rabbit hole. She wondered if, possibly, there was other documentation that wasn't being presented. Missing editions of the paper or other local publications that went into greater detail. The crossed back to the front of the store.

"Excuse me," she asked the owner. "Is there anything missing?"

"Missing?" he asked warily, as if looking for an insult. "Everything is there. What are you looking for?"

"I was wondering if there might be any other publication that went into more detail about the murder in seventy-one."

The change in the bookseller's demeanour was immediate. It was as if a door closed upon his expression, shutting out anything but distrust. "Why do you want to talk about *that*? I thought you wanted to tell the story of Mount Hugh."

"I do," she said. "But this seems like a major story."

"Murder is not something people discuss in polite society," he said. "It's unbecoming and it's not safe."

"Why isn't it safe?" she asked.

"Talking about it invites more of the same."

"But it must have affected people," she said. "I would think people would want to talk about it. They'd *need* to."

"Of course, it did," he said, his tone growing hotter with every word. "It reshaped the way we live our lives. Before that, people didn't even bother to lock their doors. But the murder changed all of that. Especially at night. Especially in winter."

Dahlia picked up on the fact that he was talking about the murders almost as if it were a bit of folklore. A fairy tale, functioning by the rules of fairy tales. Don't go out at night. Be wary in the wintertime. Don't talk about it or it'll come back.

"Well, I think it's back," she said, following an impulse. "Hugh Slaughter. Whoever or whatever that is. They mayor's wife died in the same way."

"I know," he interjected.

"Doesn't it seem like examining the earlier murders might help in the investigation of the current murder?"

The old man laughed. It was the first time she'd heard him laugh, but it wasn't pleasant. It was a cruel, pitying laugh. "You can't *solve* this. Hugh Slaughter isn't of this world. I don't know if it's a ghost or a demon or just some kind of evil presence. But it's beyond our power. There's no solving it. No bringing the killer to justice."

Dahlia narrowed her brows. She didn't believe in this kind of nonsense, but her social wit told her not to push back against his assertions. In his collection she'd seen several books of local "hauntings." In her travels, she'd seen this at the local level quite frequently. People who were in love with their hometowns tended to disseminate the local mythology, tending to suspend their disbelief when it came to their own personal legends.

"But then what can you do?" she asked. "When it returns."

"Lock your doors," he said. "And pray. Listen, you're not from around here. Sure, you were born here, but you're not *from* here. You may think we're a bunch of rubes, but we know things you don't. Everyone in town can sense it when the slaughterer is here. They can *feel* it. You feel afraid. Anxious, but you don't know why. The air feels thick. It was like that the other night. I woke up with the same terrible feeling I'd had so many years ago on the night of the first murder. I didn't need anyone to tell me that Hugh Slaughter was back. It was just a question of who he'd murdered."

Dahlia kept any reaction or judgement carefully absent on her face. She knew she'd burned away any good will she had with the bookseller. He'd categorized her now. As an outsider. As a busybody. She understood his perspective. He bought into the legends. Maybe it helped him process the murder. Maybe it was easier to believe that a demon was on the march than a human being was capable of such violence.

But what it didn't explain was why the papers hadn't covered it. There was no sign the police even investigated it. They'd never caught anyone, and the papers certainly didn't indicate any ongoing investigation.

The wheels in her head were spinning, details remixing, connections made via intuitive leaps. She thanked the old man for his time and letting her see the books. He didn't have to verbalize "good riddance" for her to get that message. She could read it in his expression. By the time she got to her car she had it. Her dissertation. The new version. The *real* story of Mount Hugh.

Simply put: it was the story of how a town created a local legend to help them process their grief and fear.

Dahlia headed back to the Watering Hole. While the old grump at the Story Shelf had clearly rejected her as an honorary Mount Hugh local, she was starting to feel like a regular at the town's social centre, greasy spoon by day and dive bar by night.

"Hey there," Daniel called as soon as she came through the door. The man was overeager in a way that was easy to interpret. He'd been fishing when she'd come in the first time, tossing bait in front of her and hoping she'd bite. Asking questions about her "husband." The problem was, although she'd made it clear she was spoken for, it didn't seem to make much difference. His line was still in the water. She'd told him she had a "partner" rather than a husband. She suspected that Daniel hadn't connected the dots and realized the partner in question was another woman. One would hope that might discourage his interest, but in Dahlia's experience, men were either slow on the uptake when it came to reasons to stop pursuit or otherwise just felt entitled and didn't give a damn. As wolves went, Daniel wasn't so bad. He was polite and friendly and not particularly overt. Still, she had to be careful. Another thing she'd learned from her experiences with men: they could turn on you in a split second, going from sweet and social to pissed off and grabby.

She found her seat—another sign that she was approaching regular status at the Watering Hole: she already had a regular seat— and plugged in her laptop at the ethernet outlet. As her computer connected to the internet, she remembered the overheard snatches of conversation she'd heard from the two detectives. That had been the first "distraction," as Naomi sometimes called them. Rabbits to chase or shiny objects to contemplate. To Naomi it didn't make sense. You went in with a plan and followed it rigorously. But that wasn't Dahlia, and it wasn't her style of journalism. If you go in deciding from the outset that you know what the story is, you sometimes miss the *real* story. Getting distracted by shiny objects wasn't just a sign of undiagnosed hyperactivity; it *was* an important part of the process. Dahlia was open to surprises, and she'd found ones when listening to the officers, the first ones that sent her down her current path.

Grayson, the older detective was a piece of work. Grouchy and combative. For him, everything was a pissing contest. There was probably sexism wrapped up in it too. She knew the type. So, in love with the old days and the old ways, anything new was threatening. He'd already decided that she was a threat to their investigation. Yes, she was looking into the same murder, or series of murders, but she had different goals and reasons. It seemed inevitable though, that their paths would cross again.

The other detective, the younger one, Elijah Riley had been his name, was a different story. He seemed open-minded, maybe even progressive. She had only encountered them briefly, but this was the impression she'd formed, and she trusted her instincts. She was usually dead-on in her impressions of people.

Her computer connected and she got onto an internet browser and began looking for information. The local papers didn't cover it, but it occurred to Dahlia that maybe the story had been covered elsewhere. No such luck. Nothing. Nothing on national news or even through conspiracy theorists. A major mysterious and *disturbing* unsolved murder that the whole world seemed to have ignored. Dahlia grew frustrated, feeling like she was getting nothing but dead ends.

In her searched she stumbled upon an article about Mount Hugh's Harvest Festival. The story and the accompanying images sent her back, triggering some of those earliest memories. Walking down main street, hand-in-hand with her mother, the festival arrayed around them. Decorations, games, food tents, a parade. Pure magic to her young mind. That was the last time she'd been happy as a child.

When they'd moved to the city, things had taken a darker turn. Her mother had sunk into desperation and that had led her into substance abuse, first an increasing dependence on alcohol and eventually harder drugs. This began a cycle that her mother never seemed to be able to get out of, like she was treading water and always a few breaths from drowning. Drugs led to desperation which led to depression which led to more of the same…

Her history with her mother ultimately denied her any closure. Things got bad —really bad —One day her mother left Dahlia alone in their roach-infested apartment saying she'd "be right back" and never returned. For Dahlia, it was the most violent and wrenching kind of wound. As shocking and life altering as losing a limb. For her whole life, Dahlia had speculated, had blamed herself. How could her mother do that to her? Was it her fault? What had Dahlia done? The questions had haunted her and even though now, at thirty, she realized rationally that her mother was solely to blame for abandoning her only child, she still felt the emotions she'd associated with the abandonment. Recognizing their irrationality didn't keep her from feeling them.

For her, it had been the beginning of a very dark period. The social workers had never been able to find a family to adopt her. This furthered her feelings of being unloved and abandoned, not only by her mother, but the whole world. She began to struggle with depression herself; at times it seemed like the tendency towards depression was the only thing her mother had left her. Over time, however, she rebuilt herself, finding purpose and strength. It had begun when she decided to throw herself into her schoolwork. At least here was something she could succeed in. She had done so well that she got a scholarship: the next step on her upward climb. Ultimately, her life had transformed when she met Naomi. Naomi had loved Dahlia for her strength, her empathy and, although it, at times, frustrated her, her endlessly inventive mind. Finally, for once, Dahlia wasn't on her life's journey alone and the support her partner offered gave her the breathing room to process and begin getting over her difficult past.

Life can break you or it can toughen you up. Her mother had been broken by life. Dahlia decided that she was going to be tough and if there was nobody to help her, then dammit, she'd do it herself. It had taken many long years, but she reinvented herself as the fighter she felt she'd always been destined to be.

Looking up, she saw Elijah at a nearby table eating his lunch. He was facing her direction, talking to Grayson, who had his back to Dahlia. Elijah looked annoyed. She wasn't surprised. She couldn't make out what his older partner was saying but she could tell from the tone of his voice that it was more of his blustery bullshit. She *could* hear him going on about his "gut" and what it was telling him. Men and their guts. It was the expertise they referenced when they couldn't back up their opinions or decisions. Do whatever the hell you want to do and then blame it on the gut.

Elijah looked miserable, like he was biting his tongue rather than tell the old geezer what he really thought of him. Watching Elijah, something clicked for her. Yes, the more she thought about it, the more she thought that he might prove useful…

She looked over at him, trying to catch his gaze. For a moment, he seemed to be looking right past her but then, as she waved a hand, he looked up, eyes meeting hers as Grayson droned on. She held a finger up in front of pursed lips. *Shhhh*.... Having non-verbally committed him to secrecy, she got up out of her chair and pointed towards the back entrance, then walked across the Watering Hole's wooden floor and stepped out.

There was a sign designating this as the smoking area, although it wasn't clear that it was off limits inside. She'd seen people smoking inside during the day and the building smelled of stale in the mornings, clear indication that the nighttime visitors felt free to light up.

She took out a joint, carefully stowed in a purse and took a long, renewing drag. She held it in for a moment, then exhaled.

"What is this?" Elijah asked, stepping outside.

"What does it look like?" she said with a grin.

"It looks like you're breaking the law," he said. "And it looks like you just invited a police officer out to be your witness."

"Is that your beat?" she asked playfully. "Busting people for possession? Don't you have bigger problems than that?"

"Maybe," he said.

"Want a hit?" She held the joint in his direction.

In spite of himself, Elijah grinned. "Don't push your luck."

"More for me, then," she said, taking a long drag. Elijah looked uncomfortable but didn't verbalize an objection.

"Well, listen," he said. "If Grayson comes out here, he's *definitely* not going to look the other way. He thinks I'm at the bathroom but he's going to come looking for me eventually."

Dahlia was pleased, having established a friendly vibe. She couldn't help but take some pleasure in this. She really was good at reading people. Maybe it had been the upshot of having nobody for so long; she'd learned how to quickly establish connections. Elijah was receptive. It wasn't exactly flirtatious. That's something she wouldn't use. It would be unfair to Naomi. But she was being playful, teasing him like a younger brother, and he was grinning in spite of himself, even as he was trying to give her a hard time.

"So, why don't you get down to business?" he continued. "Why did you call me out here?"

Dahlia smiled and took another puff.

CHAPTER SEVEN
CAT AND MOUSE

"Uh-huh," Elijah took a bite of his tuna salad sandwich. Aaron had tried to push him into ordering a burger, as if greasy food was a virtue, as if, in his skewed worldview, the ingestion of animal fat was essential to maintaining your manhood rather than just serving to clog your arteries. But Elijah stuck to his guns and ordered the tuna salad. It's not like tuna salad was a controversial choice. It wasn't 'health food.' But everything was a show to Grayson, a big production with him on the stage.

The conversation had been like that as well. A delusional monologue about how close they are to solving the case and how big a news story it was going to be, as if they press coverage were a primary concern. Elijah was trying to ignore it, but he kept getting annoyed at himself for indulging him.

"Cause when we solve it—and mark my words, we're going to solve it, we're going to blow it wide open—the press is going to be on us like a hurricane." Elijah was very familiar with Grayson's gruff exterior and was a little surprised to hear this apparent cognizance of press coverage. Was this kind of attention really important to a dyed-in-the-wool man's man? For a moment, Elijah wondered the extent to which Aaron Grayson, world-class throwback, might just be a self-conscious construction, one as recognizable and consistent as the persona of a golden age movie star—John Wayne came to mind. Maybe he had a movie star level ego as well.

"You ever worked a big case like this one?" Grayson continued. "A high-profile murder case, with shocking, over the top, details?

They eat this stuff up like its ice cream. Think of it. Headless corpse. Powerful perpetrators."

"Powerful perpetrators?" Elijah asked, honestly confused.

"Yes, powerful. The mayor and the businessman? Between the two of them they pretty much run this town."

"Did you solve the case while I wasn't looking?" Elijah asked. "Last I checked Abdoullah and Maximoff were suspects. People of interest."

"Trust me," Grayson said. "They're involved. I have a gut feeling."

Grayson and his damned gut. Was it all the burger grease that gave his gut these investigative powers?

"It's possible," Elijah said. "But unproven."

"I bet you five thousand dollars that it's the mayor," he said.

"That's a lot of confidence in your gut," Elijah said.

"Let's shake on it," Aaron said, leaning across the table and extending his hand. "Five thousand dollars."

"I'm not going to bet you," Elijah said. "It's not that I think the mayor is innocent. It's just that I have an open mind. I want to see where the evidence leads us." Elijah noticed a sour expression cross his partner's face at the term "open mind," as if an open mind was some sort of liberal concoction unworthy of God-fearing Americans.

"Well, playing hunches is a big part of police work. You get an instinct for it."

"Right," Elijah said. "But if you're oversold on your hunches, you run the risk of trying to make the evidence fit your preconceived ideas. It can get you into muddy waters."

Grayson frowned. "What? You think I'd put an innocent man away?"

Elijah honestly wondered. When your ego was that out of control, it was hard to tell what you'd do. But he wasn't about to tell Grayson that. He wasn't in the mood for a fight.

"Of course not," he said, taking the diplomatic approach. "I'm just saying be open to where the evidence leads you."

"Oh, I am," Aaron said. "But don't be surprised when it leads you to the mayor. And when don't be surprised by all the cameras in your face when it hits. And don't be surprised when afterwards, when we're celebrating, and I invite you out for a fancy meal, I rub your face in it."

Elijah just laughed and shook his head. Grayson could be very frustrating. A definite pain in the ass. But at times he was so gruff and over-the-top it was almost endearing. At that moment, he noticed Dahlia gesturing toward him.

"Got to hit the bathroom," he said to Grayson.

"Knock yourself out," his partner retorted, his face dipping down as he began shovelling bites of his country fried steak into his mouth. Grayson was like that; he'd talk your ear off but as soon as he was done, he'd eat his food as quickly as possible, as if in a race.

Elijah kept an eye towards the table as he ducked outside the side door, making sure Aaron didn't see him. It wasn't what he expected. Dahlia, smoking a joint, and giving *him*, a law officer, a hard time about it, almost as if daring him to run her in.

He had to admit he was intrigued. Her energy was playful and, in spite of himself, he responded to it. He had a moment of concern. Was she flirting? Was she interested? But no, this didn't feel like that. It was almost like she was behaving as if they'd known each other for years. Maybe having grown up together. In any case, Elijah knew that, if he was wrong about her intentions and it came down to it, he could say no. He'd heard to many men try to explain away disloyalty to their wives by saying they were tempted. What do you expect me to do? Elijah liked to think that men were more than animals and had the capacity to say no. Sure, Dahlia was a beautiful woman, but he was not on the market. He loved Helen, was committed to her, and would never do anything to endanger the unity of their family and that was that.

But, no. This wasn't that. Dahlia wasn't flirting. There was no suggestivity. No double entendres or invitingly arched eyebrows. No pointed eye-contact. No unnecessary touching, a hand landing on an arm while making a point, as if this exchange were somehow important for comprehension, while both parties really knew the truth of it, that the touch was an overture. With relief, Elijah realized that this was something else. Playful, yes? A gesture of friendship? A suggestion of allyship?

Giving up on determining her meaning through speculation he finally just asked why she had called him out. He knew it wasn't just to watch her break the law. She took another puff of her joint before answering.

"I'm not sure about your partner."

"Not sure about him?" Elijah said, chuckling involuntarily. "What is there to be sure about?"

"I don't think you can trust his intuition," she said.

"Well, no offense," he said. "But it's not really your place to be critiquing my partner." In spite of himself, Elijah felt defensive of Grayson. The old grouch was a pain, but an outside attack caused his loyalty instincts to kick in.

"Well, you guys are here to serve the public, right?" she said in the same offhand manner which he found simultaneously charming and infuriating. "You're public *servants*. And I'm the public. I get a say."

Elijah considered arguing with her but decided it wasn't worth it.

"Okay," he said. "I'll bite. What's wrong with his intuition?"

"Well, he's completely focused on the here and now, but I think the answers lie in the past. What about the nineteen-seventy-one murder?"

Elijah shrugged. "I suppose there were superficial similarities," he said. "But so far I haven't seen anything to suggest it."

"Let me ask you this: why is there so little information about it?"

"If what you're getting at is they never caught the guy, I know," he said. "But that doesn't mean anything. Do you know how many unsolved cases there are out there? It's just as likely that whoever did this tried to make it look like the seventy-one murder to throw us off his tail."

"It's not just that they didn't catch him," she said. "The whole case, the whole event, just disappeared. They ran one story in the local paper and after that: nothing. Normally with a case with this kind of headline appeal, with mysterious circumstances and grisly details, the press would be all over it. There's be national news stories and TV-movies. Everyone would know about it."

Elijah's mouth drew in tightly as he considered this. "Hmm," he said. "What are you getting at? A cover up."

"Maybe," she said. "There's definitely something weird about the way it was handled."

"That might be worth looking into," Elijah admitted. "But I still don't see how that ties it to the current case."

"It's *not* clear," she said. "But there's something in the past case that *could* inform the current one. What's the saying? Leave no stone unturned? Seems like a stone you might want to turn over."

Elijah nodded slowly as he processed this. She had a point. Of course, the danger of turning over stones was sometimes you found a snake hiding under them.

"There's definitely *something* about the seventy-one case," she said. "It's even in the way the local talk about it. It's not just grief, or embarrassment, or anything like that. Even though it's in the relatively recent past, they've elevated it to mythical status. To folklore. Maybe that's a defence mechanism, a way of turning away from whatever really happened. Whatever they don't want to think about."

"What do you mean?" Elijah asked. "Regarding folklore?"

"Well, I was talking to that old grump down at the bookstore," she said. "He told me that the locals *knew* when the killer was around. Hugh Slaughter is what they call him. In some versions he's a demon or a ghost or a monster or immortal or some other kind of supernatural killer. But he said that the locals could *feel* it when the demon was on the loose, that they'd felt it in seventy-one and they felt it the other night. They'd wake up feeling scared and anxious, feeling this thickness in the air… like a supernaturally induced panic attack. I don't know if they convince themselves after the fact that they were awakened or what; the power of suggestion and self-delusion is a powerful thing…" Dahlia trailed off. "What's wrong?" she asked. "You look a million miles away."

"Peter Lark said the same thing," Elijah said. "He described the same feelings, almost to the word, when he was talking about the night his mother died."

"What? That's weird. He wouldn't have been around for the first murder. I'd be surprised if he'd been indoctrinated into whatever sort of delusional culty coping mechanism they've got going on here."

"I know," Elijah said. "That's what's bothering me." Could it mean that Peter *was* involved, and he was using an appeal to the local myth as a part of a misdirection? It *could* fit. Staging a murder to resemble the seventy-one case and then describing awakening on that night in these locally well-known turns to suggest that Hugh Slaughter was back. It *could* be that, but Elijah wasn't sure. He'd have had a hard time putting it into words, why he felt like there might be another explanation.

Dammit, he thought, irritated at his own hypocrisy. *I'm listening to my gut.*

"So?" she asked, grinning smugly, as if she knew what he was going to say.

"I agree with you," he said, almost grudgingly. "It bears looking into. Maybe you're right and we won't be able to solve this murder unless we solve the nineteen-seventy-one murder. There are too many connections. Similar crimes…"

"Similar methods," she added.

"Similar victims," he said.

"Similar time of the year," she said, ticking off another item of the list.

"Probably both at night," he said. "And then there's this business of the creepy feeling. Whatever that means. There are a lot of connections and a lot of questions."

"Right," she said. "So, what's your plan? Let your partner lead you around by the nose? Let him pin it on whoever he's got in mind without even looking into these questions?"

Elijah frowned. He didn't like being manipulated and knew she was doing it. Yet, at the same time, she was kind of pulling it off. Something about her whole vibe, like they were longtime friends or siblings, was making it work. Part of him wanted to call her on it, to say, "hey, remember you're talking to a cop here," but he just couldn't. Was it possible this woman was just *that* good at manipulation? That good at reading people.

"Of course not," he said.

"But he's the senior partner, right? You've kind of gotta follow his lead? Or butt heads? And how will that go?"

"You've got it all figured out, don't you?" he said. "What are you proposing?"

"We'll work together," she said. "On the side. I'll dig up what I can. Legally, of course." As she said this, Elijah's eyes were involuntarily drawn to the joint she was shamelessly smoking. "I'll keep poring through the newspaper archives and maybe talk to some locals. Whatever. And maybe you can do a little digging on this case from seventy-one?"

Elijah hesitated. It was highly irregular to bring in an outsider like this, but not unprecedented. Police had some leeway to use consultants or private investigators. Even psychics. The thing that bothered him about it, of course, was that he'd have to do it behind Grayson's back as his partner was dead set on the mayor's guilt and seemed willing to pin it on him regardless of what other threads and questions remained unexplored.

"Okay," he said. "But a few ground rules. You share everything you find if it is relevant to the investigation."

"Agreed," she said. "And you do the same."

"Can't promise that," Elijah said. "I'm bound by the law. If I turn up something that I can't legally share, I won't be able to."

She didn't look happy, but agreed. "Fine. Share what you can."

"I will," he said. "And you'll require my permission prior to using anything we uncover for publication."

"It's just for my dissertation," she said.

"Even that," he said. "Dissertations are public. Anything we uncover is off the record until I say it isn't. This is important because the premature release of information can impact criminal cases."

"Fine," she said a little testily. "I get it."

"And one more thing," he said. "A bit of advice. "Steer clear of Grayson. He already doesn't like you. He doesn't like people nosing around. Or journalists. Or young people. Or women, to be honest. Especially independent ones. You're everything he hates. He's already pegged you as trouble and he's really committed to his theories of the crime. Go through me and stay out of his hair."

"No problem," she said. "I'd be happy to never have a conversation with him. I'm staying at the Mount Hugh Inn. As long as you're stranded here for the snowstorm, we can meet there to compare notes."

"Fine," Elijah said. "That's where the department put us up to wait it out. I'll look you up. But if you'll excuse me, I have to get back to lunch."

He peeked inside, saw Grayson's back was turned, and quickly slipped back inside.

"So, what's the deal?" Grayson said in an accusing voice as Elijah sat down. For a moment, he thought he'd been caught.

"What do you mean?" he asked, then noticed his partner's mischievous grin.

"You were in there a while," Aaron said. "I thought maybe you'd fallen in."

The Inn was a few miles outside of town, off the main drag and halfway around the base of the mountain. On the way, Aaron held court about Izzy Einstein and Moe Smith, two famous detectives from the prohibition era. Elijah was honestly bewildered, unable to connect the dots regarding what connection these two had to do with the current case.

"Now, I enjoy a drink or two on occasion," Grayson said. "But prohibition was the law of the land at the time and these guys were doing their jobs. Almost five thousand arrests! They were heroes, those guys, at least to the law abiding."

Elijah had heard of the two prohibition agents but couldn't imagine what they had to do with the case at hand. What thread connected their grisly murder with a string of arrests during the country's brief dry period? Was it the celebrity surrounding these two heroic agents?

"They had interesting careers, for sure," Elijah said noncommittally and then, changing the subject, "Hey, listen. I've been thinking, maybe we should look into this unsolved murder they have on the books. The one from the seventies?"

Grayson lifted a hand from the wheel and waved the idea away. "Nah. We got a good suspect. Let's not get distracted by the local ghost stories."

"Well," Elijah said, playing a hunch. "It would make a better story for the press if there were a connection. Think about it. If we brought in a decades old murder and the new one at the same time, we'd be bigger names than Einstein and Smith were during their heyday." Elijah wasn't sure about his tactic; to use press coverage as a carrot with his older partner seemed to imply that coverage was a primary concern, perhaps overriding even the arrest of the guilty party. Yet, it seemed to, perhaps, move the needle. Aaron looked like he was considering the prospect.

"Maybe," Grayson said. "But I think we've got to lean on our leads in the present."

"Sure," said Elijah. "We'll do that. But there *could* be a connection. Even if it's just some copycat inspired by the local legend. It might be worth thinking outside the box."

"Yes," Grayson said after another pause. "There could be some connection, I suppose. I don't see us wasting a lot of resources on it, but if we I'd be open to considering anything that turns up."

Elijah nodded, happy with this modest progress. He had Elijah on record saying he'd be open to evidence. If Elijah and Dahlia managed to turn up anything actionable, he could bring it to his partner, maybe keeping Dahlia's name entirely out of it.

The Mount Hugh inn was an old building that, upon first glance, seemed well kept up but closer inspection revealed that it had perhaps had a recent touch up, fresh coat of pain and steam cleaning of carpets, perhaps, and was still in need of a full renovation.

At the desk they picked up their keys. They'd taken separate rooms. The department would cover it and the two men could certainly use a break from each other. As Grayson lugged his overnight bag towards the elevator, Elijah saw Dahlia enter and approach the desk to get her own keys. She glanced his way as she crossed the room. Their eyes met briefly, and she did a little eyebrow wiggle and gave a half grin, silently acknowledging their secret partnership.

Elijah nodded and followed Grayson to the elevators. He wondered if what he was doing was wise. He'd justified it by conceptualizing Dahlia as an outside consultant, but nothing was on the books. And the fact that he had not disclosed the collaboration to Grayson, who definitely would not have approved, or his department, cause him further concern. It was important to Grayson to follow correct procedure; it was one of the reasons that Grayson's gut judgements and erratic methodology got under his skin.

Still, his job was to find a killer. It was his sincere belief that the answers lied in the past. If Dahlia could help him find them, then his course was clear. And if his partnership with Dahlia came to light and Grayson disapproved? Well, he'd deal with that when he had to.

Their rooms were beside each other on the third floor. The walls were thin at the Mount Hugh Inn: he could hear Aaron starting the shower from next door. Elijah plugged in his computer to the room's ethernet and logged into his department's police record database. The department had issued both he and Grayson laptop computers and trained them on accessing the database. For Elijah, it was now part of his standard operating procedure, and he welcomed the opportunities it opened up for convenient policework in the field. He wondered if Grayson would make use of the new tool? He was such a grumpy old dinosaur, and one of his favorite targets was technology. Anything "newfangled," as he put it, meant to improve upon the tried-and-true methods. Elijah wondered whether his partner, if he needed information, would make use of the database or if he'd just call the department switchboard and ask someone to look it up for him.

He ran a series of database searches. The first was for murder records in nineteen seventy-one. Narrowing his parameters and filtering the results did nothing to produce results of value.

Uncertain of his next step, Elijah realized that he had become so focused on the seventy-one case, led down that path by his new friend Dahlia, if she was indeed a friend, that he had been neglecting the current murder: the case that he was actually assigned to. He ran the risk of becoming hyper focused on this one idea, that there was a connection between the old and new case, that he might miss the bigger picture: the same sort of tunnel-vision he'd considered Aaron guilty of.

Regardless of what had happened in seventy-one, they had a current victim, a headless corpse and an open investigation. And, in spite of Grayson's apparent obsession, the mayor was a good suspect. The easy subject, yes, but there were good reasons to consider him. Husbands often did it. It was horrific for Elijah to contemplate, blessed with a wonderful marriage, but for many men it seemed that feeling of love could sour to the point where homicide seemed a good option. Elijah was hesitant to admit it, even to himself, but there was a part of him that *wanted* to please Grayson, a part that craved his praise. He'd been chasing the approval of older male authority figures for most of his life, since his father had taken his own life, leaving their relationship unresolved. He pushed these thoughts aside, hesitant to psychoanalyze himself and began searching the database for arrest records for the mayor, both as Abdoullah Khaled and William Lark.

As of nineteen sixty-nine, William Lark had a few DUIs on his record. Nothing of particular note, nothing to suggest a pattern or any misdeeds. DUIs were sadly common and drinking and driving didn't seem to say much of anything about a person except that they had fallen prey to a failing they shared with many other Americans.

In seventy-one, when Lark became Khaled, the DUIs stopped. Maybe the conversation had done the trick after all, helping the man get his behaviour under control. Was it *possible* that he also committed a murder in seventy-one? Certainly. Perhaps the murder had inspired the conversion. Possible, but it felt like a thin theory…

Other than that, nothing of particular note. In the database he found papers of incorporation for "Gone with the Wind Turbines," co-owned with Leonard Maximoff since nineteen seventy-one. Otherwise, he was squeaky clean.

Not that it meant anything.

Elijah found himself doubting himself. Maybe he didn't have what it took. Why did Grayson's appeal to his "gut," to his "instincts," bother him so much? Could it be professional jealousy? Maybe Grayson had the instincts that Elijah only *wished* he had. Shaken and uncertain, he decided to drop in on Dahlia and see if she had anything that might usefully change his perspective on the case.

Elijah went back down to the inn's registration area to find out what room Dahlia was in when he saw her there, sitting in one of the lobby's padded accent chairs, poring through a stack of old newspapers that sat in front of her on a coffee table.

"Finding anything?" he asked.

She looked up, surprised. "What do you think?" she said with a grin that somehow rode a line between nonchalance and defeat. "Nah. Nothing. I found a library archive a town over and talked them into letting me borrow these. I have copies of the Mount Hugh Courier, the county paper, and the local papers from nearby towns, all weeklies. I have every copy for a month after the murder. Nothing in any of them."

"I didn't do much better," he said. "No sign of it anywhere. It's like it didn't happen."

"But it *did*," she said. "And the public knows it. The man I talked to at the bookstore knew about it. Didn't want to talk about it. Was superstitious about it actually; he even said talking about it might invite it back. The demon or ghost or serial killer or whatever it was."

"Uh-huh," said Elijah, as dubious about such nonsense as she was. "So, there was another murder. Does that mean someone talked about the first one?"

"Right," she said. "And now we're talking about it. I guess that pins the next one on us."

They both laughed and then, more or less simultaneously, lapsed into a strained silence. Elijah didn't know for sure what motivated her, but in his case, it was the weight of the word: murder. He wasn't particularly superstitious, but joking about causing the next one seemed to have triggered some deeply held irrational fear. No, talking about it couldn't cause a murder. But did he really want to take a chance? Was it a good idea to joke about it? Elijah's Catholic background wouldn't let him *entirely* escape his superstitious urges.

"It's just weird," Dahlia said, intruding on his introspection. "A major crime that seemed to just fall into the void. I *do* have an idea though."

"What's that?" he asked.

"Talk to the mayor about it."

"Oh, no way," Elijah said, suddenly wondering if this girl had been playing him the whole time, getting him to agree to their little information sharing venture so she could wedge her way into their investigation. "That'd be stepping on our toes. I want to be very clear on this: we keep to our investigation of the seventy-one murder and leave the current suspects alone."

"What I'm suggesting is that we talk to him about the seventy-one murder," she said. "Since we haven't established any link connecting the two cases, I don't see any problem in talking to him."

"So, a loophole, right?"

"Not at all. He's the perfect person to talk to. He was there. He was an adult. He was actually a big player on the local scene around that time, right? With the windmill operation? He had his hands in local business and politics. *And* he doesn't strike me as the type to go evoking ghost stories and clam up. I can't think of a better person to ask."

Elijah was quiet for a moment, processing his conflicting reactions. On the one hand, he remained a little nervous. His partnership with Dahlia was uncharted waters. As an outside consultant, he had to keep her on a tight leash and make sure she didn't do anything that could adversely affect her investigation. He had to remember that her motives were not his. She was a journalist, of one form or another, so although she might be interested in finding the real killer, her ultimate goals had more to do with revealing information than punishing the guilty. Even though they both wanted the killer discovered, it was easy to imagine their differing reasons for doing so coming into conflict.

He also had to think of Aaron Grayson. As crazy as the man could drive him, he *was* his partner. As grating as the cranky old man routine could get, his whole pose of being a tough guy and a "real American," Elijah still owed him some respect. And on some level, yes, Elijah wanted to please him. Seeking that approval, he'd never had from a father figure? Perhaps. Or maybe he just wanted his partner to approve of him professionally. In any case, he wanted the old man's approval.

Maybe one way to do so was by helping him make his case against the mayor. Maybe in asking him questions about the seventy-one case, something useful would come up. Something that might help them solve the current murder.

"Fine," he said eventually. "We'll talk to the mayor."

"I'll drive," Dahlia said.

Elijah ran back up and told Grayson he was going out to get some air. He wasn't crazy about lying to his partner, but for the moment he put those concerns aside. Within a few hours they were on their way back into town in Dahlia's black Audi.

"One thing I don't understand," he asked from the passenger's seat. "Why Mount Hugh? You say you're here writing your dissertation about small towns and their reactions to grief. But you showed up right after the murder was happening. And, from talking to you, it seems like the seventy-one murder wasn't on your radar until afterwards. So, what got you here in the first place? It's a bit off the beaten path."

"One thing I didn't tell you," she said. "I was actually born here."

"Really?" he said. "That's surprising."

"Why's that?" she asked.

"When I first saw you, back at the Watering Hole, I felt like you stuck out. I saw you and thought, 'Well, she's not a local.' "

Dahlia laughed. "Is that a compliment?"

"I guess," Elijah said, suddenly cautious about his words. He didn't want Dahlia to think he was coming on to her. He *had* been impressed with both her beauty and her style. She looked almost glamorous, especially in the context of the dried-up old town. But for him, this was just a matter of almost academic interest. He wasn't interested and didn't want her to think so. "You just looked like someone from the bigger world outside, not a townie. If you know what I mean."

"Makes sense," she said. "And, to be clear, I said I was born here. Didn't really grow up here. My mom moved us away when I was small to find a better future. Figured there would be more opportunities out in that 'bigger world' you were talking about."

"And were there?"

"Not really," she said. "To be honest, it was a disaster. She got in over her head. Got in debt. Into drugs. Sank into depression. And she left me."

"My God," Elijah said, surprised by the sudden turn the story had taken. "I'm so sorry."

"That's okay. I've had a lot of time to process it," she said, but then, after a moment, continued, "Actually, to be honest, I'm still working my way through it. It pretty much broke me and I've only now gotten myself halfway rebuilt."

"Well, I know what you're going through. I went through something similar. I also had to find my own way."

"Really?" she said with an intonation that invited explanation.

But Elijah didn't feel ready to reveal more. Their conversation had been surprisingly personal, but he had just met her. He wasn't sure he was ready to go into the darkest areas of his life with her, but some impulse pushed him forward. Without consciously deciding to, he found himself telling her more.

"He killed himself." Elijah was almost surprised to hear himself saying it, but once it was out, there was no taking it back.

"Oh," Dahlia said, her face falling dissolving into shock. "I can't even imagine."

"But I think you sort of can," he said. "It's not that different than what you went through. I was just a kid. I blamed myself. You can't lose a parent to suicide without wondering. I know I wasn't the reason, but how unhappy do you have to be to leave a child behind? Even before he took his own life, my dad was not a happy person. Miserable, actually. He was hard on me and my mom. Abusive, if you want to call it that. But still, it was hard to see my way to blaming him. I always wondered if I could have done more to make him happy."

"But that's not your responsibility," she said. "It's on the parent. That's what it took me years to process."

"I know," he said. "I *know* that. But sometimes knowing doesn't matter. It doesn't keep you from feeling guilty."

"How do you go on?" she asked.

Elijah shrugged. "For years I bottled it all up," he said. "But kept it tamped down there, somewhere deep inside. To be honest, the only reason I keep it together now is I have a daughter of my own to live for. I'm determined not to make the same mistakes my father made. I'll be there for my girl no matter what."

Dahlia looked off for a moment, as if in thought. "I wonder," she said, but then followed it up with, "Never mind."

"What?" Elijah asked.

"I don't want to make you mad," she said. "I was about to psychoanalyze you."

Elijah sighed. "Go ahead. I'm just going to wonder if you don't."

"Well, I was thinking," she said. "Do you think your relationship with your partner might be informed by what happened with your dad? I mean, Grayson is difficult to please, a bit of a crank…"

"You think I'm craving his approval?" Elijah said. "To compensate for the approval I never got from my dad?" Stated out loud, it sounded silly. Like a bit of armchair therapy. A reduction of a man's complex psychology to an oversimplification.

"Sorry," she said. "I'll stop."

"Don't worry about it," he said, annoyed that her armchair therapy had been, silly as it sounded, had been so accurate. She had him pegged. He was relieved as they pulled up at the mayor's house. "We're here."

Moments later, at the front door, Elijah leaned towards Dahlia and said in a low tone, "Now remember, we're only here to ask about the seventy-one murder. If you stray from that topic, I pull the plug."

"I understand," she said, then knocked.

As soon as the door opened, Elijah could sense something was off. You could see it in the mayor's face. It was wound tight with tension, as if Elijah was the last person he wanted to see. Elijah could detect traces of cigarette smoke and booze; he wasn't sure if the scents were atmospheric or originated directly with the mayor.

"Oh, detective," Abdoullah said and then, looking towards Dahlia. "And you've brought a friend?"

"Yes. This is an associate of mine," he said. "Can we come in?"

Abdoullah reluctantly agreed. "I suppose."

Following in into the living room, they saw Leonard Maximoff, sitting on a couch, cigarette in one hand and a mixed drink in the other. If Abdoullah's face expression had been unwelcoming, shot through with anxiety at their appearance, Maximoff's seemed downright angry.

"What do you want?" he asked coldly, as if ready to throw the visitor's out.

"I'm here to ask you a few questions regarding the murder in nineteen seventy-one," said Elijah, ignoring the negative energy and pushing through with professionalism.

"What?" asked Maximoff, hot-tempered. "What does that have to do with anything?"

"Yes," said Abdoullah. "Aren't you supposed to be finding Eleanor's killer?"

"We're exploring the possibility that the two are related," said Elijah.

"We thought you might be able to help clarify what happened back then," she said addressing the mayor. "I know you were prominent in Mount Hugh at the time."

Khaled looked helplessly over to Maximoff, as if seeking prompting or assistance.

"Why dig that far back?" said Leonard. "What are you trying to accomplish?"

"The methods were similar," said Elijah.

"I'll tell you about seventy-one," Maximoff said. "That was just an outsider dumping his crime in Mount Hugh. Tainting the name of the town." Elijah could tell from the way he said it that the man felt protective of his town. It made sense. He and Khaled had brought in the windmills. They were local heroes and their fortunes rose and fell with Mount Hugh. It would make sense if he felt protective. But still, blaming the crime on an outsider seemed like a bit of a stretch, not based on any clear reasoning or evidence. Elijah turned his attention to Abdoullah. Maximoff was defensive and wary. Abdoullah seemed meek and overwhelmed. Maybe prodding him would produce results.

"So, Mister Khaled," he said in a polite but authoritative voice. "What can you tell me about the case? The information is spotty. Was there ultimately an arrest?"

"I don't know," said Abdoullah, stammering. "I didn't follow the case that closely. We were both busy, you see, with our business. The windmills."

"Listen," Maximoff said, talking to and over his former partner. "If the police choose to waste their resources digging up this irrelevant history, maybe you should consider hiring a private investigator so we can find out what really happened to Eleanor. As for me, I've had it. I'll see you later. Stay strong."

Without saying another word to Elijah or Deliah, Maximoff left, slamming the door behind him.

Elijah and Deliah made eye contact, sharing wordlessly their reactions. Maximoff was clearly shaken. They both were. Elijah, happy to have Abdoullah there alone, switched tactics.

"Listen, Mr. Khaled," he said. "I know that your beliefs are important to you and that as a true man of God you'll do whatever you can to assist in this investigation and help us find Eleanor's killer."

"Of course," he said. "Of course, I will. I want to find the killer. But I don't know anything about the older case."

"The victim," said Elijah. "Do you know anything about her?"

"No, nothing," he said, stammering. Moisture swelled up at the corner of his eyes and his voice took on a quaver. "I just… I can't help you."

The man looked like he was about to lose it. To start sobbing or have a breakdown. Yes, people under pressure might crack, but Elijah could tell that the mayor was about to slip into incoherence. Better to bide their time.

"I see," he said, simply. "Well, a good day to you sir. We'll be in touch."

Back in the car, as soon as the doors closed, Deliah turned to Elijah.

"What was *that* all about?"

"I know," Elijah said. "We poked a hornet's nest. I don't know all of the connections, but I think we know one thing definitively. These two cases are connected. Now we just need to find the proof."

CHAPTER EIGHT
KIND REGARDS, FROM THE PAST

Aaron tossed his suitcase on the bed and went to the bathroom, dropping his toiletry bag on the sink and splashing some cold water on his face. It hadn't been a particularly gruelling day, but he was already worn out. He could have some more coffee, but when he drank it all day long it messed up his sleep. He'd used to be able to go all day, seeming to have an inexhaustible well of energy, but with middle age it had all gone south. He didn't know if this was strictly true, but the impression he had was the day he turned forty-five, the bottom had dropped out on his youthful energy. Suddenly, it was a struggle to stay awake after dinner, his sleep at night was hit or miss, and he started waking up sore for no particular reason. That had been over fifteen years ago, and it had only gotten worse. Aging was the worst curse God ever visited on mankind.

Sighing, he started the shower, thinking that maybe a hot shower would wake him up, but almost immediately had a different impulse and went back out to the bedroom, just letting the shower run, steam slowly filtering out of the bathroom. Elijah was right next door. Let him assume Grayson was getting cleaned up. Let the kid underestimate him like he always did.

The bedroom had a large mirror across from the foot of the bed. He stood in front of it and looked at himself, at his greying hair and his face, now generously decorated with wrinkles, wondering where the years had gone. Staring into his reflected eyes, he worked up some defiance. Dammit, he wasn't going to give in. He wasn't going to take a nap and he wasn't going to give in on this case.

He was pissed that the case wasn't the easy slam dunk he had initially thought it to be. Why couldn't anything be simple? He felt his adrenaline rushing through his system and leaned into it.

Good, he thought. That'll wake me up.

There were just too many suspects. Too much opportunity. Too many possible motives. All of it murky. He loved to go with his gut, but his gut wasn't sure about anything anymore. His instincts for detective-work seemed to have heartburn.

There was the mayor. Obvious suspect. His business partner, Maximoff. Another good one. A man of influence with a complicated history with the mayor and his family. Then there was the son. Peter. The kid was weird. Clearly hiding something. Who knew what he was capable of? Then his girlfriend, Fawn. A Maximoff. He got a controlling vibe from her, so who knew? She was tied to both families. The whole thing was like that, all interwoven, like a tangle of wires you couldn't sort out.

And that was just immediate family and associates. Eleanor was also divorced. Not much was known about her social life, although there were rumors she got around. Hit the Watering Hole during its nightly rebranding as a bar.

He plugged in his laptop and logged onto the database through the room's ethernet cable. Yes, the switch to the new ways was annoying. When he'd started out it had all been pads and pencils and jotted down notes. But, annoyed as he was, he could recognize the value in the improvements? What would Elijah, so smug in his youth, think if he knew that his partner, under the sound screen of the blasting shower, was on the computer continuing the investigation?

As always, the kid underestimated him.

He considered the details of the case. The brutality of Eleanor's murder suggested, to him, that it wasn't random but was instead motivated by anger. This was backed up by the fact that there was no sign of forced entry. She'd let someone into her room, or at least her house. Someone she trusted. Someone who belonged there? Probably someone from that tangled list of friends and family.

The mayor had been his favourite suspect early on, but at they dug deeper it didn't seem as clear. There were many others that were equally plausible as suspects. One problem with the mayor is he was Eleanor's ex-husband. Was she really going to let him into her bedroom in the middle of the night? Given Grayson's unpleasant personal experience with divorce, it seemed unlikely. But there were others. Peter was known to have been in the house. He'd apparently slept through the whole thing, a supposition that still seemed suspicious to Grayson. But then there was Fawn. She had an easy way in through Peter.

It was a swirl in his mind. A tangle, like the threads of a spiderweb and in its centre: Eleanor. Threads of consequence, leading from Eleanor to those in her circle, one of them her killer. He thought about the vibrations that radiated down the lines of a spiderweb, alerting the spider. Similar vibrations were at play in this case, but they were, as was always the case in a murder investigation, the vibrations of means, motive, and opportunity.

For motive, he liked the mayor. Bill or Abdul or whatever the hell he called himself. They'd been married. It had soured. It ended badly. There was resentment. Probably financial motives, complicated by the mayor's business interests.

But for means and opportunity? Peter Lark, the son, seemed the winner in that category. He was the only one in the house. Opportunity. His story, that he slept through it and was then awakened by some kind of supernatural spook show, was pure bullshit. And means? Even better. The boy was training to be a surgeon. A natural fit for the clean decapitation. Grayson, a fan of investigative history, remembered reading up on the Jack the Ripper case, still never definitively solved. One of the prime suspects had been a surgeon.

But looking into the suspects, the outliers on the web, could only tell you so much. To find the truth behind these vibrations, Aaron figured the thing to do was look at the centre of the web, at Eleanor.

He typed her full name into the database, eliciting two results, both alarming.

In nineteen-seventy, around the time of the Winter Harvest Festival, she reported a rape. He opened the file and read through it. She wasn't reporting her own rape; she was reporting on behalf of someone else. The details were odd. She reported the rape of a friend, a very close one, but ultimately refused to disclose the friend's name, presumably changing her mind about reporting the crime at some time during the conversation. Ultimately, she told the officers that she'd realized that maybe it wasn't up to her to report it and that her friend might be upset that she did. Grayson considered this. Rape cases could be tough for the victims, especially if they came to trial. The courtroom experience, and sometimes surrounding publicity, could leave their own scars. Still, it was highly unusual to report a crime and then backpedal without disclosing the perpetrator or even the victim. The case was eventually closed as Eleanor couldn't convince her friend to come forward leaving the police with nothing to investigate. What this suggested to Grayson was fear; Eleanor's friend may have feared repercussions if she turned her rapist in, even with police involvement.

The second result his database search came back from the current year, ninety-six. Two hits, separated by twenty-five years. Too many ingredients in the case, and too scattered. More and more it *did* seem like the answers might lie in the previous case. But if he could *solve* it, it had all of the ingredients of a great story. Gruesome murders of women, decades apart. An unreported rape. It was high drama, the kind of soap opera story that made headlines. A sensational trial, all-day coverage. And at the press conferences, at the podium, microphone in front of him, would be Detective Aaron Grayson: the voice of the investigation. The hero who brought in the killer. A legend of a cop. *He* would be part of the story. He, who came from a humble background, who had solved cases, nose to the grindstone, living for his job, living for justice, never asking anything for himself. A life of self-denial, devoted to the pursuit of justice.

That's the story he'd tell. The spin. There were elements of truth in it, of course. The humble beginnings. The lack of a life outside of the job. But there was another way of looking at his life.

A failed life. Alone as he came closer and closer to the end. No children. No wife. The only child of long-deceased parents. Had he remained alone because he was too devoted to the job, or was it because he was too hard to live with? He knew what his ex-wife would say.

But the job *was* his greatest accomplishment. He had always been a hard worker. Had cleared a lot of cases. He was a good detective and he had produced results. At the end of the day, lacking a wife or children, all he'd have to show for having been alive would be the legacy of his casework, and the one thing he was really missing was a capstone case. A memorable, dramatic case to cement him legend, to write him into history as one of the greats.

The clock was ticking. He wasn't getting any younger. His arteries were clogging up. His risk for heart disease was high. When the doctor told him that at the annual physicals, he laughed in his face, but he was no fool. He'd been hard on his body, and the stressful job wasn't helping. One of these days the ticker was going to explode.

The upshot? He only had so much time. He had to solve his big case.

This case might be the one. It could be his last chance.

He wouldn't just fade into oblivion. He'd leave his mark. He'd be the next policing legend. It wasn't too late. He'd become a legend. He'd sell his story. Or write it himself. Maybe he'd lecture. Or set up a scholarship for promising criminologists from modest backgrounds. If he solved the case, he could write his own ticket.

A knock at the door pulled him out of his reverie and back into the present. He opened the door: it was Elijah.

"What's up?" he asked.

"Hey," Elijah said. "I was thinking of taking a walk."

"Yeah, that's fine," said Grayson. "We'll check in later and figure out our next steps. Consider yourself off the clock. Just check in within the hour or so."

Grayson returned to his unopened search result and opened it.

He narrowed his eyes, confused.

What could it mean?

She'd reported *another* crime. This time a murder. The record showed that this time she'd called it in instead of dropping by the office in person. The details were, as before, sketchy. She told the officer who had taken her call that a close friend had been murdered "a long time ago." When pressed for information, she'd hung up and didn't pick up when they rang her back. When they'd followed up with her the next day, she'd told the police that she was really drunk, didn't remember making the call, and had no idea what they were talking about. Must have passed out after the first call. She didn't know of any murder. Maybe she'd been watching the late movie and had gotten confused? Grayson didn't buy it. It wasn't clear if the officer following up did or not, but he gave her a warning about drinking too much and the penalties for making false reports.

The two police reports seemed to fit together like puzzle pieces. Could the rape victim from seventy-one been the same close friend who she reported murdered earlier that year? There was no way to be sure, but the two calls seemed too closely aligned for it to be a coincidence. The officer following up earlier in the year wouldn't have had a reason to go back to nineteen-seventy looking for hints. But to Grayson, the pattern was clear. It also seemed exceedingly likely that the body discovered in seventy-one *must* be the same person. How many murders could there have been in Mount Hugh in that random year in the seventies?

Unfortunately, of course, Eleanor wasn't around to question. So, Grayson continued digging, suppressing his luddite tendencies and getting back on the database. He accessed an online archive of autopsy reports, narrowed his search parameters for nineteen seventy-one and Mount Hugh

One report. He clicked on it.

There had been one unidentified female body scheduled for autopsy that winter that was cremated before the autopsy was complete. Case closed, but most unsatisfyingly.

Fresh rage filled Grayson's veins, as if a hypodermic needle of fire had been injected under his skin. The rage was directionless, because he didn't know who to blame, but *somebody* had tampered with the case. Somebody, somewhere in the chain of evidence, had been bought out or compromised. Someone had a motive to suppress the truth of the autopsy. Someone had something to hide. He could feel the tampering fingers reaching out over the decades, impeding his investigation.

As always, Grayson found fuel in his anger. It kept him fighting. It helped him overcome his slowing body, helped him rise above the diminished energy of a man in his mid-fifties. Yes, the anger might eventually cause his heart to self-destruct and give his life an early end, but in the meantime, it kept him going.

He jolted out of his chair and grabbed a marker from the cup on the table, one of those branded giveaways they stick in your room, hoping it will function as advertising. He went back to the bathroom, to the large bathroom mirror in which he'd, just recently, contemplated his own craggy and aging features, and began drafting. He put it all down, so he could look at it. The spider-web that, heretofore, had only existed in his brain. He knew from experience that *seeing* the pattern, whether on a bulletin board or a hotel mirror, sometimes helped you find the solution.

In the center he put Eleanor, and branching off, all of the suspects, connected by lines. So far, those closest to her. He listed their relationships, possible motives, pros and cons of each as a suspect.

Bill Lark.

Peter.

Leonard.

Fawn.

Each was compelling as a suspect but for different reasons.

And another connection: the crime from nineteen seventy-one. There *was* a connection. He was increasingly certain of it. But what? This connection was only labelled with a question mark.

His diagram complete, Grayson stood back to look at it, hoping that, in contemplation, something would reveal itself to him. His mind raced, pulled in a dozen directions at once, tossed to and fro in contemplation of disparate motives: greed, revenge, infidelity, jealousy. Or was it to shut Eleanor up? Did she know too much about what went down in nineteen seventy-one? Overwhelmed, and the adrenaline high wearing off and leaving him crashing, he fell back on the bed, still looking at the mirror.

It's here, he thought. The answer is here.

He closed his eyes.

As he regained awareness, Aaron was at the end of his life. A nobody. Another faceless anonymous elderly man living out his last days in palliative care. His frail body was draped over a hospital bed, inclined at a fifteen-degree angle. In his arm was an IV, pumping something into him, who knew what, but presumably a concoction to maintain his meagre grip on his life, his tenuous connection to the world of the living.

He was alone. Nobody to check on him, nobody to love or remember him. Nobody to even know his name. Doctors and nurses come and go. The nurses smile condescendingly, but their eyes tell him that they've already given up on him. It's just a matter of time. The doctors seem almost annoyed to be treating him. He can't know what they're thinking but he imagines: "Why am I bothering maintaining this man? He's dying anyway."

They read the name off the clipboard, but they don't remember it. Don't know him. Don't know him at all.

All of the aches and pains, the fatigue and forgetfulness, of his present was magnified. His body was one massive throbbing sore, he felt it from his head to his toes. He looked down at spindly unrecognizable arms, thin and wrinkles, as if the man inside was ill-fitted to the skin.

It's the future. His future. One in which he has failed to solve that one big case. One in which he'd failed build a legacy. One in which his name is forgotten. One in which he barely recognized himself.

He snapped back to consciousness, surging from the dream to a momentary darkness then lurching back to conscious reality. His eyes blinked open to the image on the mirror, the spider's web that gave no answers, only questions. The sun had changed its angle on the wall, indicating that some time had passed. It took him a few seconds before he realized that the phone was ringing. He looked down at the beside clock. Five o'clock. He'd been asleep for forty minutes.

He reached over and grabbed the phone, trying to force a normalcy into his voice. No reason anyone needed to know that he had crashed so early in the afternoon like an old man.

"Grayson here," he said. For a moment, the only sound on the other end was belabored breath, as if the person on the other end had run a marathon before picking up the receiver. "Hello?"

"Grayson, thank God." It was Elijah.

"What're you doing calling me?" he said, irritated. "You're right across the hall: you could've just knocked on the door. Is that too far for you to walk?

"Sorry," Elijah said. His voice sounded disoriented. Confused, maybe? And there was something else.

Fear. His partner sounded scared.

"What happened, kid?" Grayson said, dropping his testiness for a moment of sincerity. "Are you okay?"

"I'm fine," he said. "But there's been another murder."

"What?" Grayson said. His body gave him another chemical boost. "Where the hell are you?"

"I'll tell you about it later," Elijah stammered.

Grayson seethed. His partner had clearly been up to something. Where had he gone on his innocent "walk"?

There'd be hell to pay later.

"Was it the same M.O. as the other two?" Aaron asked. "Woman, head removed?"

"No," Elijah said between struggling breaths that seemed to be torn from him. "It wasn't the same. It wasn't a woman at all."

"Not a woman," said Grayson, surprised but his curiosity piqued. "Well, who was it?"

"It was the mayor," Elijah said. "It was Mayor Khaled. He's dead."

Everything Grayson knew about the case was called into doubt. All the fragments that he'd connected in the diagram, still visible on the mirror in the shading light, were scattered, like puzzle pieces thrown from an overturned table.

Back to square one.

CHAPTER NINE
CONNECTED

Having just come up empty in their conversation with the mayor, Dahlia and Elijah walked back towards her car. The sky was dark and cloudy, and the snow fell in fat fluffy flakes, almost immediately forming a layer of accumulation over the shoulders of their coats. Already Dahlia's mind was turning over possibilities, making connections. Yes, it was a dead end, but what did it really tell them? They weren't going to be able to simply walk in and ask for answers. Of course not. If it were that easy, they'd already have them. Maybe the men were involved. Or maybe they had something else to hide. In any case, the upshot was clear: they needed another way to find information.

"Okay, how about this?" she began, looking over at Elijah. If she'd had to characterize the subtext of the expression he gave her in response, it would have been, "Oh, *God.*" As if he dreaded hearing another of her ideas. She couldn't help but grin. "Just hear me out."

"Okay," he said in resignation. "Let's hear it."

"What if we drive out to where they found the first body?"

"What good would that do us?" he said. "If we can even find it? I mean, it's been *years.* It's not like there's going to be any evidence. Physical evidence doesn't last outdoors. It washes away with the first rainstorm."

"I know that," she said. "I don't expect to find something that's going to solve the case. But I don't know… seeing the space might reveal something. It might send us in a useful direction."

"Fine," he said, sounding almost relieved, as if he'd expected her suggestion to be something far more distasteful. "I can't see any harm. Just taking a walk might help me clear my head."

"Great," she said. They'd arrived at the car. She slung her backpack off her shoulder and onto the hood of her car. She unzipped the bag and began rifling around inside. "There's a good picture in the article. With it, and maybe a little help from someone in the vicinity, maybe we can find it. Here it is."

She pulled out a newspaper and flattened it across her car. Elijah leaned down to look.

A photo: shocking by the mild standards of small town newspapers. A headless body, its nudity barely concealed. What drew his eye was the necklace. A chain with a bejewelled "C" suspended from it. All the more compelling in its grotesquerie because the necklace rested on a headless neck.

It was identical to the necklace he'd seen in Malinda's house. There couldn't be two such necklaces. It was ostentatious. It was unique. The mysterious woman in the photos *must* be the victim. He wondered what the "C" could stand for. A first name? A last?

He noticed Dahlia looking at him.

"You okay?" she asked. "Why are you being so quiet? Did you figure something out."

"No," he said, fumbling through a fib. "It's just… the image is shocking."

"You're a homicide cop," she said. "I'd assume you've seen worse."

"Sure," he said. "I've seen all kinds of messed up stuff. But you get a moment to brace yourself going into a crime scene. You don't expect to see this kind of thing on the cover of a small-town newspaper."

He thought he'd sufficiently sold his lie. It was all true, more or less. He'd even had the thought about the small-town newspaper. The only part he left out was the most important bit. That he had a strong lead on their victim of the victim of this decades-old crime. Yes, he and Dahlia had entered into an unofficial partnership, but his first loyalty was still to law enforcement. To catching the killer. Yes, even to Aaron Grayson. Revealing too much to Dahlia might hinder the investigation and he couldn't allow himself to do that. He felt a twinge of guilt, as he was growing to trust and even like, Dahlia but he knew that he was making the right call.

"I couldn't make out where it was," he said. "The picture didn't give enough information."

"I know," she said. "I had the same thought. But I figure if we can narrow it down and get in the vicinity, we might be able to figure it out."

"And how are we going to do that?" Elijah asked.

"Well, I figure that even though the locals seem to have some kind of block about discussing it, most of them probably know where the body was found. I mean, it *was* big news, briefly, before they circled their wagons and started pretending it never happened."

"Well," he said. "That sounds easier said than done. Who's going to provide you with this information."

It was a valid question. Dahlia briefly considered revisiting the grouchy old man at *The Story Shelf* before recognizing what a ridiculous idea *that* was. The man had made it very clear that both she and her questions were unwelcome. She'd managed to get a little information out of him because she'd briefly gotten his guard down. That wouldn't happen again. He'd hardened against her questions at the end of their last encounter.

"How about this guy," she said.

"What?" Elijah said, braking in surprise, the car lurching in the gravel. "Who?"

Dahlia pointed at a farmer in a field by the side of the road. He seemed to be repairing a section of fence. The man wore overalls and carried a toolbox and was wearing boots that disappeared at the ankles amidst the still-gathering snow. On top he wore a wool hat that barely contained an unkempt head of greying hair.

"Are you kidding?" Elijah asked as the car slowed to a stop.

"He's as good as anyone," she said, and figured that she was right. If the experience was anything like her conversation with the bookstore owner, you had a brief chance to dig for info before the wall came down: whatever conditioning, hypnosis, or mass hysteria led the locals to pretend that the previous murder had never happened. People knew. They all knew. But none of them would talk about it. You had to surprise information out of them before those doors slammed shut.

"Let's try him," Elijah said, stepping out of the car and leading the way as they approached him. The farmer looked up, a pair of pliers in his hands. Elijah could see a veil of caution fall over his face. He recognized they were outsiders; it was all he needed to know.

"Excuse me, sir," Elijah said, Dahlia trailing behind him. "How are you doing today?"

"Fine, I reckon," he said in a clipped twang that identified him as a member of that rural subclass: the redneck. In Elijah's travels, he'd noticed that there was a strong similarity in the white underclass in terms of attitude and accent no matter what part of the country you found yourself in, it was like there was this connected culture that stretched from coast to coast, peppered among the hills and countrysides. "Gotta fix my fence so's my cows don't get out."

The man's delivery was guarded. The subtext: what's it to you?

Elijah looked up at the sky, still relentlessly unleashing the fat flakes of snow. "You have to do that now? In the snow?"

"Cows don't care if it's snowing or not," the farmer said with a little grin, as if amused by the cluelessness of the question. "Don't need them running off."

"Well, good luck with that," Elijah said, uncertain how to respond. He opted for the direct approach. He flashed his badge. "I'm officer Elijah Riley and this is an associate of mine. We're here on official business."

"My fence is official business?"

"It's not that," he said. "We're investigating the murder. You hear about it?"

The man frowned, his face tightening, closing off. "I did. But I don't see what it would have to do with me."

"Actually," Elijah said. "I have one simple question for you and I'm hoping you can help me. There was *another* murder that happened around here. About twenty years ago. A young girl, found in the forest in the vicinity. All we need to know is the location where the body was found. The records on it are unclear."

The man shook his head and suddenly seemed unwilling to make eye contact. "I can't help you with that."

"Are you saying you don't know where it happened," Elijah asked, "Or you're unwilling to tell us?"

"Listen," the old man said, his voice dropping to a near-whisper. "I don't want any trouble."

"You're *not* in trouble," Elijah said. "We're just asking for help."

"It's not you I'm worried about," he said, then clamped his mouth shut, as if worried he'd said too much.

"Then who?" Elijah asked. "Has someone threatened you?"

"Is it Hugh Slaughter you're worried about?" Dahlia, who has remained silent up to this point, said.

The old man didn't respond verbally, but the look that passed over his face made it very clear that she'd hit the nail on the head.

"I know why you're scared," she said. "I've talked to others. You think that if you talk about him, you run the risk of being his next victim."

Elijah noticed the difference in her delivery. Usually she was sassy and sarcastic, but in this case, she was exuding a calm concern, as if his fears were completely reasonable instead of a pre-modern paranoia that seemed misplaced in time: a superstition from another century. But Dahlia, in the way she spoke, let the old man know that not only didn't she think he was crazy, but that she *believed* him. He was right to be concerned.

Elijah knew this wasn't true. He'd talked to Dahlia at length and knew she didn't buy into the superstitions. No, she was just a good reader of people and a fine actress.

"I said his name once," Dahlia said, continuing. "And that's on me. I'm not going to say it again. I don't want to run the risk. But we're doing important work. If you help us, we might be able to capture him. To end his curse once and for all. And you don't have to speak his name or say anything about him. You don't have to do anything to bring the curse down upon you."

The old man's eyes were wide with fear, like a child afraid of the dark, unable to drop off to sleep after a scare story. He nodded meekly.

"So, just point," she said. "Point in the direction where the body was found."

He pointed back in the direction from which they'd come.

"Back towards the mayor's house?" she asked.

"Past it," he said, whispering. "About a ten-minute drive. An unmarked dirt road by the busted oak."

Dahlia just nodded. She didn't know what he meant by "the busted oak," but knew it was time to step away. She didn't want to push the man too far and she trusted that they could figure it out.

"Good luck on your fence," she said turning toward the car. "Stay warm."

The farmer mumbled something inaudible in response. Looking back, Elijah thought he saw relief in the man's expression, as if in ending the brief conversation he'd narrowly avoided danger.

Back in the car, they began driving in the direction the man had indicated. The road was flat and straight as an arrow. For this Elijah was grateful. Dahlia's car was, so far, doing okay on the snowy road, but he wasn't sure how long their luck would hold out. They passed the mayor's house and kept going.

"That was well done," Elijah said.

"What was?"

"They way you handled that guy," he said. "You played it perfectly."

"Oh, that?" she said, back to her snarky self. "I just figured we'd do better with him by acknowledging his concerns. I guess I have a way with people."

"I guess you do," he said, smiling. "It's a useful quality. For a journalist, I'd assume. But for a cop too. You're pretty sharp socially, and seem very adaptable to different situations."

"It's always come naturally to me," she said. "I think I had to learn to make these adjustments simply to survive when I was a kid. When you don't have much support, you have to learn to meet people where they are."

"I know exactly what you mean," he said. "I know had similar challenges, a similar lack of support. I'm not sure I came through it with all of the same tricks and skills as you though. I think I'm pretty good at reading people, but I can't get inside their heads like you can. For me, I think I just learned to approach people cautiously."

Dahlia nodded. "Me too," she said. "It took me a long time to trust anyone. It wasn't until I met Naomi that I found someone I could fully let in."

Elijah supressed the urge to raise an eyebrow. He hadn't realized that Dahlia was involved with another woman. He, of course, had no issue with that, priding himself on being forward thinking. He couldn't help but wonder how Grayson would react if he were there…

"It was the same with me," he said. "Before I met Helen, I was kind of defined by my damage. My lack of trust." Elijah realized that this was yet another connection between them. They really did have a lot in common.

"It's hard spending your life, searching for connection," she said. "But I guess we're all a product of our pasts."

"Well, in your case it's left you with a gift for interaction," he said. "I'm glad to have you on the team."

"Thank you," she continued. "For the compliment. You didn't have to say it and I appreciate it. I'm definitely getting the impression that the locals are fragile in their own way, at least where the legend of Hugh Slaughter is concerned, and must be approached cautiously."

Elijah mused on this. It was strange. The locals seemed entirely normal in most aspects, but when the first crime or the legends surrounding it came up, they reverted to primitivity and superstition. They ceased being modern Americans and became the paranoid villagers from a Universal monster movie, ready to riot with torches and pitchforks. It was puzzling; Elijah couldn't understand the disconnect.

"Oh, up here," Dahlia said.

In front of them he saw a large oak tree split down the middle, the top half resting sideways on the now-snowy meadow. He could see a hint of scorch marks along its base and assumed it had been split at some point by a lightning strike. He'd spent enough time in rural areas to understand that locals often would give directions by landmark rather than road name. Indeed, they often seemed not to know the names of roads they took every day.

Beside the oak, ran the unmarked road the farmer had mentioned. It was a dirt road, choked with snow.

"Okay," Dahlia said, taking in the scene. "That's a pretty small road. Looks bumpy and rutted out. Let's park. We'll have to go in on foot."

Elijah noticed that the small road was a straight shot from the mayor's house. The road between the two location was flat: a direct line. She parked and they got out and approached the fence that blocked the small road. Their footwear wasn't really up to the task. Neither was wearing boots. But they did the best they could, trudging through the snow, now accumulated to easily eight inches. The snow moistened Elijah's slacks to halfway up to his knees. It didn't take them long before they were to the location.

"See that?" Dahlia said, bringing out the picture. "That rise? The little hump and the big rock? This is the place."

But it looked quite different from the card. Where a large birch tree had stood in the seventies, now stood a wind turbine: massive on an entirely different order of magnitude. It was huge, at a scale that almost made you question your sanity.

"Why don't you stay with the car and keep an eye on it?" he asked.

"What do you think's going to happen?" she asked. "Someone's going to steal it? Out in the country? During a blizzard? Or are you worried Hugh Slaughter is going to hotwire it?"

He grinned, enjoying her sarcastic barb in spite of himself. It occurred to him again that this new acquaintance was almost like a long-lost younger sister. They had so much in common and had easily settled into a playful sibling combativeness.

"Listen" he said. "I think it's your turn to compromise here. In terms of our agreement. I'm still a cop. This is a crime scene."

"A twenty five-year old crime scene," she said.

"Regardless of that," he said. "I want you at the car."

He said this with a hint of steel in his voice. Not angry but making it clear. He had a backbone, and he was putting his foot down.

"Fine," she said, sulking like a kid. "I'll wait at the car."

He reached down and took the picture from her hand.

"It's definitely the spot."

"It's so weird," she said. "Such an iconic murder. I mean, even though they don't want to talk about it, *clearly* it looms large in the minds of the people of Mount Hugh. You might almost say their superstitious fear of it is a defining thing about the area. How strange that the only monument to it is this wind turbine. No shrine, no tombstone, just a giant fucking windmill."

"Yeah," he said. "That's the weirdest thing about this case. The reactions of the locals don't fit any of the usual patterns. Yes, denial is a thing. People might not want to admit that evil turned up in their town. But not like this. It's almost like hypnosis."

"Yes," she said. "Or mass hysteria."

He tucked the picture into his pocket and took another step towards the location.

"Keep the engine running," he said. "I don't think this will take long. There's not going to be any physical evidence. I'm just looking for insight."

"You got it, boss," she said with some degree of sarcasm. "Don't get lost."

Elijah trudged through the snow which was blown into higher drifts as he approached the site where they'd found the body, marked only by the huge turbine. There wasn't much to see. Of course, any physical evidence would be long gone. And even the roadway of the little dirt lane was covered with snow. He looked around, scanning the road and the horizon for anything that might give him some insight. It was isolated but not *that* isolated. It was closer to the road than he'd thought. In the distance, he could see the lights from the mayor's house, car in the distance. Whoever this woman was, the woman with the "C" necklace, was known to the Maximoffs and presumably the mayor as well. He glanced up at the turbine looming above him. Overwhelming, mysterious. It felt *too* large, impossibly so, like it didn't belong on the planet. The more he looked at it, the more certain he became that it couldn't remain standing. How could it? Wasn't it about to come crashing down and crush him? Wouldn't simple gravity ascertain that it did?

He pushed these irrational thoughts down, surprised at their intensity. No, it was just a turbine. A glorified windmill. He resolved to approach it more closely to see the exact spot where the body was found, fairly easy to determine from landmarks that remained from the photo. As he approached closer, the woods seemed to take on an eerie atmosphere. The sun was setting, and shadows were growing more prominent. Familiar objects took on sinister aspects. The bare limbs of trees looked like claws. Icicles hung from them like daggers. Emptiness all around, a soulless expanse, inducing pure terror. And above it all, the turbine loomed, like an ancient god, a celestial visitor from afar. It's giant blades slowly rotated, each one incomprehensibly huge. Irrationally, he felt like the motion of the blades had some significance, as if it were a message and if he could only decode it, it might reveal some terrifying truth about reality.

This is silly, he thought. You're not superstitious, not like the locals. There's no reason to be concerned…

He walked closer but the effort to lift his feet became almost too much. It wasn't the snow that was making walking difficult, but the fear that sat crouched in his heart. Waves and waves of fear washed over him, and with them a corresponding panic. Suddenly the shadows, the areas of darkness in the forest, seemed to hold threats. Terrors. Ghosts? Supernatural killers? Perhaps the spectre of Hugh Slaughter. He felt like he was in clear danger and for a moment considered running. It became more than he could handle and without consciously willing it, almost as if by a self-protective instinct, Elijah found himself with his gun in his hand. He looked out over its sites into the forest. Didn't he see movement out there? Hints of it amongst the shadows? Figures moving. Planning. Waiting for the moment to make their move…

He'd act first.

Elijah thought he saw it again, movement. What was it? Certainly not human… He turned his gun towards the sound. Towards the threat. And still, the fear washed over him, filling him. He began to shake. Tremors in his hands made it hard to hold the gun. He felt like he could hear his heartbeat in his ears, an unnaturally fast rhythm. On some level he recognized the irrationality, but he was helpless to stop it. He knew that he either needed to fire or to flee. Fight or flight. Those base instincts were all that was motivating him at the moment. Overheard, it seemed that the blades of the turbine spun faster and faster, and his fear seemed to ratchet up with turning, as if it was an engine driving his terror.

He heard the car honking. Looking over, he could no longer see it. The world had darkened in the wake of the sunset, and the snow had again picked up. The view was so obscured by the field of falling flakes that it created the illusion that he was alone in a dark world, disconnected from everything…

Moments earlier, Dahlia had sat inside the car in the driver's seat, the vent from the heater pointed hat her face. It had begun to warm her up, but she suspected her toes would remain chilled until she got back to her hotel room. Elijah had disappeared into the shadows of the trees that lined the small dirt road beyond the fence.

Thoughts spun in her head like the turbine in the distance. A web of connections, her attention traveling down strands, trying to map them into a coherent pattern. One thought that had impressed itself upon her: the mayor had lived through this grim and gruesome murder, yet had chosen, along with his partner, to place the massive turbine on the exact spot at which her body had been found. It was bewildering. Was it possible that the placement was somehow a coincidence? Something unfortunate chosen by committee? Or had they chosen the spot knowingly. To her, it felt like more erasure. In the same way that the newspapers suppressed the story after its initial publication, and how the locals pretended it never happened, wasn't placing the base of a massive wind turbine at the spot of the mystery woman's death another way of wiping the slate clean? As she wondered that the mayor's motive, she looked down the road towards his house. To her shock, she saw flames of bright orange, leaping like demons. Smoke tearing toward the sky. That was when she had pressed on the horn, and then Elijah didn't immediately appear she'd pressed it again. Again. Then just leaned on it.

Not knowing what to do, she stepped out of the car squinting towards the house, trying to get a better view. The whole thing seemed to be going up. The entire shape of the house, which has been clearly visible earlier before the sunset and onset of heavier snowfall, had been overwritten with a red-hot outline of flame. She felt herself seized by fear, helpless to move, staring into the distant flames. What was going on? What forces were at work?

Suddenly, a hand gripped her arm and she screamed.

"It's me!" said Elijah. He seemed winded and there was a wild look in his eyes. "It's okay, it's only me."

Dahlia wouldn't have admitted it to anyone, but the first thing that had occurred to her panicked mind was that Hugh Slaughter had stepped out of the past, out of local folklore, and had grabbed her to pull her down to hell.

"They mayor's house," she said, barely able to get the words out. "We have to get back there."

Elijah followed her gaze and immediately understood. They got back in the car and started back down the road, making the best time they could on a roadway that had grown increasingly slick with accumulated snow.

"Are you okay?" she asked from behind the steering wheel. She'd been creeped out herself, but Elijah's panicked expression as he'd appeared beside her had startled her.

In response to her question, he just shook his head.

"There was something out there," he said eventually.

"What?" she said. "I didn't see anything."

"I didn't see it clearly," he said. "But it was out there. Watching. Moving in the shadows. I could sense it."

Sense it? Dahlia wondered if her new friend was losing his mind.

Dahlia was confused and uncertain what to say. Elijah wasn't acting like himself. Frankly, she found his whole demeanor a little upsetting. Normally, she'd have just hit him with a quip or sarcastic comment, playfully questioning his ridiculous assertion that he could sense something in the woods. Instead, she chose her words carefully.

"Doesn't that sound irrational?" she asked.

Elijah paused for a long time before answering.

"I know it does," he said his eyes somehow simultaneously doubting and freshly terrified. "You're right. All I can say is I felt it."

She didn't question him further. Her intuition told her that whatever he'd experienced in the woods would pass from him like a dream. She'd felt her own moment of terror, and already it was fading. Maybe with some distance and time they'd be able to make sense of it.

The car pulled up at the major's house. It was as she'd deduced from the distance. The entire house was engulphed in flame. It wasn't consumed yet, but it looked as if fire had sprung up at several points along its walls simultaneously.

"Hey there," a voice called out. Dahlia saw that it was the same farmer she'd encountered in the field earlier. He has a small gardening hose, spraying it at the front of the house. The thin stream of water made small progress against the flames but wasn't enough to turn back the tide of their progress. There were a few others. Another farmer, this one a bit younger, and a heavyset woman. Another few neighbors were approaching the house from the direction of the backyard, carrying buckets. "They're getting water from the creek behind the property," the farmer said.

Elijah saw that the front door was slightly ajar. It was soaking from the stream of the hose. It was dangerous, but things would only get worse. As his head began to clear somewhat, still wracked by irrational fear but with a hint of a return to the consciousness he was used to, Elijah knew that this might be his only chance to look inside. He pushed the wettened door open with his foot and stepped inside.

There, inside, in the foyer, a body. He could recognize it as the mayor's from the clothing he was wearing. He could recognize it although the head had been removed. And, if there had been any doubt, there, a few feet from it, positioned on the top of a series of three small interior steps, was his head, clearly recognizable, dead eyes looking out at the house was consumed in flames.

A moment later, Elijah ran out of the house, coughing, smoke clinging to him. His eyes were wide, empty. He looked sick and overwhelmed.

"Don't go in," he said to Dahlia and the crowd. "There's no point."

He slumped in the front passenger's seat of Dahlia's car, shaking with what appeared to be tremors of panic. He took out the police issued emergency phone and dialled.

"What did you see?" she asked and then, when he didn't answer, "Who are you calling?"

"My partner," he said, waiting for the phone to be picked up. "Grayson, thank God…"

CHAPTER TEN
HINDSIGHT

"Goddammit," he growled. At the night. At the snow. At nothing. At everything.

The big gas guzzler slipped and slid around the turns which he took a little too fast. Aaron Grayson knew how to drive on snow. He'd been countersteering like a pro for decades. But, given his mental state, perhaps he was being a bit risky with the sudden moves. But he didn't care. His case, the perfect wrapped-up-in-a-bow case that he'd first come upon had continued to spiral further and further out of control. What had seemed open and shut became further and further muddled and confused by diverging possibilities.

Now, the mayor was dead. His favorite suspect. Head removed from shoulders, house burned down. The killer was still out there and all of Grayson's theories had gone up in smoke, just like the burning building growing larger through his windshield.

The car slid and skidded in for a halt in front of the blaze. Many locals were gathered, desperately hosing down the house's front and ferrying in water from a nearby creek in a sort of assembly line of buckets. It didn't seem to be making much of a difference. The fire had already won; everything they did now only served to slow the inevitable consumption of the mayor's home.

Grayson got out of his car to hear a heavy-set farmer declare.

"The curse is back. Hugh Slaughter is back."

The woman he was talking to, a wrinkled lady with bleach blonde hair wearing a nightgown, glared at Grayson before responding. "It's the outsiders that had brought him back. They kept digging around until they woke him up."

It took everything Grayson had not to get in their faces. He wanted to grab them by the shoulder, shake them and say, "Get your head out of your asses. You're spewing fairytales. There's a killer on the loose. Not a monster or a demon or what-the-hell-ever…"

But he didn't. He bit his tongue and bottled it up. But he was *pissed.* His investigation had gone south, and the situation was worsened by all of the superstitious nonsense the locals were spreading around.

Grayson roughly shouldered past the couple, almost knocking the man over in the slick snow. He moved through the crowd until he saw his partner and beside him, that nosy reporter. Of course, she was involved. On a level Grayson understood, rationally, that Elijah was not at fault. He hadn't cause anything, he'd only been on hand to uncover the murder. But he was out on his own. On some kind of errand, apparently collaborating with Dahlia, that suspicious sneak. Emotionally, Grayson couldn't help feeling that Elijah was botching his case, that his bumbling had screwed it up.

And he was pissed.

He stepped up to Elijah and, putting his hand on his younger partner's shoulder, turned him around so they were face to face.

"Okay, kid," he growled. "What the hell is going on?"

"I was out doing a little legwork," he said lamely. "Looking into the case from the seventies."

"Oh yeah?" Grayson's voice was venomous, dripping with sarcasm. "So, you just took that on yourself, did you? Decided to go in a different direction than what we discussed?"

"I know, I know…" Elijah said. "We talked about it. And you thought…"

"It's a fucking distraction," Aaron said. "It's unrelated. At best, the killer now is using it as a reference to try to get the locals worked up. But we don't need to be solving some decades-old cold case. We need to be finding evidence and following leads from the shit that's happening in the present."

"I just thought…"

"I remember my exact words," Grayson said. "I said we didn't need to be wasting resources on the old case."

"But I was off the clock," Elijah said in a wheedling tone, as if he wasn't sure he believed his excuses himself. "I don't see how *more* information could hurt."

"Bullshit," Grayson said. "That's all bullshit and you know it."

"If I hadn't been out investigation, I wouldn't have been the first on the scene to this murder…" His excuses were growing thinner and thinner.

"And what the hell does that have to do with anything? That's being in the right place at the right time. It's fucking coincidence. It has nothing to do with the fact that you superseded the chain of command. You intentionally ignored my directives for this investigation. You went behind my back. And you brought in this civilian…" At this point, Grayson gestured at Dahlia who stood by quietly watching the confrontation. "This busybody who came in with no clearance, stepping on our toes. In what world do you think this is okay?"

Elijah, chastened, had run out of excuses. "You're right," he said. "I overstepped. I shouldn't have done it, done anything, behind your back. I'm sorry."

"Damn straight," Grayson said, his temper flaring. His fists were clenched tight, nails digging into his palms, his knuckles standing out white and bony. He felt like punching something. "And if you pull any more of this kind of bullshit, you're off the case. I'll send you back to the substation with a reprimand. Do we understand each other?"

"Yes, sir," Elijah said, not meeting Grayson's eyes.

Grayson nodded, feeling a little stability return. At least this one thing was under his control.

"So, fill me in," he said.

"We were down the road," he said. "At the… uh… the location of the earlier murder. When we saw the house going up. There were a few locals here already when we got here. Trying to put it out. I went inside and found the mayor. Beheaded, like the other victims."

"Victim," Grayson corrected. "This is our second. Until we have a better reason to think there's a direct connection, we're leaving that seventies murder behind. Maybe it was inspiration. Maybe this murderer is an obsessed local. A copycat. But we've got to focus on the here and now."

"Right," Elijah said. "Anyway, I wasn't able to recover the body. The flames were too bad. But I can verify the condition of the body."

"The way I figure it," Dahlia said. "The murder must have happened fifty minutes or so ago…""Excuse me, Miss Crane," Grayson said gruffly. "But did anyone ask you?"

"No," she said meekly. "But I just wanted to share my observations."

"We don't need them," he said. "We don't need amateur interference. This is an official investigation. The fact that you're curious, that you're playing Nancy Drew, doesn't mean a damned thing. Tell me, do you have any background? Did you go to the police academy?"

"No," she said.

"Did you study forensic science?" he didn't wait for her to answer before continuing. "Were you granted a badge or any kind of licence from any official body? No? Well, then you can leave my crime scene. Either grab a bucket and start helping put out this fire or step the hell back. Past the edge of the driveway. That's where the yellow tape is going up."

Elijah stepped forward and for a moment it seemed like he was going to speak up in Dahlia's defense, but Grayson silenced him with a look. Elijah knew he was on thin ice. Grayson didn't really understand the nature of his relationship with this girl, this loose cannon, and he didn't really care. All he knew was he didn't need her sticking her nose in. He'd dealt with enough busy bodies over the years. They did nothing but muddy things up.

Grayson swung his arm, indicating the edge of the driveway. "So, get back there. You're not a part of this. The point is, you have no credentials, and we don't know you. For all I know you could be working with the killer, interfering in our investigation. A distraction, trying to get us moving down the wrong path." He was talking off the top of his head, but even as he said it, it made a kind of intuitive sense to Grayson. If the killer was intentionally invoking the earlier murder, perhaps to obscure a real motive behind local folklore, wouldn't it also make sense to try to sway the investigation in that direction? Maybe Dahlia was working with the killer? Maybe she was *behind* it.

"Abdoullah…" Aaron turned at the sound of the voice, calling out plaintively. It was Leonard Maximoff, apparently having just arrived on the scene. Sure, he sounded distraught, but Grayson wasn't convinced. He'd seen convincing performances from guilty parties before. Call it what you want: acting or simply lying. Sociopaths sometimes gave amazing performances.

Maximoff approached Aaron. "Officer Grayson… is he?"

"He's gone," Aaron said. He wasn't particularly concerned with revealing this fact. The gathered locals were already talking about it. "Killed and his house apparently set on fire."

Maximoff fell to his knees in the gathering snow, letting out a sob. "No…" he said.

"It's their fault," said one of the yokels. "It's Hugh Slaughter. He's back. They set him free. Invited him back." Grayson felt fresh fury at this idiocy. The idea that talking, asking questions, could incite a supernatural murder. It was hogwash.

"He was my oldest friend," Maximoff said, tears welling, streaming down his cheeks.

Yes, a convincing performance.

"You have my condolences," Aaron said, not bothering trying to sound sincere. "Maybe *you* can tell me where you were for the past hour or two?"

Maximoff blinked away the tears and looked up, surprised.

"I was in bed," he said. "Malinda was with me. She can vouch for me."

"Uh-huh," Grayson said. Just like the tears, it meant nothing. He let out a short laugh. "It wouldn't be the first time a spouse vouched for a killer."

"Now, listen," Maximoff said, angry but clearly shocked at what Grayson had said.

"I'll need to talk to her," he said, steamrolling over Maximoff's objections. "She back at your place?"

"Yes," Maximoff said, nodding uncertainly.

"Good. I'd also like to be the one to explain the situation with Peter. In the meantime, I think you'd be useful here, helping keep the locals in line. Keep them calm. And set up a time for the townsfolk to gather for safety instructions. Curfew, that sort of thing. You read me?"

Grayson put a little steel in his voice on the final question, making it clear that although it was delivered as a request, there would be consequences for noncompliance. Grayson was sick of nobody taking his authority seriously. It was time to crack down. In any case, it seemed to work. The combination of a chance to contribute and the implied threat seemed to be enough.

"You got it," Maximoff said.

"Come on, Riley," Aaron said to his partner. "You're back on the clock."

Elijah followed Grayson towards his car. "What about the caution tape?"

"Local law enforcement can do that," he said dismissively. "I called them in. They'll be here any minute. Besides, any useful evidence has already been incinerated. I'm sure that was the point of the fire. This crime scene is useless. Already compromised all to hell. We're going to the Maximoff's. I want to ask them some questions before they've had a chance to talk to anyone."

Grayson paused and turned. Dahlia was following them.

"I thought I was clear," he said. "You're not wanted here."

"You *need* my help," she said.

"Doesn't look that way from where I sit, Miss Crane."

"You don't know how to do your job," she said. "You're too stuck in your ways, too hung up on your habits and outmoded ways of thinking. And they haven't got you anywhere. If you'd listened to Elijah about how the previous murder was connected to the recent one, maybe you could have solved this case before another murder happened under your nose."

On a level, Grayson was surprised. He'd been throwing his weight around. Like an alpha dog. Intimidating people. It had worked on Elijah, and it had worked on Maximoff. It was surprising that this troublemaker was coming at him. But on the other hand, he took some satisfaction in the fact that he'd successfully gotten under *her* skin. In a weird way, it made him feel more in control.

"Is that your professional opinion, Miss Crane?" he said, emphasizing the name as if to underline her lack of official qualifications. "As a freelance journalist? A college student? Are you gracing me with your expertise in this performance review?"

She reddened. Good. He was getting to her.

"Listen," Elijah said, seeming to find a bit of backbone. "Let's *all* be professional. The fighting doesn't help."

Grayson nodded. "Sure. Let's go Riley. We have work to do. Stay out of our way, Miss Crane. It's a crime to obstruct an investigation, and if you don't think I'd put you behind bars for getting in our way, then you don't know me very well."

He turned his back on her, a satisfied smile on his face.

Grayson drove. His winter-driving skills had returned. He felt back in charge, in some degree of control. The rage at the setbacks in his case had subsisted somewhat.

"That's behind us," Grayson said. "I said my piece and we have work to do."

Elijah nodded. "Right."

"So, what was the idea?" Grayson asked in all sincerity. "What did you think you could find at a twenty five-year old murder scene? Outdoors? Any evidence would have been obliterated a long time ago." It bugged him, made him wonder at his young partner's judgement.

"I don't know what I was looking for," Elijah said quietly. "But I felt like there might be some value in seeing the place it happened. It might suggest something."

Grayson shook his head. "I expect better from you, partner. That sounds like a bunch of mystical mumbo jumbo. Like you're expecting some kind of revelation."

"I did find… something," Elijah said uncertainly.

"Something useful?" Grayson pressed. "In our investigation."

"I don't know," Elijah said. "It was strange."

"Well, lay it on me," Grayson grumbled, training his eyes out the front window, at the arcing snowflakes, flashing in reflecting the headlight's beams like falling stars.

"I sensed a present. When I was up by the turbine. Something there. Watching me. I *felt* it. And a fear. Overpowering."

"Seriously?" he asked. "Jesus Christ, kid. You're a mess. Stumbling through the woods, running from shadows. I can't believe you're buying into this bullshit, the local legends and superstitious malarkey they're selling around here."

"It's not that," Elijah said. "It's real. I felt it."

"And maybe it's your buddy there, too," Grayson said. "Crane. You've got her leading you around. Talking you into bad ideas. I gotta say, I expected more from you. This is disappointing. You're supposed to be a leader. An authority. But instead, you're just blowing around from one thing to another, latching on to every bad idea that comes down the pike."

Elijah looked away, hurt, almost as if struck. Grayson felt only a moment's remorse at the look on his partner's face.

It needed to be said, Grayson thought. He needs to get his shit together.

As they arrived at the Maximoff house, Malinda greeted them at the door. She'd dressed and was clearly expecting them, opening the front door as Grayson's hand was poised to knock. He was annoyed; he'd been counting on catching the Maximoff's off-guard and making the most of the advantage of surprise.

"Here we go," he muttered behind his hand to Elijah as the door was pulled open. "Leonard alerted them. They've got their stories together. Get ready for some bullshit."

"Hi Ms. Maximoff," he said, turning, his demeanor changing completely. "Mind if we come in and ask a few questions?"

"Of course, Detective Grayson," she said, wiping tears from her face. "Leonard called me from Bill's house. It's so terrible. He was one of our oldest friends."

Apparently Maximoff has a cellular telephone in his car. Grayson supposed he shouldn't have been surprised. The man had money so, of course, he had all of the latest toys. His plan to keep him busy so he could use surprise strategically against the family had been subverted.

"Tea and cookies?" she said as they followed her into the kitchen.

Grayson thought it an odd choice in greeting a lawman in the middle of the night to talk about a murder, but he said yes anyway. His feet had gotten cold at the sight and the idea of hot tea was appealing. Elijah followed closely behind, minding himself and following the chain of command, for the moment at least. He still seemed to be stinging from the scolding.

"Can you call Peter down?" Grayson asked when he was seated in front of a steaming mug of tea.

"He stepped out," Malinda said. Grayson found the answer evasive but decided to let it stand for the moment. He noticed that Elijah was still more withdrawn than usual, more of an observer than an actual participant. Although he often got on Grayson's nerves, Elijah did contribute his share of good ideas. Aaron wondered if he'd been too hard on him. But, no. The boy had gotten out of line. Grayson had given him too long a leash and he'd paid for it. This was a needed correction. And Grayson had to admit that, on a level, he was enjoying his partner's submissiveness. Maybe now he knew his place.

"Officers," said Fawn, turning the corner on the stairs from the second floor.

"Fawn," Grayson said with unearned familiarity. "Did you ever get your hands on that university letter we were asking about?" He delivered the question with unmistakable sass and an eyebrow arched challengingly.

To her credit, Fawn wasn't going for it, wasn't going to be bullied or chided into spilling the beans. "You can talk to Peter about that," she said. "It's *his* business. He should be here in a minute."

"Suit yourself," Grayson said with a chuckle, amused because, from what he'd seen, Fawn was the one who wore the pants in the relationship. It was funny, her saying it was his business when she clearly led the boy by the hand through his life. But he'd get to the bottom of things. The Maximoffs were used to having their way, used to throwing their weight around. That shit was *not* going to work with him. They could play their games, circle their wagons, get their stories together, obfuscate and delay, but Grayson would outwait them. He was like a gator; once he got his teeth locked in, it was only a matter of time before he'd pull you into the water and devastate you with a bone-crushing role. "Listen, I don't know what's going on between you and Pete. Who knows? Maybe he finally had enough of your mind games."

"Listen," Malinda said. "You don't need to come in here insulting…"

There it was. Entitled rich folks treating cops like they were service workers. They really just didn't get it.

"My apologies," he said sarcastically. "It the simple request was too much for you folks, with everything that's going on, maybe we should make the call to the university ourselves. Officer Riley, you could do that tomorrow, couldn't you?"

"Absolutely," Elijah said, seeming to perk up a bit. "First thing in the morning. As soon as their offices are open."

"No," Fawn said. "I said we'd handle it. Please, just wait for Peter to get here."

The side door to the kitchen opened and Peter entered. There was a moment, one of those frozen moments of time, where he looked on, surprised at the police presence in his presumably safe domestic space, and Grayson and Elijah took looked him over. He was covered in snow, wet up to his angles from fighting snowdrifts. He looked rough, like he'd rolled down a snow-covered hill.

"So, where you been, Petey-boy?" Aaron asked. He was getting a kick out of watching these stuck-up bigwigs squirm.

"Out," he said in a distracted voice. "Walking around the hill."

"Walking around the hill," Grayson said. "That all you got?"

"That's what I was doing," he said.

Grayson turned to Elijah. "How does that square with you, partner? As an alibi?"

"Listen," Elijah started. "Maybe we should…"

"You know what we're talking about, don't you son?" Grayson said turning his attention back to Peter. "There was another murder tonight."

"I know," Peter said, suddenly overcome with emotion. "I saw the fire. I heard people out there talking."

"Your father," Grayson said. "Taken out."

Peter's face was blank. Yes, grief could suck the reaction out of you, but so could sociopathy.

"Both of my parents," Peter said numbly. "Murdered."

"Yeah, that's right," Aaron said. "It implies a connection. Doesn't seem like a serial killer lashing out randomly, does it? Seems kind of like someone picking people for a reason. And, as we know, murderers tend to be people close to the victim. A lot of times it's husbands or angry exes taking out the women, but we're a bit past that now, aren't we?"

"Please," Malinda said, raising her voice. Irate, as if she were about to ask if she could speak to the manager. "Take it easy on him. He's going through a lot."

Grayson only responded by casting her a threatening glare and holding a hand up, gesturing that she should pipe down. He took a step towards Peter. "You had no real alibi for the night of your mother's murder. You found her. You had hours to do it. And now, here we are again. Walking around the hill? I don't guess anyone saw you, did they? About an hour ago? That can vouch for you."

Peter's brows knit and his lip trembled. "No," he said. "I don't guess."

"And then there's the business about your lying. About this medical school nonsense. Why are you lying to us Pete? What's the real story? It wouldn't be a bad time to start fessing up."

Fawn stepped forward, putting herself between Aaron and Peter, as if she were trying to break up and impending fight. Aaron ignored her, leaning past her to continue.

"It's looking bad for you, kid. Cooperating, telling us what's going on, will go a long way towards building back some trust with us."

"I did lie," he said. It came out halfway to a sob, as if it had been torn out of him. "It was for my parents. I did it for them. My plan had always been to be a doctor, a surgeon, and they wanted it for me. They were proud of me. And I… I couldn't handle it. The pressure. I failed out. So, I made up the lie about the transfer, not realizing that Dent didn't have a medical school. I didn't want to disappoint them."

He paused for a long time, looking down at his hands, before continuing. "But I suppose that doesn't matter now. They're both gone."

"It's true," Fawn said. "I was helping him. Assisting him in getting back to school."

"You *lied*?" Malinda said. "To all of us. Me too? You're not going to be a doctor?"

"I am," Peter said. "Eventually. I hope to. But I just have a lot to work out first…" He trailed off here, as if recognizing the wheedling bullshit tone in his own voice and finding it unconvincing.

"I am *so* disappointed," Malinda said and, turning to her daughter, "Fawn, this is not the kind of man to connect yourself to. He's dishonest, he's weak. He seems unstable. He has no value to your life. He contributes nothing."

Aaron smiled grimly. When people had money, that was all they cared about.

"Why are you saying, mom?"

"Well, that maybe it's time for you to move on. You've put too much effort into this boy."

"How can you say that, mom?" Fawn asked. "After all he's been through. Is it any wonder that he's having trouble keeping it together." As if by way of demonstration of this point, Peter's head collapsed onto his folded arms, and he collapsed into low sobs.

"His problems started before the recent tragedies," Malinda said. "They've always been there. Like it's his fundamental nature."

Grayson remembered how Malinda had come on like the perfect hostess, offering tea and cookies. But now, here she was, showing her true colors. Like a striking viper. He almost felt sorry for Peter, as much as the spineless boy disgusted him.

"So, it's all about maintaining wealth, isn't it?" he asked Malinda. "That's what it's always about for you people, isn't it? The bottom line? Once you've got your hands on wealth it's always about keeping it."

Malinda turned on him. Now that the viper was out of its cage, she seemed to have stopped pretending. The calm matriarch was gone, and the venomous snake was fully revealed.

"What do you know about wealth?" she asked, looking him up and down. "Look at you. In your discount suit. Trying to cultivate a sense of style. You *want* to be important, don't you? To be wealthy? That's why you're always puffing out your chest and throwing your weight around. I may value wealth but at least I'm honest about it. You look down your nose at the successful while coveting their success."

For a moment, Aaron was shocked into a fuming silence. He hadn't expected the outburst and was even more pissed off because there was an element of truth to it. Nobody liked having a mirror pushed in their face.

"Now wait a damned minute," he said once he'd recovered his composure.

"Peter," she said, imperious, as if she were a queen dictating policy. "I want you to leave. And stay away from Fawn."

"Ms. Maximoff," he said in a voice weak, desperate.

"Mom," Fawn said. "What the hell?"

"You've attached yourself to a sinking ship, dear," Malinda said with surprising compassion. "When you do that, there's only one thing that'll happen. You get pulled under."

"It's *my* life," Fawn said. "You're not in charge."

"No, but I have my hands on the purse strings, dear. So, I want you to carefully consider your priorities."

"Come on," Fawn said to Peter. "We're getting out of here."

"Before you do," Aaron said to Fawn. "In spite of your mom's hissy fit, we're running a murder investigation here. I need to talk to both of you. Everybody's a suspect, so don't leave town."

"We won't," Fawn said.

"Where will you be?" he asked.

"We'll figure something out," Peter said.

Grayson frowned, anticipating having to track them down.

"Meet us at the hotel," he said. "Tomorrow at eight a.m. The lobby."

"Yes sir," Fawn said and the two left the house.

As the door shut and a silence fell over the room, the sort of conversational vacuum that sometimes descends in the aftermath of an argument, Elijah suddenly came alive.

"So, who is this woman?" he said, a seeming non sequitur.

"Excuse me?" she asked, apparently just as confused as Grayson felt at this unexpected query. He looked over and saw that his partner was holding a photo he'd taken from a shelf in the front hall. Grayson resisted the urge to yank the leash and bully his partner back into line. He'd see where this went. Maybe he was onto something. Grayson leaned in and looked at the photo. In it, Eleanor and Malinda stood on opposite sides of a third woman, a petite blonde. They were leaning back on a convertible and from the make, the hairstyles, and other context clues, Aaron surmised the picture was from the late sixties. Grayson realized that he'd seen several other pictures of the trio on display, but he hadn't given much conscious thought to what now seemed an obvious question.

Who was the other woman?

With a twinge of annoyance, he felt like Elijah must be back on the connection he'd been trying to force between the contemporary murders and the one from the seventies. But still, his gut told him to see where it led. He realized that Malinda had been silent for a moment. Why pause? It was an easy question. You have the girl in a frame. You know who she is? Why not just say it. Unless you're hiding something.

"Well?" Grayson asked gruffly. "Officer Riley asked you a question."

"She was a friend of ours. Eleanor and mine. For a time, the three of us were very close but we grew apart. This woman never had partners or a husband. She was always so focused on education.

Over time, it came to feel that we had little in common and that she thought herself better than us."

"Where is she now?" Aaron asked, with no idea what Elijah had been getting at, no idea, indeed, where *he* was going in this line of questioning. No, in the moment he was completely following his gut which, despite what Elijah might think, rarely steered him wrong. He was following his gut and it felt good.

"To be honest, I don't really care. Around the time we stopped hanging out, she left town, not bothering to tell us where or even say goodbye. One day, she just left. Who knows? Probably for some educational opportunity, some scholarship. If I had to guess, I'd say she's probably a professor somewhere…"

"This woman *was* your friend. At least before you drifted apart. And you're saying you never were the least bit curious?" Elijah asked.

"No," Malinda said curtly. "Not even a little. We were done with each other and that was that."

Grayson remembered how casually she'd cut Peter from her life and her daughter's, complaining that he had nothing to contribute. Was it that simple, when the bottom line dictated your life, to hack away the bits that didn't serve your narrowly defined interests?

"I'm sorry," she said. "But I don't have any information on her. Did you have something else I could help you with?"

"Yes," said Elijah. "In the picture's she's wearing a necklace. The letter C." Grayson frowned, wondering where his partner was going with this. "Do you remember the significance of that?"

"Why, yes," Malinda said. "Eleanor gave her the necklace. For no particular reason, that I can remember, except perhaps as a gesture of friendship." There was a strange bitterness in her voice as she said this. What was it jealousy? Something else? Aaron wondered if he was catching a whiff of a previously unsuspected motive. "She wore it all the time, and the significance of the 'C' is obvious. It stood for her last name. Crane. Her name was Lucy Crane."

Grayson turned and met Elijah's eyes as the revelation seemed to hit both of them simultaneously.

Lucy Crane.

Crane.

Could there be a connection to Dahlia?

Chapter Eleven
Hugh Slaughter

Dahlia drove slowly back to the hotel. It was the middle of the night, and she couldn't afford to slide off the road in the icy conditions. She didn't want to end out stranded.

Also, if she was being honest, she'd have to admit she was a little shaken. By everything. Of course, by the new murder. By the feeling of impending doom that seemed to surround everything in Mount Hugh. The creepy vibe she got from the locals, with their vacant terrified eyes, as if they weren't seeing the world in front of them but instead were looking into themselves, or into a primitive past, and seeing nightmares come alive. And then, to see that same look on Elijah's face. Elijah, her fast friend with whom she'd quickly bonded. Her own traumas, too, were close to the surface. The conversation with Elijah in the car about their pasts had dredged up some unpleasant thoughts.

Then, the fire. The murder. And then, Aaron Grayson, the old overconfident bastard, going on the attack. He accused her of interference but clearly, *he* was the one botching his own case. He was too blinded by his own preconceptions, his own simplistic mindset, and he'd stood by and done nothing to prevent a second murder. She *knew* that she and Elijah had been onto something. For her it was like there was a pattern that she couldn't quite see, but as she gathered information and retrieved missing pieces of the puzzle, the pattern started to cohere into something comprehensible. In her mind, the picture had gained focus. She was almost there.

But had she lost Elijah's assistance? And now Grayson was threatening to throw her in jail if she kept investigating. Should she just back down? Was it really her fight?

Like hell she'd back down.

More than anything, she needed an outside perspective. As soon as she got back to the hotel, she used the phone in her room to call Naomi. Naomi was her rock. Her anchor. She was the first person that Dahlia had really learned to trust, and, in that way, she had completely changed her life. She made Dahlia feel stronger, like maybe she had the strength to do what needed to be done.

But at times like these, she needed her. Needed to lean on her stability.

"Babe," Naomi said as she picked up. "I missed you. How goes the adventure in journalism."

"Great," Dahlia said. She didn't believe it herself and, of course, Naomi could see right through her.

"What's wrong?" she asked. "It's late there. What happened?"

Dahlia recounted the events of the evening, leading up to and including the fire and murder.

"A second murder," Naomi said. "Are you in danger there, babe?"

"No," Dahlia said although, as soon as she said it, she wondered if that was really true. "Whoever's behind it is targeting locals."

"Hmmm," Naomi said. "But you were born there. Doesn't that make you worry?"

"No," Dahlia said. Another lie, of course. She *was* worried. She didn't know what was happening or what was going to happen. Until she saw the full pattern, that big-picture version, she couldn't really know who was safe and who wasn't. But she wasn't going to tell Naomi that, because she knew that the second Naomi was worried that she was in danger, she'd start trying to convince her to come home. Indeed, her beloved partner was probably already fighting the urge to talk her into returning. Naomi supported Dahlia in her ambitions and efforts. That was one of the wonderful things about her, her support was unconditional. Even when Dahlia's studies and journalistic goals had been merely a pipedream, Naomi had been there encouraging her to pursue her dream. Every step of the way.

But, of course, if she felt like Dahlia's *life* was in danger, it would be a very different dynamic.

"I'm completely safe," Dahlia continued. "I'm always around other people. Some of them police officers. The killer has only struck when people were isolated. It's the same pattern from the original murder, the one from the seventies."

"Then why do you sound so worried?"

"I don't know," Dahlia said, struggling to put it into words. "The locals around here are strange. Superstitious. They believe that talking about the murders invites them to happen. I think it's somehow tied to the lack of press coverage too. Perhaps these attitudes are so evasive they even infected the fourth estate. But in any case, in Mount Hugh, they have a whole mythology around it. They have a name for the killer. For the monster."

"That's insane," said Naomi. "Completely irrational. Maybe that's just how they process their fear? I don't know. That's more your wheelhouse than mine. But you said the monster had a name. What do they call it."

For a moment, Dahlia paused.

"What?" Naomi said. "*You're* not afraid, are you?"

"No," Dahlia said. "Well, consciously no. I know it's crazy. And I'm not a superstitious person. But the fear of these people is kind of infectious. You can laugh at it or be creeped out by it, but it *gets* to you."

"So, what's it called?"

"They call him Hugh Slaughter," Dahlia said, almost in a whisper.

Naomi laughed.

"Hugh Slaughter," she repeated. "That's a bit 'on the nose,' don't you think?"

Dahlia laughed along with her but didn't really share her irreverence. "I'm sure you're right. These people are scared and there's some kind of psychological phenomenon going on. Mass hysteria or mass self-hypnosis or something. Something weird but probably not something unprecedented. Weird things happen when people deal with tragedy. It's natural. The original murder was never solved so the people felt the need to give a name to the killer. And, making up a story, they naturally built it out into a myth. A killing force, a demon or something, that might go dormant that could return at any time if you looked too closely or spoke its name too loudly."

"Right," said Naomi. "Like one of those urban legends. The one where you turn off the light and say the monster's name three times in front of a mirror."

"Exactly," Dahlia said. "I recognize intellectually that this all makes sense. Saying it out loud helps. But there are times that the fear gets to me. It's real. Palpable. It hangs in the air like smoke. I made friends with one of the police officers. A man named Elijah. We hit it off conversationally…"

"Should I be jealous?" Naomi asked playfully, not really worried.

"No. It was like finding a long-lost brother. We just immediately got each other in that rare way that new friends sometimes click. Anyway, he and I went off to explore the connections between the two murders and we were both talking about how funny it was that the locals are acting like extras in a Frankenstein movie. Superstitious villagers about to take up torches. He was right there with me, on the same wavelength. But he went out into the forest, just off the roadway, where the first murder had happened, and came back… different. He was panicked, irrational. It was like the superstitions of the townsfolk was a virus and it had infected him."

"That's weird," said Naomi. "But you said yourself it seemed like a mass hysteria phenomenon. The power of suggestion is strong. And it seems like now it's getting to you."

"Maybe it is," Dahlia said. "I just have this feeling of… I don't know… I guess *dread* is the best word for it. When I was a kid and my life was a mess, I used to worry about disaster coming at any moment. It had happened enough time. I'd learned that life was unpredictable because mine was, so I knew a turn could come at any time. It created this nervousness, this anxiety, that I carried inside me. Like a coiled spring about to pop. I thought I'd gotten over it in recent years. Since meeting you, since getting my life together. But now it's back. I feel like the disaster is back. And yeah, maybe all of this Hugh Slaughter is contributing. It's giving *me* a name for the fear I feel. The instability. That idea that the rug could get pulled out from under you at any moment."

"Do you need to come home?" Naomi asked. That's how she phrased it. As a question. She wasn't demanding, wasn't trying to convince. Just checking in.

"No," Dahlia said hesitatingly. "Not yet, in any case. I think I just needed to talk."

"Well, let me tell you two things," Naomi said. "First, I support you. One hundred percent. I support what you're doing and what you want to learn and accomplish from the project. As always."

"I know," Dahlia said, feeling the warmth of love thaw some of the anxiety that had invaded her psyche. "And I love you for it."

"But also know this: if you feel like it's time to go home, I support you in that as well. It's not a failure to know you need to take a step back. That's a good thing. It's wisdom. But what I'm hearing is that you're not at that level."

"I'm not," Dahlia said. "I really want to see this through."

"Then you should," Naomi said. "Because if that's where you are with it, backing out is going to make you judge yourself harshly. See it through."

Dahlia smiled. Nobody knew her like Naomi.

"One more thing. You have to take care of yourself, babe, because you're not just living for yourself anymore. You're living for me."

"Thank you," Dahlia said. "I will. I'll take care of myself."

"Have you been getting enough sleep?" Naomi asked.

"Not really," Dahlia said. "It's hard to stop thinking about this stuff. It keeps me up."

"Then that might be contributing as well, right?" Naomi asked. "When you're sleep deprived, your emotions become heightened. You become more reactive, less logical."

"That's true," Dahlia said.

"Then get a good night's sleep," Naomi said. "Get a fresh start tomorrow. Well-rested. I bet everything will look different to you in the light of day and you'll find that the anxiety you're feeling tonight was just a blip."

"Good advice," Dahlia said. "I'll do that."

"I wish I was there to join you," Naomi said. "I miss you."

"I miss you too," Dahlia said. "I love you."

The Mount Hugh Inn was three story brick building, easily a hundred years old and one got the sense that it had been in operation as a hotel for all that time. What it lacked in modernity or amenities it made up for in the sense of character and history that it exuded. The rooms felt like well-preserved time capsules, appointed with furnishings giving a nineteenth century flavor. Each room had a tidy oak writing table, four poster beds and, by the window, a cushioned lounge chair.

That's where Dahlia sat, in the lounge chair. She'd changed into the plush bathrobe that hung from a hook on the bathroom door, had fixed herself a cup of tea, and now stared out into the night. Mount Hugh shut down early, as did most small towns. They "rolled up the sidewalks," as she'd heard the locals say, when the sun went down. In small towns, there wasn't much of an expectation of night life; people went home to their families and if they wanted a drink, they generally did it behind closed doors. The one exception was the Watering Hole, catering to the restless spirits in the populace, but they were several blocks down and not visible from her vantage point.

Now, looking out, she saw barely a light in the street below and it gave her the feeling that only she was awake. Snowflakes drifted past the streetlights outside the window, they dipped and dove, reflecting the yellowish glare. Dahlia sipped a glass of tea and pushed the red recording button on her handheld tape recorder, took a deep breath, and started talking, letting her thoughts, all the subconscious connections she'd made, come out in a rambling stream of consciousness. She'd found this method helpful in the past. It had functioned as a kind of self-therapy for her before and she hoped that here it might help her solve the mystery. It spoke to a truth; ideas, when locked in your head, tended to lead you in circles. It was only when they got out, when they were spoken, that you could break that pattern and move forward. In the absence of conversation, Dahlia had found that her method of talking to her little tape recorder was the best way to break mental logjams.

"Why am I here?" she asked herself. She almost laughed. It sounded like such an existential question, such a portentous place to start. "What am I here in Mount Hugh?" she amended, continuing, "I am here to learn about the communities. Communities in general. This was my purpose, at least initially. To learn about how communities such as Mount Hugh survive in the face of a changing world. To finish my dissertation on this topic. And maybe, while I was at it, to reconnect with my past. Process it. But those goals have changed."

She pressed pause and sipped her tea, still hot from the kettle. Outside the snowflakes continued to dip and dive. Down the street, a snowplow turned a corner, pushing through the drift, shoving snow off the road and into piles on the sidewalks. She resumed her recording.

"So, what is my goal now? To help, I suppose. To help the community. To help them heal? Maybe. Clearly, this community is damaged in their relationship to trauma. They seem to have an almost pathological aversion to dealing with it. Twenty five years ago, an unknown woman was found beheaded. They almost immediately retreated into denial, pretending it never happened. And now, as it has happened again, they blame those asking questions, those searching. In this way, the sin becomes not the murder, but the acknowledgement of it. If pretending it never happened lets us maintain the fiction that we live in a perfect town then, by logical extension, by acknowledging it, we make it real. And in their mythology, it's literal. Hugh Slaughter is waiting. Asking questions, talking about him, releases him into the world."

She could feel it. Connections, waiting to be made. Maybe something important. To solve the case? To process her past? She wasn't sure, but her subconscious was fully engaged, charged, as if by an electrical current. She pressed on.

"I am no stranger to trauma," she said. "And I am from here. Is my own journey really any different? Haven't I too suppressed and denied? Why was it important for me to come back? My work in dealing with small communities has taken me all over the world looking for answers. Mount Hugh is, in many ways, a typical town. There is nothing here of inherent importance to my project. So why did I feel it was important that I come home. What truths, what motives, have I been supressing."

Anther sip of tea. Outside the window the snowflakes fell, one after another, with no end in sight, the only witnesses to her late-night monologue. She mused on the fact that this recording, which had been meant to explore the questions of the mystery she struggled to untangle, had turned into another self-therapy session. No matter: she would press on. She could feel answers, swirling invisible around her head, dipping and darting like the snowflakes, just beyond her fingertips. If she could manage to make the right connections, she'd find truth. About herself or the murders? Who knew? All she knew was that she had to speak the feelings, to get them out into the world, to change her relationship to them so she could improve her understanding. So, she could break the cycle and move forward.

"I was born here," she said. "It's where I started. And it's where the pain I've spent so much of my life trying to deal with started. It was my home, but I feel like an outsider, still. More than ever. I've never felt like I belong anywhere. That feeling of displacement has followed me since childhood. Maybe the only way I can ever get past it is by returning to the source and working it out here." It made a kind of intuitive sense. To fix her damaged psyche, she had to return to the wellspring for her trauma, to that original context in which the damage had occurred.

"I've always felt alone. Unloved. Without a community. Without a family. Maybe that's why I gravitated towards communities as the subject for my dissertation. What are the bonds that sustain them? These are bonds I've never felt in my own life. So, in my life's work so far, my subject of dissertation, I've really been trying to come to understand how the bonds of community are formed, as if by learning this perhaps I could heal myself and learn how to find love, to find a family, to find my place in a community."

She paused the recorder for a moment, thrilled with the connections she'd made, feeling the almost electric charge of revelation in her mind as her understanding expanded. She delved back further, narrating to her recorder her thoughts on how she'd been shaped by her circumstances. She wondered at the different ways that her lack of support and love had affected her. It had damaged her ability to trust. She even wondered if it had indirectly impacted her sexuality; had the loss of a central woman in her life left her looking for love in other women? It sounded silly, saying it out loud, typical Freudian conclusions, but there might be something to it. She could see a version of the same search in her newfound friend, Elijah. No, it hadn't affected his sexuality, but wasn't his complex relationship with his partner a version of him seeking approval from a surrogate father figure? And *that* got her thinking about fathers. She didn't have one. She'd had a mother, but she had no clue as to her father's identity. He was nothing. A cypher. A void. She had never imagined his face, and her mother had never spoken about him.

"So, what is my project about? Getting my PhD? Exploring the nature of communities? Or am I seeking to reconcile my identity. To fill in those gaps."

She saw a pattern. It wasn't the answer to the mystery, but it was the way in which all the different pieces were connected. Communities. Families. Trauma. Her identity.

Murder.

Suddenly, unbidden, an idea bubbled up. It was one of the happy side-effects to her habit of narrating in the recorder. It was almost like a meditative state, a trance, one in which the speaker was very close to the subconscious, and sometimes surprises emerged from the darkness.

"The first victim, the first modern victim anyway, was Eleanor. She seemed to be a lonely person. Estranged from her husband for reasons that are still a little unclear to me. I don't know what her relationship to Peter was, but *he* seems damaged. Perhaps by the breakup. She seemed to lack strong connections." Dahlia could relate to this, which might have been part of what drew her mind to Eleanor. A damaged woman. A mother. "She was known to attend the Watering Hole. At night. When it functions as a bar." She paused for a minute, taking a sip of the tea, which had dipped to lukewarm. "It's popular among the locals. Locals who knew Eleanor. Who know the Larks and the Maximoffs. And there would certainly be those barflies, the old timers, who remember something from around the time of the original murder. And even if they have those barriers, the strong psychological block from talking about or even acknowledging the murders, and the myth of Hugh Slaughter, they're *drinking*. They're lowering their inhibitions. Maybe if she talked to the right local, at the right time of the night, she could get some truth, unguarded by a fear of supernatural retribution. Not a bad idea. She'd have to swing by the Watering Hole in the evening and see what she could dig up.

She looked at the clock on the bedside table, digital numbers burning blue. 10:32pm.

Fuck it, she thought. No time like the present. I'm going.

She started getting dressed.

Dahlia found it easier to walk down the middle of the road, where the snowplough had gone. Its passage had thrown snowdrifts onto the sidewalks that were three feet deep and trudging through them would have been snow going. Her car had so much snow thrown on it that the prospect of digging it out in the cold night air was less appealing than the walk.

The Mount Hugh main street was empty, and she hadn't seen any vehicles except for the plow twenty minutes earlier, so she didn't have to worry about traffic. And if a car *did* come by, it would be driving slow because of the conditions. She hugged her heavy jacket close to herself, nuzzling into its faux fur collar.

She wondered what Naomi would say to her if she could see her.

You're crazy, babe. She could hear her lover's voice in her head. Not an attack, not an insult. Amused. The subtext: you're crazy but the good kind of crazy. The endearing kind.

But there was the other question. Of safety. As the thought occurred to her, she began to look around, to the shadows in the thin alleys between the buildings on main street. Could a killer be waiting? Watching her even in that moment?

She pushed the thought aside. It was only two blocks down. She was surrounded on both sides by buildings, most of them two or three stories, many with storefronts on the bottom and apartments up top. Her killer, whether a human with a worldly motive or a folkloric demon, was not going to attack her walking down the middle of the road with so many potential witnesses. It wasn't how the killer operated. And now, having clarified her thoughts, she found that she really did believe that the killer had a motive. The fears she'd expressed to Naomi really were the product of overthinking and a lack of rest. Paranoia induced by a paranoid atmosphere. No, the killer was killing for a reason. And the reasons had nothing to do with her.

When she arrived at the bar the lights were out. Daniel, the friendly bartender who still approach her with a mildly flirtatious vibe. Stood out front. A broom and shovel were leaning against the wall.

"Hi there," he said, turning and seeing her. He looked surprised. "You picked *tonight* to come out for a drink?"

She smiled and shrugged. "I was bored." She was slightly nervous. So far, she'd felt like she could handle Daniel. He seemed like a sincerely nice guy and although he was interested in her, she hadn't gotten an aggressive or creepy vibe. But things looked different at night and people tended to behave differently at night, especially when they'd been drinking. She didn't know if Daniel imbibed on the job, but everything added up to a somewhat heightened threat level, worsened by the fact that she'd been thinking of serial killers and murdering demons on the walk over.

"Well, we're closed. I sent everyone home a while ago. I was just about to lock up. I have regulars in walking distance but some of them drive. You always have to watch out for your regulars, make sure they don't drink more than they can handle and try to drive home. Night like this makes it worse."

Dahlia smiled. He clearly had a conscience. She imagined other bar owners might have stayed open for the revenue.

"Can I talk to you for a minute?" she asked.

"What about?" he responded, his interest piqued. She wondered what was going on in his mind, if he was wondering if she was about to make a romantic offer.

"It's about the town," she said, not revealing too much about her goals. "It's about my research. My article."

She smiled, making eye contact. Although she felt a twinge of regret at doing it, she knew that Daniel liked her. Maybe he'd be more willing than some to talk if it was to a girl, he had a thing for. If he'd had a few drinks, that wouldn't hurt either. As usual, Dahlia leaned into her natural instinct for how to playthings, how to meet each person where they needed to be met in order to get the desired result; the sad side effect of her lack of connections in her life was her heightened ability to make short-term shallow connections. To manipulate.

"We could talk at my place," he said. "Right above the Watering Hole. It's comfy." He smiled but she could see in his eyes that the offer might have strings attached.

"It'll only take a minute," she said, giving him what she hoped was a winning smile. "Can we just step into the diner?" She instinctively called it a diner, although at this time of night, "bar" was the more appropriate term.

"Sure," Daniel said, returning the smile. "You're the boss."

They stepped inside. He turned the lights back on as she brushed snow from her shoulders.

"Want a drink?" he asked, possibly hoping to loosen her up with alcohol.

"Sure," she said. "That sounds great. I'll have a water."

If he was disappointed in her order, he didn't show it. He sat down beside her in a corner booth, both of them armed with a glass of water, and she started asking questions.

"So, you closed early?" she said. "I'd have thought there would be regulars that were willing to brave the elements."

"Honestly, yes," he said. "I have regulars that live down the block. They can always make it back home. It wasn't just the weather."

"Then, what?"

"It was also the vibe," he said. "They were afraid."

"Of the blizzard?"

"No," he said. "Of the killer. Of 'Hugh Slaughter' as they call it."

Dahlia felt a chill run down her back but, at the same time, felt a modicum of relief. The story was scary, but that's all it was. A fairy tale. It was nice to see a resident of Mount Hugh who understood that. On a level she wasn't surprised. The "true believers" she'd encountered had been older than Daniel. The superstitious fear seemed stronger among the older population. But then, there *had* been Elijah. That had been particularly surprising. Elijah was young and had struck her as extremely rational. What had happened in the woods that had so rattled him? That had, in turn, rattled her to the point that she had begun to question reality herself.

"So, your locals packed it in early because they got a weird vibe?" He seemed not to have heard about the latest murder yet, and she opted not to tell him, lest the knowledge affect the information he was giving. No, he wasn't superstitious, but if he found out that his regulars' feeling of dread had seemed to correspond to the murder, it might make him more reticent to talk.

"Yes," he said. "A few hours ago, there was a change in the air. I felt it too, but I didn't attribute it to any supernatural killer. Some kind of psychological effect that we were sharing. You know how it is? Sometimes the week seems to be lasting forever, and everyone you talk to agrees. You say, 'This week's lasting forever,' and it seems like everyone's on the same page. But the week's the same as any other. Seven days. But, for whatever reason, through subconscious cues people are sending and receiving, everyone has the same idea."

Dahlia smiled, again, relieved. She was pleased to find that Daniel had more going on upstairs than measuring drinks and flirting. And he had a good point. Ideas could spread like viruses. There seemed to be no limit to the effects of the human subconscious.

"So, you don't think he's a ghost? Or a monster? Some kind of demon?"

At this, Daniel laughed. "Of course not. I don't believe in that kind of garbage. Never have. No reason this should be any different. I mean, the murders are horrifying. Awful. But I don't need a demon to explain that. Maybe that's the problem with the old fogies, like the regulars who got freaked out and wanted to go home tonight. They don't want to believe that a human being could be capable of such evil. They don't want to live in a world where people are like that, and they've got to invent a demon to explain it. Well, my eyes are open. I know how bad some people can be."

Dahlia nodded, her thoughts focusing into further clarity. "That's my thinking too. It's not a monster. It's not going to kill every time we think about it or talk about it. That kind of thinking is just to *keep* us from catching him. If you shut down your search out of fear it'll happen again, then the killer has won and will never be caught."

Daniel nodded and she felt like he'd had the exact same thought. "That's exactly right. The killer's a person."

"Yes," Dahlia said. "He's a person. Somebody from town."

"Stands to reason," Daniel replied. "I mean, it seems like he committed similar murders years apart. Probably never left."

Dahlia pulled out a small notebook out of her purse and took a pen from its spiral binding. "You okay with me taking notes? You're the first local that's agreed to talk to me about this stuff."

"Happy too," Daniel said. She could see from his expression, his pleased eagerness, that he still thought he had a shot at her. Maybe he thought she'd eventually say yes to his invitation to visit his apartment. Unfortunately, she'd have to let him labor under that illusion for the moment. Perhaps it was wrong to do so, but she needed his cooperation and wasn't willing to risk it.

"So, you've heard your patrons talk about it. According to them, what exactly *is* Hugh Slaughter?"

"Well, some people seem to think he's some kind of monster. Almost like a bigfoot or the Moth man. Something that roams the woods and feeds on people. Others talk like he's an evil spirit. Occasionally, I'll hear people talking like he's a person, but one of exceptional evil. Like he's possessed or somehow favoured by the devil. It's a different story depending on who's doing the talking, but anyone using the name, talking about Hugh Slaughter, seems to believe there's something unnatural about him."

"Do you have any idea who could have started these myths?"

"No idea," he said. "I've never heard any indication of who started them."

She wasn't surprised, knowing how these local myths and legends tended to grow and spread, mysteriously seeming to blossom up out of nowhere to become part of the local common knowledge.

"Have you ever heard the mayor mention it?" she asked. "When he came in here? Or maybe in a campaign speech? Do you think he might have been the one to create the rumour?"

"No," Daniel said, sounding certain. "It's the locals. The ones who have been here for generations, working the soil. The mayor, although he's been in town for decades that this point, isn't that type of local. And neither are his friends, the Maximoff's. It's not a myth that originates with the wealthy, it comes from common folk. They're the ones I hear talking about it."

Dahlia frowned. It still made so little sense, the degree to which the idea seemed to have deeply taken root. Yes, weird ideas could easily spread, like a virus, in the laboratory of a small town. She'd seen it before in her work in other areas for her dissertation. But usually, there was a gradual nature to the development of local folklore. This seemed to have sprung up relatively quickly in the aftermath of the first murder and now, a couple of decades later, seemed completely ingrained and unquestioned. The idea had spread like a virus. A plague.

"Have you ever heard anyone, one of your regulars or someone else, talking about actually *seeing* Hugh Slaughter?"

He thought for a moment before answering. "No. I have to say that I haven't. It's always the same. A sense of dread. You can tell. The happy drunk start staring down into their beers. They say they can sense him, out there, but they only speak of it in whispers. And one thing that that I've noticed is that it gets worse every winter."

"When did all of this start?"

He paused, thoughtfully. "Well, I guess it was around the time of the murder, back in the seventies. People were getting creeped out, you could tell, and then the next thing you know, it had a name. Hugh Slaughter."

Even though he didn't believe in the myth, Dahlia thought she saw a hint of nervousness cross his face, like the shadow of a passing bird of prey.

"And the mayor and Leonard Maximoff… was this after they moved to town?"

"Yes," said Daniel. "It was right after they hit the scene. I was just a kid at the time, but I've heard the stories. They were big news. Revitalizing the town. It was right after they started put up their turbines. 'Gone With the Wind Turbines.' A lot of people thought it was a joke when it started. Small towns are naturally suspicious of new technology. But they made a big change. Kept the heat running through the winters better than ever before."

Dahlia smiled. It was funny. Of course, turbines were basically windmills, a source of power that preceded modern fossil fuels. But as turbines were marketed as an environmentally friendly alternative, they rubbed the old-timers the wrong way, those grumps that had to always put on a show about how life used to be better. Dinosaurs, like Aaron Grayson.

"But many resisted the change," he continued. "And I've heard some of them tie it all together. Saying that Hugh Slaughter was some sort of supernatural punishment for interfering with the natural way of things. As if outside investment and clean energy had called up a demon from hell to terrorize the population."

It sounded ridiculous, of course, but in the quiet room by the window facing the darkened desolate street, it was still easy to feel a quiver of fear.

"But you say you've felt it? The fear?" What was the word he'd used? "The vibe?"

He nodded. "That's right. When I hear my old-timers growling about Hugh Slaughter, I've felt it myself. Fear. Paranoia. Running over me like waves."

"But you don't think it means anything?"

He shrugged. "I don't know. But it doesn't mean that all of a sudden, I believe in ghosts or demons or whatever. I've never believed in that kind of stuff."

Dahlia nodded. It had been similar to her experience. She had felt it too, *something*. It had shaken her, had taken her a while to shrug it off, but she did. And she remembered Elijah, as rational and sensible as they'd come. That look in his eyes when he'd emerged from the woods where the unnamed body had been found. Like he was walking out of a nightmare.

"The myths have been around for years, but just as sort of a boogeyman thing, you know? Behave yourself or Hugh Slaughter is going to get you. That changed with Eleanor."

"How so?" Dahlia asked.

"When she died it hit close to home. Then it felt like an attack on all of us, on the community." His frown deepened, as if he could still feel the pain. "The mayor was popular enough, but his wife – his ex-wife – was beloved." For a moment, Dahlia felt fresh guilt that she'd let him go on this long without revealing the latest murder. But she said nothing. "She was everyone's favorite. She charmed everyone when he was first running for office. To be honest, I think she had as much to do with him getting married as anyone. She was one of those rare personalities who could fit in anywhere, talk to anyone. She was just as popular with the struggling farmers as she was with the bigwigs. And after her divorce she remained just as beloved. She had no official title or duty, but she was as much a part of this community as anyone."

Dahlia, in her studies of small towns, had run across the type before. Lynchpin personalities that seemed to pull everyone into the orbit of their friendship and good humor. "And she was a regular at the Watering Hole?"

"Well, she came in to the diner all the time, during the day," he said. "Sometimes at night. But she was all class. She'd have a glass of wine or two and chat with friends and leave. And *everyone* was her friend. From the wealthy lawyers to the hopeless drunks. She didn't judge anyone, unlike many members of her social class. It was like she was royalty, holding court, and I never heard anyone say a bad word about her. And the guys never hit on her. Not even the ones who were always cruising for action, the total horndogs, and Eleanor was a beautiful woman. But there was just something about her, something elevated, that made you want to protect her. That's why it hurt so bad when she was taken from us. And in such an ugly and violent way."

He paused, seeming to need a moment to master his emotions before continuing.

"After she died, it got worse. People started talking about Hugh Slaughter as if simply saying his name could call him up. As if he were a punishment, God's vengeance, or a demon out of hell, our judgement. And the fear got worse. I saw grown men break whimper like children when it hit."

"Was Eleanor from Mount Hugh?"

"She was," he said. "Maybe that's what made the difference with her. Why she never seemed to think she was better than everyone else like some of those others. The Maximoff's and the mayor himself aren't from here, of course. They came from the outside, promising big changes. Maybe that's why there were so resented. Didn't help that people got the impression they thought they were better than us."

Dahlia wondered if this could somehow be connected. Could the killer be trying to strike back against the outsiders? She wasn't sure this made sense. If Eleanor was a beloved local, would it make sense to kill her to strike back against other members of her social class? She wasn't sure but ruled nothing out.

"Tell me more about the Maximoff's," she said, continuing to take notes.

"Well, they are outsiders. Never stopped being outsiders. And they seemed to come here with a mission: to change the community. They were close friends with the mayor but not with the locals, and even though they spent a lot of time with her due to Leonard's business ties to Lark, I never really felt like they never really connected with her. At least, that's how it seems to me."

Dahlia nodded. Daniel was an observant man. She considered how, as someone who served people food and drink, he was uniquely positioned to have the lowdown over what was really going on.

"I was still very young when the first murder took place," he said. "But I remember hearing about Eleanor. I had aunts that were very much part of the Mount Hugh social scene, friends of Eleanor from the ladies' clubs, and they talked about it. How she changed as Lark and Maximoff unveiled their plan for the town. She became devoted to keeping the town safe while Lark, influenced by his business partner, saw the community as one big cash grab. I suspect that's the reason they divorced but I've never heard firsthand."

"And what about the kids?" Dahlia asked. "Peter and Fawn?"

Daniel frowned, as if tasting something bitter. "Fawn is as bad as her parents. Worse, maybe, because she thinks she's entitled to everything and hasn't worked a day in her life. Just like her parents, all she cares about is power and money. And Peter, well, he's just like his dad. Easily influenced. Just like Mayor Lark, he fell under the influence of wealth and power. William Lark wanted was pulled into the orbit of Leonard Maximoff, and Peter was pulled in by his daughter, Fawn. Through it all, only Eleanor remained uncorrupted."

More pieces of the puzzle started to click together. Yes, the fear might have been a spontaneous reaction, a kind of mass hysteria, but the story of Hugh Slaughter must have had an author in the material world. *Somebody* came up with it, someone coined the term. It may have dovetailed perfectly with the hysteria, but someone told the story first. Dahlia thought it was significant that Hugh Slaughter first reared his ugly head not only shortly after the first murder, but also not long after Malinda and Leonard arrived in town. It was easy to hear such a story and imagine it had been handed down as an old wives' tale for generations. Indeed, the Hugh Slaughter anecdote had that feeling. But it wasn't folklore. It came into being after the first murder. A mere twenty five years earlier, not in previous generations.

What Dahlia began to wonder was this: perhaps the most logical explanation was that someone from the outside with an interest in manipulating the local populace had come up with the legend and the more she thought about it, the more her prime suspects became

Malinda and Leonard: outsiders with something to gain. They'd come to town to profit off it. They'd manipulated their way into power. And what did they have to gain by inventing a legend? Was it to cover their tracks in a murder, or for some other reason? Dahlia wasn't sure, but she was growing increasingly convinced that the Maximoff's, one or both, were behind the Hugh Slaughter myth.

Dahlia knew her next course of action: to return to the Maximoff estate with some questions of her own. She'd leave Elijah out of it this time; she'd gotten him into too much hot water, and she didn't think he really had the stomach for going outside of his chain of command. And as for Aaron Grayson and his threats? Well, the hell with him. If he wanted to arrest her for interfering, he was going to have to slap the cuffs on her himself. Maybe she could solve a murder before he had a chance.

She looked at the clock on the wall of the Watering Hole. It was almost one o'clock. Too late to pay the Maximoff's another visit. She resolved to go to their house first thing in the morning. Maybe then, she could catch them off guard.

"Listen, Daniel," she said. "I should probably be going."

He frowned. "I see," he said. "Got what you need?"

"Yes," she said. "But I hope you don't think I'm using you. That's why I'm here. To try to find answers. I really appreciate you talking to me."

"I never had a shot at you, did I?" he asked.

Dahlia considered. Which would be more cruel? To tell him she was already in a committed relationship, or that she wasn't into men? In the end she simply said.

"I'm sorry, but no," adding, "But if I was in the market for a man, I could do a lot worse than you. Good night."

The walk back was uneventful. For whatever reason, the shadows didn't scare her as much. Maybe it was all the thinking she'd done, digging in rationally with a level-headed person. If proximity to paranoia could suck you in, then perhaps exposure to rational thinkers could do the converse. For whatever reason, she made it back with no issues. Her mind was racing, yes, but with ideas. She felt closer.

She could almost see the pattern.

She went to bed and eventually her racing mind calmed down and let her sleep for a few hours. It woke her at dawn with a surge of adrenaline. For a moment she was confused. It was that feeling when you, half-asleep, remember something important. A meeting. An obligation. You'd forgotten to set an alarm. She awoke with a surge.

What had she forgotten?

She realized that this was it: it was time to pay the Maximoffs a visit.

The plows had been by and although the sky was clear and the sun shining, the air was still frigid. If it kept up, she imagined that the snow might start to melt by midday, but it was equally likely another blizzard would blow in. The air moved so fast in this part of the country. Her breath condensed into clouds of vapor. It was a pain, but she dug out her car with her foot-long ice scraper. She nosed it out from the curve and its wheels found traction on the snow, piled thick by the passing plows. Conditions on the road were better than expected but she still took it slow. According to her dashboard clock it was 5:45 when she pulled into the Maximoff's driveway. An early time to pay a visit, arguably rude, but she knew what she was doing. She wanted to catch them off balance. They'd gotten a lot of milage from coordinating carefully planned stories. She suspected that the whole clan made a point of "getting their stories straight" before talking to anyone. If she came in early and strong, maybe she could circumvent that.

Malinda Maximoff had other ideas.

Before her tires had even crunched to a stop on the snow packed driveway, Malinda, in a winter coat and heavy boots was marching determinedly towards the driver's side door. By the time Dahlia stepped out, Malinda was there, standing atop a snowdrift that put her a foot above her visitor, giving the psychological advantage: the appearance of dominance.

"You need to leave," Malinda said simply. "You are not welcome here."

Dahlia was thrown. She'd come in, planning on making an aggressive push for answers, but Malinda had outflanked her with aggression of her own. Not knowing what else to do, Dahlia attempted a countermove.

"First I have a few questions," she said. "It will just take a minute, but it's important."

"Important?" Malinda said with a sneer. "Look at you and your arrogance. You have no right to anything, young lady. No authority to ask me anything. I invited you in, sympathetic to your story of your well-meaning dissertation, and then I find out you're just here digging up dirt on everyone."

"That's not true," Dahlia said. "I'm trying to…"

"I don't care *what* you're trying to do," Malinda said. "You're not a police officer. You're just a nosy busybody. And you're trespassing. Those police officers were here last night. They were looking for you. They thought you'd be at the hotel."

Dahlia wondered at this but brushed it off as a lie.

"Maybe I'll call them and tell them where to find you. They can arrest you for trespassing, although I suspect that might not be the only charge."

For a moment, Dahlia almost backed down. But as was often the case in those moments, when arrogant people saw her as an easy target to bully, she felt her spine harden into a thing of steel. She'd been pushed around her whole life, and when people thought it was okay to do it, she went on the attack. It was the same ingrained reaction she'd had the previous afternoon with Aaron Grayson.

Dahlia stepped towards Malinda, joining her atop the snowdrift. Now, standing toe to toe, she was taller, easily a half foot. She leaned towards Malinda, staring down into her eyes. Perhaps involuntarily, Malinda dipped back. Dahlia knew the type. She was used to throwing her weight around. Used to everyone following her orders.

Try me, bitch.

"Hugh Slaughter," Dahlia said. "The locals all talk about Hugh Slaughter."

"What of it?" Malinda stammered.

"It's a fairy tale. A distraction. A red herring. But someone invented it," Dahlia said. She pointed a finger toward Malinda's chest as if threatening to poke her in the sternum. "It originated here, didn't it? In your house?"

Malinda laughed. A nervous laugh. Was the laughter because she thought Dahlia was unhinged or because she was close to the truth.

"You're insane," she said. "You perverted masculine loon."

Name calling. She seemed unbalanced. Dahlia had her on the defensive. She pressed on.

"Here's what I think happened – you tell me if I left anything out. The first murder, back in the seventies, I figure your husband was behind that. I don't know the exactly why or how it happened, but I think he was in some way responsible. And then you and your husband tried to cover it up. Circling your wagons, as you always seem to do. Leonard probably bribed the mayor, maybe got him to put some pressure on the papers, maybe paid them off too, and then created the fairy tale of the vengeful spirit to discourage the townsfolk from talking about it. I know how news travels in a small town. Gossips and their daily phone calls. Men at the barbershop, women at the salon. You two could have just dropped it here and there, as something you'd heard and were repeating… and in no time the story took hold, and the murder conveniently went away. Wiped clean like it never happened."

Malinda was quiet and for a delusional second, Dahlia thought that she had her. That a confession was forthcoming. But then the corners of Malinda's mouth turned up into a wicked sneer.

"Listen," she said. "If I wanted to commit a murder, I'd do it with no fear and no need for any fairy tales to cover it up. My family line, and Leonard's are the finest. We have money. And power. Can you really be so naïve that you don't realize what money and power can do? The rich and powerful make people disappear all the time. Wealth buys you that. You don't need schemes and conspiracies.

You just need money and the power that it buys. And if you don't stop sticking your nose in where it's not wanted, maybe you'll have to see firsthand what we are capable of doing to you. The same thing that was done to your mother."

"My mother." The words came out almost as a whisper. Dahlia was completely thrown. What did her mother have to do with any of this? "Why did you bring my mother into it?"

"When I first saw you, I saw the resemblance. I had a hunch. Maybe that's why I invited you in on that first day. Curiosity. But when I learned a little more, I was able to confirm it."

"Confirm what?"

"She, the first victim, was your mother." Malinda paused as the information hit Dahlia like a sledgehammer, and then added. "And she deserved it."

"You don't know my mother…"

"Lucy Crane," Malinda said. "We were friends. The three of us. Me, Lucy, and Eleanor. But it was a complicated dynamic. Eleanor didn't come from money, but she had a natural class and she married into our social class when she married Lark, and he formed his partnership with Leonard. I liked Eleanor. Lucy was different. She and Eleanor were close – they were both locals – but Lucy was different. Whereas Eleanor had grace and manners, Lucy was trash. Pushy, brash, unrefined. She pushed her way into our circles, putting bad ideas into Eleanor's head, turning her against me, against Leonard. She didn't know a woman's place. Didn't think she needed a man; thought she could go out and grab whatever she wanted. And she was a whore. She slept around. I'm sure she angered someone in town. A man whose heart she broke, or a maybe woman she wronged by leading her husband astray. To this day I have no idea who killed her, only that she had it coming. And yes, I'll admit it. I spread the story of Hugh Slaughter. The inbred yokels around here ate it up, just like I knew they would."

Through this monologue, Dahlia was seething, seeing flashes of red. Her head throbbed and she felt like she might pass out. All the anxiety, all of the rage, all of the unchecked emotion she'd spent years trying to master came back to her in a rush. Still, she managed a question.

"Why?" she said, for the moment leaving everything else aside: the slander to her mother and the implied insults to her, the disgusting arrogance and class snobbery. "Why invent the myth? How does that help anyone?"

"I didn't want it to taint the town. My husband had just made a very large investment in this community. The first turbines had just gone up. If a scandal exploded across the headlines, it could have tainted the town, given it a bad image, and completely gutted the return on our investment. I wanted everyone to lose focus on the victim and whatever trashy personal drama led to her death. The fairy tale shifted the focus. It was a distraction. And it worked."

"You..." Dahlia was so mad she could hardly speak. "You *bitch*!"

She stepped towards her, arms outstretched. Dahlia was not a physically violent woman but in that moment, she was ready to act. Her arms were extended, her hands open, but she had no plan. Would she push her down in the snow? Punch her in the gut? Wrap her fingers around her neck? Everything was on the table.

But she didn't get a chance to find out what she was going to do because at that moment, Malinda pulled a pistol out of her coat pocket. It was tiny, almost looking like a toy, but Dahlia had no doubt: it was real, pointed at her, and the simple pull of a trigger could end her life.

"Don't step any closer," Malinda said.

Dahlia dropped her hands to her side, suddenly stricken by how far out of control she'd let things get.

"You had your chance to leave," Malinda said. "You know, the community will find it very easy to believe that you were the killer." She raised the gun; it had been pointing at Dahlia's midsection, now it was centered on the middle of her forehead. "That you came back to town to take revenge on the town for your mother's death. Making them feel even more unsafe. Once I tell the story, nothing else will matter."

Dahlia could see the wheels turning in Malinda's mind. She who, from her elitist vantage point, felt entitled to rewrite the myths of the locals she saw as inferior. Dahlia would be the new Hugh Slaughter, the new boogeyman.

"You'll never get away with this," said Dahlia. "I swear on my mother, you'll never get away with it."

"Nobody would question it. You were trespassing when I came out. You were reaching for me. Pretty much what happened. Shooting you would have been justified."

At that moment, Dahlia leapt from the snowbank towards her parked car. Malinda pulled the trigger, but the shot went wide, kicking up spray in the snow that lined the driveway. Dahlia hopped in the car, slammed it into gear and backed out of the driveway going inadvisably fast, given the weather conditions.

She saw Malinda aim and fire again. Then again. If her feet hadn't slid in the snow, the bullets might have found their mark. As it was, they took out one headlight and the passenger's side mirror. The car spun frictionlessly at the end of the driveway and, by some miracle, stopped moving pointing towards town. Dahlia floored it, fingers crossed that the tires wouldn't slide off the still slick roadway, still hearing firecracker pops as the pistol fired again in the distance.

Dahlia's heart was racing. In fear. In anger. Adrenaline surged, and she felt a tingly feeling in her scalp. Malinda had been trying to kill her. She still didn't know for sure if that the Maximoff's were guilty, but Malinda had been ready to kill her, had felt justified, and had been confident she could get away with it.

But as she drove towards the hotel and everything began to sink in, Dahlia's perspective shifted, and the *real* issue emerged.

She'd identified it the night before, with her tape recorder. Her reasons for returning to Mount Hugh. To connect with her past. And she was beginning to do so, but what she had found out was throwing everything she thought she knew into chaos. She hadn't really known her mother at all. Was what Eleanor said true? Was her mother a horrible person? Dahlia had thought she could return to her hometown, process her past, and emerge with a stronger sense of identity, of stability.

Instead, she felt everything shifting. As if her life, her past, everything she thought she knew about herself, had been built on a foundation made of sand.

CHAPTER ELEVEN
SHATTERED HOPE
1984

The sounds of the shouting men drifted to the teenage boy as he hurried down the cracked street, his head lowered. He held his bag tightly against his chest, as was the routine. The argument had clearly gotten more heated as now, he could hear pained screams. A piercing scream cut through the late afternoon as two men fell from a balcony two stories up, right in front of the boy. He gulped, frozen as the men continued exchanging blows.

"Get out of here, boy!" Old man Blake, the local grocer hissed at Elijah as he grabbed a wooden broom and started hitting the men, yelling, "You trash! Get off my patio!"

Elijah did not need to be told twice. He ducked and sprinted around the corner. He finally let out a sigh of relief when he turned the block and found himself leaning against a chipped picket fence which surrounded one of the better-looking houses in the neighborhood, and that was saying a lot. His brown eyes looked up and he took in his surroundings.

Directly across the road was a tall apartment building that had seen better days. Next to it were a few others that were a mirror of its state. The cracking walls, the broken windows, the trash strewn surroundings, they were common characteristics for most of the homes in this part of town. Only a few even bothered to do anything about it, and clean up just a little.

Letting out another sigh, the boy turned and ran the rest of the way home. Weaving in and out of short alleys that he knew like the back of his hand, he finally arrived in front of a rundown four-story apartment building. Once he was inside, he ignored the elevator that had never worked since they had moved there when he was barely three and took the stairs. Years of running up and down the stairs had left Elijah with enough endurance to take the stairs two at a time steadily without breaking a sweat.

He made his way into the dim hallway on the third floor. The boy looked up and frowned at the sole flickering bulb. To think the man living at the end of the hall had changed it just last week. The glow cast a dusky shadow over the peeling wall paint. At the entrance to his apartment, he fumbled in his bag, searching for his keys, when the door opened inward and he saw his mother.

"*Buenas noches, mamá,*" Elijah greeted his mother.

"Welcome back, *cariño,*" His mother, Virginia said softly as she took his bag from him. Elijah pecked his mother on her cheek and she hugged him. Elijah quirked a brow at the sight of his mother's face. Whenever her face was tight, when her smile did not reach her eyes, he knew exactly what was going on.

His eyes flitted over to the other side of the room where the television was. The room was dark but for the light from the box. The TV was bright enough for him to see the frown lines on his father's face.

"I am back, dad."

"Hmmm… hmm…" Patrick Riley grunted. His mother rolled her eyes and stormed into the room with his bag.

Elijah sighed. The tension in the room could be cut with a knife. He could tell that they had gotten into one of their fights. As slowly as he could, he trod across the floor.

"Why are you back so late, Elijah? Does the bus at that fancy school of yours not work anymore?" HIs father suddenly snapped, causing Elijah to freeze where he stood.

"I… I…" he swallowed hard. His father stood up and turned around to look at him. While the overhead light was not on, the light from the television as well as sunrays filtering in from the two windows in the room that his mother painstakingly cleaned every week, cast enough light for Elijah to see the sullen expression on his father's face.

"I, what? Is your tongue tied?" His father hissed.

"I… couldn't take the bus, because…." Elijah lowered his head. Then he said, "I could not take the bus because we have not paid the fees this semester."

His father scoffed, "Of course, of course, more bills! More bills from that blasted school of yours!"

"That's enough, Patrick!" Virginia hissed, running into the room. She glared at Elijah's father. "We are not going to keep talking about this. It's useless. Go on in, *mi hijo*. Your tutor will be here soon. Go and wait for him."

"Why? Why should he go in? Why shouldn't he be here as this is all his fault?!" Patrick snapped. "I cannot for the life of me understand why you chose to take this boy to that posh school! All it does is suck our money, money we don't even have! All our savings, gone into that school, for bills, bills and more bills. And now they ask for more money so he can ride the bus?"

Elijah lowered his head, tears pooling in his eyes. Virginia wrapped a hand around Elijah's shoulder as she said to her husband,

"Patrick, we talked about this. It is important that Elijah goes to a good school, gets a good education and…"

"And what? Are we going to die just so the kid can get to play around and act all posh with his snobbish pals? Are we going to starve? Because we sure as hell have no more money after you pumped all our savings into that school! Which we cannot afford! Now, we cannot eat, we cannot even use the bus. Elijah, it is about time you stop living off us. You have got to be independent, son! Stop being such a dunce! You should contribute to this home too and…"

"That is enough, Patrick. You have said enough," Virginia glared at him. "You will not talk to our child that way. We are his parents and we should care for him!"

Virginia's large brown eyes sparked in anger and despite her tiny frame, Elijah and Patrick shuddered. Patrick mumbled something they did not hear and fell into the tattered couch. He quickly turned back to the television.

"Come, *mi hijo*," Virginia led Elijah to the room gently, "You do not need to worry about anything. Do not listen to everything your father has just said, and do not trouble yourself about our finances."

"But *mamá*…"

Virginia wiped his tears away and smiled softly, "All you need to do, *mi hijo*, is study. Concern yourself with only that. *Mamá* and *Papá* will take care of everything else."

"I am so sorry, *mamá*. I am so sorry that I am not competent, I am sorry that I am so incapable."

"Oh don't say that, *cariño*! I am so proud of you! You are not incompetent! *Por favor*, don't listen to your *papá*."

"*Por favor* mamá, why don't I stop the tutoring sessions? I can continue to study on my own. That way we can save more money, and… and…. I can find a job, I can find a job, and we can earn money too. We don't need to have the tutor, we don't need to spend so much money."

"Oh, *mi hijo*," Virginia touched his cheek gently, "I am grateful to have been blessed with a child like you, a child filled with so much *amor*. Don't worry, it will be fine. You will not stop the lessons, you will not leave your school and you will not work part-time either. *Mamá* will take care of everything."

"But you already work so hard, *mamá*, and the bills keep piling and…" Elijah's eyes got wet again.

His mother shook her head and stroked his hair, "It is a dangerous world out there, *mi hijo*. It is not worth it. Do not worry about adult problems. We will not talk about this anymore, *mi amor*. Now, go prepare for your lessons."

"*Si, mamá.*" Elijah nodded and headed to his room.

Elijah switched on his desk lamp and pulled his lesson notes out of his bag. He sighed as he spread them out. *Don't worry*, his mother had said. But how could he not worry? His school expenses and his tutoring sessions took the brunt of their finances and he felt so bad. He could not help feeling he was burdening his parents. He was so lost in his thoughts that he did not hear the slight rap on the open door of his room. A clicking sound caused the boy to look up. The surprised boy found himself staring into the amused face of his tutor.

"Penny for your thoughts?" The blonde-haired young man called Russell said as he settled into the second chair in the cramped room.

Russell was a junior at the University of Philly, and he was a star pupil, straight As, star basketball player, secretary of the university's Business Students' Association, a known community volunteer, a hard worker and an all-round nice guy. After seeing his resume, it had taken Virgina all but a minute to hire him to tutor Elijah. Including Elijah, Russell tutored six high school students. While he was on a full ride scholarship, he was also the third in a family of eight children and two deadbeat parents. He had been lucky enough to be the first to get out and see the walls of the university, but that also meant that the burden on his shoulders significantly increased. Elijah had no complaints. Russell was like the big brother he never had. He was nice to him, and also very patient.

Elijah looked at the twenty-one-year-old and sniffed. Russell was someone he truly admired. His strength and dedication always amazed the teenager. And just like always, he found himself wondering how Russell was able to handle it all.

"You started working at thirteen, right?" Elijah blurted out.

Russell quirked a brow and he crossed his arms, "Why do you ask, Elijah?"

Eljah shrugged, "I want to work and *mamá* says I should not. She says it is dangerous out there and…"

"Your mother is right," Russell said quietly.

"If it is so dangerous, how come you were able to do it? See? You turned out well, didn't you? And you're still doing well. You are going to graduate soon too."

Russell smiled ruefully. Absent-mindedly, he ran a hand through his blonde hair as he said, "Elijah, our situations are completely different."

"How so?" Elijah asked stubbornly.

"You have parents who pay attention to you and care about your education. They care about your meals, they care about your health. I had parents who spend half of the time high on drugs, and the other half intoxicated and clutching to bottles of beer. My eldest brother broke the head of the neighbor in an altercation and ran off, missing till date and my eldest sister got pregnant and shacked up with the father of her child, in a place worse than our home." There was a faraway look in Russell's eyes as he said. "And me? I was left to fend for my five siblings because there was no one else to do it."

Elijah's hand brushed against his eyes, wiping away tears. Russell smiled softly and patted Elijah's shoulder, "I started working so early out of necessity, Elijah, not because I wanted to. It was either that or my siblings were going to starve. Someone had to step up, and I chose to. Understand that all your mother wants is what's best for you. She does not have everything but she is trying her best with what she has."

"But I want to help her too…"

"Well, have you thought that doing well is really just what she needs?" Russell pointed out.

Elijah nodded his head slowly, "I just feel so guilty. *Mamá* says it is okay but I know dad is right. My education is a burden and I should contribute more to the home."

"Well… if you study hard, and you get into a good school and you are able to finish and get a good job, won't you be able to contribute to the home then?" Russell reminded him.

"But that is such a long time away."

"Well, we better start studying then," Russell's eyes glinted with determination.

"O…kay," Elijah nodded and turned to his books.

About an hour later, Elijah watched Russell as he graded the quizzes he had just finished. A smile broke across Russell's face as he looked up. He tapped the book as he said, "Well done, Elijah. You have made so much improvement. Look here."

Russell moved a book which had a blue leather cover close to Elijah. It was a scorebook.

"Can you see? Your grades in the quizzes have continued to go up steadily. You are doing better in our classes. And from the test papers you got back from school today, I can see all-round improvement."

Elijah managed a small smile, "Thanks, Russell.'

"Mm hmm… and English, it's your best yet. Why, this gladdens my heart, Elijah, especially when I think about where we started from. Well done. You should be happy."

"Uh huh," Elijah nodded. The top thing occupying his mind at that moment was what his improvement meant. Without a doubt, this would convince his *mamá* that the tutoring sessions were the best option.

"There are a few things you need to work on though…" Russell was saying when he trailed off. He tapped the table lightly. The young boy tilted his head as he said, "Did you hear what I just said, Elijah?"

"Things I need to work on?" Elijah supplied.

"Right…" Russell nodded slowly, "You need to have more confidence in yourself and trust that you know the work."

Elijah opened his mouth to speak but no words came out. Russell smiled softly and tapped the graded examination booklet that Elijah had shown him earlier. At the top of the page, PHYSICAL SCIENCE, was written boldly. Russell tapped a question, saying,

"Do you see what I mean?"

A confused Elijah shook his head and looked at Russell expectantly. Russell tapped the answer keys.

" Here, you initially chose option A, then, you erased it. The crease left behind is still a little visible."

Elijah looked down at the page. The question had been "Dogs can hear certain _______________ outside of the range of human hearing." The correct answer, which had been Elijah's first instinct, was C) frequencies. But he'd second guessed himself, choosing instead A) volumes.

"Oh." Was all Elijah could say. The boy scratched his brown hair, trying to recall what he had been thinking when he answered the question. Why hadn't he gone with his first instinct?

"And it is not just for this question," Russell continued. "I also noticed this pattern in your other papers. You were right but you probably did not believe or trust yourself and the answer so you ended up choosing the wrong one. You would have scored higher grades with more confidence."

"Oh…" Elijah muttered.

Russell smiled sympathetically and patted his shoulder, "Cheer up, Elijah. You are actually doing very well. With grit and determination, you are going to continue to improve. And with loads of confidence too, of course. You study so hard, and you work so hard, so you should trust your instincts more. All right?"

"Yes." Elijah said with a nod. "Thank you, Russell."

"That's okay. So, how about we do a few more exercises, your reading work, then we can end our session today?"

"Okay," Elijah said quietly.

A little while later, Elijah walked out of his room with Russell. A sole bulb was glimmering in the living room. The TV was now off and his father was nowhere in sight. To minimize the power bills, they alternated the electrical sources and appliances. With the lamps now on, there was no way the television could be left blaring. Virginia hurried to them. She smiled brightly at Russell,

"Thank you so much, Russell. Would you like some food? You can join us for dinner."

"Oh no, that's okay, Mrs. Virginia, you don't have to," Russell started protesting but she was already dragging him to the kitchen.

"Nonsense. Here, I will pack some for you since you are in such a hurry to leave."

From the doorway, Elijah watched the scene, a small smile playing on his lips. It was always the same thing. Russell always turned down the food and his mother always forced him to go back with some. She knew Russell loved her food, evident from his gusto and appetite the first night he tutored Elijah. Back then, Russell had probably had no idea that it would be a regular from that moment. It was not easy to say no to the Mexican spitfire that Virginia Riley was.

Elijah watched his mother hand over a white envelope and a bag containing a Tupperware.

"I am so sorry I could not pay last session's fee that day. You'll find the fee for today and the last session in the envelope."

"Like I said then, it's okay, Mrs. Virginia." Russell lowered his head apologetically, "And you really don't have to feed me."

"I hope you enjoy it. It should be enough for three servings. You are going to the dorm, right? Or are you going home? I can give you more for your siblings."

"I am going to the dorm, yes. Thank you so much, Mrs. Virginia, but I feel bad about this," Russell said, lowering his head. "You are always so nice to me and I charge you and… you don't have so much either and…"

"Nonsense, *muchacho*, don't you dare say that. You work so hard and you deserve your money. Know your worth and don't let anyone shortchange you, all right? You are good. Continue being good, understand"

"*Yes*," Russell nodded slowly, "But you don't have much and…"

"No matter how little I have, it will never be too small to feed others, *muchacho*, what more a good kid like you. Don't worry about it! Now, how is *mi hijo* doing?"

Russell smiled and nodded. He was smart enough to know when to give up the fight. There was no winning over Virginia Riley. "He is doing very well. He has shown tremendous improvement. You should be proud."

Virginia clasped her hands together in glee, "*Gracias, gracias, muchacho.*"

"*De nada*, Mrs. Virginia. It is my pleasure teaching Elijah. He is a bright kid and he did all of this by himself, he put in so much work."

"I know, I know," Virginia beamed. She pointed at Russell and her smile widened, "Ooh… your Spanish is getting better."

He chuckled and said, "I have just picked up a few things from you. *Gracias*, Mrs. Virginia, for your kind words, for your care, for the food, for the payment, for everything."

"Oh, don't bother about it," she waved her hand. "Next class will be on Friday, is that okay?"

"*Si*, Mrs. Virginia. I will see you both then."

They headed out and Elijah hurried to Russell. Russell placed a hand on Elijah's shoulder and smiled, "I'll see you on Friday, kid. Take care of yourself and don't forget to do your exercises."

"Thanks, Russell."

As soon as the door closed behind Russell, Virginia swept Elijah into a tight embrace.

"Oh *cariño*, I am so proud of you! You have done so well! You make your m*amá* proud. Come on, help me set the table. I made your favorite, fried chicken and mac and cheese. You'll love it as always, *mi hijo*. Come!"

Sighing, Elijah followed his mother into the kitchen. He doubted he was going to be able to make her see reason and understand why he wanted to stop the tutoring sessions.

The sound of the front door opening reached them just as the last plate was set on the table. Patrick stormed into the kitchen, his face in a scowl. Virginia and Elijah watched him as he fell heavily into his chair and immediately reached for a drumstick. He took a large bite and munched angrily. Virginia motioned to Elijah for him to sit, and she took her seat as well.

"I thought you would be calmer by the time you return." Virginia said quietly as she took a small bite of her mac and cheese.

"Oh, I was very calm, until I saw that tutor kid with a bag of food and I was reminded how much money we are throwing away," Patrick hissed.

Virginia's brown eyes glowed and she glared at Patrick, "You didn't say anything to that poor *niño*, did you? He did nothing wrong."

"Of course I didn't. I do not lack manners, you know." Patrick's frown deepened.

"These days, I highly doubt that," Virginia muttered, loud enough that her husband heard though. Elijah swallowed hard and tried to munch on his chicken quietly. He already knew that the fight from earlier was about to resume. In that moment, he wished the ground would open up and swallow him.

Patrick shouted, "We are barely surviving, barely making ends meet, yet you are giving away food!"

"He is our son's tutor and a very good one. And even if he was not, food should never be kept from others," Virginia retorted.

"It is always about the kid's schooling! Are we going to bleed dry to give our son the future you envision for him? All these expenses, it will eat us out of home and food. We are barely scraping by!!"

"Patrick…" his mother said softly. "Elijah's grades have improved tremendously. Just a little more and he will achieve the best grades to get him a full ride scholarship to high school. Elijah is very bright and it's just a little more time."

Patrick visibly relaxed and took a sip of his water. Elijah shut his eyes, breathing in relief, when his father thundered again,

"He needs to learn to be independent. He does not need a tutor, or a fancy school. Why can't he study by himself? Why? You have got to learn accountability, son. You have to be responsible! You have to understand that money doesn't grow on trees. If you cannot be independent, you will ruin us even more!"

Virginia slammed her hand on the table, causing Patrick and Elijah to jump. She glared at Patrick as she said, "Can we talk about something else? Otherwise, I'll leave this table."

Patrick grumbled inaudibly and turned to his food. Elijah's eyes drooped as he turned to his meal. His mother's food was the best but that night, he tasted nothing but the disappointment he felt in himself, and his incompetence. His mother might say otherwise but he could not stop thinking that his father was right. He felt like such a nuisance.

"Are you okay, Elijah? I heard what Ms. Watson said."

The sobbing Elijah looked up to see his best friend, Barry staring down at him, his eyes filled with compassion.

Elijah brushed his tears away. He could still hear the teacher's voice in his head, resounding. Normally, he would have been able to hold himself but as soon as she left, the waterworks were released. He was just really frustrated at himself these days.

"You have to work on your confidence, Elijah, else, it is going to keep holding you back. You prepared such a unique and informative poster on Mexican folklore, but you could not even present it. You kept stumbling and looking at the cue cards. Another teacher would think it was not your work and you were not the one who prepared it, but I know you did the work because you are a hardworking student. You are creative and smart, now I need you to have some more confidence and courage," Mrs. Watson's words floated in his head.

"I am sorry, Mrs. Watson," he had managed to say, his lips already trembling.

"Your grades were not great this time and were split, because you didn't do well in the presentation aspect. I hope you can do better next time."

"I am sorry, Mrs. Watson. I'll work on it, I'll be more confident..."

Elijah shut his eyes and pressed his fingers against his eyelids. Thinking about the conversation only made him more pained. Mrs. Watson had said the same thing Russell said days ago. Why was he such a loser?

"It's going to be fine, Elijah," Barry patted his friend's shoulder and helped him stand up. "Are you walking home or taking the bus today?"

"Walk…" Elijah replied hoarsely.

"I'll walk with you then. Is that okay?"

Elijah nodded and the pair headed out of the classroom. They had been friends since kindergarten. Barry was from Ireland and they had both clicked since the first day and gotten closer over the years.

"Do you want to talk about it?" Barry asked softly as they headed down the road.

Elijah sighed and ran a hand through his hair, "I wish I am more like you, Barry. You are so confident and never afraid, whatever situation you are in."

"Oh, Elijah, you should feel proud of yourself too. You also work so hard, remember? It might not seem that way, your results right now, but you should be proud, my friend. It's not only the confident ones that should feel proud."

Elijah sighed and looked up at the sky, "You truly have a way with words, my friend. I wonder where we will both be in high school. Will we still be together? Will I be walking down the street by myself?"

"I'm sure we will! You are my best friend, don't worry so much about these things." Barry suddenly stopped and tugged on Elijah's sleeve. "Ice cream! Let's get some."

"Uh… I don't have money," Elijah lowered his head.

Barry smiled softly and dragged him to the truck at the end of the street, saying, "It's fine, I have enough for two."

A little while later, the friends continued their walk, Barry wielding a vanilla ice cream cone, and Elijah holding a chocolate ice cream cone.

"Can I ask you a question?" Elijah blurted out. There was something he had been wondering about for some time, but it never seemed like the right time. Barry nodded and waited, "Do you like boys?"

Barry was visibly taken aback and Elijah opened his mouth to apologize when Barry smiled ruefully and said, "You are my best friend so if no one else, i should tell you the truth, right? I like boys and girls, Elijah."

"Huh?" Elijah asked in between bites of his ice cream.

Barry nodded slowly, "Yes, I like boys and girls but I don't know if it's a right feeling. But please, you don't have to worry, Elijah. I don't like you that way. I see you as a brother."

"I am not worried. I'm just not sure…. Is it morally... correct?"

Barry shrugged, "That I cannot say, but I see morals as a choice, you know, everyone has different choices, some like vegetable pizza and others like pineapple pizza. At the end of the day, aren't morals subjective and selective?"

Elijah shrugged, "Like choosing the strong character instead of the weak one in a video game?"

"I actually prefer choosing the female character. I feel empowered," Barry grinned, causing Elijah to laugh.

The boys continued their walk, discussing everything and nothing. They finally got to a crossroad where they had to separate. They said their goodbyes and started heading in different directions when Barry called.

"Hey, Elijah!"

Elijah turned around. Barry walked closer and said, "Promise me that if you ever need anything, you won't hesitate to let me know, whether financially, academically or mentally. Let me know if you need my help."

A grateful smile spread across Elijah's cheek, "Thank you, my friend."

"See you next week!" Barry waved as he ran off.

For the first time in a while, Elijah felt light. Talking deeply with his friend had helped greatly. He felt seen and heard. Still smiling, he headed toward home.

The closer Elijah got to his home, the heavier his feet fell. The happiness he had felt was now dampened by the thought of going up to the apartment to see the disappointed face of his father. His *mamá* was his only comfort, like the sun peeking through the clouds on a gloomy day.

He stopped in front of the door, his hand frozen on the door knob. Unlike always, the door was not opened from the inside by his mother. On impulse, he turned the knob and his eyes widened, realizing it was not locked. He heard a strained groan and his instincts heightened. Had they been robbed?! Was someone hurt? Elijah made his way in. His eyes went even wider at the sight of his father seated at the kitchen table, holding his head, his body racking with sobs. Never had he seen or heard his father cry. *Mamá!* Did something happen to her? Elijah gasped and ran in.

"Dad? Did something happen? Where is *mamá*?"

Patrick looked at him with red eyes. It was obvious he had not heard him come in. His father reached out to him and placed his hands on his shoulders, "Elijah, you have to be strong, we have to be strong."

Elijah swallowed hard. His mouth was suddenly dry and he could feel his heart pounding in his chest, "Dad, did something happen to *mamá*? Please tell me."

"Your mama, she… she has been struggling to find work, to… sponsor her work visa. It's been hard, so hard. No luck. She… overstayed and the immigration, they picked her up, son."

"No…" Elijah whispered as his eyes clouded with tears. He could not believe what he was hearing. It wasn't true. He had to be dreaming.

"They've… taken her to the deportation centre and will be sending her back to Mexico indefinitely. I don't know what we are going to do. We cannot pay a lawyer, not right now, we… can't afford it."

"We have to bring her back, dad! We have to… this is all my fault…" Elijah wailed, falling to the floor, his head in his hands. "*Mamá* struggled so hard because of me."

Patrick placed a firm hand on Elijah's shoulder and pulled him up. "No! No blame games here, son. You have to be strong. This is no time for pity parties. We have to be strong and work hard. If we want to see your mother again, if I want to see my wife again, if we want to bring her back, then we need to be strong and fight this. You got that?!"

"Yes, dad…" Elijah wailed.

"Come here," Patrick pulled his son into an embrace. They shook as they sobbed harder.

CHAPTER THIRETEEN
SHATTERED MEMORIES
1971

The bright yellow wallpaper in the small room had several red hearts scattered all over it. The peeling wallpaper tapered up and ended in a grayish-white ceiling. A particular section of the ceiling was stained brown and just below it on the floor was a large pail. Water gathered there whenever it rained and Lucy had decided that there was no point in moving it around. It was in the corner so out of the way from hurting her five-year-old daughter, Dahlia. That never stopped her from constantly reminding the little girl though. Secondly, they never received guests, so why did they need to keep up appearances? What mattered was having a roof over their heads, and living in a clean home.

The apartment was made up of two small rooms: the toilet, and the living room, which held a mattress that was elevated from the floor slightly with bricks. In the corner was a hotplate and sink which served as their kitchen. The other furniture in the room was a threadbare armchair and a velvety pillow they had found at a Goodwill downtown. It was in this room that five-year-old Dahlia sat in front of the old black and white television, while her mother caught some sleep on the bed behind her.

Dahlia's eyes were glued to the TV as she murmured. She held her hand against her stomach again as she frowned. The little girl turned to the bed. She stood up and quietly made her way to her sleeping mother. Dahlia gently tapped her mother's shoulder as she said,

"*Eomma*, I'm hungry…." Dahlia nudged her. "*Eomma…*"

Lucy Crane's brown eyes fluttered open and she found herself staring into the small face of her daughter. She reached for her half-asleep, saying, "Are you okay, *nae ttal*?"

"I'm hungry, *eomma…*" Dahlia murmured. Her hand rubbed her stomach and her bottom lip trembled. "I want to eat."

Lucy groaned as she turned on the bed. Her eyes closed once more and she pulled Dahlia into an embrace and kissed her cheek. "*Eomma* will make you some food, but let me sleep just a teeny little bit. Is that okay?"

"O…kay, *eomma*.," the girl replied softly as she tried to disentangle herself from her mother's grasp.

"Oh wait, check my bag for some cookies. There should be some there."

"Okay, *eomma*," the girl murmured as she slipped off the bed. She hurried to the side of the bed where her mother had dumped her bag last night.

Little Dahlia unzipped the bag with enthusiasm. She reached in and pulled out her hand gripping three small cookies that were wrapped in individual paper packages. Her eyes glinted as she ran back to the bed and touched her mother's shoulder gently,

"*Eomma, gomawo*." Dahlia whispered.

"Mm hmm…" An already asleep Lucy murmured.

Excited about her stash, Dahlia reclaimed her space in front of the TV and munched on her snacks. The sound of amused laughter caught Dahlia's attention and pulled her eyes away from the TV. She looked in the direction of the window. The rundown apartment had paper thin walls. Not only could they hear the constant fighting of the couple next door, they could also hear the passing cars and people. Dahlia shuffled over to the window and gently pushed away the embroidered lace curtains her mother put up when they first moved in. It was one of the few good things in the house and a contrast to the threadbare blanket her mother was currently sleeping on. They were also a family heirloom. All the little girl knew about it was what her mother had told her. It had been a wedding gift from Lucy's grandmother to Lucy's mother. She had not approved of her daughter marrying an African American after sending her to the United States to work but she had sent that down with a note *'For you to start your home with'*. And Lucy's mother had passed it to her before she died. Through all their moves across different cities, and living in the most deplorable places, the curtains had been with them, blocking them from the eyes lurking outside, like a wall.

And now, from behind the curtains, Dahlia watched the children that ran by the window with their mothers. They were heading to the park across the street. She had a perfect view of the park and she watched the laughing children. Play in the park… it was something she had never done. Dahlia splayed a hand across the window glass, watching the children longingly. She could see a few boys tossing a ball around and on the other side, some girls were skipping. The monkey bar was crowded too. Dahlia's eyes followed a particular kid who was stuffing her mouth with a corn dog. Dahlia's stomach grumbled in hunger as she licked her lips. She had never tried a corn dog. How did it taste? The child wondered. Was it as crispy and chewy as it looked? Would she ever get to try out the golden-brown fried snack? She murmured softly, feeling hungrier the more she thought about food.

"Dahlia Crane, what do you think you are doing!? Get away from the window!"

Dahlia jolted, shocked by her mother's voice. She scuttled away from the window.

"Eomma…"

"You know the rules, right?"

"Yes. I am sorry."

Lucy sighed as she hurried to Dahlia's side. She placed her hands on her shoulders and said,

"It's not safe out there, Dahlia. Please be careful and listen to *eomma*."

"Yes, *eomma*," the girl nodded, her head lowered.

"Good girl," Lucy said, pulling her into a hug. "Now sit and watch TV and I'll get you some food."

Dahlia nodded and reclaimed her spot in front of the TV. Every few seconds though, her eyes and thoughts returned to the window and the park that seemed so far away.

Lucy sighed and headed to the kitchen area. She turned on the tap and frowned as a thin stream of water streaked out. Her eyes strayed back to her daughter. She watched her look at the curtains and sighed again. Lucy splashed water on her face, just before she glanced over the small box that held their groceries. Seeing how scant it was, she groaned inwardly. The young woman pulled out a can of beans and poured it into a pan. After much trial, she was able to turn on the hotplate and the pan was set on it. Lucy leaned against the metal sink, running a tired hand through her hair as she heated up the food. Occasionally, her eyes strayed to her daughter who she caught trying to take a glimpse of the world beyond the window.

Lucy's eyes flitted over to the bed. In a little nook close to it, there was a plastic bag that held a gift for her daughter. She had managed to get it dirt cheap and had been saving it for Dahlia's birthday. Was this the right time? Her eyes followed her daughter's movements. Giving it to Dahlia meant taking her out and… Lucy's eyes shut tight as she breathed deeply. The world out there was so scary and she wanted nothing bad to happen to her child. She had experienced it firsthand. No one had protected her and she had to protect her child from all of it.

A low sizzling sound pulled her back to the present and her eyes wide, she turned back to the hotplate. Lucy switched it off and stirred the beans. Lucy scooped the hot beans into a plate, and after retrieving Dahlia's water bottle which was still half filled, she headed to her child. She set the food in front of Dahlia.

"Here you go, *nae ttal*. Eat well."

Dahlia nodded and grabbed a spoonful. She was about to shove it into her mouth when Lucy tapped her hand gently and brought it down.

"Slowly, *nae ttal*, it's hot."

Lucy took the spoon from her, blew air on it and fed Dahlia who latched onto it and swallowed happily. Lucy passed the spoon back to Dahlia and she took a few more careful bites by herself this time.

"How is it? Is it good?" Lucy watched her daughter.

Her mouth occupied, Dahlia nodded and gave a thumbs up. Lucy smiled softly and stroked Dahlia's brown hair. It was so like hers, down to the curls, which were due to Lucy's father's African American roots for sure.

"Dahlia…" Lucy started. Her daughter was currently munching and her eyes were back at the window. It seemed she had forgotten the TV a long time ago.

"Mmm…?" Dahlia said, looking up at her mother.

Lucy smiled ruefully. She reached up and using the tail of her shirt, wiped off some food stains from the corners of Dahlia's mouth. Dahlia smiled and took a sip of water.

"I'll be working late tonight, *nae ttal*."

Dahlia's smile immediately fell and her large brown eyes clouded, "Again?"

"Yes. I'm sorry, Dahlia. I just have to work so hard, for us. I'll try to be back as early as three am. All right? I promise."

Dahlia lowered her head and said in a soft voice, "I never get to spend time with you, *eomma*. I never get to do anything with you. You're always working and when you're not working, you're too tired from working. When will you ever spend time with me?"

Lucy blinked back tears and quickly looked away. She took a deep breath to calm herself and turned back to her daughter. Gently, she lifted her chin up with the tip of her finger.

"I'm so sorry, *nae ttal*. I promise you that once things get better, I will spend every minute with you. Please just be patient with *eomma*."

Dahlia sighed and nodded. She turned back to her food and took another bite. She looked at the window again and this time, she had a faraway look in her eyes. Lucy nodded. Her decision was made.

"You know what?"

Dahlia looked back at her expectantly.

"Why don't we go to the park after breakfast? We can spend some time playing there. How's that sound?"

"Really, *eomma*?!" Dahlia's eyes widened in delight and she broke into a grin. She threw her arms around Lucy. "Thank you, thank you, *eomma*!"

Lucy grinned when Dahlia finally pulled away. "Now finish your food, I'll go take a shower."

"Okay!" Dahlia nodded vigorously, turning back to her food.

"And eat slowly." Lucy reminded her as she stood up.

She turned to the TV to switch it off when she saw that the cartoon program that Dahlia had been watching was gone and replaced with a news report. Her eyes widened and her eyeballs darted rapidly at the sight of the people on the screen. Slowly, she reached for the knob on the TV and turned the volume up.

The banner at the bottom of the screen read, SMALL TOWN OF MOUNT HUGH WITNESSES REDUCTION IN ELECTRICITY BILLS AND REDUCED POWER SHORTAGES DUE TO WIND TURBINE INVESTMENT BROUGHT IN BY LOCAL BUSINESSMEN.

"This is a groundbreaking feat indeed. The town of Mount Hugh is very grateful to you both, Mr, Lark, Mr. Maximoff. What would you like to say?" The reporter was saying.

It was a newsroom. The two men were seated on the other side of the reporter, displaying bright smiles and looking like the world's best humanitarians. On the screen behind the three of them was a large picture of several wind turbines sited in some area in Mount Hugh. Lucy's mouth went dry and she felt a sharp pain in the pit of her stomach as she watched on in horror.

"Well, what can I say? It's all for the people, the people we love so much. Mount Hugh is my home. I grew up there and so did my fathers before me. It's only right that I give back, don't you think? With these wind turbines, our power shortages as well as our power bills have drastically improved. It's a win for everyone," one of the men flashed a smile, revealing perfect white teeth. A small banner rolled in front of him as he spoke, displaying his name: *William Lark, Entrepreneur and Investor.*

The camera zoomed in on him and Lucy swayed on her feet. Her hands flailed around as she searched for something to hold onto. She could hear the deafening pounding of her heart and gasped for air.

"*Eomma*, are you okay?" Dahlia was immediately at her side. "*Eomma!*"

Lucy managed to look at her daughter who was holding her with one hand and touching her head with the back of her other hand. Unsteady, Lucy pointed at the TV. Immediately, Dahlia switched it off.

"Eomma?"

Shakily, Lucy shuffled to the bathroom. She managed to lock the door behind her to keep Dahlia from entering. She did not want her daughter to see her that way. As soon as she was inside, she emptied the contents of her stomach into the toilet, and it was not a lot, considering it was last night she had her last meal. Lucy held onto the toilet bowl, groaning. There was soft knocking on the door, followed by Dahlia's worried voice.

"*Eomma*, are you okay?"

"Yes, Dahlia…" Lucy managed to say, "Go finish your food, *nae ttal. Eomma* is fine."

"But…" Dahlia started protesting.

"I am fine, Dahlia. I think I ate something bad last night. That is all. Do not worry. I will be out soon, after I take a shower."

"Okay, *eomma*…" her daughter replied reluctantly.

As soon as she heard Dahlia's retreating footsteps, Lucy turned back to the toilet bowl and heaved some more. She stood up, still unsteady on her feet and flushed the toilet. The woman stripped off her clothes and got into the shower. As the cold stream washed over her, she let the tears fall. Her shoulders ached and shook as she wailed, trying to be as quiet as she could be.

On the other side of the door, Dahlia stood, listening to her mother's crying. The sound of the water could not muffle her mother's tears. Dahlia wiped off her tears. She did not know why her mother was sad, and she did not think her mother would tell her why either. But she would be the best daughter ever and make her mother happy always, the determined little girl decided.

A short while later when Lucy came out, she was surprised to find the pan and dish in the kitchen had been cleaned and kept away. She hurried over to Dahlia.

"*Nae ttal*, what did I say about going around the kitchen area without my supervision? I don't want you to hurt yourself."

Dahlia shook her head, "I can help you out too, *eomma*. I'm a big girl now."

Lucy touched Dahlia's cheek gently as she said, "You're still my little girl. Besides, you're just five."

Dahlia shrugged. "Five enough to help out."

Lucy chuckled at that. "And smart as always. All right, time for your shower, then we can leave for the park. Is that okay?"

"*Eomma*, you were…"

Lucy pulled her daughter into a hug as she said softly, "I am fine, *nae ttal*. Everything is fine. Come on, time for your shower."

Dahlia followed her mother, her resolution from earlier still strong in her heart.

Lucy and an antsy Dahlia stood at the edge of the park, their hair whipping in the light breeze. Dahlia rubbed her hands in glee and looked up at her mother.

"Can I go and play now, *eomma*?"

Lucy crouched so she was at Dahlia's height and touched her daughter's cheeks gently.

"I'm so sorry if I've failed you as a mother, Dahlia, I'm sorry if I've been a bad mother. I know that I haven't given you the best that life has to offer and I've made you feel so alone. You mean everything to me, *nae ttal*. You are my world, and I love you so much."

Dahlia shook her head vigorously and touched her mother's cheek. She planted a kiss on her mother's forehead and said, "You can't say that *eomma*, because it's not true."

"What?" Lucy whispered.

"You are not a bad mother and you haven't failed me. You are the best and most beautiful mom I've ever seen. You are the right mom for me."

"Dahlia…" Lucy whispered and pulled her into a tight hug. She sniffed as tears rolled down her cheeks.

When she finally let Dahlia go, Dahlia wiped her tears away with her small hands saying, "Please don't cry, *eomma*. I'm sorry for making you cry."

"No, no, Dahlia. These are happy tears. You didn't make me sad. You never make me sad. I'll always be here to protect you, dear. No harm will ever come to you as long as I am alive, and even when I'm dead. Do you understand, *nae ttal*? I'll never let anything hurt you. I love you."

"I love you too, *eomma*." Dahlia grinned.

Lucy stroked her daughter's hair and dabbed her eyes with her other hand, "All right, go on and play some football. I'll be right here watching you."

"Uh… I'll just go to the swings, *eomma*. I don't have a ball and I don't think the boys will let me play with them," Dahlia said thoughtfully, her eyes on the football game going on in the distance.

"Who says you don't have a ball?" Lucy asked, her eyes twinkling.

"What?" Dahlia turned back to her mother, confused.

Grinning, Lucy pulled a plastic ball out of the bag she had taken out of the apartment before they left. Dahlia's mouth fell open and she bounced on her toes, her eyes twinkling.

"*Eomma*! Is it for me? Thank you! Thank you! *Eomma, gomawo*!"

Lucy laughed as she handed the ball to her daughter, "Silly, who else will it be for? I bought it for your birthday but it's still months away. There's nothing wrong in getting gifts when it's not your birthday, right?"

"Thank you, thanks, *eomma*!" Dahlia hugged her again, before running off, kicking the ball ahead of her.

"Be careful and don't go far, Dahlia!" Lucy called to her.

Dahlia stopped, turned around and blew Lucy a kiss. Lucy made a catching gesture and held her hand to her heart. She blew back a kiss and Dahlia caught it and held it to her heart. Lucy tilted her head, a soft smile playing on her lips as she watched her daughter play with the ball. A couple little girls joined her and she watched the girls play enthusiastically. Dahlia's curly hair blew in the wind as she ran around. Her cheeks were rosy and her eyes twinkled as she laughed. Her child was happy. Lucy blinked back tears. She had not seen her child this happy in a very long time. She was happy, she was among her peers and she was being a normal child.

Lucy's eyes flitted over to the other children. Shiny new sneakers, good clothes and her eyes flitted back to her daughter. She was close enough that she could see the solitary hole in her knee length socks and her jumper, it was clean but so old. She could not even remember when or where she bought it, which was proof enough. Lucy sighed and pressed her eyes with her fingers. Her daughter deserved so much better than this. She deserved a good life and she deserved good things. How could she make that possible? She held a fist to her chest as she watched her daughter playing.

Her beeper buzzed just then. Absent-mindedly, she reached for it. She frowned when she saw it was a message from her boss. She had to call him. Her eyes darted around and she saw a payphone at the edge of the park. She still had good view of Dahlia.

"Dahlia!" Lucy called to her daughter. Dahlia turned around and looked at her questioningly.

Lucy pointed at the phone booth and made a call gesture and pointed at herself. Dahlia nodded in understanding and turned back to her ball game. Her eyes still following her daughter, Lucy headed to the payphone. She tapped her foot impatiently as she waited for the person inside to finish. *How can I get us out of poverty and give you the life you deserve?* Lucy wondered again, staring at her child.

The sound of the door closing jolted her back to the present and she turned to see that the previous occupant of the booth was walking away. Lucy quickly slipped into the booth. She slipped a coin into the slot. While she waited for her boss to pick the call, her eyes were glued on her daughter.

"It's me, Lucy," she said immediately the click was followed by the sound of heavy breathing.

"Ah… good… good… I wanted to inform you ahead. A client has requested a personal dance session with you, at 11pm, so don't be late. And well…"

Lucy frowned, "Well what, Mr. Higgins?"

"Well, he paid quite a lot so, you know…" Huggins trailed off again.

"I don't know, Mr. Huggins," Lucy gritted her teeth.

"Well… something extra can be added on top, if you know what I mean."

"I will not be sleeping with a client, Mr. Higgins. Pole dancing is what I do," Lucy said tightly.

"Oh, come on, Lucy, it's just a little roll in the sack."

"Sex for money, Mr. Higgins, call it what it is, prostitution. I'm not a prostitute. Besides, it's illegal!!" Lucy shout whispered.

"Oh Lucy, you won't be the first here to do it. Besides, I won't tell if you won't tell. And the client certainly won't tell."

"I will not be doing this, Mr. Higgins."

"Lucy… do you know how much you will be raking in if you just bend back a little and do this?"

"Last I checked, Mr. Higgins, you own a strip club, not a whorehouse," Lucy's frowned deepened. She was getting very uncomfortable. "Besides, what if I get pregnant? Have you forgotten that abortion is illegal here and contraceptive pills, oh that's just something I cannot even spare money on. What will happen then?"

"Lucy, it's good money. The client is paying you 150 dollars, and just for two hours. Think about it."

Lucy's eyes widened and she cleared her throat. Instantly, she did some calculations. Their rent was 300 dollars. If she did this, that was already half of the rent settled. And… she would just need to get the remaining half and… money for groceries. This was good, really good. She shut her eyes and sighed.

"Are you still there, Lucy?"

"Fine, fine, I'll do it. But only this time, never again." she slammed the receiver down and ran a hand through her hair, feeling frustrated.

Lucy looked up and her eyes widened when she did not find Dahlia. She ran out of the phone booth, her heart pounding erratically.

"Dahlia! Dahlia!" She shouted, her eyes darting around. Tears streaked down Lucy's face as she searched for her child.

"*Eomma*!" Lucy turned around and ran toward a confused Dahlia.

"Where have you been? You scared me!"

"I'm sorry, *eomma*," Dahlia whispered. "The ball rolled behind that tree so I went to get it."

"Please don't do that again. Stay where I can see you."

"I'm sorry, *eomma*." Dahlia planted a kiss on her cheek.

"I'm fine, you can go play."

Lucy settled heavily into a park bench and held her head in her hands. She wiped her tears away and, in that moment, she felt a sharp pain in her head as memories flooded her, memories from that horrible night in February of Nineteen-sixty six.

"Here you go, Lucy. I got this for you. 'C' like your name, Lucy Crane," Eleanor smiled as she helped Lucy put on the pearl necklace.

"It's so beautiful, Eleanor, too beautiful for me. It doesn't belong on me, just like I don't belong at this party."

Lucy looked down at the excited and sophisticated people dancing in the ballroom below.

"Nonsense," Eleanor said, swatting her hand lightly. "You might not come from wealth, Lucy, but the wealth of our friendship is so much more important. Don't look down on yourself or how valuable I hold you, my friend."

Lucy nodded, her eyes filled with tears. Eleanor linked hands with her. "Now come, let me introduce you to a few friends.

Lucy blinked and shook her head as she tried to fight the memories to no avail.

"Please go back, William," Lucy hissed as she hurried to her car.

William continued to trail her, "Oh come on, Lucy, just a kiss, a little kiss, and let me feel you up a little."

Lucy spun around, glaring at him. "Stop this madness, William. You are my friend's fiancé and she's in there at the party. You shouldn't be acting this way even when you are drunk."

"Come on, baby. Do you feel that?" William grabbed her arm and pulled her against him so she was against his bulging crotch. She struggled against him and managed to get away.

"Leave me alone!" She shouted and ran toward her car. The strong smell of whiskey descended on her as she got her keys in the lock.

Lucy gasped and her eyes flew open. She touched her wet cheeks. Her heart was pounding. That night was the worst of her life, one she always relived in her nightmares. The only good thing it had brought her was Dahlia. Lucy stood up, her eyes on her daughter. She knew what she had to do. She made a beeline for the phone booth.

Lucy took a deep breath and looked at the phone. She set it back on the cradle and turned to head out. She shook her head and reached for it again but her hand fell to her side. Her eyes drifted to Dahlia, who was now playing on the swing with her new friends and Lucy shut her eyes tight and steeled herself. She had to do this for her daughter. It was the only way her daughter could get out of this life. It was the only way Dahlia could have the chance to be better than her. Lucy dialed a number that she had dialed so many times in the past. A number that was ingrained in her head no matter how many times she had tried to forget it. A few rings and there was the voice,

"William Lark. Who is this?"

A chill ran through her spine and the phone fell out of her hand.

"Hello?" The voice asked again. Clumsily, she set the phone back in place and took deep breaths.

For Dahlia, for Dahlia, she chanted in her head like a mantra. Lucy grabbed the phone again and dialed.

"William Lark. Look, if this is some prank…"

"It's Lucy Crane." She said quietly.

There was a moment of silence, then his slimy voice returned, "Lucy Crane, by my word! I never thought I would hear that name or this voice again. Where did you disappear to? There has been no news of you since the party. How are you?"

"I didn't call to exchange pleasantries, William," Lucy said tightly. "And for my health, it's been doing miserably since the party, all thanks to you."

"I have no idea what you are talking about, Lucy."

"Are you really going to pretend, William? You know fully well that you assaulted me that night when I got to my car!"

"I don't know what you're talking about, Lucy. The only thing I remember from that night is that everyone, including you, had fun.

Why do you want to make a fuss over something that happened a long time ago?"

"You raped me, William, and I got pregnant. How can you pretend nothing happened? How do you live with yourself? Oh, my goodness! How many women have you done this to?"

"Get off your high horse, Lucy. I never laid a hand on you. If you got pregnant, it had to be one of your numerous man friends. Everyone knows you were a whore."

"That's not true! Malinda started that slimy rumor because she was jealous of my friendship with Eleanor. She started that to tarnish my image and ruin me! If you don't believe me, we can have a paternity test, William," Lucy said firmly, her eyes blazing. She had had enough of being walked all over by the powerful.

His laughter resonated through the phone, "That's ludicrous and not going to happen. Why did you call? I'm sure it's not to reminisce over your false accounts of that night."

Lucy swallowed hard. This was it. The moment of truth. "I… I need some money, William. Please. I just need enough for my daughter to have a good life, a normal life."

Once again, she was greeted by his bellowing laughter. "You really are a gold digger, Lucy Crane. You just made all this up to get money from me. I bet you heard of our recent successes and you decided to crawl out of the woodwork."

"I am not asking for much, William. I might just have to go to the police then."

This time, Lucy was greeted by silence and heavy breathing. She could hear the anger in his voice when he finally spoke.

"Fine, meet me in Mount Hugh tonight. Let's discuss this."

"That's not happening. We can talk over the phone."

"Phone? No, Lucy. How do I know you're not recording this? Let's meet in a neutral place in Mount Hugh."

Lucy tapped her chin lightly as she thought about it. She was not looking forward to meeting William again, certainly not on his turf. Still, what he said made sense. And, it would certainly be better if someone else was there. Her eyes found her daughter and she sighed softly. She would finally be able to give Dahlia the life she deserved.

"Fine, I'll return to Mount Hugh alone and meet you, only if someone else is present. I won't meet you alone, William, never."

"Someone else? Fine. That can be arranged. Don't worry and leave it all to me. You can trust me completely, Lucy… completely."

"I will see you tonight."

Lucy hung up after getting the details of their meeting spot. She looked at Dahlia again and heaved a sigh of relief.

"For you my child, I'll do anything," she muttered under her breath.

CHAPTER FOURTEEN
SHATTERED EGO
1962

A small radio set next to the wooden fence blared *The Beach Boys* at top volume. Around the offending little object were five teenagers, tapping along to the music, with blunts hanging between their fingers and lips.

"The Beach Boys… they are the ultimate best," one of them drawled as he took another inhale of his cigar.

"Tell me about it," another one murmured.

A third boy scratched his head and said, "Hey, what's the time? We have to be back at school before the lunch bell goes."

"Oh relax…" the tallest of the boys grunted from his perch next to a hollowed-out tree. "We've got plenty of time, Little Larry. There's no need to be so antsy."

"If you say so, Aaron," the one called Little Larry said with a frown. At seventeen, Larry was small for his age and was used to his friends towering over him. It was why they had nicknamed him 'Little Larry'. At first, he had protested but the name stuck. He had learned to accept it and even introduced himself as so sometimes. What he had going for him, he always said, was his great hair. *It will get me far*, those were his regular words.

"So, Johnnie, you heard back from Philly?" Kevin asked, scratching his dyed whitish blonde hair.

A smile spread across John's face as he nodded, "You got that right. I got the mail yesterday. Full ride, baby!"

"Ha!" Little Larry pumped the air and bumped fists with John. "Playing football was worth it after all, huh?"

"Well, it's about time you douse that blunt, man," Gustov said with a slight shake of his head. "I bet you'll be having what? Weekly tests? You got to lay off the weed, man."

"Oh, you don't have to tell me," John grinned. "It will be sad saying goodbye to my friend here though."

The four of them laughed while Aaron frowned. He took another inhale of his blunt, his frown deepening.

"What about the factory, Larry? Heard from them yet?" Kevin asked.

"Uh huh, uh huh, I got an interview set for next week."

"Well, I bet you'll knock them dead with your eloquence," Gustov grinned.

"What's so special about working at a factory? Or studying at North Philly?" Aaron grunted. "I've been to Philly and there's nothing there but gray clouds, and what's a factory if not a load of work, resulting in acting joints and backs?"

The smiles on the faces of the others fell and Kevin rolled his eyes and turned to Aaron.

"You hear back from the college yet? Or that job down in South Creek?" Kevin asked tightly. The other three also looked at Aaron, their brows arched. They were not expectant. They knew what the answer would be.

Aaron's mouth clamped shut, but only for a second. The next moment, he shrugged and said, "Oh, definitely soon. You know what they say, greatness takes time."

"Indeed, indeed," Kevin nodded slowly.

"It's only a matter of time now. I mean, they literally have no choice. Oof… it's going to be so difficult for me to choose between the options coming my way soon."

"You realize that the year is coming to a close, right? I don't think you have much time left. Maybe you should try making more efforts than you currently are."

Aaron frowned, "There is no way I will not have opportunities lined up for me. Surely you know that, Kevin. It's too early to worry about any of that."

The four boys exchanged glances and their lips twitched.

"You don't say… you are just the perfect candidate and they'll just be killing themselves over you," an amused Kevin added. It was not just known by the boys, but also public knowledge that Aaron Grayson was failing his classes. In a small town, news travelled fast. Even the seemingly mundane things became news when there was nothing else going on.

"You got that right! I'm telling you guys, my name is going to be known all over these parts, and everyone will know who I am. Everybody will know my name and those who were rude to me, will be so sorry!" Aaron declared.

"You could be known as the worse criminal that our town produces, you know. It's not too late. I mean, that's still a reason for tongues to wag in your direction," Kevin commented, causing the others to burst into hysterical laughter.

Aaron jumped to his feet, glaring at them. "You're all fools. Mark it, you'll eat your words."

He stormed off and Kevin shook his head as he snuffed out his blunt. "There goes troubled Aaron."

Larry frowned, "We are no less troubled than him."

"Oh, Larry, Larry, Larry," John placed a hand around Larry's shoulder and leaned closer to say, "Yes, we are all troubled, but Aaron is our fitting leader."

Kevin grinned. "He is more troubled than the rest of us."

"Uh huh. Did you hear all that nonsense he said just now? Who is going to hire a failure like him? What school will even accept him?" John rolled his eyes.

"Still, I don't think it's fair to call him that…" Larry started saying when Kevin cut in,

"Look the guy is troubled, more than the rest of us. He clearly has deep-seated problems, that's the only explanation for the facade he puts up and…"

"Oh crap! We are going to be late! Aaron already left us behind!" Gustov shouted as he stomped on his blunt, dousing it. He immediately lunged in the direction Aaron had headed only moments ago.

"That bastard Aaron! Why didn't he tell us? The principal is going to have our heads!" Kevin shouted. "Oh, Little Larry, leave the radio!"

"But…" a confused Larry stuttered.

"Let's go!" John shoved him forward.

The boys ran at full speed. They knew without a doubt that they were late and they blamed no one else but Aaron. They had snuck out of school during lunch period with the plan to return before the bell rang. Aaron had been their timekeeper but he had clearly headed back without informing them, just because he was pissed.

"The bastard always has to make it about himself!" John shouted over the wind.

"He always has to be the star!" An angry Kevin shouted back.

The boys raced each other, the tails of their partly buttoned shirts whipping in the wind behind them, as well as their long and untamed hair. As they ran, they kicked potted plants and pushed over a few newspaper stands.

"Bastards!" One of their victims shouted.

Laughing, the boys stuck out their tongues and continued running.

In tandem, they all let out huge sighs when they saw the looming gate of the school. Just a little while earlier, they had jumped over the fence, with the intention to return before the bell rang. Now that plan was moot, they all thought as the first peals of the bell reached them.

The boys skidded to a halt. Leaning against the fence was a frowning Aaron. He was glaring at a man blocking the entrance. The boys swallowed hard when they laid their eyes on their principal, Timmy Briggs. His round stomach covered by his white shirt, bulged out over his brown slacks. He looked like a vanilla ice cream cone. The man turned his rotund head in their direction as they slowly walked up. A brow arched, he clapped slowly.

"Well, well, well, look what we have here. I was beginning to think you were not going to return today."

"Uh… Mr. Briggs…" Kevin started saying but the man raised a hand, silencing them.

He clasped his hands behind his back as he walked from one boy to the other, shaking his head slowly.

"The miscreants of our high school, that is the identity you all have procured for yourself and it is clear you have no reservations about it. So, while your mates, the diligent ones spend their breaks in the cafeteria, and then return to class, you lot gallivant around town, terrorizing everyone in your sight and…"

He froze in front of Gustov and frowned. His nose twitched and he leaned forward. Gustov leaned back as he tried to get away from him. The principal's glare stopped him. Briggs' frown deepened and he stepped back, "Smoking too. Why am I not surprised? The lot of you clearly lack future ambitions. Miscreants! That's what you all are!"

"I am no miscreant," Aaron hissed.

Five pairs of eyes turned to him in annoyance. Four of them, the boys', held strong glares.

"What are you doing there? Get over here!" The principal hissed, motioning to the queue the boys were currently standing in. "Join your partners. You are the leader of this stupid gang, are you not?"

Aaron rolled his eyes and stood his ground but in seconds, the principal was at his side, swatting at his shoulder with a paper fan.

"Stupid! Stupid! Stupid!"

He pushed the glaring Aaron to the queue. Mr. Briggs pointed the fan at Aaron and shook his head as he said snidely, "You, Aaron Grayson, are a disgrace. How is it that you and Quinn come from the same stock? Are you not ashamed of yourself? Your younger brother is doing so well, but here you are the complete opposite! I bet your brother will go off to college while you will be bundled off to the county jail. It's just a matter of time now."

The boys snickered while Aaron glared at the principal, his mouth trembling. It was not the first time the principal was comparing Aaron to his brother, neither was he the first person who was doing it. And Aaron knew that he also would not be the last. He had heard it so many times already but that did not stop it from stinging. Briggs waved the fan in front of Aaron's face and hissed,

"Hey, stop glaring! Get that look out of your eyes, you bastard."

"Make me…" Aaron growled.

Briggs opened his mouth to say something but he seemed to think better of it because he stepped back and said, "Detention after school, for the rest of this week. Let's see how the lot of you enjoy being cooped in a classroom longer than you need to. Now get out of my sight, you dunces."

The boys shuffled away quickly. Only Aaron took his time, ensuring that his glare lingered on the principal for a second longer.

"That bastard," the principal muttered under his breath. "One of these days, one of these days."

The bell for close of school rang and with it, Aaron and his gang members groaned. Since they returned to the classroom, they had not spoken to each other, but now, it was time to move to the detention hall. Stepping into the hall, Aaron stopped short when he saw Quinn, his fifteen-year-old younger brother. Quinn was leaning against the wall, his hands crossed and his backpack slung over his shoulder. His sneakers were shiny, just as they had been that morning. Aaron looked down at his feet. His were scuffed, a contrast to his brother's. Quinn's brown hair was neat, every strand in place, despite the fact that he had had PE today. And Aaron once again looked down at his dyed black and blue hair which fell to just below his shoulders. His brother, Quinn Grayson, perfect in every way looked up at him just then and waved. A small smile played on Quinn's lips as he straightened up. While he was two years younger than Aaron, he was already almost taller than him. It was only a few years now, Aaron was sure.

"Ready to go home?" Quinn asked.

"I'm not going home yet," Aaron said flatly.

Quinn's smile slipped as he said quietly, "Why? Where are you going to, Aaron? Didn't you hear what dad said last week? He said we should also always return home together."

"Well, newsflash, little brother, things don't always go the way your father wants them to."

"Hey, aren't you coming to the basement, Aaron?" Larry asked as he and Gustov brushed past the brothers.

"I'll be there soon," Aaron called back.

"The basement? Wait... you got detention, didn't you?" Quinn turned back to his brother with narrowed eyes. "Did you sneak out again? How could you?!"

"I don't need to stand here and listen to your nagging," Aaron hissed as he made to walk around his brother.

"I am so going to tell mom and dad about this! When will you stop this? What's so hard about staying in school during school hours? What's so hard about sticking to the rules?!" Quinn hissed.

"Well, not all of us can be you, Quinn. Look, it's none of your business, all right? Stop being such a bug and hovering over me and my business. Being brothers does not mean we are hitched at the hip. Stop being a helicopter and stop concerning yourself with what concerns me!"

Quinn shook his head slowly and looked up at his brother, his eyes brimming with disappointment, "Do you know how much I wish I can stay out of your business? Do you know how much I wish not to be associated with you? Do you think I want to be known as the brother of Aaron Grayson, the one who leads a gang? Well, I don't! But still, I am a Grayson just as you are and your business will affect me and possibly ruin my future opportunities! Everyone knows you, even the police! And if you continue this way, you'll end up ruining not just your life but mine and our parents too! So, no, Aaron! As much as I want to not be a helicopter brother, as you so put it, I can't! Because the stain you cause to our family name will affect us all!"

The fuming Quinn turned around and stormed off. Aaron sighed. Running his hand through his hair, he leaned against the wall that just moments ago, his brother had been leaning against. He knew Quinn was right. In small towns like this, it was easy for you to be judged based on your family name. The same way people compared him to Quinn was the same way Quinn was compared to him and judged. He shook his head and headed off to the detention hall. He wouldn't dwell on any of it now. Besides, there was nothing he could do but face what was in front of him.

As soon as he stepped into the basement classroom, he received a duster in his face.

"Hey!" He shouted as he spat out dust. "What was that for?"

"That's for leaving us behind and not notifying us of the time, you bastard," Kevin hissed.

Aaron rolled his eyes as he walked into the class. "It would have made no difference. Didn't you see that I was caught too? And you know fully well that I'm the best runner in town. If I couldn't get back in time, there's no way the lot of you could have returned in time."

The other guys rolled their eyes and John said, "That's for us to decide, Aaron. You never can tell."

"Yeah whatever. You can drop your anger, all right? I'm here with you guys, proof enough that none of us escaped the punishment."

"The least you could do is apologize, man. You did leave us hanging, you know," Little Larry said quietly.

Aaron looked at the four guys and they looked back at him expectantly. He rolled his eyes and shrugged,

"Fine, my bad."

"Your bad? That's…" Kevin started saying when Gustov tapped his shoulder and shook his head slightly.

"That's the best we are going to get, you know that. Let's just leave it be."

"So we good?" Aaron arched a brow.

"Yeah, whatever," the guys murmured. Before they could say more, the door swung open, revealing Briggs.

"This is not a vacation. To your seats, you miscreants! The next few hours are going to be long."

Groaning, the boys settled into their seats to face their punishment.

A few hours later, the laughing boys emerged from the school building. The sun was overcast and was slowly moving into the horizon.

"Should we stop over at *Lay's* on our way home?" Aaron asked his friends.

"Uh… I don't think that will be possible," Gustov stated with a gulp as the boys froze.

"Why? Don't tell me you guys are still mad…" Aaron started saying as his eyes followed the boys' gaze. He froze as well when he saw the dark brown pickup truck with the local police logo parked in front of the school gate. Leaning against it was a tall and lean man in a brown uniform. His silver badge glinted and though his hat was lowered over the upper half of his face, Aaron could feel his penetrating glare.

"See you, man!" The guys called as they ran in the other direction.

"If you're still alive by the morrow," Kevin added with a slap on Aaron's back before sprinting off.

Slowly, Aaron made his way towards the truck. Once he was at the vehicle, the man did not say anything but instead, turned around and climbed into the cab. Aaron swallowed hard. His mouth felt dry as he slipped in. For a moment, they sat in silence, then the man glared at Aaron and the seatbelt. Aaron fumbled to lock it in. As soon as it was in place, the man pulled away from the curb.

"Dad, I can explain," Aaron started.

"What else can you say, Aaron? You were given detention because once again, you and that bunch of loafers you call your gang snuck out of school. Am I correct?" His father asked through gritted teeth.

"Quinn has a big mouth," Aaron grunted.

His father suddenly stepped on the brake and Aaron jerked. If he was not wearing his seatbelt, he would have most likely been thrown through the windshield.

"Have you no shame?" Martin Grayson bellowed. "You are a complete nuisance, to our family and to this town! Your brother snitching on you is the least of your worries! How much longer are you going to keep being a mess, Aaron?"

"Dad… I…" Aaron stuttered.

"Do you think you can go around doing anything you want and you'll be able to claw your way out? Do you think because I'm the deputy chief of police, you get to act without consequences?! What gives you such audacity?"

Aaron lowered his head, not speaking. Martin Grayson started the car again, his angry fists holding the steering wheel tightly as he maneuvered through the street. Silence loomed for a moment, then Martin said,

"What's your plan for your life, Aaron?"

"Dad, I…" Aaron trailed off. He looked straight ahead, unable to look at his father.

"You've got no offers, from colleges, from universities or even any jobs. Your grades are in the trash! What do you see yourself doing in the future, Aaron?"

"There's still time," Aaron said softly, his lower lip trembling.

His father scoffed, "Time indeed. Time waits for no man, Aaron, and from where I'm seated, all you're doing is wasting the time you got. You say there's still time? That's you lying to yourself. Take a look at your brother, he already got so many offers and he's not yet done. He'll decide the best and…"

"I'm not my brother!" Aaron shouted. "Why do you always have to make everything about your golden child? You know, the only reason your son is so perfect is because he has no autonomy. He does not have any freedom, he makes no decisions of his own and is just a crazy bootlicker, a simple yes man!"

Martin arched a brow, "Is that what you tell yourself? Is that how you sleep well at night, Aaron? 'Oh, my brother is not better than me because he has no mind of his own', is that what you think!? Have you ever thought that that's just who you are, that you're describing yourself? Don't you live your life trying to impress those buffoons you go around with? Isn't that why you hang out with that crowd, running around and constituting nuisance? Isn't all of this because you want attention? Because you have nothing substantial to offer? I wonder who's the real bootlicker."

Aaron blinked back tears and quickly turned to the window. He felt a sharp pain in his chest and a lump in his throat. His shoulders slumped and he could not speak. As his father's words hung in the air, Aaron, compressed under the weight of them, could do nothing but sit limply and watch the town roll by. Thoughts swirled in his muddled mind: *Is he right? Are all my actions due to attention-seeking? Is this all because him and mom never gave me opportunities or attention?*

By the time they arrived at the two-story white thatched house with brown shutters they called home, Aaron was still in his shell.

He slid out of the truck and mindlessly headed to the door. As soon as they were inside, his father said,

"There's no point punishing you because you'll still do whatever you want to do."

"Aaron, what happened?" His mother hurried to his side.

Ignoring her, Aaron headed to the stairs, taking them slowly. His parents' voices reached him.

"Martin, what happened?"

"The usual. Nothing to talk about. Where's Quinn?"

Aaron slammed his door shut and his back slid down it to the floor. He looked forward, his eyes glued to the window across him.

Aaron had no idea how long he sat there or what he thought about but the sound of laughter pulled him back to reality. His room was close to the stairs and bits of conversation from his family on the first floor reached him.

"So, what did he say?" He heard his mother ask.

"Well, they'll be sending the project to the Model Science Fair at the state capital," he heard Quinn say.

"Oh, that's amazing, son! Last week it was the painting, now this! We need to celebrate!" Aaron's mother exclaimed.

"Of course, of course, I'm not surprised. He takes after me." Martin chipped in.

Aaron rolled his eyes and raised his hand to his face. His mouth parted softly when he realized his face was wet. He had been crying without even realizing it. He shook his head and jumped to his feet.

"Screw them all," Aaron hissed. "They can have fun with their favorite child. I'm going to go have my own fun."

He crossed the room to the window across the door and lifted it. He tapped the long pipe outside and gently and slowly, let himself out. A few minutes later, he landed on his feet in the yard. His eyes darted around and once he confirmed no one saw him, Aaron sprinted down the street.

"Little Larry! Larry!" Aaron shout whispered, knocking on Larry's window.

Larry's face popped up on the other side. His blonde hair was a mess and it was clear he had been sleeping. Larry opened the window and stared at him.

"What, Aaron?"

"Wanna go have fun?"

A smile spread across Larry's face, "You don't need to ask twice. And my parents are out to town till the weekend. I can stay out as late as ever!"

"Oh yeah! Come on, Let's go get Gustov," Aaron led the way.

"What of Kevin and Johnnie?"

Aaron frowned, "They're on the other side of town, let's just hang without them."

"You mad at Kevin?" Larry asked knowingly. He hurried to catch up with Aaron's long strides.

Aaron's frown deepened as he said, "He has been mouthing off recently. I don't want to see him right now."

"Fair enough but I hope you all smooth things over soon," Larry, ever the peacemaker, said.

Aaron grunted and looked at the house they had just arrived at. They made their way through the backyard. They didn't need to knock as Gustov saw them first.

"What are you guys doing here?" He hissed.

"Going to have fun, come on." Aaron turned to leave but Gustov said,

"Nah, I'm not going anywhere. I've been grounded, which means I'm already living on thin ice."

"You're not serious, so you'll really stay back because you were told to? You're such a coward," Aaron rolled his eyes.

"Come on, man, let's go," Larry tugged on Aaron's sleeve.

"Coward!" Aaron shouted as Gustov slammed his window shut.

"So, what did your father say?" Larry asked Aaron as they walked into town. The sun had set and it was getting dark.

"Oh… 'I'm disappointed in you, your brother is better', the usual brouhaha." Aaron shrugged, like it had not bothered him.

"I'm sorry, man."

"Mm hmm…" A distracted Aaron said. His eyes were focused on a car that had just pulled up in front of the grocery store. He watched an elderly man alight the car and slowly head to the shop's entrance where there were several bags. He picked up two and with difficulty, lugged them to the car. From what Aaron could see, there were still about six to seven more bags. Aaron heard himself say, "Is he preparing for a zombie outbreak?"

"What are you looking at?" Larry's eyes followed his. "Ooh… grandpa has a journey ahead of him."

"Let's do this," Aaron said, heading to the car.

"We're helping him? That's strange of you."

"Stealing the car. Who said anything about helping?" Aaron asked incredulously.

"What?" Larry shoved Aaron behind another car a few feet away. "You can't be serious. Why would we do something so stupid? I'm not stealing a car."

"For fun, Larry, for fun. Come on, don't be such a weak man. Wanna be like Gustov? Be my guest and leave."

Larry sighed and shook his head, "But why do we have to go this far, Aaron? This is too much."

Aaron's eyes darkened as he freed himself from Larry's grip. He said flatly, "How else will I get the attention of everyone? All they care about is the well-behaved Quinn Grayson, the deputy chief's son. No one sees me. Maybe now, they will."

"Still man..." Larry started protesting but he saw the determination in his friend's eyes. He sighed and said, "Fine, but we won't go far, just around the block and we return. Deal?"

"Deal. Now!" Aaron ran to the car and grunting, Larry ran after him.

Just as Larry shut the door, the old man turned around from the shop. He shouted and threw an egg at Larry who hustled to lower his head. Aaron skidded and sped away.

"Crap, I think he saw me. Once around the block and we go back," Larry groaned, wiping away egg yolk. He looked at Aaron who was speeding up. "Are you listening to me?"

"Shut up, man!" Aaron shouted as he was flooded by the voices.

Your brother is so much better than you!

How are you both from the same stock?

What plans do you have for the future?

You're a nobody!

The county jail beckons to you…

He gritted his teeth and stepped on the gas. He would show them.

"Are you insane?" Larry reached for the steering wheel and started struggling with Aaron.

The car veered off the road and flipped over twice. Just before it rolled into the woods, it was stopped by a tree smashing into the trunk.

Aaron's eyes flitted open and he winced. He unbuckled the seatbelt he had remembered to lock in back at the grocery store and groaned. His eyes flew to his side and he saw an empty seat. Shuddering, he looked forward and saw a human shaped hole in the windshield. The car was upside down and Aaron managed to crawl out.

"Larry! Larry!"

He froze when he saw Larry, face down. He must have been thrown out. Had he been using his seatbelt? Aaron swallowed hard. He trembled as he reached forward to touch him but he stumbled before he made contact. Aaron scrambled backward on his palms. His eyes darted around. The moon illuminated the accident scene but he could see no one. *What am I going to do?! What will I do?!* He screamed internally. Sparing one last glance at his friend, he stumbled out of the woods, wincing from his pain.

Aaron winced as he sneaked into his house through the back door. He froze in the kitchen, waiting to hear any sounds. There was nothing. The clock above the sink showed it was just past seven-thirty. He struggled through the kitchen and gently made his way up the stairs where he found the hallway light was on. He tried to move as quickly as possible. His mother was most likely on a call with her sister at this time and his father would be at the station or on patrol. And as usual, Quinn would be studying. No one would notice him, he was sure. He was also sure that no one noticed he had been out too.

Once he was in his room, he slipped off his shirt. He groaned when he saw the pieces of glass that scattered across the floor. His torso was covered with bruises and the pain in his leg told him there would be more in his lower half. He would have to cover it all up with his clothes. No one could know. He shut his eyes tight trying to fight the memories of the accident. Why? Why did he have to do that? He groaned inwardly. This whole evening was a mess he wished never happened. And Little Larry… was he…? He shook his head, trying not to think about it.

"What happened to you and why do you have so many bruises? Did you get into a fight?"

Alarmed, Aaron's eyes flew open. He turned to see Quinn at his doorway, his mouth agape, a glass of water in his hand. Aaron's room light was off but the hallway light cast enough glow for him to be visible.

Oh crap, he thought to himself. He had been in such a hurry and did not ensure his door was shut well. It must have creaked open.

"What…" Quinn started, pointing at him when Aaron stepped forward.

"Mind your business." Not waiting for a response, Aaron slammed the door and headed to the shower.

Aaron retired to bed a nervous wreck.

Chapter Fifteen
One Snowy Morning In Mount Hugh

Grayson looked up at the old clock hanging on the wall in the lobby of the Mount Hugh Inn. An antique but it still kept time. Grayson could relate to that. Take a lickin' and keep on tickin', just like in the Timex commercials. The clock's hands stood poised at ten minutes to eight. The spoiled rich kids, Peter and Fawn, would be there any minute. He looked over at Elijah, sitting in one of the cushioned chaise lounge chairs that stood in the lobby. It was time to go over the game plan.

"Okay, Riley," he said. "You're going to follow my lead."

"Of course," Elijah said.

"Really, kid," Grayson said, still feeling the sting of the multiple betrayals and missteps of his young partner. "It's important. We're in this together. Just you and me against the world. Against all the kooks in this town." He was including Dahlia of course. He didn't have to mention that in order for Riley to get the message.

"I understand," Elijah said. "So, what's our angle?"

Aaron nodded, pleased at Elijah's compliance. What's the angle? What's the play? Part of the problem that had been nagging Grayson was the fact that there were simply too many suspects. Good ones, juicy ones. He'd initially been quick to arrive at his own conclusions, seeing the mayor as a particularly appealing suspect. Likely to have done it and perfect to sell the story. But now the mayor was out. Struck off the list in the most violent and final way possible. Rather than simplifying things, it complicated them. Deprived of his favorite suspect he was forced to recognize how packed the list of contenders was. So many of them. Close connections, all rich, all greedy, all corrupt. On a level, it was annoying. Grayson felt a twinge in his gut, like a bit of errant indigestion, from the lack of clarity. He followed his gut. Always had. It had never steered him wrong. And he could feel in his gut that this case hadn't solidified. He'd been getting these signals since he'd arrived in this shitty mountain town three days ago. He remembered trying to sell Elijah on the virtues of the small town, a bastion of American tradition. Aaron Grayson wasn't one to eat crow, but on a level he wished he could retract those words. Mount Hugh could go to hell. The town was filled with loonies. Rich assholes who thought they ran the world and superstitious locals who believed in ghosts and supernatural serial killers. And snowstorms? In April? Grayson was determined to whittle down the suspect list by the time the weather cleared up.

He noticed Elijah looking at him expectantly.

"Yes," he said, slowly, playing off his distraction as a ploy for dramatic effect. "Our angle. Our angle is as follows…" He continued, some of the plan unfolding as he'd had it constructed in his head, some of it improvised on the spot. "We've got too many suspects. Too many decent to excellent suspects. It's unworkable. We need to start eliminating some of them. Or better yet, solve this damned case."

He didn't say it out loud, but it wasn't lost on Grayson that their prime suspect *had* just been "eliminated," although not at all in the preferred manner. For a second, Grayson wondered if Elijah was biting his tongue to avoid pointing it out.

"Agreed," said Elijah. "We do. Too many suspects and no path to whittling them down."

"Great," Aaron said. "So, Peter and Fawn, we know they're full of shit, right?" Elijah nodded assent. *Good, he's with me so far.* "I mean, both of them are highly suspicious. Both have been caught in at least one mutual lie. And beyond that, there's other suspicious stuff. Peter's alibis for the two murders are thin to non-existent."

Here Elijah broke in. "That's true, but it doesn't mean they did it."

"Don't assume you know where I'm going with this," Aaron grumbled. "Give me a chance to talk, here. What I was going to say was that being full of shit doesn't make them murderers. People cover stuff up for all kinds of reasons. We know that. Pretty much everyone we've talked to in this case has lied about *something*. I'm sure of it."

Elijah again nodded, but Grayson could tell from his expression that his young partner was surprised to be agreeing. This, in itself, felt like a barb and spurred Grayson on.

"They've all a bunch of rich spoiled creeps who clearly think they're above everyone else. They're used to getting their way and used to the rules bending in their favor whenever their interests require it. And they clearly have interests. No doubt about it. Leonard and Malinda have interests: maintaining their wealth and position, their daughter's future, the fucking windmills. Lark was just as bad, although we can strike him off our list. Peter, well, it's obvious what his interests are and the fact that he was willing to lie to try to weasel himself out of disappointing his parents further condemns him. Think about it. He dropped out and feared nothing more than disappointing people. This much is obvious from the convoluted ruse he and Fawn have kept going, this show they're putting on for her parents. Maybe his mom found out about him dropping out and laid into him. Maybe he snapped. He was studying to be a surgeon. It's not too much of a stretch to imagine he's got a doctor bag full of sharpened scalpels stashed away somewhere. Peter's weak willed, yes. It's clear he's got no balls. He lets the women in his life lead him around. But he fits a profile. These weak-kneed panty-waists can snap. They take out their frustrations. You know, like the guy from Psycho."

Elijah nodded condescendingly. That was the problem with these overeducated know-it-alls; they were so secure in their superiority, they didn't think you could see it when they were being condescending. "You got a problem with that theory?" Grayson growled.

"Well, I don't know," Elijah said cautiously. Grayson took a little pleasure in the fact that his partner seemed a little gun-shy after the dressing-down he'd given him. Good. "There are a couple of things. One: these murders *do* seem to replicate the ones in the seventies, for whatever reason. If Peter killed his mom because she found out about him dropping out, or in the middle of an argument or whatever, then why replicate the circumstances? How would he even know about it? He wouldn't remember it and nobody talks about it. The whole town pretends it never happened."

Grayson shrugged. "I don't see it as something to get hung up on. Who knows what kind of sick shit this kid is into. If he's a Norman Bates type. Maybe he's obsessed with the earlier murder because he fantasises about chopping people's heads off. Or maybe it was just to throw us off his trail."

Elijah didn't look too sure but didn't say anything.

"What else you got?" Grayson asked. "You said you had a couple of reasons."

"Well, you kind of alluded to this yourself, but Peter doesn't seem to have it in him, He's young, weak-willed, and naive. I don't see him planning and carrying any of this out. He seems too fragile. He seems like he'd have caved and confessed."

"Yeah, but that's what I'm saying," Grayson said. "Maybe he's got a double life going. There's the weak kid we see and the killer hiding in his skin. You're supposed to be the education one. Psychology and all of that B.S. Don't they teach you that people suppress stuff? That there's a whole other person under the surface."

"You're right about that," Elijah said grudgingly, conceding the point but not the argument.

"Well, how about *this*," Grayson said. "I said Peter did it, but I didn't say he was working alone. Fawn's clearly pulling his strings, maybe she pulled those strings too. Maybe she's the brains of the operation."

"I don't see it," Elijah said. "We've seen her protecting Peter. That seems to be her whole thing. Clearly she is in on the lie about the school. I'd believe she was the string-puller behind *that*. But that's for Peter's benefit. Why would she throw him into danger by pushing him into a murder?"

Grayson felt his jaw muscles tightening. Yes, Elijah was being more respectful, appropriately chastened after their recent dustup, but he just never stopped. Shooting down Aaron's every idea. Such a know it all. Such a little Mr. Perfect. Grayson became aware of something shifting in him, A reaction Something buried.

"Well if you hate all of my ideas so much, what the hell is the answer? If you're so damned smart?" Grayson was surprised at the sound of his own voice, its vehemence, the tense tremble at his words. His emotions were getting the better of him.

What was this all about?

"I don't think I have the answers," Elijah said, his face registering an irritating concern. "I just think it's important to keep an open mind."

"Who says my mind isn't open?" Grayson's growl increased in volume until it approached a roar. "Just because I have a theory doesn't mean my mind isn't open. What, am I supposed to proceed as a blank fucking slate?"

"I'm sorry," Elijah said with seeming sincerity. "I didn't mean anything. I just wanted to make sure you were open to other ideas…"

"Of course I am," Grayson retorted hotly. "If it was settled I'd be making an arrest instead of conducting interviews. You just think you know it all, don't you? Think you're perfect." The words had a familiar feel in his mouth, like they were ones he'd said again and again and then it hit him with the force of a sledgehammer, memories buried for decades, unearthed. He remembered his little brother, Quinn. He'd always been his dad's favorite. How did it take him this long to realize that Elijah's smugness, his confidence in his own superiority, reminded him of Quinn?

Everything came rushing back. Memories long unexamined, like a flood released by a bursting dam. His perfect brother. The dad who he was never good enough for. The reckless theft of a car. The accident. Little Larry.

And after that? Running away in fear he'd get caught.

"Are you okay?" Elijah asked. Grayson looked over enraged at the look of concern he saw on his young partner's face.

"Of course I'm okay," he growled. "What a fucking question."

Keep it together, man, he thought to himself, annoyed at the cathartic flood of emotion. What am I? One of these limp wristed pansies? Haunted by my childhood. Man up!

"Just follow my lead, okay?"

He glanced up and the second hand passed the twelve. Eight o'clock. Right on schedule, Peter and Fawn entered the hotel lobby. She was wearing a sweater and he a nice polo. Like a couple of preppies going to the country club. They crossed the hotel lobby with what seemed like a rehearsed reserve and Aaron knew that the script had been written by Fawn.

"Have a seat guys," Aaron said, gesturing to a couple of well-padded chairs by the lobby's large central area. Peter looked towards Fawn as if seeking permission.

"We doing this here?" she asked. "Shouldn't this be somewhere private?"

Grayson shrugged. "Why? We're just having a conversation. Nobody here cares what we're talking about." Just another way to keep them off balance. Fawn looked towards Peter and gestured with her eyebrows: a prompt.

Peter nervously cleared his throat. "I'd, uh…. we'd like to have a lawyer present."

"A lawyer?" Grayson said with a harsh chuckle. "What do you think this is? You're not under arrest. We're just having a *conversation* here. I'll be honest with you, I was pretty disappointed when I found out about the bill of goods you were selling, to your family, to us, to everybody. That right there is enough probable cause, enough suspicion to arrest you, Pete. It looks like someone trying to establish an alibi. But I decided to give you a chance to explain yourself. So, you really want to go down that road? Bring in the lawyers? Make this official instead of a friendly conversation? Or are you going to let me give you a second chance?"

As Grayson spoke, Peter's eyes darted around frenziedly: an animal caught in a headlight.

"Don't sweat it, kid," Grayson said in a mocking tone. "It's going to be alright. Just let us help you."

Peter stammered, then looked over at Fawn. Her brows were drawn in a tight line across her forehead.

"Fine," she said. "Let's have a conversation."

"Great," Aaron said, then made a point of turning his back towards Fawn, focusing his attention instead on Peter. The weak link. "So, Pete. How did you feel about your mom?"

"How did I feel about her?" he said with what seemed like sincere bewilderment. "I loved her. She was my mom. I loved her so much."

"Sure, you did," Grayson said noncommittally. "How about you, Fawn?"

"You did?" Aaron said, poking randomly hoping for a reaction. "She didn't give you a hard time? Busting your chops for trying to take her only son away from her?"

"No," said Fawn. "I was closer to her than I was my own mother. She was like family to me." Grayson could see that. Malinda was a real piece of work. No wonder Fawn was looking for a mellower mother figure.

"Okay," Aaron said. "Well how about your dad, Peter?"

Here, Peter frowned. "To be honest, detective? I didn't feel that close to him." Aaron noticed Fawn's eyes narrow as if she was worried her boyfriend was saying too much. Grayson didn't take this as evidence of collusion on a crime, necessarily. She just didn't want the boy spilling his guts and accidentally making them look guilty, whether they were or not. In any case, Peter kept going. "We didn't connect too much. He became so devoted to his religion and it wasn't one we shared so it, at times, made him almost feel like a stranger. His new beliefs pushed a wedge between him and mom too and it was hard not to see this as one of the instigators of the divorce. So I think I had some resentment."

Aaron nodded. He had to give the boy points for speaking his mind, although it really did nothing to clarify the question of innocence or guilt. "Well, I get where you're coming from. That Muslim stuff aint for everyone. I don't know about you, but it always rubbed me the wrong way how the women are pretty much slaves to the men. And they wrap them up like a bunch of mummies. Creepy stuff."

Grayson noticed Elijah roll his eyes and Peter and Fawn looked appalled. He couldn't help but grin, getting a kick out of the poking and jabbing he was doing.

"It's not like that," Peter said, suddenly coming to the defence of the same belief system he was throwing under the bus thirty seconds earlier. "He didn't take on a bunch of socially conservative or old fashioned views. It's that Islam became such a driving force in his life. He became so devoted to his God that he had less time for the rest of us. But the effect was it drove us apart. The only way I had to connect with him at all were those rare moments when we could connect *through* his beliefs. Like when I needed advice. He became very thoughtful, very wise at counselling me on moral questions like forgiveness. ”

Elijah, who had remained mostly silent, suddenly jumped in. “Why forgiveness, specifically?” Aaron had been annoyed when Elijah opened his mouth but when he heard the question, appreciated the angle his partner was exploring.

Unbidden, Fawn answered on her partner’s behalf. “Abdoullah always said that everyone sins and thus everyone needed repentance. It wasn’t something he viewed as specific to him in particular; it was a general principle. Since people inevitably sin, seeking forgiveness or repentance is something everyone needs in their lives. The concept was important to him; it was something he mentioned frequently.”

Aaron couldn’t tell whether this was a real answer or some kind of diversionary tactic to send him in the wrong direction. He knew, however, that he’d do better grilling Peter than Fawn. Fawn was too clearly calculating in her answers and suggestions to Peter. Strategizing. Peter, on the other hand, was all emotion. If Aaron pushed the right button he might let something slip.

“How old were you when he converted?” Aaron asked.

“I only remember him as a Muslim,” Peter said. “My whole life. That’s why it always seems weird to me when I hear someone call him Bill. He’s always been Abdoullah as far as I’m concerned.”

“But you said the religion drove in a wedge? How’s that if it was always a factor?”

“It’s just that over the years it became a bigger part of his life,” Peter said. “Eventually, it seemed to push almost everything else out.”

"Did you ever hear why he converted?" Aaron said. "I don't really know," Peter said.

"It always sounded to me like it was a sudden conversion," Elijah suggested, speaking half to Peter, half to Aaron. "Almost a surprise to the people in his life."

"That's true," Peter said. "That's what I always heard."

"But I guess that's the nature of these moments of religious inspiration," Elijah said. "They come over people suddenly."

"Inspiration?" Aaron said quietly. "I don't know. To me it sounds more like influence than inspiration." Elijah, thankfully, didn't take that bait and turn it into some kind of argument. Aaron found himself annoyed at the direction the interview was going. It had turned into some kind of lecture on comparative religion. If Lark's religion had anything to do with the murder's it was logistical, circumstantial, not tied to the doctrine of his belief system. They were wasting time on this topic, getting into the weeds, not doing anything to cull their suspect surplus. Time to get back to their main focus.

"So, Pete, did your mom find out that you dropped out of your program? Did she find out about the lies?"

Peter became visibly nervous, his face reddening and the muscles in his neck tightening. *Good,* Aaron through. *Squirm.* Grayson enjoyed turning up the heat because he knew that Peter was such a good candidate for caving under pressure.

"I don't think she ever knew," he said with what sounded like contrition. "But she suspected. She asked a lot of questions."

"Hmmm," Aaron said, "And so, I guess that's the reason you killed her?"

The mood in the room shifted drastically from one of submission to outrage. Peter started stammering and Fawn's eyes flashed with an anger that she seemed to have inherited from Malinda.

"This interview is over," she shouted.

"Hold on, hold on…" Elijah said, placing himself between the couple and the door. Grayson slumped back into one of the comfortable chairs and pressed a finger to a suddenly throbbing temple. Everything seemed to be swirling around him.

Dammit. He had to admit, that one was a misstep. He'd been doing what he always did: following his instincts. He had a sense that cracks were forming in Peter's resolve, that he might be one big push away from shattering and admitting what he'd done. At that moment, the accusation seemed like a good idea. Obviously, in retrospect, not one of his best. Maybe he'd been doing it too long. Maybe he was losing his mojo. He wasn't as young as he used to be. He'd been up late thinking the night before. Has it accomplished anything or only worn him out? Draining the energy out of his old man's brain and preparing him for a morning of failure. Suddenly, a half-remembered dream bubbled up, him in hospice at the end of a life full of regrets. For as long as he could remember, Grayson had been driven by the goal of recognition, acclaim. Ever since childhood when nothing he did seemed to be enough for a father unreasonably enamoured by a "perfect" son, he'd wanted to throw his success in the face of the world. His old man, his superiors on the force, his critical ex-wife: everyone. Aaron Grayson wanted to be the top of his field, the country's best detective, and he wanted everyone to know it. But was it too late for that? Wasn't fame a young man's game?

At that moment, he felt a gentle tap on his shoulder. He opened his eyes. It was Elijah.

"I've talked them into staying," he said, continuing in a very sincere and respectful tone. "But they're skittish. I think it might go better if they talked to me. Can I take a shot at it?"

For a split second, Grayson felt the rage build up. How dare he try to take over his investigation? But it faded. No, Elijah was right. Grayson had spooked them, Almost scared them off. It was the cliche. Good cop bad cop. They'd had enough of the bad cop. Grayson had scared them, annoyed them. It was time to bring in the friendlier approach. Sometimes it worked. Sometimes the bad cop loosened them up so much that they spilled when faced with the friendlier partner. After facing aggression, the friendly face could lead them into a false sense of security, wrongly believing that this cop is their friend, loyal to their needs rather than the truth.

"Take a shot at it kid," Aaron said.

"Okay," Elijah said. "Can you let me do it my way? Even if you're not sure you agree with me or where it's going, just let me ask my questions? Just trust me, I have ideas and, believe it or not, I have instincts that I follow too. They may not be the same ones as yours, but I'm capable of going with my gut just the same as you are."

Grayson smiled, feeling an almost fatherly affection for the young detective. Because that's what being a dad was like, right? Elijah drove him crazy, frustrated the hell out of him, but he also took pride in his accomplishments. He was a smart kid and, yes, he was smart about making connections and has a strong sense of intuition. It occurred to Grayson that maybe *this* was his path. Maybe he was too old to distinguish himself as a super cop. As a rockstar detective. But perhaps the problem was trying to do it all on his own. Hell, even Dirty Harry had a partner.

Maybe the way to distinguish himself *was* as a part of a team. Elijah could be the youthful facade, the good looking face, photogenic and ready for the cameras. Grayson could distinguish himself as the wise veteran. Between the two of them they could hit the front page if they could clear up this mess. They could be the new Einstein and Smith. A duo to catch the imagination of the public. He decided he'd let the kid take his shot. He'd try to step back and let the kid ask what he was going to ask, even if he didn't agree with it. He wouldn't undermine him while he was asking questions. He'd save any feedback for after, when they had some privacy.

We'll see how this goes….

"Thanks for asking, kid," Aaron said. "You got it. I'm giving you the wheel." He grinned. "Don't fuck it up."

Elijah adjusted his tie and approached the couple. He tried to push down feelings of anxiety but they were undeniable. Did Grayson really trust him or was he only taking him up on his offer out of pity. He *had* disappointed his partner recently. His psyche still stung from the dressing down he'd received after briefly joining forces with Dahlia. He'd talked himself into it, saying that they were running a parallel investigation to the main one and that theirs, focusing on the older case, wouldn't interfere with the primary one. But he had to admit he was wrong. Even if he wasn't outright lying to Grayson, he'd been lying by omission. There was no justifiable reason not to include his partner in his plans.

He was not going to make the same mistake again. He'd be honest with Aaron, even at the risk of his wrath. And now, he had permission to pursue his investigation as he saw fit.

Here goes, he thought. Elijah addressed both of them simultaneously as he asked:

"Do you believe in Hugh Slaughter?"

He watched them closely for any reaction to the name. The reaction was hard to ignore: laughter.

"The local boogeyman?" Fawn said, as if she were not a local herself: sheltered, perhaps, by her wealth and privilege.

"Of course not, detective," said Peter.

Elijah had been hoping for something, perhaps a glimmer of tension or recognition that might reveal that one or both of them had been using the myth to their own advantage, but there was nothing but derision and dismissiveness. In a way it was a relief; the two were not superstitious. Perhaps this would help ground the investigation in reality. As much as Hugh Slaughter did seem to be a factor at play, Elijah felt off his game when dealing with the supernatural and/or mythological elements. It was all beyond his police training and beyond the usual imaginings of his rational mind.

He was aware of another reaction. Still seated in his comfy chair in the hotel lobby, Grayson rolled his eyes. Elijah could almost feel his elder partner holding his tongue.

But could he rule out the supernatural so quickly? He had experienced *something* in the shadow of the wind turbine in the woods the previous night. Something had come over him. Was it a ghost or demon or something else? Who knew? But the fact that it was beyond his ability to explain suggested that it at least met some definition of "supernatural." He remembered that Peter had made a comment about a, perhaps similar, feeling overtaking him the night of his mother's death.

"Peter," he said. "You mentioned that the night your mother was murdered that you *felt* something.

"That's true," Peter said. "I did. But it wasn't Hugh Slaughter. I don't believe in that nonsense. I wasn't raised to believe in fairytales"

"Fine," Elijah said. "It wasn't an evil spirit. It wasn't Hugh Slaughter. But *was* it that you experienced?"

"Frankly, I have no idea," Peter said. "It was like I could feel something in the air. Pulses of fear and anxiety. The air got thick and it felt like something was there. A presence of some kind."

"Me too," Fawn said. "I've felt it twice."

Peter nodded. "Yes."

"When was the second time?" Elijah asked.

"The second time was last night," Peter continued, his eyes haunted. "Right before I found out about my dad."

Twice. One on the night of each murder. And Elijah had felt it, felt something, on the previous night as well. Perhaps the same thing.

Still, to Elijah, it sounded just as supernatural as the local myths and theories about Hugh Slaughter. It was the same kind of unscientific language, the language of folklore and conspiracy theory. Part of his brain fought against embracing this seemingly magical thinking.

"But doesn't that sound a lot like Hugh Slaughter?" Elijah asked. "A presence? How is that different from a ghost or some kind of supernatural killer? That sounds like the same type of superstition you guys were just condemning."

"I don't know *what* it was," Peter said. "I never said it was a ghost. *You* did. You're trying to put words in my mouth. I don't believe in the local legends. I'm only reporting what I felt. That doesn't mean I buy into the stories."

He was right. And the important fact was: Peter's experience mirrored his own. Elijah was not inclined to believe urban legends, but he too had experienced mysterious sensations that overwhelmed his emotions. They had *all* felt it. At the same time.

"Hey, uh, guys," Aaron said. Elijah looked over. "I know I said I'd leave you to your line of questioning, but is this it? If we're going to discuss thoughts and feelings and ghosts instead of facts, maybe we should let these two. You and I can speak privately, Detective Riley."

Elijah, still haunted by the revelation that this same weird state that had overcome him was experienced by others, simply nodded.

"Sure," he said. "You two can go."

Elijah had half-convinced himself that the agitation he had felt in the shadow of the turbine was simply a mild emotional disturbance, perhaps brought on by fatigue or the nature of the case. Something internal. But if it had been experienced, nearly identically, by these two, then it *had* to be external. But what? It was completely outside of his experience, outside of the rules of both science and police work.

What had come over him?

"We're not done with you two yet," Aaron said as they walked towards the front door of the hotel. "Don't leave town."

Peter scoffed and Fawn said, "The storm will see to that. The roads out of town are impassable."

Elijah saw a quick grin pass over his partner's face. Grayson always got a kick out of a successful barb. Aaron watched them go and then, when the door swung shut, turned to his partner.

"Okay," he said. "So what the hell was that about?"

Even given the dismissive attitude, Elijah could sense that something had shifted, that his partner was at least trying to give him some benefit of the doubt. For this small favor, he was grateful.

"I know this is going to sound crazy. It does to me too. But I'm just going to say it. Last night, before we found out about the murder, Dahlia and I went to find the location of the seventy-two murder."

"What was that supposed to accomplish?" Grayson asked. "I know you think the earlier murder was relevant to the case, and you know what I think about your theories, but even if I agreed: what's the point of visiting a decades-old murder site? Any physical evidence is going to be long gone."

"I know," Elijah said. "I just thought being there might reveal something I hadn't thought of. The site was close to one of those turbines and as I was investigating, I was overtaken by this weird feeling. Like someone was pacing behind me, unseen. Or watching me from a distance. It was like this jerk I could feel, tugging on my consciousness."

Aaron shook his head. "Well, what's that supposed to mean? That it was Hugh Slaughter sneaking up on you? Or a ghost? Little green men from Mars, maybe?"

Elijah frowned at his dismissive tone. "I'm not saying that. I don't know *what* it meant. I only know what I felt."

"Feelings," Aaron said in a disgusted tone. "What is it with people talking about feelings like that proves something? Like it's evidence? Evidence is what you can see or feel. It's something you can measure. How you feel doesn't mean shit in a murder investigation. Listen, we can't go down this road. We can bring in suspects and ask them about folklore and fairytales. It's nonsense. You want to know what I think happened? You told me that you went there thinking the location would 'reveal' something to you." Elijah started to object but Aaron stopped him by holding up his hand, palm-up. "Let me finish, okay? You wanted the murder site to show you something. I don't know if you even know what you mean by that, but it's not police work. It's not what they teach you in the academy. It sounds like you came into the situation primed to experience something, so open-minded you were practically begging to see or feel something out of the ordinary. Maybe all the local hogwash about Hugh Slaughter had gotten to you and part of you wanted to join in on the fun."

"That's not it," Elijah said. "I swear it isn't. Listen…"

But Grayson cut him off before he could continue.

"Or maybe it was Dahlia. You know, I smelled weed on her when we first talked to her." Grayson tapped the side of his nose. "I've got a hound-dog's nose. Always have. And even now, with my creaky bones and failing eyesight, my nose never lets me down. I know she's a druggie. Did you smoke a joint with her?"

"What? No…" Elijah was insulted by the suggestion but, still, felt a twinge of guilt because Dahlia had offered when she'd first suggested a partnership.

"Well, maybe she slipped you something. A hallucinogen, maybe. LSD. Maybe she drugged you and what you felt was drugs."

"Why would she do that?" he asked.

"Maybe she came to town to do some killing, avenging her mother's death, and is trying to get you on her side to help push suspicion away from her and towards Hugh Slaughter."

"That's preposterous," Elijah said.

"More preposterous than a creepy feeling having a bearing on a murder case."

Elijah had to admit that he had a point.

"But that's what I've been trying to tell you, Grayson," he said. "It *wasn't* just my feeling. Fawn and Peter just said it. They felt the same thing."

. Aaron scoffed. "Those two would say anything to throw us off track."

"They mentioned it. I didn't say a word about my feelings. The feeling had to come from somewhere."

"Again with the feelings. Kid, it doesn't mean anything. Just that you're too fucking sensitive."

"Listen," Elijah said, in the most sincerely pleading delivery he could manage. "Let me try one thing. It'll seem crazy. Maybe it is. But just give me a shot."

Grayson grumbled but agreed. "Fine. Whatever. We're partners. We can try something your way on occasion. But you promise me, if it doesn't lead anywhere, drop this and let's get back to the real world."

"Fine," Elijah said, then led Grayson upstairs to his room. When they were there, he placed a call to the reception desk and put it on speaker.

"Good morning, sir," a man said with refined politeness.

"Hi. I'm Detective Elijah Riley and this is my partner, Aaron Grayson. We're conducting an investigation and would like to ask you a few questions."

"Of course, sir," the man said with practiced manners.

"I was wondering if you felt anything unusual yesterday."

"I'm not sure I know what you mean," the man said, his voice clearly reflecting confusion.

"I mean, yesterday evening, shortly after sunset, did you feel any surprising emotions? A feeling of panic? Or paranoia? Being watched or in danger."

"I did," he said, his voice suddenly lowering to a near-whisper. "I was on duty when I suddenly felt something just like what you're talking about. Chills down my spine. It hit me in waves. Fear. Paranoia. I felt like someone was hiding, about to spring on me. And it wasn't just me. Other customers in the lobby, locals having dinner in the restaurant, came to the reception desk making similar complaints. One lady asked me if I could call the police and when I asked why she couldn't say beyond the fact that she didn't feel safe. I felt so unsettled that I left my station and locked myself in the staff room until it passed." Here he paused for a moment. "When whatever it was, passed."

Elijah looked towards Grayson, who shrugged, whispering behind his hand. "I don't know. It could be an act. Or mass hysteria." Although he didn't agree, Elijah could tell from his delivery that he was a bit bewildered and knew that his scepticism was getting hard to justify.

Elijah nodded. "Let me ask you another question," he said. "Did you ever experience anything like this before?"

"Yes," he said. "Once. Recently. I was working security that night because we were short staffed."

"And what night was that?" Elijah asked. "Did anything noteworthy happen that night."

"Oh yes," the man said without hesitation. "It was the night that Eleanor Pomeroy was murdered."

Elijah looked over at Grayson with a triumphant look. His partner, for once, seemed to be at a loss for words.

The moment was broken by a knock on their door. As Elijah thanked the receptionist and hung up, Grayson moved to the door and opened it.

Dahlia was there.

Grayson smirked as if he'd been expecting her. "Well, look what the cat dragged in," he said.

CHAPTER SIXTEEN
THE UNHOLY TRINITY

Dahlia had been offered and taken a seat. A wooden chair, by the window, overlooking the snow covered street. She realized now that this had been a mistake because as soon as she sat. Grayson stood and began pacing in front of her, pacing, asking questions.

She thought she'd agreed to a seat, to a conversation, but now it was clear: she'd stepped into a trap. She was being interrogated.

"So, I'm on your list now," she said, trying for a defiant tone but not pulling it off. She could hear the nervousness in her tone.

"Damned right," he said. "I was just telling your buddy Elijah that we've got too many suspects but you're quickly becoming my favorite."

"I didn't do it," she said.

"Uh-huh," Grayson said as if barely hearing her. "See, here's the thing: you rubbed me the wrong way from the beginning, horning in, throwing your weight around, trying to derail our investigation. You were doing that from that first conversation and then it got worse when you tried to steer my partner off the straight and narrow into your wild theories and bullshit and this seemingly irrelevant cold case. And I've dealt with interference before. The press, sometimes. Families of the victims can be a pain in the ass. Well-meaning locals. But I didn't really get your angle. But now that I know it, it all falls into place. Like the pieces of the fucking puzzle. You're from here but not from here. You're doing a dissertation on some bullshit topic, the special bonds in a small town or what the hell ever, but suddenly you're horning in on this murder that just happens to occur. You're a pain in the ass, but I totally don't get your angle. NOW I do."

Dahlia tensed up for what was coming.

"Because we know that the seventy-one victim was your mother, Lucy Crane. Suddenly, a story emerges. Your mom was murdered and you're coming back to take revenge. You know about these assholes that she hung out with. The rich folks who looked down their noses at her. Decided she was trash. Low class. Kept her around as a joke, maybe? You think they killed her. Maybe you know something? I haven't figured that out yet… but in your mind or in reality they killed her. Whether they did or not we can work out later, but the important part is: there's your motive. And suddenly it's all simple. You come back. You take out Eleanor. Then you start stirring shit up. Getting the locals all agitated. Doing the same to my partner. You divert attention to your mother's murder, suggesting that maybe it's the same guy. Maybe it's related. The irony is, the answer *does* lie in the seventy-two murder but you're in the clear because your mother was never identified. It's perfect. Maybe it's extra satisfying for you, using your own mother's murder to get away with killing her killers."

Dahlia had to admit, it was a pretty compelling story. And a hard one to listen to. She knew it wasn't true, of course. It was wrong in most of its details. She'd had no idea her mother was murdered. She'd only just found out herself. Maybe she'd lied to herself about her reasons for returning. In a sense she'd returned for a bit of self-therapy, to work out where she'd come from. But all the dark secrets in her mother's past had been secrets to her as well as everyone else. Still, Grayson's story got to her. Her mother's death still throbbed in her soul like a fresh wound and his story was like a shower of salt on the gash. Part of her *did* crave justice, revenge on whoever had murdered her mother. If it was the Larks, then maybe part of her would have wanted to kill them. It was all almost too much to process. She felt her breathing tighten and her eyes moisten. She didn't want to give Grayson the satisfaction of an emotional response, didn't want to give him emotion to misinterpret and didn't want to provide fodder for his shameless gloating. She took a breath and pulled herself upright, determined to fight through, to fight him.

"You were running around thinking you'd outsmarted us but we finally got you!"

"That's a nice story," Dahlia said, trying to force ice into her veins to suppress her emotions. "But it's all a figment of your imagination. Besides, I have alibis for both murders."

"Maybe you had an accomplice," Grayson spat, sounding uncertain of himself even as he said it.

Dahlia laughed derisively. "An accomplice? Who? I don't know *anyone* in town. I haven't been here since I was a child. Besides, if I *had* done it, which I obviously didn't, do I really strike you as the type to need an accomplice? I've been on my own my whole life."

"Well, why have you been trying to rope Riley into your schemes then?" Grayson said. "If you do it all yourself."

"Listen, the connection between the current case and the one from the seventies, that was *me* that made that connection. My connection with Riley was mutually beneficial. I benefited from a police contact and he benefitted from the connections that I made *on my own*. And all along you were on autopilot, sticking to your gut and your presuppositions."

The corner of her mouth turned up into a half-smile at his reaction. She'd pushed a button. His face reddened, the veins on his neck and temple popped out. He was furious.

"Admit it," she shouted, flecks of spit spraying as he did. "You did it. I haven't worked out all the details, but you're behind it."

"Listen," she said. "I didn't come here for this kind of treatment. Your accusations are full of holes. It's clear you've never liked me but you've never been able to clearly explain what it is. It's pretty clear to me that you've got a problem with women. A problem with them thinking for themselves, for not immediately submitting to your wishes. You hate what I represent as a modern woman." Grayson began to interject but she continued. "Like I said, there's a reason I came here. To share information. As I said, my and Riley's partnership was to our mutual benefit. He's got some good ideas and access to resources. I have ideas of my own. I've turned up something new and I came here in good faith intending to assist you in your investigation. So, do you want to hear it or not."

Grayson stammered, clearly unprepared for this. Eventually he said, "You'd better. If you have information you're not sharing you're obstructing this investigation. A crime. You might be aiding and abetting the murderer."

"So, I'm not the murderer now?" she said with a laugh. "And you'd like to hear what I know?"

"Yes, dammit," Grayson said.

"Say pretty please," she said, with a girlish grin.

"Don't push your luck," he said. "Or I'll slap you in cuffs."

Dahlia didn't respond to that jab and instead said, "Malinda invented the Hugh Slaughter myth. She admitted it to me right before she took a shot at me with a pistol."

Elijah's eyes widened. "She *shot* at you."

"That's right," she said. "She didn't admit to the crime but the attempt at murdering me seems to confirm it. If she didn't do it herself, maybe her husband did. Maybe she invented Slaughter as part of the cover up. I just found out *all* of this, including the fact that my mother was the victim. If I'd know, maybe I would have come back for revenge, but I didn't. I never knew a thing."

"And why did you come to us with this?" Grayson said with a neutral expression. "After all the trouble we've had."

"Because my mom was murdered," she said. "I wasn't sure why I was looking into things before, but now it's even more important to me. Someone killed my mom, mutilated her, and left her to rot like trash. I want them brought to justice and you guys are my best bet at making that happen."

Elijah had been listening with interest. This was huge. His senses were charged with the revelation, and he could almost feel his skin tingling. Without consulting his partner, he jumped in with his own revelation. "I've made my own connections, Dahlia. I just established that the weird reaction I felt right around the same time as the murder wasn't just a figment of my imagination. Peter and Fawn both felt it and we've established through an unbiased interview that a random sampling of hotel employees and customers felt the same thing. *And,* people felt it at the time of the first murder, Eleanor's."

Dahlia's brows narrowed. "But what does it mean?"

"I don't know," Elijah said, honestly stumped. "But your information is valuable. Malinda's admission solidifies the fact that the Hugh Slaughter myth is meaningless. There was no Hugh Slaughter, no supernatural murderer, and the ill wind that seems to blow through town whenever there's a murder isn't a demon returning from hell to haunt Mount Hugh. It's…. something else."

"But what?"

Elijah shook his head and shrugged, presenting his empty palms as a visual demonstration of his cluelessness. "No idea. But the weird feeling, which felt very disturbing and very real at the time, and all of the talk had me halfway believing something supernatural was going on. Now I know better. Whatever the explanation is, it's something in the real world. Something that can be measured and tracked. Right now, this is our main question: what is triggering this feeling?"

Aaron resisted the urge to just let go. To explode, to let his temper go. It sometimes felt good to do so, and he imagined it would be gratifying after the nonsense he'd been hearing. These two young people, trying to hijack his case with a bunch of nonsense. Still, he supposed there *were* things that required explanation. Like it or not, there did seem to be an independently verifiable effect that gripped people around the time of the murders. He had no more idea than the other two what this might be, and the only small consolation he took was that Elijah had just made it clear that he would look for answers in the real world. In evidence. In science. At least that was something he could understand and, when they uncovered an explanation, maybe it would all make sense.

Aaron had grudgingly realized that his best path to fame might be at the side of his partner, just like Einstein and Smith. Was it possible that this girl would prove useful as well. He pushed down the impulse to lay into these fools and forced himself to hear them out.

"But how does this help us solve the case?" he asked. "I mean, maybe there's a mystery here. A gas leak or something in the water? But what does it have to do with the case? Is your theory that the same thing that's making people feel all worked up is causing them to commit homicide?"

"I don't know," Dahlia said. "Maybe not. But maybe someone is using this. Whatever it is that causes this fear, maybe someone has been using it to their advantage. To aid in their crimes, or maybe to hide them. The fact that it corresponds so closely to the two murders has to mean something. If there's a connection, then finding the source might lead us to our killer or at least help us narrow down the field."

Elijah nodded assent. Grayson grumbled. He hated this. "If this gets out of control, with the supernatural stuff, it's going to make us look like fools in the media. I don't want your tangents to ruin my image."

"Why are you so concerned with your image?" Dahlia asked. "Sometimes it seems like that's more important to you than solving the case."

"I just don't like being made to look foolish," he said, but inside his mind he continued considering the angles of press coverage. He didn't like the direction these two were going, but if their unorthodox methods could help catch the hero, then the result was ultimately the same. He could reap the rewards: branded by the media as a hero. Maybe the press would have fun with the daughter of the victim helping them solve related murders and the young partner, but *he,* Aaron Grayson, would step in as the lead investigator. The one in charge. The hero. So he'd try to stop fighting, start working *with* them and see if there was any benefit to be wrought.

Grayson let out a deep breath before speaking. "Okay, kids," he said. "Against my better judgement, I'm going to agree to look into this bullshit. It's annoying, I don't know what it means, but it seems like it might be *something.* But we need some ground rules. We'll investigate this stuff and see if it leads to anything. If it leads to a killer being captured."

"Okay," said Dahlia. "But what are these ground rules?"

"Glad you asked," Grayson said with a sarcastic grin. "When you write about this case, you include me in your story as the lead investigator." He glanced at Elijah. "Riley too. Put him in there."

Dahlia, again, was completely bewildered by his continued preoccupation with press coverage. She looked over at Elijah and saw it in his eyes. Imploring. *Just agree with it.* She was annoyed because she didn't like being controlled but, on the other hand, couldn't see the harm in it. She hadn't been planning on writing the mystery and its resolution up as that kind of narrative but she could be flexible. "Okay, fine," she said. "You got it, Grayson. I'll include you in whatever I write up. Both of you. I'll agree to it because nothing is more important to me than bringing the killer to justice."

"Great," said Aaron. "So, we're working together. Let's try not to drive each other crazy. Where do we start?"

After a moment's thought, Elijah answered. "A timeline. Let's note the times, as accurately as we can, of everything from the mass murders to the bouts of hysteria."

"That's good," Dahlia said. "Then we can look for patterns."

"Okay, great," Grayson said without much enthusiasm.

The room's phone rang and Elijah answered.

"Phone call for Dahlia Crane," said the receptionist's voice. "Is she there?"

"Yes," said Elijah in mild confusion.

"Connecting," said the receptionist.

"Hello, babe," said a woman's voice.

"Uh, it's your partner," said Elijah, holding his hand over the receiver.

"Oh, thanks," said Dahlia. "I was expecting the call and told them downstairs where I'd be."

Dahlia took the phone and walked over to the corner of the room and began relaying recent events and revelations in a low tone while Elijah and Grayson began building their timeline. Elijah took notes on a portable dry erase board they'd brought for this type of notetaking.

"So, we have our two main events: two periods where this mysterious thing has overtaken people," said Aaron. "What do we think this is? Hypnosis? Chemicals?"

"I don't see how," said Elijah. "I mean, it affected me out in the field and these random people in town, pretty much simultaneously." As he said the word "simultaneously" he indicated their timeline. "I don't think chemicals could manage that precision. And obviously, there was no hypnotist out on the edge of the forest."

"Well, I guess a hypnotist could have planted a suggestion earlier..." Even as Grayson said it, he knew he didn't like it. He was floundering in the weeds with annoyingly contrived theories. The kind of conspiracy theories delusional men who imagined a world of impossible secrets indulged in. Wackos who lived in basements.

"When would the hypnotist have gotten to *me*?" asked Elijah.

"I don't know," Grayson said. "The hotel? You were at the hotel and so were the other affected folks we know of."

Elijah shook his head. "Doesn't hold up. How was it triggered at that specific time? What could have possibly been the signal?"

"You're right," said Grayson, almost embarrassed at his inane thought process when forced to deal with this intractable problem. "It's dumb. Garbage. But how the hell do we make sense of this?"

Across the room, Dahlia's hand, holding the phone, was trembling.

"Your *mother*?" Naomi said.

Dahlia stifled a sob, swallowed it, and the result was more trembling. She couldn't afford to let Elijah and Grayson see her losing it. Especially Grayson. She was the unwanted partner and Grayson clearly resented her womanhood. If he saw her breaking down it would seem to confirm to him all of his biases. She was weak. She couldn't hack it.

"That's right," said Dahlia. "Murdered by the side of a road out in the wilderness. Alone."

"Come home, babe," said Naomi. "Let the police handle it. You shared what you know. Let them finish it. It's their job."

"I can't," Dahlia said. "The storm has completely clogged the mountain passes. Nobody can get in or out of town until it's cleared. Maybe tomorrow."

"What was that sound?" Naomi asked with sudden concern.

"I don't know what you mean," Dahlia responded.

"Was that a gunshot?" Naomi said. "And I feel like I hear a helicopter in the background. What's happening there?"

Dahlia looked around her in confusion, glancing out the window.

"There's nothing…" she started but then she felt it. Something dangerous lurking just outside her vision. Hidden but ready to spring. She felt an attack of vertigo, nausea, the world spinning. She sat on the edge of her bed.

"You feel that?" Elijah said in a terrified whisper.

"Yes," Grayson said reluctantly, through clenched teeth. "Dammit, I do."

"What is it, babe?" Naomi asked with increasing tension. "What's happening there? Are you in danger?"

"It's nothing," Dahlia said with a certainty she did not feel. It was all so confusing because while her senses of sight and sound told her that there was no danger present, *another* sense, one that was outside of the usual five, told her a different story, that danger was imminent, that it was everywhere. There were eyes on her. A crosshair. A twisted finger curled around an invisible trigger. "Just stay on the line with me, baby. Stay with me. We'll get through it together."

"What is it?" Aaron said. "What is this feeling?"

"Does it feel like there's something behind the walls?" Elijah asked. "Something nearby that's hidden?"

Aaron nodded, almost unwillingly. "Yes," he said. "I can feel it. Something coming for us." He closed his eyes. It was like something from a half-remembered nightmare. An unthinkable terror pulled from his deepest subconscious. He tried to fight it but could feel it pulling at him, like an undercurrent threatening to suck him down into the depths of fear. Aaron took a deep breath and then walked over to the window. Looking out, he saw locals running, half-sliding in the snow, running towards their homes, panicked. The effect had clearly spread beyond their room. Aaron pulled his gun from his holster and moved towards the door.

"I don't know what this is," Aaron said. "We might be under attack."

Elijah followed behind him. "Stay here," he said to Dahlia who was huddled in the corner.

"Don't be scared, Naomi," he heard her say between sobs. "I feel it too, but don't be scared…"

Aaron shakily put one foot in front of the other, picking his way stumblingly down the hall. Every shadow seemed to hold the threat of attack. Even the walls, mundanely papered in a pattern of small yellow flowers, seemed to hold the threat of an impending ambush, as if there were forces laying in wait to emerge.

Fuck, thought Grayson. Maybe this is something beyond human understanding. A ghost or a demon.

Aaron could feel it. Everywhere and nowhere. Pressing down on him, like an intangible weight. Not seen or heard or smelled but somehow sensed, vaguely, as if by some vague vestigial sensory organ. Aaron pressed his eyes closed and massaged his temple, still holding his pistol with the other hand. At any second it could emerge. To attack.

"Stay back, Riley," he said. "Go back to the room. It's too dangerous."

"No," Elijah said. "We're partners. In this together."

There's got to be an explanation, Grayson thought, but the evidence he *felt* told him differently. It was a tug of war between his rational, grounded, mind and this primitive fear he felt coursing through his consciousness. Was he sensing something supernatural or maybe *hearing* something? Something growling? A noise vibrating through the pipes?

Grayson felt his knees begin to buckle and then… nothing.

The sensation faded just as quickly as it had appeared. The world made sense again. Grayson straightened up, fighting the wobbliness he felt in his knees. Grayson looked at Elijah and an understanding passed between them.

"Damn," Grayson said. In that moment, the two shared a rare moment of mutual vulnerability. For that brief instant, Grayson's carefully maintained gruff persona had fallen away like a curtain blown back in the wind. His aggressiveness, his exacting critique of the world around him, was gone. Similarly, Elijah faced him, an open book. "You better go check on the girl," Aaron said. "I'm going to check downstairs."

The lobby was in panic but this seemed like the normal version, not the artificially amped up fear and paranoia they'd experienced a moment before.

"What happened?" he asked the man behind the registration desk.

"There's been a murder," he said, clearly in shock.

"What?" Grayon half-shouted, presenting his badge.

"At the main dining room of the hotel." Grayson was very familiar with the room. He and Elijah had shared breakfast there a little over an hour before, prior to their meeting with Fawn and Peter.

Another murder, thought Grayson. Just what we need…

Back in the room, Dahlia hung up the phone. Peter leant over here where she huddled in the corner beside the bed.

"Are you okay?" Peter asked.

"I'm fine now," she said. "But it was rough there for a while."

Elijah leaned down, holding out a hand to her. Grasping it, she let him help pull her to her feet.

"There was no denying it this time," she said.

"I know," Elijah responded, as the two walked towards the room's window with its view down on mainstreet and the mountain rising in the distance. "Even Grayson felt it."

"And it wasn't just him," she said. "*Naomi* did too."

"What?" Elijah said, shocked and excited at this new information.

"She thought she heard gunshots and helicopters. She was terrified. We both were. It was like she was somehow experiencing the terror over the phone line."

Elijah's mind raced. Suddenly, an answer suggested itself. If the fear was being spread across the phone line, then its delivery system must be sound. But what could produce such a sound? His eyes, scanning the tableau visible through the window, landed on the answer, in the distance.

He looked up and Dahlia's eyes met his. A look of understanding passed between them. She'd pieced it together too. In the same moment.

"The turbines," she said.

Elijah nodded. "It's the only possible explanation." They shared a grim smile. They were close now. "If the killer is using the turbines to sow paranoia and fear, maybe to cover his tracks, then he's very clever."

"Maybe so," said Dahlia. "But I'm clever too. And I have a plan. We'll take this killer down." As she said it she made a promise, not just to herself but to her mother as well. She would be remembered.

She would be avenged.

Chapter Seventeen
Busted Part 1

He wouldn't have admitted it to anyone, but he was shaken.

Grayson was used to being in control. Sure, Elijah might argue that he lacked a certain measure of *self*-control. He'd heard that one before. He'd even been pushed into a few meetings with police psychologists over the years that had been selling that hogwash, that had told him he had "anger issues," but the fact remained that Grayson was the one steering his own ship. Everything he did was a result of his decisions. If he flew off the handle it was his own impulses leading him to do so and he was okay with that. Often, as he'd seen so many times over the years, losing it could be the right move. It was all about timing. Flying off the handle had broken more than one case. Anyway, regardless of whether it worked out or not, whether he had anger issues or not, it was *him* behind the steering wheel.

But this had been different. When that weird spell had overtaken him and everyone else in town apparently, that mass hysteria or whatever you wanted to call it, he hadn't been in his right mind. He was thinking like a different person. Frankly, that was scary. Grayson was getting older. He already had worries about losing his grip and slipping into senility. His dream of himself alone in hospice care crept unbidden into his conscious mind.

When he'd heard about the latest murder, he was happy at the excuse to get out of the hotel. To move, to act. Doing something would help him to get out of his mind, to get away from the unsettling implications of the recent episode. People were still milling about, there was still panic in the air, but this was a panic he recognized. A panic of the everyday world, not the realm of spirits and demons and other such mumbo-jumbo. Now people were panicked because someone was dead, and the word was spreading. This was something he understood, and it was almost with a sense of relief that he attended to the situation.

He followed the crowd out into the street and started working his way towards The Watering Hole. He briefly considered driving but rejected the notion for a couple of reasons. He didn't feel like digging his car out of the snow but more importantly, he knew he would benefit from "walking it off," getting the weirdness out of his system, expelling the excess adrenaline, clearing the cobwebs from his mind. He inhaled deeply, drinking of the brisk morning air, letting it fill his lungs and clear his head. Yes, walking would suffice. Besides, it was only a few blocks down Main Street. He'd probably get there just as quickly.

That's it, he thought, drawing more oxygen in, filling his lungs, letting the chill air kickstart his system, *Get your shit together.*

He heard rumblings from the townsfolk he passed, people gathered in loose clumps, stumbling, confused, untethered, like the survivors of a downed ship at sea, struggling to stay afloat, clinging to debris. Were they looking at him? For a moment he thought it was paranoia, but no, they were. He noticed a glare on an old lady's face, eyes turned towards him accusingly. A middle-aged man with a missing front tooth, pointing an outstretched finger accusingly. Multiple faces from out of the crowd, giving him the evil eye. Among the overlapping voices he picked out snatches of conversation.

It's their fault…

They brought the madness with them…

The outsiders…

In spite of himself, Grayson grinned. The jackasses. Here was something he could hang on to. He let his anger grow and it cleared his head even more quickly than the crispness in the air. So, these yokels were going to point their fingers at him? Accuse him of bringing evil or bad luck into their little town like a bunch of villagers from a monster movie? Just who in the hell did they think they were? In his mind, Grayson leaned into it, wallowed in it. Fuck 'em. Fuck the lot of them. The anger burned it all away. The confusion, the doubt. In its place, Aaron Grayson's persona reasserted itself. Yes. This was it. Time to act.

He was a man with a job to do. Murders to solve. And another one had just been served up fresh at the local greasy spoon. He pushed his way in through the front door of the Watering Hole. The place was full of hysterical people. Women crying. Men panicked, some enraged.

Well, that just wouldn't do.

"Everybody, out of here," Grayson said, managing somehow to growl with the full volume of a shout. The room dropped into silence, and in that vacuum, which seemed to beg for an explanation, he elaborated. "Everyone who saw something, wait over there," he shot a finger decisively towards a corner. "Everyone else… out!"

"You can't do this," a well-dressed man in a blazer and a red tie said. He looked like he had money or at least a sense of self-importance. Saw himself as a bigwig. Grayson knew the type. Not so different than Lark and Maximoff. Who was this asshole? A real estate agent or town council member? Well, he was about to find out something about the balance of power. "You aren't local," the man continued. "You come in here stirring things up."

Grayson set his jaw, gritted his teeth, pissed but welcoming it. Another version of the frantic villager scene he'd observed on the way to the diner. This guy thought he could throw his weight around. Grayson stepped up to this man and stretched himself up to his full height, correcting his generally atrocious posture tactically. He leaned down into the man's smug face and practically spat his response.

"Did I fucking stutter?" The man shrunk back. "Did you observe the attack?"

"No," the man said.

"No, *sir,*" Grayson corrected, going full drill sergeant. People, particularly entitled assholes like this guy, weren't used to an authoritative voice. It was a trick Grayson had used more than once. If you took your authority for granted, didn't try to convince but instead commanded, and did so with enough confidence and fire that it implied dire consequences for insubordination, a lot of your puffed-up overconfident types would fold almost immediately. It was like a pack of dogs. The top dog, the alpha, cowed the other males. A game of dominance. And it worked.

"No sir," the man repeated, flustered, his voice quavering. The big dog was now a whipped pup. He didn't know how to deal with it when a real man pushed back. "I heard the commotion and came from next door."

"Thank you for explaining," Grayson said in a lullingly calm voice, and then, cranking his volume back up. "Now, I would appreciate it if you would most kindly get the fuck *out!*"

The man practically ran from the establishment.

"Any of the rest of you that are just here to gossip and rubberneck, you can follow him. This is now an active crime scene and I'm the officer in charge. You got no right to be here. And if you don't think I'm serious, I'd be more than happy to slap the lot of you in cuffs. And if I run out of those, I got a pack of zip ties. If we run out of jail cells, I'll find somewhere to stow your ass. If you don't think I won't arrest the whole damn town if need me, then go ahead and try me."

Without a word, a half dozen locals immediately fled, leaving the once-crowded diner suddenly much more manageable.

Those remaining in the establishment, presumably only those who had been present for the incident, cleared the way in front of him. Walking up to the bar he saw a dead body and a couple of familiar faces.

Grayson immediately recognized the body. Although he was facedown, his graying red hair was distinctive. It was Daniel, the main server at the bar. Grayson had assumed he was also the proprietor; he seemed to carry himself with the kind of pride characteristic of a business owner, like he was personally invested in happy customers. It was a shame. Daniel had struck him as a friendly guy.

The familiar faces: Leonard Maximoff and Peter Lark. Although Grayson hadn't anticipated seeing them, he wasn't surprised. It seemed to fit the pattern. The interconnections. Of course they'd be here.

Peter was holding a dishrag across his back. The rag was partially saturated with blood from what seemed to be a fairly serious wound. Leonard was similarly applying direct pressure to his abdomen.

"You guys okay?" Grayson asked, trying to temper his usual gruffness.

"As you might imagine, officer," Maximoff said with a barely suppressed rage that threatened to bubble to the surface. "We're not doing so great."

"Somebody call the ambulance?" Grayson asked.

"They're on their way," Peter said meekly. His face was pale. Grayson didn't know if it was from blood loss or shock. Sometimes the idea of a wound was as bad as the wound itself.

Grayson looked down at the body. Poor bastard. Clearly dead, but he checked for a pulse on the neck and wrist anyway. Just in case. Standard procedure. The body was still warm but there wasn't a hint of life. The paramedics would be here in a minute, but they wouldn't have much to do. There are only so many ways you can take a pulse.

There was a series of wounds dead center in the man's back, what looked at first glance like a trio of stabs and two broad slashes. Based on the blood patterns seeping from beneath the body, Grayson surmised that there were other wounds he wasn't seeing on the man's front. The floorboards were suffused with blood. Whoever had attacked him had really done a job. Was it an aggressive man who had worked his way around, front to back, or vice versa? Or had there been two attackers?

"So, what happened?" Grayson asked, in that moment not ruling anything out. Who knew what this was? Was it an attack or a knife fight?

"We were attacked," Maximoff almost spat in his rage. There was also something in his eyes, a confusion. Was he in shock or still struggling through the aftereffects of the strange spell that seemed to have overtaken the entire town?

"Okay," Grayson said testily after a pause. "You're going to have to give me a bit more. Who did it?"

"It was Hugh Slaughter," he said. "He killed the bartender and then attacked me and Peter."

"Hugh Slaughter?" Grayson said, not bothering to hide his exasperation. "The local boogeyman? I thought you bigwigs were to fancy to believe in small town urban legends and fairytales."

Maximoff shook his head back and forth. It was a frantic gesture, as if he were trying to clear out unwelcome thoughts from his mind. "Right before the attack you could *feel* it. You could feel him coming. Like he showed up out of hell."

Grayson rolled his eyes. Not helpful at all. He'd get a description eventually, but for now he'd just let the guy tell the story. "Okay. Well, let's not worry about your theories about where this guy came from for now. Just tell me, in detail, what happened. Start with what you two were doing here." Grayson had to admit, he'd wondered. Seeing these two, both prime suspect and clearly interconnected to the morass of secrets they were wading through, activated a conspiratorial mindset. Had they been here planning? Concocting a cover story? Could he believe anything they said?"

"It couldn't have been more than ten minutes ago."

"Right," Grayson said. "I was down the street. Around the time the screaming started."

Maximoff nodded, seeming to calm a bit. Perhaps telling the story was doing something to center him, to lower the heartrate. "I was meeting Peter to talk."

"About what?" Grayson asked. It seemed like a reasonable question. Their families were close, but the two had no particular relationship. Maximoff was a former business partner of Peter's late father. It was a connection they didn't even have a name for. And, sure, they might be friendly, but showing up at a restaurant in the morning kind of implied they had something in particular to discuss. Naturally, Grayson's mind returned to his conspiracy theories. What had these two been up to?

"Do I really have to explain it?" Maximoff said, the anger again rising to the surface. It was understandable that the man, shaken up by the attack, might have a short fuse, but Grayson wondered if there might be more to it than that. He'd interviewed a lot of suspects over the years. A hell of a lot of them had been guilty but the majority were, of course, very hesitant to admit to anything. One tactic he had seen time and time again was the attempt to deflect with anger. If you were getting close to information, this brand of suspect would immediately turn on the outrage, putting on a big show of it. *How dare you? How could you even ask that?* The years of dealing with guilty bullshitters had conditioned Grayson's internal alarms to go off when confronted with this kind of indignation. Was Maximoff sincerely pissed at the question, or had Grayson hit too close to home? Had they actually been up to something?

"Yes," Grayson said coldly. "If you didn't have to explain it, I wouldn't have asked. So just answer the questions and save the commentary, okay?"

Maximoff backed down a little at the show of strength, although he hadn't totally surrendered the way the asshole in the red tie, had. Maximoff's concession seemed more strategic, less grounded in fear. He let out a breath and explained in a tense but controlled tone. "Peter has been through a lot. He's just lost both parents in a very short time. Everything about his life is in question. He's hurting and he needs someone to talk to. As you may have heard, Peter hasn't been close to his father for years. As that relationship soured, he and I have struck up a friendship of sorts. Where possible, I have stepped in to try to help him in what ways I can. With support and advice."

Grayson looked over to Peter, who was nodding assent.

"So, you've kind of been filling in as a father figure?"

"Exactly," Maximoff said. "And right now, this poor kid needs someone to lean on more than ever."

"I get it," Grayson grumbled. On its surface it made sense, although it did gall him to hear everyone talking about Peter like he was an eight-year-old. Sure, he was a young man, but he was a man. Peter's biggest problem was that everyone treated him with kid's gloves. "Well, get on with the story. You were meeting up to give Pete a shoulder to cry on or whatever. What happened when you got here?"

"I was walking down the street, checking my watch. It had stopped, I was looking down at it, about to wind it when I opened the door. When I did, I saw it, standing there. The bartender was already on the floor, dying. I *think* he was still alive when I came in. But the damage was done. Too late. And the man had turned with the knife on Peter. The scene I saw as I opened the door, Peter was lying on the floor, already wounded."

Grayson wasn't sure about anything, but there was no denying that Peter had been cut. The dishrag he was holding had been stained clear through with blood and droplets were dripping from it to the wooden floor.

"Okay," Grayson said. "And then?"

"I ran at him, screaming. I yelled, get away from him. I didn't know what I was going to do, but maybe I made a big enough noise. He turned and ran out the side door. I followed him down the alley. I wasn't really thinking. I cornered him at the end of the alley, at the wire fence. I was trying to climb it, and I grabbed for his leg. That's when he slashed at me with the knife." He nodded down to his own wound. He was still applying direct pressure with a washrag. It didn't look to be as deep as Peter's wound.

"Uh-huh," Grayson said and then, turning to Peter. "That about how you remember it?"

"Yes," Peter said. "I was waiting for him when this guy went after Daniel. Just came in out of nowhere, didn't say a word, and started stabbing." Peter paused, shuddering. "I pretty much passed out from shock, and I guess Leonard came in and chased the guy off. I'm sure he saved my life."

Grayson nodded. He didn't like it when interviewees started supplying their own conclusions. It could feel like they were trying to sell you on an interpretation. Grayson liked to gather the facts and come to his own conclusions.

"Fine," Grayson said noncommittally. "And did either of you get a good look at this guy?"

"He was, uh…" Peter said. "It all happened so fast. It was confusing."

"Right," said Grayson. What the hell kind of description was that? Regardless of how shaken up someone was, Grayson would expect certain details. Height, race, hair color. All he knew so far was that the attacker was male. He wondered if Peter's confusion could be somehow related to the mass hysteria that had undertaken the town. But why bend over backwards trying to explain it away?

The real answer was, of course, that he was lying. Covering something up. Grayson, catching movement out of the corner of his eye, saw Elijah pulling up outside. Without that interfering Dahlia, thank God. "Excuse me gentlemen," he said. "I need to check in with my partner. I want both of you to try to get yourselves calmed down and see what you can remember about this attacker. We need information, at least a basic description, if we're going to have any chance of catching him. Anything. Height, eye colour, clothing. Rack your minds."

With that, Grayson headed over and met Elijah at the door.

"It's the bartender," Grayson said, not bothering with a greeting. "That guy, Daniel. Stabbed a bunch of times, front and back." He nodded towards the body, splayed flat on the floor, blood pooling. The paramedics are probably going to check him but there's no chance. He'd had it. Body's still warm, but he's done."

"Daniel," Elijah said with a frown.

"I know," Grayson said. "He was a good egg. Made sure you got plenty of refills."

Elijah gave him a look as if he couldn't decide if that was intended as a joke or not. It wasn't. Perhaps insensitive, but Grayson had meant it as a compliment. Keeping the coffee topped off was something he appreciated.

"And it's not just him," Grayson said. "Don't know if you noticed this or not, but Lark kid and Maximoff both got slashed."

Elijah was looking in their direction. "I noticed. What do they have to say?"

"Not much," Grayson said. "Can't get a decent description out of them and, so far, no idea of what it was all about. Apparently, the guy just popped up and started stabbing."

"What's bothering you?" Elijah asked, making Grayson realize he'd been frowning.

"I don't know," Grayson said slowly, trying to work it out as he responded. "It doesn't feel right."

"Well, for one thing, it doesn't seem like it fits our pattern," Elijah suggested with a shrug.

"That's right," Grayson responded, latching onto the idea. "No decapitation. And the stabbing. Way messier."

"No surgical precision," Elijah said nodding.

"Right. We talked a lot about how carefully the previous victims had been dispatched of and arranged. It was like the guy thought he was a chef or an artist or something. It's part of the reason we were looking at Peter, with his surgical training. This is different." As he spoke, a team of three paramedics arrived. As predicted, one of them, a slightly heavyset blonde woman, leaned over the bartended and checked for vitals. The procedure took less than a minute before she let Daniel's wrist drop and looked up to her companions and shook her head sadly, mouthing the word, "This one's gone."

"And it's not just that," Aaron said, piecing it together as he spoke. "This one happened in broad daylight. In public. The others were at night in isolation."

Elijah nodded. "Well, what do you think it could mean?"

"Could mean a couple of things, I guess. I mean, it *could* be a different killer. Unrelated to the main murders. Could be that."

Across the room, the paramedics had draped a sheet over Daniel and were attending to Peter and Leonard, checking their wounds and taking vital signs.

"True," said Elijah. "But you don't sound convinced. Are you talk thinking about who the victims were?"

"I was," Grayson said. "It's another difference. The main victim, this Daniel guy, is disconnected from the other three. At this point, our main murders don't seem random. The mayor and his wife. Obvious connections there. And the earlier one, if you want to throw that one in too." Grayson felt disgruntled about it, but he had to admit there was a clear connection to the earlier murder. He'd resisted it for a long time, but given what they knew about the victim's connections, it all seemed to tie together in terms of potential motive. "I mean, Crane knew these people. Was part of their circle at some point. Makes the whole thing seem very much *not* random."

"Right. But then why Daniel?" Elijah asked.

"Think about it," Grayson said with a grin. "It fits perfectly if they were trying to throw us off their trail. Throw in another victim that doesn't fit the motive pattern. Then put themselves in the mix as victims. If we buy their story, Peter and Leonard's, it seems to let them off the hook. For all of the murders, presumably. *If* we think of them as victims, that is. But are they victims, or just clever perpetrators trying to cover their tracks."

"So, you think they did it?"

"Not necessarily," Grayson said. "But it's all tied together." He couldn't help but smile, pleased at the conversation, that Elijah was, for once, asking questions but not arguing about everything that came out of his mouth in response. "Listen kid, I think we're close.

I can feel it. And I appreciate you, okay?" It went against his every instinct as am inveterate grump to say it, but it felt like the moment for a bit of sincerity. "You've got a good mind, kid. We may not always be on the same page, may not always agree, but you think like a detective. And I think our best way forward is together. If we put our heads together and without getting in each other's way, I think we can solve this case."

Elijah's face brightened. "Thanks, Aaron. I appreciate that."

Grayson felt the urge to undercut the moment, to say something dismissive, "don't let it go to your head, kid," or something like that, but ultimately he didn't. He let the sincerity stand. "Just so you know, I know it may seem like I'm trying to take control of the case. Like it's about my ego or whatever. But I've always been motivated by a desire for justice. Getting the right guy has *always* been my goal. One hundred percent. When we're butting heads, it's been because of a sincere disagreement over who the right guy is, or what we need to do in order to find him."

Elijah nodded. "I hear you, man. I think that's all either of us ever wanted."

"Great," Grayson said. "So, let's get out there and knock it home. Let's forget about our squabbles and try to actually find this guy."

"Detective Grayson?" said a voice from behind a bar. Grayson looked up. It was a middle-aged woman, one of the cooks. Her hair was bleach-blonde, and her face was streaked with tears. Undoubtedly, she was still processing the death of Daniel.

"That's me, darling," he said sympathetically. "How can I help you?"

"Phone call," she said, handing a receiver to Grayson over the bar.

"Thanks," he said, taking the phone. It was unexpected. Who else could know he was here?

"Hello?"

"Grayson," said a familiar voice, that of his superior from the regional headquarters.

"Captain Sloane," he said. "Surprised to hear from you. I'm at a crime scene."

"I gathered that," Sloane said. "I called for you at the hotel and they told me where they figured you'd be. How is this case going? You're really racking up those bodies."

"We're close to a breakthrough," Grayson said. "The pieces are coming together." Even to his own ears, it sounded weak. Like the kind of vague statement a detective might make when he really had no idea. But Grayson believed it. They *were* getting close. "But listen, you didn't call me at a crime scene for a general progress report. What's the urgency?"

"We've decided to let the Feds take over," Sloane said. "You two are to return to base."

"What?" Grayson said, shocked. "Listen, this is a complicated case. Lots of moving parts. I know things have been crazy, but we haven't even been here a week."

"You're doing fine," Sloane said. "I trust you and I know you'd get results. I don't want you to think that this decision reflects negatively on your performance."

"Then what *does* it reflect on?"

"You don't need to worry about that," said Grayson's superior. "All you need to know is you're being reassigned. If you're worried about this reflecting poorly on you, don't. It won't be considered in performance reviews and you don't get any bad press."

"Glad to hear it," Grayson said. He appreciated this note; Sloane knew that his reputation was important to him. But still, that wasn't his only concern. He also had some professional pride in his ability to untangle these complicated cases. To have it taken away when he was so close... "But seriously, sir. What's the justification."

"Nothing I can get into," said Sloane. "It's above my paygrade. When the Feds show up, you and Riley debrief them then return to base."

Already, Grayson's wheels were turning. They'd maybe have a little time. At most a day or two to try to wrap things up? If the roads remained impassable, maybe a little longer? He understood the directive and he didn't intend to disregard it, but there was nothing telling him he couldn't crack the case while the Feds were en route. "Understood, Captain."

"Great," said Sloane. "I have to spring this on you, but I appreciate that you're a team player."

Grayson hung up.

"What?" Elijah asked. He must have seen the disappointment in his face.

"They're taking the case from us. Giving it to the Feds."

"Why?" said Elijah, bewildered. "The crimes didn't cross state lines. They were all within a few miles of each other."

"No reasons were given," Grayson growled. "And it was made very clear that none were forthcoming. The general message was bend over and take it with a smile."

"It's weird," Elijah said.

Grayson wasn't sure what he was getting at but felt like he had something in particular on his mind. "How's that?" he asked.

"It's just that it reminds me a lot of the older case. From twenty five years ago? This is from the same playbook. Remember what I was telling you? How shortly after the murder it was like every mention of it was wiped from the local records? Even the investigator's name seemed to disappear. There was almost *nothing* on it, either in the journalistic or police records. Just the one article right after it happened."

"Before somebody somewhere pulled the strings," Grayson said, completing his young partner's thought. "Before they shut the whole thing down." Elijah nodded, then Grayson continued. "They're doing the same fucking thing to us now."

"That's right. *Somebody* doesn't want us solving this. Somebody with power. With reach."

Grayson looked across the room. The paramedics had professionally applied field dressings to the wounds. Peter was being hauled out on a stretcher and Maximoff had his arm draped over the shoulders of a medic for support. An ambulance waited outside, just past the picture window.

"Just a second," he said, quickly crossing the room.

"Detective?" Leonard Maximoff said.

"We weren't done with our conversation," Grayson said icily.

"Can't this wait?" Maximoff said. "We've been through a lot and the doctors need to look us over in a hospital setting."

"You aint gonna bleed out if we chat for a few more minutes," Grayson said. He noticed a medic give him a dirty look which he chose to ignore.

"Listen, Detective," Leonard said, "I've been through a lot. I need medical treatment. And furthermore, Peter is in pretty bad shape. I need to be there for him. I'm the closest thing to a father he has. I can't stay and talk to you." It was an interesting mix of anger and recrimination. A classic indignant guilt trip.

Exactly the kind of nonsense guilty men tended to throw out there, trying to distract from the real story.

"That's real interesting," Grayson said. "I'd think that someone who is grieving the loss of two friends, who just watched someone who is just like a son to him get stabbed, who just got stabbed himself, would be a little more interested in finding out who did the stabbing. And the decapitating. It seems strange to me that you're more interested in getting all outraged by how I use your time than you are in helping me find the perpetrator."

Grayson looked over and Elijah who nodded, conceding that it was a valid point. For his part, Maximoff just stammered incoherently. Bluster. Outrage.

Bullshit.

"Of course I want you to find him," Maximoff said, changing his tune. "Of course. I want to give you all the information you need. I just need to go to the hospital now. And to be with Peter. You understand…" It was weak. Paper thin. Grayson wondered why Maximoff hadn't been at the top of his suspect list the whole time.

"Oh yeah," said Grayson with thinly veiled sarcasm. "I understand. Of course. You care. You want to help. But you just can't spare a few sentences right now. Well, I think you're going to want to talk to me, because I know who did it. I know who the killer is."

"You *do?*" Maximoff failed to repress his reaction.

"Yep. So, you're definitely want to continue this conversation after they get you patched up. And since I know how much you care, I'm sure you'll want to do it as soon as possible." Grayson had considered following the ambulance to the hospital but wondered if that would be ideal. It can be hard to conduct an interview with doctors milling around. It was a case where everyone thought their own job took precedence and people ended out stepping on each other's toes. He'd rather have more control of the conversation. "Listen," he said to one of the paramedics. "How serious is this?"

"This man's wounds are superficial," the female medic said, gesturing towards Maximoff. "We'll treat him, but he'll be out later this afternoon. The boy might take a little longer."

"Can you meet us back at the hotel when you're released?" Grayson asked Maximoff.

"That's fine," said Maximoff in a resigned tone. "Although I don't know what else I can really tell you."

Grayson nodded. "We'll see. We just have a way of doing this. Certain questions we like to make sure we ask. Head over to the hotel when you're out so we can get it over with."

Maximoff's grumbled response was barely audible as he let himself be led from the diner by the attending medics.

"I don't know about you," Grayson said to Elijah as the door shut behind the paramedics. "But I'm thinking he might be the guy."

CHAPTER EIGHTEEN
BUSTED PART TWO

It was late afternoon by the time Leonard Maximoff made it over to the hotel. Grayson wasn't surprised he'd dragged his feet. While his mouth had been working overtime to sell how helpful he wanted to be, his actions had said otherwise. Grayson and Elijah had agreed; Maximoff had been doing major stonewalling, completely out of character for someone who had a vested interest in finding the killer. It was opposite behavior. You threw obstacles in front of investigators when you were worried it would be *your* head on the chopping block. Maximoff had automatically, perhaps subconsciously, begun stonewalling. At the very least, he was worried that the investigation would turn up something he'd rather remained buried. At the worst? He was a killer covering his tracks. The irony was it was his stonewalling that had cemented his position in the top spot. The most likely killer, the most suspicious. He'd done a quick one-eighty, backpedalling with his schtick about how damned much he cared about finding the killer, but it was too little too late. The damage was already done.

He was suspect number one.

So, when he took his sweet time making it back to the hotel, nobody was that surprised. Grayson knew he was full of it. He had made it clear that he wasn't on their side, and there was no reason to expect that he was acting in good faith or to believe anything he said.

Perfect, Grayson thought. Can't wait to poke holes in his story.

When he finally *did* show up, Maximoff has suggested that they meet in the hotel lounge downstairs. Aaron's gut reaction was annoyance. It was a power play. Grayson had decided to hold the meeting in the hotel, on his "home turf" in a sense, and here Maximoff was trying to control the venue. But Grayson decided to go with it. He might lose more leverage by showing it bothered him than he would in losing control of the venue.

"You ready to go down?" Elijah asked. They'd met in Grayson's room to discuss the case prior to their meeting. Both men were on the same page as far as this was concerned: Maximoff was not acting like an innocent man. He was hiding *something.*

Grayson looked at his watch. "Nah. Let's let him wait a few minutes. I can play this leverage game as well as he does."

When he did finally head down, the two men took the elevator to the first floor. They hung a left at the reception desk and went into the lounge. Leonard was already seated at the biggest table in the otherwise empty room. He was in a high-backed chair upholstered in an elegant green with gold threads interwoven and was seated at the head of the table. Grayson realized he might be overthinking, but it was hard not to see this as another power move, although it was certainly undercut by the fact that the table was empty. Maybe he saw himself as the important man, the king, as it were, but if that were so the message was that he was a king without subjects.

A young man who Grayson had seen undertaking duties as both a bellboy and security guard came up and handed Maximoff a drink. Dark liquor over ice. The boy said nothing but simply handed him the glass, as if there was an unspoken understanding: your regular, sir?

"Thank you," Maximoff said.

"My pleasure, sir," the young man said, practically bending over backwards in his deference and eagerness to please. Grayson was disgusted. He supposed it must mostly just come down to money. It was a small town. Fortunes were few and far between. But Maximoff was a bigwig. Everyone knew he had cash. Hell, he was probably the richest man in town, and he was treated with a deference beyond that which the mayor had entertained. Everyone seemed to treat him like he was the fucking king of England or something.

Yeah, this asshole was getting too big for his britches. Time to take him down a peg or two.

"Gentlemen," Maximoff said as the two police officers approached, almost as if it was he that had called for the meeting.

"Hey, Lenny," Grayson said, with an unmistakable lack of deference. As he and Elijah approached the table, Grayson pulled out two chairs, but he pulled them far from the table, well past the head, at opposing angles. No, he wasn't going to give this asshole the satisfaction of pretending he was holding court with underlings. Elijah didn't say a word – who knows if he got what was going on with the seating – but they both sat. Their position forced Maximoff to turn his chair all the way around until he had his back to the table, facing two men, both aimed at him on forty-five-degree angles. Maximoff's little bit of stage direction had been reworked. The new layout suggested an interrogation.

"Okay," Grayson said. "Let's get started."

"Fine," said Leonard and, again trying to take the wheel. "So, who's your suspect? Who did it?" He said it as if he was just as curious and concerned as anyone else but, of course, that meant nothing. Killers were liars too. Almost always. And this time, Leonard had had plenty of time to rehearse his performance. For all

Grayson knew, that was the reason for the delay: strategizing how to best bullshit his way through the meeting.

"We'll get to that," Grayson said, casually waving away his questions but inwardly pleased that his bluff had clearly gotten under Maximoff's skin. "But first, I have a few questions for you. Things we never got to in our earlier conversation."

"What is this? Are we just having a conversation or do you consider me a suspect? Is this an interrogation?"

"Nah," said Grayson. "We're just trying to solve the murder. We're all on the same page here." Grayson pushed through quickly. There was always that hint of suspense, that fear of those dreaded words that any cop hates to hear, "I'd like to contact my lawyer." Grayson had determined that the way to keep Leonard Maximoff talking was to play against his ego, his need to feel powerful, to feel like he was winning. "I know you want to help us find the guy who did this." Grayson bit down on the sarcasm he felt as he said the line, trying his best for a flat and seemingly sincere delivery.

"Of course," said Leonard.

"So, first things first. I wanted to make sure we got your alibis sorted out."

"Alibis?" he said, his eyebrows lifting in concern.

"Sure," said Grayson. "You have to understand how we do this. We have a whaddayacallit? A standard operating procedure. Like in the Army. We're trained and we have this checklist and one of the things we do is we check in with everyone we talk to about alibis." Not strictly true, but generally so.

"I still don't see how…"

"And I know you're not worried," Grayson said. "And you have no reason to be. Because, like you said, you're here to help us. You've got nothing to hide. And I gotta say, we really appreciate your cooperation on this. You're really helping us solve this case." A little ass-kissing never hurt. Grayson knew who he was dealing with, and he was trying to give him what he wanted. Just enough deference and respect. The semblance of performance. That would be the cheese in the mousetrap and, if the conversation went the way he hoped it would, Maximoff would walk right into it. "We need to account for everything. The murderer that we've identified might have had an accomplice. We have to make sure everyone is clear." Grayson took out a little pad and golf pencil he kept in his coat pocket for notes.

"So, uh…" Maximoff began awkwardly. "Which murder?"

"All of them," Grayson said in a perfect deadpan. "Might as well be thorough, right? Starting from the most recent, I suppose?"

"Well, for the one today, as I told you, I was on my way to the restaurant as the murder was taking place. I spoke to people on the street. It shouldn't be hard to verify."

"Perfect!" said Grayson. "This is exactly the kind of stuff I'm talking about. This helps tremendously, and it lets us keep you out of the whole business. Great, keep going. The next one, if we're going in reverse chronological order, that'd be your friend. Lark."

"Right, poor William," Maximoff said in his best distraught tone. "I had been at his house earlier, but your partner and that…" At this point he gestured vaguely. "…that reporter chick, saw me leave."

"Right," said Grayson, but thought to himself: that doesn't mean you didn't go back. For the moment, he chose not to press this issue but instead pushed on. "Great. Well, let's keep going back. Tell me about Eleanor. Where were you for that one?"

"At home," he said. "With my wife. My daughter was there too. She can vouch for me."

"Well, no," said Maximoff growing flustered. "But my wife can vouch for my whereabouts too. I was at home. Naturally."

"I'm sure she can," Grayson said. At home. The wife. Weakest alibi in the book. Wives covered for their husbands. They covered sometimes without even knowing they were doing it. Time "at home" was a generalized mess. It was downtime where nothing was happening, empty stretches of hours of people mindlessly sharing a space. Sure, he was home. Does that mean he couldn't have left for an hour and a half in the middle of it? Did it mean he *didn't* drive the twenty minutes between their houses to do his dirty business? Would his wife even have noticed. He nodded as if he agreed but on his notebook under the column he'd created labelled, *L. Maximoff Alibis*, he jotted down, *Eleanor, home with wife, alibi weak*. But the fact was, that although "at home with the family" wasn't a great alibi, it *would* hold up in court if the Maximoff's were good on the witness stand. And Grayson had a feeling that they *would* be. Although he was backed against the ropes right now, Leonard was a slimeball. A rich guy. If he was opening his mouth, he was lying. He was used to it. And he was the type of "impressive" man that could often win over a jury. Malinda and Fawn were both cut from the same cloth. He had a strong suspicion they'd both lied to their faces during the investigation.

He needed more.

"So, is that it?" Maximoff asked.

"Well, there's the matter of this *other* murder," Grayson teased.

"What other murder? This all started with Eleanor."

"Not exactly," Grayson said, throwing in a generous pause. He felt like he was fishing, out on a lake, letting the fish run with the bait, about to yank on his line to sink the hook. "There was this other murder. Around twenty years prior."

"Around twenty years?" Maximoff was overplaying his bewilderment.

"Sure," Grayson said. "You know about it. You mentioned Hugh Slaughter, right? That one."

"Oh, right," Maximoff said. "They found that woman in the woods, right?"

"Yeah," Grayson said. "She was missing her head. Same as Eleanor. Same as Lark. Now, I'm no mathematician but my calculations all three of these folks were exactly one head short." He couldn't resist. He had Maximoff on the line. Time to start destabilizing him. He noticed a subtle smile play across Elijah's lips; the kid was pleased to hear his partner tying in the earlier murder.

Maximoff's brows narrowed. "Are you playing games with me detective?" he said. "What does this have to do with me? If some poor random unidentified woman is found in the forest?"

"Ah, but that's the thing, Lenny," Grayson said, tapping the golf pencil against the pad for emphasis. "We've recently had a break in that one. We've determined, with some certainty, that the woman they found in the forest was one Lucy Crane. That name ring a bell?"

"Ah… no," Maximoff said, his eyes suddenly darting left and right. Grayson recognized the move. When you had them up against the ropes it set in. The survival instinct. Maximoff knew he was in trouble. His instincts were setting in. He was scanning the room, asking himself, *Do I run for it? Do I stay here and try to talk my way out of it?*

"That's strange," he said. "I think she used to be part of your little crowd. Saw a picture of her with you and your wife back at your house if I'm not mistaken."

"Oh, Lucy *Crane,*" Maximoff said, managing to pull it together. "I remember her. A friend of Malinda's from back in the day. This was a long time ago, you'll understand. She may have been part of our social circle briefly, but I think she eventually drifted away…"

"Might have happened right around the time *somebody* took her head off her shoulders." Grayson said. "I'm sure you'd remember her. Pretty girl from what I gathered. I'm sure she was there at some of those parties you used to host. In fact, I believe we can establish she was at one of your parties the night she died."

"Well, I wouldn't be much of a host if I murdered my own guests would it? And besides, if I was hosting, I was, obviously, at my house." Maximoff's voice was almost trembling as he said it. He sounded defensive, nervous. Good. But Grayson knew he was risking overdoing it. He felt that he was about two second from Maximoff shutting it down and lawyering up. It was time to pull back. So far, he didn't have enough to build his case.

The feds would be coming in shortly. They might have been paid off, or misdirected in a certain direction. It certainly seemed likely that Maximoff had pulled strings, higher up, to get Grayson and Riley booted off the case. That suggested that they'd gotten too close for his comfort. But one they were out, they were out. What he really needed was physical evidence. Grayson knew that this interview might be *it.* There'd be no chance for them to build a case through fingerprints or forensic evidence at that point. Everything relied on what he could get Maximoff to say during this interview. So, Grayson switched gears. It wouldn't do to have the fish slip from the line this close to being reeled in.

"Anyway," he said. "I'm sure you're as outraged as I am that this same person who killed your best friend and his wife, also took out this innocent girl back in the day. This guy is preying on those closest to you. *You* could be next."

"That's right…" Maximoff said slowly, not sure he was buying it. Time to stroke his ego.

"That's why your help is going to be so valuable to us. You're connected to all of these people. You can help us verify my theories and catch the person I know is responsible."

"Right. And you said you know who did it, right?"

"Oh yeah," Grayson said. "We've got him. Just need a little more line and we can reel him in."

Elijah suddenly stepped forward. He cast a look at Grayson, one eyebrow subtly raised, the unspoken question, "You might if I try something?" Grayson gave the barest hint of a nod. *Go for it, kid.*

Elijah handed Leonard a piece of paper, a small square of hotel stationary, and a pen.

"What's this?" Maximoff asked, confused.

"Would you mind writing your name for me? Proper spelling? I've seen it written different ways in different documents and want to make sure it's correct in the report."

Maximoff looked to Grayson and raised his eyebrows slightly, as if saying, "what is this?" Grayson shrugged with a hint of a smile, suggesting, "humour him." It was an amusing moment of camaraderie between the two who had just been pitted against each other, and Grayson willingly played the part, letting Maximoff think that his partner was a pencil pusher of questionable priorities. But Grayson thought he might actually know what Elijah had up his sleeve…

Maximoff scribbled his name on the pad with hie *left* hand. The wound, on his lower abdomen, was on the left, and it was a nearly perfectly vertical cut. This suggested, but didn't prove anything conclusively but it suggested something. Maximoff had thought the placement of the cut odd. For an attacker to have made it the angles seemed unlikely. It wouldn't make sense as a self-inflicted wound from a right-handed person. If he were right-handed, Maximoff would have had to reach across his chest and down and the cut would have almost definitely been made on a diagonal. It also seemed unlikely that anyone would cut themselves with their non-dominant hand. It simply defied normal behaviour. Seeing Maximoff's left-handedness strongly implied that he might have made the wound himself. Grayson covertly made eye contact with Elijah, giving him an encouraging glance, to let him know that he understood what he'd been going for.

"Thank you," Elijah said, taking back the slip of paper, and then, to support his cover story, "Two f's. That's what I thought."

"Listen," Leonard asked, apparently feeling confident enough to express frustration. "I feel like I've given you all the help you've asked. You told me you knew who the killer was and implied that you'd tell me. I want this killer brought to justice just as much as you do." Grayson was annoyed, his bluff called. How long could he lead this guy in circles before he called for his lawyer?

"We'll do that," Elijah said, stepping forward. "But first I had a couple of follow up questions I was hoping you could clear up."

Grayson grinned. He realized that he'd gained some confidence in his partner's approach. No, their theories weren't always aligned, but Elijah came up with interesting stuff when left to explore. He realized it had been a mistake to keep him on such a short leash. They *were* on the same team, after all.

"Fine," Maximoff said, huffily. "What is it?"

"Well, you had an alibi for Eleanor and even though it was a long time ago, it seems like we might be able to find people who could vouch for you on the night that Lucy Crane died. I was a little unclear on what your alibi was for Abdoullah Lark. You said that I'd seen you leave his house. That's true. But where did you go after that?"

"Well, I went home eventually," he said.

"Eventually," said Elijah.

"I didn't get back for a few hours. First, I drove around a bit. Around the hills."

"That ain't exactly an alibi," said Grayson. People took aimless walks and drives he supposed, but it was classically weak as an alibi. No chance anyone would see you and no real reason for the activity.

"Listen," Maximoff said. "I don't know why you're giving me the third degree all of a sudden. I was just attacked as I fought off the man who killed Daniel and stabbed Peter."

"Right," said Elijah. "And what did this killer look like exactly?"

"He was…" Maximoff gestured aimlessly as he sought the words. "I'd never seen him before. He was tall. Uh… dark hair."

"Okay," said Elijah. "Please elaborate. The more detail the better."

"There was something about him… something strange. It was hard to really process what I was seeing at the time. It's hard to explain, but everyone was feeling so weird… that weird spell that seems to hit whenever Hugh Slaughter, or whatever it is, attacks. His eyes were dark, you know? It was like they were all pupils. Like the eyes of a shark. And his skin was pale, like he hadn't seen the sun in a long time. He was wearing a long tattered overcoat. Filthy, covered in mud. So were his shoes."

It was all Grayson could do not to roll his eyes. This wasn't a man remembering a description: it was a man improvising. Inventing. He was trying to imply Hugh Slaughter, the supernatural explanation, without coming out and saying it, describing someone who'd clawed his way out of an open grave. Trying to send the investigation down that dead-end road.

"And it was almost like there was something else there with him. It's hard to explain, but I felt like there was a presence floating there with him. I felt chills looking at him, I swear."

"Huh," Elijah said, looking down at a little pad he'd produced from his pocket. "That's interesting."

"What do you mean?" Maximoff said.

"Well, it's interesting because that's nothing like the description Peter gave." He looked down at the pad. "I managed to get him on the phone over at the hospital a little while ago. He was feeling a little better and was able to tell me in more detail what what he saw. He said it was a man in a ski mask and a baggy jacket. Just a regular guy. Average height. But he mentioned that at a certain point he got this weird feeling, at a certain point, that the guy wasn't human. A *feeling*." He glanced at Grayson as he said it and Grayson understood the implication, that Peter might have been overcome by the feelings of paranoia that had seemed to overtake everyone, Grayson included. This made Peter's story seem the more reliable of the two. The killer wasn't a ghoul from beyond the grave. He was a regular man, and his attack coincided with the strange wave of paranoia that affected everyone's perceptions on the emotional level.

"Well, you know what they say," Maximoff said. "When there's a robbery or something, you know, men flashing guns around, the descriptions from eyewitnesses are wildly inconsistent. When people are panicked, they see things differently…"

"They do say that," Grayson said noncommittally. It was true to an extent, but this was clearly bullshit. One person didn't see a ski mask and another an uncovered face. Maximoff was lying.

"So, did Peter actually *see* you get attacked?" Elijah asked.

"Well, he said he did, didn't he?" Maximoff said defensively.

"No, he didn't exactly say that," Elijah said. "It sounded more like he was repeating what he'd been told. It sounds like the first he saw you was when you ran inside *after* you say you chased the man in the alley. He saw you coming back in with the wound."

"Okay, fine," said Maximoff. "I didn't have time to stop and say hi. I was trying to catch the attacker."

"Uh-huh," said Elijah and then, after a pause. "So, did *anybody* see you going after the attacker?"

"I don't know," he said. "How would I know? It was Hugh Slaughter, okay? If you see him, you'd understand. He's not a normal man. And that weird feeling? When he appears? You felt it, right? It must mean something, right? There's something unnatural out there. You both felt it. I think that feeling… it's what he… I don't know… what he *releases* when he's coming."

It sounded desperate. Out of character. A man throwing out whatever he could think of. Throwing it as the wall and seeing what would stick.

"So, you're a believer now, huh?" Aaron asked. "Mister sophisticated getting down and dirty with the superstitious locals. I thought you were one of these classy, educated types. You just as ignorant as the rest of these rubes? The ones that were born here? Going to spend their whole lives in the same town? You a true believer just like the waitresses and the janitors?"

It had the desired effect. Maximoff's jaw clenched. Grayson had played his ego against his bullshit story. If he admitted he didn't believe, he was admitting his story was bogus. If pretended he believed, he had to deny his superiority to the people of Mount Hugh that he had been looking down his nose at for years. At the same time, Grayson could see the vein in his temple enlarging, his cheeks reddening in anger. He could see the tension playing out on his face.

Good, you bastard, Grayson thought. Get mad. Let me have it. Say something. Give us some rope to hang you with.

"So, which is it, Lenny?" Grayson asked with a smirk calculated to enrage.

Elijah had stepped over to the window. He had a curious expression on his face.

"What?" asked Grayson, wondering if, perhaps, there was some new madness occurring on the street. Another murder? Nothing would surprise him at this point.

"Are those turbines supposed to be moving that fast?"

Grayson stepped over and looked up.

"Holy shit," he said. "It's like they're about ready to take off."

Leonard shot to his feet, bolt upright, like he'd received an electrical jolt.

"No no no," he muttered under his breath. "If you gentlemen will excuse me, I have to go…" His voice sounded distant, trembling. He rushed from the hotel.

"Now just a damned minute," Grayson said moving towards the door. "I didn't say you could go."

"Let him," said Elijah, placing a hand on his partner's shoulder. "Let him go. Just let him get out far enough ahead that we can follow him. I have a sneaky suspicion that he'll lead us to all of the answers we've been looking for."

"Great idea," said Grayson but then, suddenly, he felt something rising up within him. Fear. Anxiety. What was this feeling?

They were going to crash…

Little Larry. Dead.

It was his fault.

You can never outrun your sins. Never atone.

They were going to get him… he'd have to pay for what he'd done.

Feelings. Fears. Decades old. Grayson felt them just as intensely as if they were happening to him in that moment.

"Oh God," he said, almost losing his balance. He caught himself on the edge of a table, pushing himself back up to standing on wobbly legs.

Other worries.

The future. The past. The unknown.

He'd never be good enough. As good as Quinn.

He'd die alone. Unremembered.

They were gunning for him. Hiding in the shadows.

Ghosts. Demons. Hugh Slaughter. His father.

"You're fine, Aaron," said Elijah gently, so gently, placing a hand on his shoulder. "Stand up, buddy."

Aaron looked down and realized that he'd sat. Noticing moisture on his face, he realized that he'd been crying. What the hell? He wiped his face with his sleeve.

"Sorry, Riley. Don't know what got into me."

"Don't be sorry," Elijah said. "It's not you. Look." He gestured towards the lobby outside the lounge. Locals were stumbling in circles. Panicked. Crying. Afraid. Angry. It looked like a scene from an open-air asylum, one with no locked doors. "Everyone is feeling it. But it's not real."

Grayson could hear the tenderness in Elijah's voice. Uncharacteristically, it didn't piss him off. In his weakened, vulnerable state, he recognized that he needed connections. His partner had his back.

"The same thing is hitting everyone," Elijah said. "And I'm sure that Maximoff knows something about it. We need to follow him now so we can clear up this whole mess once and for all."

"You're right, Riley," said Grayson, trying to push through the anxiety, the fear, that threatened to shut him down. He knew he had to act, but part of him wanted to collapse under the weight of a lifetime of fears suppressed, anxieties tamped down, anger misdirected, despair ignored. Grayson stood up.

"Good," said Elijah. Grayson could see something of the fear in his eyes, but he seemed to have it under better control. "Let's go. One step at a time. Remember… none of it's real."

Chapter Nineteen
Whispered Eulogy

She could see them, on the hillside. The turbines. Somehow, they were behind all of this. Dahlia and Elijah had just pieced it together in the same moment. It had to have something to do with the sound. The vibration.

Elijah put down the phone. "That was Grayson," he said. "There's been a murder. Down at the Watering Hole. He's going over to check it out. I should probably head down there and help out. Are you going to be okay if I leave?"

Dahlia didn't exactly feel okay. She was still overwhelmed from the… she didn't even know what to call it… the incident. She'd been on the phone with Naomi and somehow, they'd both been pulled into the same delusion, the same hysterical energy. Paranoia and enhanced emotions, pulling them both in random directions. She still felt weird, like she'd been shocked and could still feel the aftereffects of lightning arcing over her skin. It was a weird tingle. But they'd all been through the same thing. Presumably the whole town. She had no special claim or need.

But what she *did* feel, very clearly, was anger. And this wasn't part of the incident. It wasn't an externally applied emotion. No, this anger was hers, it was earned. It had meaning. Now that they were closing in on answers, answers that somehow included the wind turbines, put on the hillside by the late William Lark and his erstwhile business partner, Mr. Leonard Maximoff, Dahlia felt a lot of things clicking into place. No, she hadn't really known, at least on a conscious level, why she'd needed to come back to Mount Hugh. Her half-baked thesis was, she realized now, a misdirection, a justification. No, what she knew now was that she'd returned to find out what had happened to her mother. And now that she knew: she was here to punish those responsible. She leaned into the anger and the last lingering effects of the incident seemed to dissipate, like smoke being blown into nothing by a strong wind.

"I'm fine," she said. "Do what you have to do. Get that bastard." Dahlia was surprised to hear the venom in her voice. Elijah noticed too; she could tell from the look of concern that crossed his face.

"I will," he said. "You know I will. We're all on the same page here. We want to catch this guy. We'll bring him in."

Dahlia nodded. "Good," she said. "I'll make sure of it."

Elijah moved towards the door, then paused. Looking back, he said, "If you want to help, you could go up to the turbines and see if there's some way you can test our theory. I want to bring Aaron in on this but based on our most recent conversations with him, I'm afraid he'll just reject the suggestion if we don't present him with something solid."

"That makes sense," she said. She stood up, happy to have a part to play. "Unfortunately, he's going to resist the idea no matter how we present it."

Elijah nodded. "He's so bull-headed. Drives me crazy."

"You know, I had some thoughts about that," she said. "I think we've been approaching him wrong. Yes, he's intolerable. A total crank. But you can't win if you just go in butting heads with someone like that. If you fight him, he'll fight harder. That's his nature."

"I agree with you so far," Elijah said with a hint of a smile. "So, what do you suggest?"

"Well, I'm sure you have to do this when you're dealing with suspects, right? You just have to play to his personality instead of playing against it."

Elijah nodded. "Yeah, you're right. Interrogations are a big mind game. You have to figure out where a suspect's weak spot is and exploit it. Some people will cave if you come on strong. Others will give in if you pretend you're their buddy. It differs."

"And what do you think Grayson's weak point is?"

"His ego," Elijah said without hesitation. "He wants to be taken seriously. It's the reason for all of the bluster."

"Right," she said. "So, how do you get what *you* want from a guy like that?"

Elijah paused for a moment, thinking. "You flatter him. Stroke his ego. Let him think he came up with the idea."

She nodded. "That's right. It's hard because he's pushing your buttons so hard the last thing you want to do if butter him up. But I think it might work."

He grinned. "I think you might be right. You know, you're pretty observant."

"Thanks," she said appreciating the compliment. It was one of those things she knew about herself; she was naturally good at playing off people's personalities. She'd been making the same mistake with Grayson, letting him get under her skin. "You try to get him on our side. I'll head up to the hillside and try to get some ammunition we can use to convince him."

Elijah headed downstairs to find his partner and Dahlia, after splashing a little water on her face, followed suit. Retraced their steps from the previous night towards the turbines. Now that she saw their importance she couldn't help but notice you could see them from almost everywhere in town. They were gigantic and dominated the mountain in the distance. She imagined that if you lived here, you'd naturally stop noticing them. They'd recede into the background of the subconscious. But driving towards them, she noticed they had a formidable presence. They were massively tall, and their blades were unimaginably huge. When you focused on them, they almost didn't seem real because of their scope: like optical illusions somehow inserted into the everyday world. What was this strange power they had to unsettle and disrupt everyone unlucky enough to be in their shadow? Every turn she made, she'd see them on the horizon and, eventually, it began to engage her anxiety. She began to feel that she was moving toward a confrontation with the turbines themselves, that they were engines of evil. How could one possibly win that fight?

Don't think about it. Don't psych yourself out. They're just machines. Towers of metal. We just need to figure out how they're affecting people. A scientific explanation…

Instead, she looked down at the road passing, her hands upon the steering wheel, anything but the turbines in the distance. As soon as the anxiety cleared from her mind, something else bubbled up.

Images of her mother. Memories from childhood. Her mother, crying for reasons that Dahlia had been too young to understand.

Her mother, high on God knows what. Angry, desperate. To Dahlia, it was like she was possessed.

Her mother, leaving the house. The last time she ever saw her.

"I'll be right back, pumpkin," she'd said. It was a moment of normalcy. In that moment, her mother seemed like herself. No sign of the demons that haunted her. On her way out the door, she'd flashed Dahlia a smile and it had been like she remembered. In happier times. But hadn't there been a hint of sadness in her eyes as the door closed behind her?

And now she knew where she'd ended up. Dead, on the side of the road. Cast out like garbage. Mutilated. Killed.

It was hitting her hard. Really hitting her. A delayed reaction to everything that had happened, everything she'd learned. It had been too much to process, too much going on, but she felt it pressing down on her like a weight, a terrifying gravity that threatened to flatten her.

Tears ran down Dahlia's cheeks and she was overtaken with violent sobbing, cries that seemed to tear themselves out of the deepest part of her, shaking her like earthquakes. She was too overwhelmed to drive and had to pull over.

Naomi. I have to call Naomi.

She hadn't spoken to her since the terrifying shared spell had listed. And she had so much to say to her.

And, more than everything, she needed her.

She strategically parked beside a large oak that blocked her view of the distant turbines. She'd be facing them soon enough. She dialed.

"Baby!" Naomi said, her voice heartbreakingly full of concern and desperation. "Are you okay?"

"Are you?" Dahlia asked.

"I'm fine but…" she paused, confused. "What was *that*?"

"It's this town. One of its mysteries. I want to ask you about that but first… I love you. I'm okay. Yes, things have been rough here. But we're close. Almost done."

"Come home," Naomi said. "Just come home."

"Soon, baby," Dahlia said.

"You can't tell me you're safe there."

Dahlia's pause was all the answer Naomi needed. Eventually Dahlia said. "I have to see it through. That's all I can say."

"If you get killed, I'll never forgive you."

"I won't," Dahlia said. "I promise."

"Fine. Let's pretend that's a sufficient assurance. Tell me what's going on."

"Well, it's been a crazy afternoon. There was that incident… which I want to tell you about. And there was another murder."

"Right. You told me about that. The mayor, right?"

"No. After that. This afternoon."

"My God," Naomi said, halfway to a shriek. "How many murders have there been?"

"This is three. Four, actually if you count my mother."

"Baby," Naomi said, her tone lightening. "You *can't* be okay. That's going to take a while to process."

"You're right about that," Dahlia said. "It's only starting to hit me. Just now. It's the main reason I called."

"Well, baby, you never really grieved," Naomi said. "Your mother disappeared. You never got to say goodbye. Never got to even acknowledge, really, that she was gone. The sadness has always been there but since you couldn't really process it, you threw yourself into other things. Taking care of others. Your studies. Your thesis." Her voice was so tender, so sympathetic; Dahlia could feel some of the tension ease. She needed to feel loved, to feel supported and with Naomi's words she could feel her strength begin to return. "Sound about right?"

"It does," Dahlia said. "But it's all coming to the surface now. Feelings. Memories. Finding out what happened to her has pulled everything out of the shadows. But it's bad, baby. So complicated. Her fate was so much worse than anything I could have imagined. And that's why I have to stay, baby. I have to see this through. I have to make sure the people responsible get theirs."

"You need to let it go," Naomi said. "If you think revenge is going to satisfy you, you're wrong."

"Listen, babe, you talk a lot about processing trauma," Dahlia said. "I need resolution here. Seeing this through is the only way I'm going to get that."

"Just be careful," Naomi responded. "Seriously."

"I will," Dahlia said. "Now, here's the part where you can help me. You're the math professor. The smart one."

"I don't know about that," Naomi said with a strained laugh.

"Certainly, relative to me," Dahlia said. "This weird effect seems to happen around the time of every murder. You felt it yourself. It's a panic. An emotional destabilization. I was chasing my own tail trying to explain it satisfactorily, and everything was leaning supernatural. That's how the locals seem to think of it. And I almost got myself convinced that was the answer."

"I remember that," said Naomi. "You even sounded like you were halfway there to believing in the local boogey man."

"I was," Dahlia said. "But I'm thinking more clearly now. I've never believed in that stuff. I've always been more of a 'believe-it-when-I-see-it' type of girl. But there is *something* going on. What we've realized, however, is that it must have an explanation in the real world. In science."

"Well, math isn't science," Naomi said. "I don't know if my expertise will help you."

"Ah, you know you can," Dahlia said. "You're more scientifically minded. You subscribe to *Scientific American.* I read novels, you read *Brief History of Time.*"

"I'll try," Naomi said. "No promises."

"Fine," Dahlia said. "It's something that causes everyone to panic. Originally, I'd thought it must be radiation or some kind of poison or something like that, but since our phone call I realized the most likely source was sound. And I think it might have something to do with the turbines. We've got a couple of hints of that."

"Okay," said Naomi.

"That's it," Dahlia said. "Come up with a theory."

"Oh, geez," Naomi said. "You're putting me on the spot." Then there was a pause. "Wait a minute. Hold on." The sound of papers shuffling coming over the line. A minute stretched by. "Here it is," she said. "They call it the ghost frequency."

"The ghost frequency?"

"Yeah," Naomi said. "I have an article on it here. From one of my science magazines. Sound is a wave, and it resonates at different frequencies. A wave has two qualities. One is amplitude; that's how high it is. In sound, amplitude equals volume. The other is frequency. That's how long it takes a wave to repeat, and we hear that as pitch. Longer repeating waves sound deeper, and tightly packed high frequency waves sound high pitched. The ghost frequency is 18.9 hertz."

"Is that high or low pitch?"

"Extremely low. It's considered infrasound, which means its below the standard range of human hearing. So, you wouldn't even know it was there. Anyway, this ghost frequency is thought to cause unease among the people exposed to it. It can induce hallucinations or anxiety and is often associated with paranormal phenomena."

"Wow," said Dahlia.

"Sound like your problem?"

"It does," Dahlia responded. "Do you think wind turbines could generate these frequencies?"

"I don't see why not," Naomi said. "Turbines would definitely generate frequencies on the low end. I'd imagine that depending on the materials and how they are arranged, a turbine might generate infrasound at that particular frequency. And the thing about low frequencies is they travel farther than higher frequencies. It's no unreasonable to imagine these frequencies affecting a whole community."

"This could be it. If the turbines are somehow generating these frequencies, it would explain the weird and paranoid superstitions, the delusions, that the locals seem to have, and those periods of protracted anxiety."

"Does it explain the murders?"

"It might," Dahlia said. "It might at that. But I need more information first."

"And you're going to get that information now?" Naomi said with obvious concern.

"Yes," Dahlia said.

"You're putting yourself in danger again, aren't you?"

"Not at all," Dahlia said. "I'm just gathering data. Or evidence, I guess."

She hated to lie to her, but Dahlia wasn't sure. As they finished their conversation and she got back on the road, approaching the turbines in the distance, ominous and omnipresent, she was felt very much like she was walking straight into a potentially dangerous situation.

Soon, she was back at the turbine where Elijah had experienced his own personal spell of anxiety and confusion the previous evening. She pulled over on the deeply rutted and snow-covered road, careful not to end out in the ditch in the treacherous weather. There, on the hillside, it stood. The turbine. Looming threateningly. She was very aware that this very spot, which might hold the answers they sought, was also the location where her mother's headless body had been found. As she walked up to the turbine, she almost felt sick with conflicting emotions roiling in her gut. Fear. Anger. Grief. But, so far, natural emotions. She wasn't feeling the hysterical effect.

Feet away from the central tower a massive construction of sleek fiberglass that supported impossible massive spinning blades hundreds of feet overhead.

"How do you do it, you bastard?" she said, looking up to the blades.

Now she had an idea of that. The ghost frequency. But standing there she began to puzzle out the why. The ghost frequency theory was compelling, and it explained a lot, but it didn't explain a series of nearly identical murders. The frequency, at least as described by Naomi, wouldn't do that. It wouldn't turn you into a serial killer.

She and Elijah had surmised that the Hugh Slaughter myth was invented, and Malinda had confirmed it. Suddenly, the pieces seemed to lock into place. The ghost frequency caused panic every time there was a murder. Peter had reported it when his mother had been killed. Townsfolk had felt it during the subsequent two murders. The prevailing theory among the locals was that the weird feeling was proof of Hugh Slaughter's existence, that these spells of panic and fear were proof that a demon was on the loose. But Dahlia could see now that the opposite was true. The panic didn't cause the murders, and it didn't appear as Hugh Slaughter appeared; the panic was created just prior to the murders, or perhaps right after, in order to cause hallucinations among the public. It was part of the two-pronged campaign to convince the locals that their killer was supernatural: spread rumors about a demonic killer, and cause panic with the intentional use of the ghost frequency. The pieces fit, including the necklace, a gift from Eleanor to her mother, a connection between two victims. She knew the plan. And she had a pretty good idea whose plan it was: all signs pointed to Maximoff. The mastermind. It was just a matter of sorting out the details.

She noticed footprints in the snow and followed them over to a nearby electrical box. Against its edge the snow was disturbed, digging around in her gloved hands she pulled up a duffel bag. Its zipper was clogged with snow but after some tugging, she managed to open it. Inside was an axe. She examined it closely. There were tiny specks along its blade. Blood? Rust, maybe? She couldn't be sure, but her gut told her this was the axe used to kill the mayor. The other murders had been surgically precise, probably set dressing to allude the paranormal serial killer cover story, but maybe this time he'd been in more of a hurry. Maybe that's why he burned down the house. She ran her thumb along the edge of its blade. It was certainly sharp enough.

She leaned the axe against the electrical box and dug around in the bag. It still had weight. There was something inside. For a moment she thought it was a stone or a brick, but as she pulled it out, she saw a book. Chillingly, she realized that it was a copy of the Quran, the Muslim holy book.

Lark…

She flipped it open and it, as if of its own accord, turned to a particular page, as if the spine were used to being opened to that particular page. A particular passage was highlighted. Dahlia was only passingly familiar with the Quran from a half-remembered undergraduate class on comparative religion. The highlighted verse was chapter four, verse ninety-three of Surah An-Nisa. She remembered that this book had concerned the proper treatment of women. Her eyes scanned the text.

And whomever slays a believer intentionally his punishment is Hell, where he will abide. Allah's wrath is against him and He has cast His curse upon him, and has prepared for him a great chastisement.

Dahlia's mind raced. The passage was relevant. Damning. She'd been certain that Maximoff was the guilty one, that the bag had been his. But this new piece of evidence suggested otherwise.

She didn't know everything about Maximoff but felt certain that he had no interest in the Muslim faith. That was all Lark.

She took a deep breath to clear her head, remembering the reason she'd come here: to untangle the mystery of the turbines and their sinister affect. Quickly she ran her hands along the inside of the duffel bag. The only other thing inside was a small key. Just the right size for the electrical box. She opened it and looked inside.

In front her she saw switches and trailing wires in a complicated arrangement that, of course, meant nothing to her. Not knowing where to start, she pushed the biggest button she could find, which she assumed was the power button. Presumably she was right because immediately she could hear a humming. She didn't feel anything weird but, glancing up, she could see the blades of the turbine slowly moving.

Okay, she thought. So far, so good.

She wasn't surprised that she hadn't been instantly seized with panic. The turbines ran frequently. The hillside was covered with them and some of them seemed to be running all the time. She didn't know the strategy, but imagined they might alternate between turbines so some could take a break and avoid wear and tear. Uncertain what her next move should be, Dahlia looked over at the other switches. Her heart seemed to stop in her chest when she noticed one of them was stained with blood. It made sense. If the killer caused the ghost frequency to cause panic while he committed his murders, then he'd need to turn it off afterwards. Seemed natural that the switch was bloodstained. Looking closer she saw that this switch adjusted the speed of the turbines. This made sense, she supposed. If sound was a wave generated by the motion of the blades, then changing the speed might naturally change the frequency, right? Impulsively she flipped it.

For a moment, it seemed that nothing had happened. Then, looking up, she saw that the blades spinning faster. It was a gradual change; they seemed to move faster with each rotation as they approached top speed.

Then everything changed.

Dahlia felt fear. The most overpowering fear she'd ever experienced in her life. She felt it pulsing through her like the blood in her veins had been replaced by pure liquid terror. Looking down the hillside, she saw her mother's headless body in the road.

"Mommy," she said in a meek voice and then the body seemed to stand up and stumble towards her, like a poorly piloted marionette. Panic seized her. She felt like running. Hiding. Burying herself in the snow and letting the cold take her. It got hard to think. Her thoughts seemed to bounce around in her head, her consciousness a turbulent sea, a tsunami of anxiety.

She squeezed her eyes shut. Shut it all out. Mommy's not there. What you're feeling isn't real. She could imagine the people in town. Fear seizing them. They'd be certain that Hugh Slaughter was coming for them. They'd been conditioned to think so. She managed to calm her brain somewhat when she heard a sound. Opening her eyes, she saw a car tearing down the small rural road, too fast in the ice and snow. Toward the turbines. Towards her. Irrationally, her first thought was *Hugh Slaughter* as if the supernatural killer would show up in a BMW. She knew that first thought wasn't entirely wrong, however. It was Leonard Maximoff. The killer returning to the scene of the crime?

She didn't think he'd seen her yet, so she quickly locked the electrical box, stowing the key in her pocket, grabbed the axe, and moved behind the turbine tower so she'd be invisible to him as he approached. She heard the car screech in beside hers. It was a miracle he didn't slide off the road. She heard his footsteps as he clambered up the hill, heard him grunt as he lost his footing and fell in the snow. Then, he was there. She peeked around the tower and watched him as he dug a remote out of his pocked and opened the electrical box. This suggested to Dahlia that there must be multiple sets of controller, that he wasn't necessarily working alone. He ducked into the box, and she heard a switch being flipped. Immediately, the revolutions of the gigantic fan blades slowed towards a stop and the panic and anxiety she'd worked so hard to tamp down seemed to fade.

Then, he bent down and began furiously digging in the snow. Looking for the bag. And the axe. She could hear him cursing under his breath.

She stepped out from behind the tower.

"Looking for this?" she said, holding the axe in front of her as she advanced.

For a moment Leonard only stammered, but then he seemed to gain control and compose himself. He was a tall man, impeccably groomed and dressed, wearing a stylish black overcoat. He had a healthy head of silver hair. Everything about him spoke to his wealth and power.

"Miss Crane," he said. Of course, he knew who she was. She imagined that Malinda had told him something of their earlier encounter.

"Yes," she said through clenched teeth. "I believe you were acquainted with my mother."

He hesitated for a moment, then said, "I was."

"Why did you kill her?"

His brows narrowed into an unconvincing performance of mock concern. "I swear to you, I'd never do such a thing. She was just an acquaintance of mine, many years ago. That's all."

"There's more to it than that and you know it, you son of a bitch."

Even as Maximoff's face reshaped itself into a placating smile, a mask of insincerity and condescension, his hand dipped towards his pocket.

Without thinking she stepped forward and swung the axe quickly at his legs. His eyes widened and he inhaled quickly, anticipating agony. The head of the axe, the blunt end, collided with his legs. She'd spun it mid-flight, deciding in a split second that she wasn't ready to use the sharp end. Still, the blow landed hard. He grunted and crumpled into the snow. He clutched his leg and groaned in pain.

"Dammit, girl," he said.

"Toss it in the snow, asshole," she said, raising the axe high, aiming it for his forehead. "The gun."

His face twisted with pain, the hand in the pocket emerged with a small pistol lying sideways across his palm. She could see it in his eyes. He was thinking about risking it and taking the shot. She could imagine the calculations he was running. Could he drop her before she swung the axe at her head? Maybe he was questioning his speed, his accuracy.

"Last chance," she said, and then let the axe drop a few inches, a quick lurch. His eyes widened and he tossed the pistol aside.

But even in that moment, he was calculating. The pistol landed in the snow a few feet away from him. Just beyond his reach. She saw his eyes dart over, assessing the situation. The pistol had disappeared into the snow but had left a ruffled spot where it had broken the surface. His eyes were alive, calculating. Could he dive for it? Spin and shoot her?

Dahlia was good at reading people. She could assess their motives, their emotions, could untangle their truths from lies. It was one of her greatest gifts, one developed over a lifetime of feeling insecure around other people, and in that moment she knew just as clearly as if she were reading his mind that he was biding his time, waiting for his chance.

Fine, she thought. *I can use that.* Dahlia knew that, in Maximoff's mind, their confrontation would end with her dead in the snow, crumpled in a heap a few dozen yards from where her mother had been found. She knew that prolonging their interaction put her at distinct risk. He was looking for a chance to kill her. But as long as that was the case, maybe she could get him to talk. In the back of her mind, she could hear Naomi's voice.

If you get killed, I'll never forgive you.

She had to risk it. *Sorry, baby,* she thought.

"Tell me what you know," Dahlia said. "Tell me what happened with my mother. Or next time I'll use the sharpened end. And I suspect you might know how sharp this axe is. And I'll aim for the head. Seems appropriate."

"Fine," he said, making a show of being grudging in his compliance. It was a performance. She could see the wheels turning. *Let her think she's got me. Then, when I get my chance...* She was counting on that mindset keeping him talking. "Your mother was a hanger-on. She was trashy. Low class. But she wormed her way into our circle."

Dahlia could feel the onrush of blood to her head as anger filled her like a fire, but she repressed any reaction. She knew the venom on Maximoff's voice was real. In his world, he looked down on those he considered low class. People without money. But that wasn't the whole story. But she'd found her wedge. His class-snobbery had motivated him to reveal the first bit of information. He had so looked down on her mother that he felt no guilt for her murder and no compunction about assassinating her character decades after the fact.

"Wormed her way?" she said, suppressing her rage as she dangled her bait. "I mean, you were all young people, right? How was she different than the rest of you."

As she'd predicted, Maximoff couldn't resist. He scoffed. "The fact that you could even ask that tells me all I need to know about *you.* She had no class. Didn't belong in our circle. I knew it from the beginning. She was a flirt and a tease. Trying to sleep her way into a better situation for herself."

Another wedge to be levered. A flirt and a tease. Sleeping her way to the top. This was the key to what had happened. Dahlia's brain, her reactions, were so compartmented at that point that she felt almost lightheaded. Part of her brain was piecing it together, dangling bait, part of her was grieving for her mother, and a part of her was as angry as she'd ever been. Part of her wanted to swing that axe one more time.

"A flirt and a tease," she said and then, piecing it together as the words came out of her mouth. "It was Lark, wasn't it?"

"Bill got frisky with her one night at a party." Maximoff said this dismissively, as if "getting frisky" wasn't such a big deal. But she could read between the lines. Of course it was. It made sense. The passage, promising hellfire to killers, spoke to guilt. So did his conversion, which followed the first murder. Lark had killed her mother and spent the rest of his life struggling with it.

"When was this?"

Maximoff paused for a second. "Sixty-six, I think. February. Anyway, she was acting all coy and cute and Bill went for her. She went and called it rape but," he shrugged it away. "They were drinking together. She was flirting. To be honest, I think she was asking for it."

Dahlia imagined the real story. An insecure girl, unused to attention, trying to fit in. Flattered, vulnerable. Maximoff was blaming the victim. Of course he was. He had to blame the victim in order to remain the good guy in his own head.

"Go on," she said between clenched teeth.

"Word got out and your mother ran away. Her reputation was shot in the town. Her fling with respectability was over. People saw her for what she was." Dahlia pieced together the timeline in her head. When she'd fled from Mount Hugh, she'd gone to raise Dahlia on her own. That had been the beginning of the change in her mother too. She'd began to drink. To use drugs. To lose her grip. Because of what these people did to her. She'd been crushed. But had she been mad too? "She came back, though, didn't she?"

"Looking for a handout," Maximoff said. "She called it 'financial support,' but I'd call it extortion. Blackmail."

"From Lark?"

Maximoff nodded. "Of course. He was the one she blamed so he was the one she came for."

Of course. It wasn't a matter of Lark's guilt. It was a matter of the fact that she had dared to hold him accountable. But Dahlia knew that wasn't all. The passage she'd read in the Quran, promising hell to murderers. The spine of the book had been cracked, permanently marking the page. The passage, highlighted, pored over. It spoke to Lark's guilt, as did his conversion.

"He killed her." Not a question really. A statement. As she said it, she knew it was true. On a level she was glad to know, but on another it was horribly disappointing. There would be no confrontation, no justice, with the man who had killed her mother. He was already dead.

"Bill was a different man back then," Maximoff said. "You didn't know him. He had a temper. Didn't mess around. Wasn't going to some tramp manipulate him. Threaten his money. His marriage."

Dahlia had to admit, she'd almost bought it. As astute a judge of character as she was, she'd not seen through Lark's gentle demeanour. That was a persona constructed out of guilt. Atonement? Or a con?

"And then you stepped in," she said. "To help him cover it up. With the turbines."

"You know about that?" Maximoff said, for a moment, sincerely surprised.

"I do," she said. "The ghost frequencies. That's why I was here."

"When we'd been putting up the turbines, when I was in the field running tests, I hit on this one speed. When you ran the blade at that speed, you'd get freaked out. I hit on it by accident." As he talked, his fingers crept along the surface of the snow, slowly, barely perceptibly, inch by inch, towards the gun buried in the snow. By the time she noticed it, he'd already positioned his arm a foot closer. If he lunged, he could have it in his hand in a single move. "I felt like I was losing my mind, and I could see workers in a nearby field doing the same. Running in terror from something that wasn't there. I learned not to run the turbine at that speed and had pretty much forgotten about it until that night."

"And you used it to cook up your cover story. The myth of Hugh Slaughter."

As he continued, Maximoff sounded almost proud of himself, as if the most important thing in the story was his cleverness. "It was my idea was to turn the murder into a myth. A fairytale. I ran this turbine at the magic speed for a while that night so the people would have nightmares then dressed up the body so it would look like a ritualistic murder. In the weeks that followed, Malina and I started seeding the fairytale around town. Hugh Slaughter. I'd say it like it was something I'd heard someone else say, something I was repeating, and soon everyone was saying it."

Maximoff's hand crept closer and closer towards the gun's location. Dahlia pretended not to notice, but she could feel her heartbeat, feel the blood racing in her head. She had him on the line, had almost everything she needed, but she had to keep him talking…

"And you used your money to shut down the story?"

"The police chief was happy to take a handout. So were the editors at these small town papers." Dahlia had seen that the results had been effective.

"I know the rest," she said. "Lark couldn't live with himself. Had a religious conversion. Changed to a life of peace. Maybe he wanted to turn himself in? But you blackmailed him. Threatened to take him down, his family. Used him. Increased your own power and fortune. That it?"

"That's not exactly how I'd characterize it," he said. "But I did what I could to protect myself." The hand dipped down into the snow. Maximoff made it look like he'd lost his balance, like he'd thrust out his hand to catch himself, counting on the fact that she wasn't thinking about the gun. But she was. She hadn't forgotten for a second.

Keep him talking, she thought. If you can just keep him talking for a little longer…

"And somehow, recently, Eleanor found out."

She could see his hand moving under the surface of the snow. Seeking the pistol.

Leonard nodded affirmation. "She'd been the only one that could ever really stand your mom. No idea why. Maybe she felt sorry for her. But she found out. That's why she and Malinda had their falling out. Malinda had always seen your mom for what she was. Eleanor couldn't move past it and was pushing to reopen the investigation. She'd been diagnosed with cancer. Had less than a year. I think she'd always known but decided it was time to come clean. To have us turn ourselves in."

"And you killed her," Dahlia said. "Reproduced the murder. Started up the turbine to sow the seeds of panic. To get the locals repeating the myth."

"This time you're wrong," he said. "It was Bill. Years of his devout life didn't change who he was in his core. When Eleanor threatened his freedom, he snapped, same as he had all those years ago. That's the difference between me and Bill. He was a creature of emotion. They'd get out of hand and he'd react. I am a man of rational action."

Rational, yes. Calculating. "So, you covered it up. Again. Ran the turbines. Set dressed the scene so it'd look like a ritual."

"That's right," he said, admitting to his part. But was there a gleam of triumph in his eyes? Was his hand, still beneath the snow, wrapped around the pistol.

"But the investigation got too close," she said. "And Lark couldn't be trusted. He'd managed to suppress his guilt over the first murder by converting. By living a pious life. But now he'd killed again. Someone close to him. You knew he'd crack eventually. So, you killed him. Not an act of passion but, as you said, the act of a rational calculating man."

"I did what I had to." Maximoff seemed almost relaxed. Confident.

"But you got in over your head. Too much suspicion was on you for Lark. So, you cooked up the murder at the Watering Hole. To throw us off your track."

"I was going to meet up with Peter there, but showed up early in the ski mask and went after the bartender with a knife. Cut Peter and then myself. Made it look like I'd stepped in."

He was revealing everything now. Like he had the upper hand.

He definitely had the gun. Under the snow, she was certain his finger was wrapped around the trigger.

"To eliminate yourself as a suspect?"

"Yes. And make it look like the murders were random. Not all tied to my immediate social circle. Congratulations. You figured it out. You can put the axe down. I'm ready to surrender. Turn myself in. You got me."

Put the axe down.

She saw it. She'd waited too long. He had the gun in his hand and would fire the moment she put down the axe. She'd waited too long, had backed herself into a corner, where her only options were to swing the axe or risk him shooting her. She lifted the axe again, aimed it squarely between his eyes.

"Put it down," he said gently, soothingly. "Do it for your mother. She wouldn't want you to go down this path." It was, definitively, the wrong thing to say, evoking her dead mother, the mother in whose death he was culpable. Dahlia felt the constraints with which she'd controlled her anger slipping.

"You have no idea what my mother would want," she said, suddenly overwhelmed with rage. It would be so easy to let the axe fall. Just let gravity start the job. Stop resisting its pull. Then maybe, apply the strength of her muscles towards the downward momentum. The easiest thing in the world. And wouldn't that be justice? Besides, what other choice did she have? The confusion and disorientation that had been swirling around in her head, overtook her. So many emotions. So complex. It was like a dam had burst and all of the self-control with which she had been acting was washed away and in the aftermath, it was all so clear. She *had* to do it. She owed it to her mother, to all of the people of Mount Hugh who had suffered...

She just had to swing it down, to bring it down with all of the strength in her arms, and end it. It was the only way. Her vision seemed to narrow, it was as if darkness or flames were crowding her field of view into a small circle of existence right in front of her. Maximoff. She willed her arms to funnel their strength into swinging the bladed implement.

"Put down the axe!"

The command wasn't coming from Maximoff. She looked over. Aaron Grayson had spoken. He stood halfway up the hillside, his gun drawn, aimed at her.

"It's okay," Elijah said, standing behind his partner. "We heard everything."

CHAPTER TWENTY
THAWED

"It's over," Grayson said, his voice echoing in the crisp air. "Drop the axe or I swear to God, I'll shoot you."

"If it's going to be over, it has to be me," Dahlia said. She sounded odd, strangely unemotional, as if hollowed out inside. The axe hovered above her head, ready to be released. "He has a gun. It's the only way."

Maximoff's eyes widened. His hand came up out of the snow and he tossed a pistol away from him.

"I'm unarmed gentlemen," he said. Elijah saw the move for what it was; perhaps Maximoff had been about to shoot Dahlia, but he now recognized that he was outnumbered.

"I'm the only one that can end it," Dahlia said. "I have to end it."

Elijah could see Grayson squinting, steadying his aim.

"No," Elijah said softly, quietly enough that only Grayson could hear him. "Let me talk to her."

"You've got a minute," Grayson growled under his breath. "But if she makes any sudden moves, I'm taking her down."

Elijah moved towards her, his hand outstretched. As he approached her, he noticed that her eyes were moist, tears welling up. "It's okay, Dahlia," he said. "We got him. You don't need to do this."

"Do we?" she said with an audible hint of hysteria. "Think about it. His money, his influence, has protected him so far. He paid off the authorities to ignore the case. He's paid his way out of trouble for years. They're all corrupt."

"That aint us, honey," Aaron growled. "This rich asshole doesn't sign *my* checks. Put the axe down before I put a bullet in you."

Elijah glared at his partner, annoyed. It wasn't the time for threats, but Grayson only had one approach. "Let us do our job, Dahlia. His money won't protect him now. We'll put him away and he'll never see the light of day."

The axe wavered but remained raised. At her feet, Maximoff crouched, his eyes sharp, like a cornered animal looking for an opening. The dam broke and tears rolled down Dahlia's cheeks.

"He's killed," she said. "He's terrorized this town. They're living in fear because of him. There have been heavy consequences for everybody *except* him."

"He'll get his," Grayson said. "But so will you if you don't stand down."

"Grayson," Elijah said, in a rare moment of stark defiance. "I got this."

At that moment, Elijah heard a click, then the sound of an engine powering up. For a moment, he looked around, trying to piece together what was happening. He looked up at the turbine as its blades began to move, grinding into motion and picking up speed quickly. Puzzled, he looked down; the click had been much closer. He saw a simple remote controller in Leonard's hand, like a tv remove but simpler. Just a few buttons. It looked jury rigged. In a second, Elijah puzzled it out. Of course he had a controller. He needed to be able to start the blades at will.

But this was the last coherent thought Elijah was able to manage, for the blades, now spinning at a high rate of speed, dangerously fast, as if they might shear themselves from the turbine, sent a shockwave of panic into his mind. It was almost as if the blades themselves were blowing his perceptions from his mind, slicing his composure and focus into ribbons. The fear hit him hard, like an earthquake, and he fell to his knees. He'd felt it before, but this was different. They were, after all, merely feet from the turbine. As Elijah went down, he noticed, out of the corner of his eye, Elijah dropped his gun and also begin to lose his footing. Dahlia still stood, still held the axe tremblingly aloft, but her eyes darted wildly around, expressive of rampant paranoia.

It's not real, Elijah thought. *Nothing to be afraid of.*

But he was afraid. Of everything. Of nothing. The fear was vast, undifferentiated, overwhelming.

He was afraid of this father, reliving scenes from childhood. He was afraid of losing his family, his daughter, his wife. He was afraid of Grayson. Of Dahlia, turning the axe on him. Of the spinning blades, shearing off and impaling him as they fell to the earth.

Looking up, he saw Maximoff standing. It took effort, he could see that, but as everyone else was overcome, Maximoff managed to find his footing. Through the noise the effect had on his consciousness, Elijah managed to wonder: had Maximoff so frequently exposed himself to the effect of the blades that he had developed a tolerance, or was it his drive to escape, to survive, that allowed him to overcome it?

Whatever the case, Maximoff stood and wrenched the axe from Dahlia's hands and, as an extension of the same move, brought its blunt end swiftly into her chest. With a gasp she fell on her back, then collapsing into sobs.

Having had a moment to recover, Elijah managed to get his feet under him. Standing, he saw Leonard running away, up the snowy hill. He looked over at Grayson who was blinking the fear and confusion away. Grayson looked up the hill and saw Maximoff's retreating form.

"Let's get that bastard," Grayson said. The words tore harshly out of him, as if he had to force them. Elijah understood. He was under the same pressure, a psychological disturbance so strong it felt physical. Like gravity or some other fundamental force. As Elijah forced himself to ignore the sensations and move up the hill, it felt like he was trudging through something holding his legs down. The feeling reminded him of something he'd experienced in nightmares as a child. No matter how hard he tried to pump his legs, they didn't seem to want to work.

Suddenly, the fear, the anxiety and paranoia, moved beyond the generalized. Haunting voices from Elijah's past called to him.

It's your fault…

"Father?" Elijah muttered. Although his memories of his father were dim, he recognized the voice. Blaming him. For his mother's deportation. For risking the family's finances on his dreams. For what he is.

You'll never be a man, the voice said, *you're weak.*

"You're not real," Elijah said. "You're dead. Gone." It was the same voice that had shaped his life. Everything he was had been defined *against* the pressure of a harsh and unloving father. And although Elijah was proud of the man he was, the man he had singlehandedly shaped himself to be, it did gall him that his father had been such an influence, albeit a negative one. He didn't want to be such a product of the man. To that very day, it shaped his relationships. The way he had to prove his strength, while still setting himself apart from the type of masculinity the old man represented. Recently, this had manifested itself in his relationship with his partner. Grayson had stirred up all of Elijah's insecurities, and their relationship mirrored his relationship with his father. Grayson had become a sort of stand in and, in spite of himself, Elijah had brought the baggage of his childhood to the partnership.

Looking over at Grayson, he could see that his partner was being haunted by something unseen as well. Voices from the past? Phantoms come to haunt him? Characteristically, Grayson's emotions manifested as rage. He did look afraid, terrified in fact, but rather than being overwhelmed by it, shutting down or trying to escape, he lashed out defiantly, turning his head down the hill, eyes focusing on nothing apparent, and snarled. "Damn you, Larry. Stop hounding me! Will it never be enough?"

Larry? Elijah had no idea but was glad for the momentary distraction. Observing Grayson's own struggle with the ghosts of his past had diverted his attention from his own. Attempting to build some momentum, Elijah forced a single thought into his head. The answer to his father's criticisms. The answer to his life: a simple phrase that he knew, on some level, was true although he was endlessly beset by doubts and residual trauma.

I am a man, he thought to himself. *I am strong.*

He knew it to be true. He was a better man than his father had ever been. His father had been angry, fragile. But that's not the same as being strength. Sure, it's often mistaken for it, but often the loudest voices, barking out in anger like wild dogs, were merely masks for underlying insecurities. Elijah knew this. He knew that his dad's anger was weakness rather than strength. The same must be true of Aaron too. Seeing him struggling up the hill, haunted by voices from his own past, seemed to prove this. No, Elijah wasn't weak. His only problem was that he left others cause him doubt as to this fact.

His footsteps grew lighter. No longer did he feel like he was trudging through three feet of glue. Halfway up the hill, as his head cleared, he realized that he could have simply turned off the turbine, but the desire to move, to flee, had been too strong, his rational mind stirred into confusion. In any case, it was too late. If he turned down the hill and back to the turbine, he'd be giving Maximoff time to escape.

Grayson seemed to have recovered more quickly, almost as if his angry reaction was the fuel driving his engine, his rage giving him the strength to push himself, one step in front of the other, up the snowy slope. Elijah could see it in his face, the set of his jaw. He was pissed. Although Grayson's angry reactions contributed to some of his questionable decision-making, in this case, it was welcome.

Go with it, Elijah thought. *Let it drive you. Get that bastard.*

But at the top of the slope was a treeline, and as Grayson's angry feet pushed him to the summit, Maximoff suddenly leapt out from behind a large oak. He'd been lying in wait. An ambush, and Grayson had walked right into it. He swung the axe at Grayson, and the older detective ducked back, narrowly avoiding the weapon's sharpened blade but losing his balance in the process. Grayson's gun flew from his hand, disappearing from view upon impact with the hill's snowy surface and Grayson himself, having shifted his center of balance, slid backwards, his legs flying out from under him. He skidded backwards on his back, suddenly frictionless on the sharply sloping hillside.

For a moment, Grayson saw a childish look of triumph on Maximoff's face as he looked down. Here was a man used to getting his way, having made it through life thinking rules didn't apply to him. Dahlia was certainly right in a sense. The man had bought his way out of trouble and has presumably never had to face a consequence. Elijah raised his own gun, but hesitated. He had never shot a man before.

Just do it, he thought, but in that moment couldn't bring himself to. He was unable to determine if he was facing natural and sincere doubt or if his doubts were still being compelled and magnified from the sinister effect of the turbine's blades, that unearthly frequency that somehow dredged the fear and weakness from the subconscious of anyone within earshot. Instead, he continued up the hill, trying to find strength. If Grayson's rage could propel his feet, then perhaps Elijah's sense of duty could do the same. Within a few seconds he was upon Maximoff who had, perhaps, tarried a moment too long exulting in his triumph. Elijah could see that he was winded from the trek up the hill.

"Put it down," Elijah said. "Drop it or I shoot." He didn't know if he would or not. Could he pull the trigger when the moment came? Although his words echoed the threat Grayson had made to Dahlia at the bottom of the hill, there was a difference. When Grayson threatened to shoot, you could hear it in his voice that the threat was real. He *would* follow through. In his own voice, it sounded more like a question. An attempt at negotiation.

Presumably hearing the same thing, Maximoff smirked, saying, "I don't think you will detective." Upslope, Maximoff was well placed. The king of the hill. Without another word, he swung the axe. Elijah leaned to the left and the axe swung past his midsection, zipping closely enough that he could feel its passage as a hint of wind on the chill wintry air. Immediately it came back around, this time aimed directly at Elijah's head. This time he ducked and if he'd been a second slower, the axe would have struck him in the temple. Having learned from his partner's misstep, Elijah was determined not to undermine his footing, but the consequence of this was his only option to avoid the arcs of the axe head was leaning in either direction or ducking. Diving would run the risk of sending himself sprawling down the hill, down to where Grayson was still trying to find his footing. Elijah lifted his gun. He had a shot. It was easy. Maximoff was mere feet away. He couldn't miss if he tried. The smug millionaire's chest was exposed. Center mass. An easy shot.

But he couldn't.

He heard an echo in his head. An angry male voice.

You're weak. When it comes down to it you don't have the balls to do what needs to be done?

Was it his father or Grayson?

The moment passed. The axe swung again, this time aimed directly at Elijah's hesitating hands. This time, Elijah didn't have time to react strategically. He'd been taken off guard, distracted by the voice in his head, undoubtedly put there by the mysterious spell of the turbine. Instead, his hands spasmed back at the last second. The axe missed his wrist, missed severing his hands by inches, and instead struck his service revolver along the gun barrel. Had his finger instinctively pulled the trigger, it would have all been over, but it didn't and instead the gun was knocked from his hands, to spiral off to the side.

Without thinking, Elijah lunged forward, his hands grasping for the axe. Soon, both men held it, four hands overlapping each other in their grasps across the handle. Elijah put his full strength into trying to wrench it from his opponent's grasp and while he felt that he was undoubtedly in better shape than the older Maximoff, more fit and trained, Maximoff seemed to be tapping into some resource of strength. Was it desperation? Arrogance? Maximoff was capable of murder; who knew what else he could manage?

The two struggled, each yanking on the axe handle, pulling each other two and fro in their attempts to gain control. And all the while, the voices intruded, forcing themselves into Elijah's head. It threw his mentality off balance, destabilizing his focus. If he was going to lose, it would be through this disadvantage. Clearly, Maximoff was less susceptible to the turbine's effects. Indeed, at this point, he didn't seem to be affected at all. For Elijah it was another story.

His father: *You're nothing. A disappointment. You'll never be anything.*

His mother. Saying goodbye. Deported. *Because of you.* Again, his father.

Grayson. *You don't have what it takes kid. You've got no backbone.*

He even heard his beloved wife's voice, telling him that he was letting the family down. *We need you, Elijah.... why aren't you doing more for us?* This wasn't a voice of the past, not a real complaint, but his deepest fear manifested into something that, in that moment, *felt* completely real. He worried about his duties as a husband, a father. His own father's harsh approach had instilled this kernel of doubt that wouldn't go away. Was Elijah truly a man? A husband? A father? When it came down to it, could he do what needed to be done? A man's duties?

Under this assault, imposed from outside but seemingly originating within his head, Elijah weakened. His grip faltered. His hands began to lose their strength.

Maximoff began to get the upper hand.

For Elijah, he was losing focus. Almost forgetting where he was.

Helen... Elijah pictured his wife, her brows narrowed in concern for the security of the family.

Dora... His beloved daughter. Beautiful. Innocent. An angel. Only two years old. Helpless. To his disordered mind, his failures were endangering her. Making her unsafe. Threatening her with neglect. Starvation.

Maximoff wrenched the axe free. For a moment he lost his balance, Elijah's loss of grip sending him plunging backwards.

No!

Elijah wouldn't let the turbine determine his fate. He wouldn't let it so instil his mind with doubts that he'd fall before this arrogant manipulator. That was the problem. People like Maximoff had the luxury of confidence. It was easy when everything was handed to you. But people like himself, Dahlia, even Grayson... They struggled. They had doubts. The good people had doubts. But he wasn't going to believe the lies of the turbines and the voices in his head. Lies that had originated in childhood with his unloving father.

Elijah was strong. He was a man. And he would be damned if he'd ever let his family down.

He felt it. Rising. Like a wave to be ridden, one of righteous anger to lift him above the fear. He channelled the anger into his hands and threw a punch, striking Maximoff across the face. Another landing in his gut. A third, an uppercut, striking Maximoff under the nose, sending him tumbling back, the axe dropping from his hand.

Elijah had opened the door, letting the anger in. Was this what it felt like for Grayson in every waking moment? He didn't know, but he had to admit, if he was being honest with himself, that it felt good.

He advanced upon Maximoff, now lying in the snow.

"It's over," Elijah said, out of breath, his lungs burning with exertion.

But Maximoff was smiling.

"You're a fool," Maximoff said, then Elijah saw it. A gun in the corrupt tycoon's hand. Elijah's own gun. Apparently Maximoff had stumbled across it in the snow when he'd fallen. For a moment, Elijah was overwhelmed with the unfairness of it. What kind of world was it where men like Maximoff get away with everything, protected by their wealth and privilege, and even now fate seemed to smile upon him?

"Put it down," Elijah said. "You're going away. That's a certainty. Don't make it harder on yourself."

Maximoff stood off, brushing snow from his coat with one hand while he held the gun steadily trained on Elijah with the other. His laugh was harsh.

"You really believe that?" he said steadying the gun, his finger poised on the trigger. "A certainty? The outcome is certain, sure. There *is* only one was this can end."

As if completing the sentence, describing the preordained outcome: a gunshot. Then another.

A bullet tore into Maximoff's chest. Another struck him in the right leg. He fell backwards into the snow, the red of his blood staining the white powder.

Elijah turned. Dahlia stood there, eyes narrowed, holding Grayson's gun, smoke still wafting from its barrel. He remembered the tense exchange with her only a few moments before. She'd said that Maximoff would get away with it if she didn't do something. It had almost happened.

"You can stop shooting," he said. "He's down."

She nodded numbly and let the barrel of the gun dip towards the ground.

Grayson had made it to the top of the hill. Wordlessly, he held out his hand and Dahlia gave him his gun. Elijah expected him to be angry. A civilian discharging a police officer's gun was as out-of-protocol as it got. But instead, Grayson grinned.

"Nice shooting," he said.

Elijah stepped over to Maximoff.

"Did I kill him?" Dahlia asked. He couldn't tell from her voice what she hoped the answer was.

"No," Elijah said. "You hit him once in the leg and one grazed his chest. He's passed out from shock, and he'll definitely feel the pain when he wakes up, but there's nothing life threatening. He'll survive."

"Yeah," Grayson said. "Then he'll spend the rest of his life behind bars."

A few hours later, Elijah and Grayson stood under the clearing sky at Malinda's house as she was taken into a squad car by the local police. She was being arrested for being an accomplice to the crimes. And the charges to her *would* stick. They'd make sure of that.

It had been a much different scene when Maximoff was arrested, of course. He was unconscious. They'd radioed in for aid from police and paramedics to the location of the turbine after first, of course, disabling the turbine. Grayson was of the mindset to take the axe to the controls of the wicked device, but Elijah coaxed him into waiting. It wouldn't do to damage the property, even if it belonged to a known murderer. Best to not give Maximoff's defense team anything to bring up in trial. Instead, they called a local judge to get an order to decommission the turbines until their danger could be studied. When the paramedics arrived, they got him in a stretcher and, with some difficulty, down the snow-covered hill. The team took him to the hospital and Elijah and Grayson followed. They were on hand when he was taken into the hospital for treatment, revived. They arrested him on the spot and left him handcuffed to his hospital bed with an armed guard. The hospital had been overrun with people feeling the effects of the turbine, people having panic attacks, undergoing accidents while overcome. More than one person had been driven into cardiac arrest by the incident. Still, Elijah noticed a feeling of relief, of restore normalcy among the local populace, underlining the important work they'd done that day. They'd freed them of the curse of the turbines, and they'd never have to suffer its effects again.

At Malinda's, she complained and threatened and begged but the two officers merely watched stony faced as she was cuffed and the officers on the scene led her to the back seat. Hers were the typical complaints of the smug and privileged when they were finally faced with consequences from their actions.

As Malinda was driven away, Fawn and Peter watched in stunned silence.

"How about us?" Peter asked grimly.

"Well, you are free to go about your business," Grayson said. "We haven't uncovered any connection to the crimes."

"Of course not," Peter said. The boy looked rough. His eyes were red and he choked back tears, a mix of confused emotions playing over his face. Elijah felt very bad for the young man. He'd certainly made mistakes and bad decisions, but he'd been through a lot. Grayson didn't seem to share his sympathy. "He killed my parents," Peter continued.

Elijah looked over to Fawn, who had remained quiet. She didn't look sad. It was hard to say what was going on in her head. Her eyes darted around. Panicked, desperate. For a moment Elijah wondered if she had been involved but it seemed unlikely. No, the more reasonable explanation was she was frantic, realizing that her life, and the benefits she reaped from her parents' fortune, was likely to change.

"But what about *us*?" he repeated, looking over at Fawn for guidance. She nodded, encouraging him to speak. Clearly it was something they'd discussed.

"I don't get your meaning," Grayson said dismissively.

"Our *money,*" Fawn said, frustrated.

"Yes," Peter said, picking up the thread. "Her family and my family. Their assets."

"Oh," Grayson said smugly. "You're worried about your allowance? Well, Fawn, your folks are going to be sinking a lot into lawyers for their murder defense, I'd imagine. And for both of you, expect your family fortunes to be under attack. Your parents casually, and seemingly knowingly, stuck up towers that have caused an ongoing public health threat for decades. There are going to be lawsuits. Probably from the city whose finances were impacted by the turbines, as well as a class action from the affected public. Anticipating an attempt to move assets around to avoid the fallout, we've already got an order from a judge freezing all assets."

Elijah watched their faces fall, exhibiting an impact greater than he'd ever seen from them. Parents killed, parents arrested, none of it hit as hard as the loss of the fortune.

"So, what do we do?" Peter asked, sounding lost.

"Well, you might think about getting a job," Grayson said sarcastically. "Or go back to school if that works for you. Try to make a better go of it, this time. And don't expect the fancy houses to stick around for long either. It's all going to go away."

"We'll be out on the street," Fawn shrieked. "Get a job? How? What am I supposed to do? We won't be able to afford rent."

"Maybe see if they're hiring down at the Watering Hole," Grayson said with a smirk.

Back in their car, Elijah noticed that his older partner couldn't start grinning.

"That was pretty satisfying, wasn't it?" Elijah asked, his own face warming into a similar grin.

"You're damned right, it was," Grayson said. "Feel like I've been waiting for a long time to take this crew down a couple of notches."

"I agree," Elijah said. "It's cathartic."

Immediately, he regretted the choice of words and braced himself for a reaction, anticipating that Grayson wouldn't be able to resist. He could almost hear him. "Cathartic? What's that?" Even if he knew, Grayson would feign ignorance. He hated know-it-all, hated fancy language. It was all part of his persona. His crusty old cop schtick. "One of them ten-dollar-words," he'd say.

But, no. Instead, Grayson looked over at him with what looked suspiciously like approval. Warmth, even.

"Listen, Elijah," he said. "Thanks. Seriously, kid. We wouldn't have pulled this off without you. Even though we didn't see eye-to-eye every step of the way, the push and pull, the clashing ideas, was necessary I think to get to the finish line. To put it simply, I guess we make a pretty good team."

"We do," Elijah said. "I know I pushed back against you a few times. Maybe made some mistakes. Didn't take you – or your instincts – seriously enough. But you know your stuff. I appreciate all of your guidance, even when delivered harshly."

Grayson laughed. "I gotta be me," he said.

Elijah, too laughed. "Well, I think we get each other now. And I'd love to keep working to you." Earlier in the week, Elijah would have been surprised to hear himself saying the words, but things had changed. Maybe it was the experience on the hillside, beset by ghosts of the past while closing out the case, but Elijah felt like his understanding of his partner and their relationship had fundamentally shifted.

Grayson wasn't his father. Not at all. Maybe he presented himself similarly. Both men had a damaged center of anger. But Elijah's father had been cold on the inside. Lifeless, dead, compassionless. Grayson was anything but. He could be harsh, and he could be a pain in the ass, but he *was* fundamentally a good person. On the right side. Maybe Elijah's trauma over his relationship with his dad had made it hard to see that, but now he did.

"Absolutely, kid," Grayson said with an unusually sincere smile. "We're partners for the long haul. So, listen, what say we head back into the city? I don't want to waste another day in this town."

"Sounds good to me," Elijah said and the two headed back to the hotel.

"You pack up kid," Grayson said, dropping him off. "I'm going to swing by to the local cops to fully debrief them on everything that's happened today for their records. Gotta make sure they don't drop the ball on this case. Should be back in about ten minutes."

"Won't you need to pack?" Elijah asked.

"I never *un*packed, kid," Grayson said. "My shit is ready to go."

Elijah didn't take long getting his suitcase ready. He was happy to leave too. Although he felt some satisfaction with the outcome of the case, his stay in Mount Hugh had left a bad taste in his mouth. Faced with such corruption and such obstruction from all sides, from the perpetrators, those in their circle, and most of the local population as well. Sure, the turbines were partially to blame for the strange mentality of the locals, but Elijah couldn't help but also blame general small-mindedness.

There was one person, however, who he'd miss.

He saw her in the lobby, dropping off her key, pulling a suitcase with wheels and a long handle.

"Dahlia!" he said.

She turned, smiling, but with a lot behind it. Sadness, damage, something bittersweet. Perhaps her own catharsis.

"Hey, Elijah," she said, grinning as if in spite of herself.

"Listen," he said. "I just want to thank you for everything. Your work, your ideas, your humanitarian impulses, helping people with no reward. For putting up with Aaron Grayson. For saving my life." He could feel that this little speech was a sort of echo of the one Grayson had given him in the car, but there was so much left unsaid. How to tell her that he felt that she was a kindred spirit? That she felt like a long-lost sister?

"Thank you," she said. "And likewise. It's been good working for you."

"I see you're ready to get out of here," he said.

"I am," she said. "I have a woman who loves me at home. It's killing me that I can't vent to her. That I can't seek comfort in her arms."

Elijah, for his part, understood. He missed Helen and would definitely be taking some time to revel in the comfort of her affection.

"Are you okay?" he asked. "After today?"

"Everything is a process," she said. "I finally have answers. I found the villain in my life, and I confronted him. I have a lot to process. I'll do that with Naomi. Probably with therapists too. It'll take time, but I'll get over it. Hopefully, for the first time in my life I can really move on from the damage of my childhood."

Elijah was tempted to say that he felt the same way but wasn't sure if that was a conversation he was ready to get into. Instead, he said, "You know, for what it's worth, I'm always just a phone call away if you need any support. If you need anything at all. Maybe you can Naomi can come for dinner sometime? I'd love for you to meet my wife and the little one."

Dahlia brightened at this prospect and, quickly accepting it, exchanged numbers with Elijah. Then it was time or seemed to be. Time to say goodbye. Immediately, Elijah regretted those things unsaid. But there was no context for it. How did you tell someone, a stranger who you had no connection to besides working together on a case, that you felt such a connection?

It was Dahlia who tore down the dam. She spoke, her voice suffused with emotion he hadn't heard before. "Mount Hugh *has* changed me, Elijah. I came here not sure what I was looking for, maybe subconsciously seeking answers, and stumbled onto them. I can finally grieve, Elijah. My mother's disappearance, always a big question mark, something I didn't know whether to feel sad or mad or betrayed about, is finally clear. She left me to protect me and I feel like I know her again." Tears rolled down her cheeks.

"She'd be proud of you. Of what you did here," Elijah said. Then, moved by her sincerity, her willingness to expose her vulnerability, he overcame his reticence to reveal his own feelings and continued. "I don't know if you feel it the way I do, but I feel like we have a connection." She didn't answer verbally, but her expression told him she had noticed the same thing. "After my mother was deported, my father blamed me. He blamed me for my ambition. In his mind, we couldn't afford an immigration lawyer because of the money that went to my tuition."

"That's unfair," she said. "To put that pressure on a child. It's a parent's job to make the world better for a child, not to blame the child for the way things are."

"I know," he said nodding. He knew that she was talking as much about her situation as his own. "There are so many unfair pressures put on children when they should be protected and nurtured. And maybe that's why I feel the connection to you. We were both dealt a bad hand by life and we both overcame it."

Dahlia smiled tentatively. "You did," she said. "Whether I have or not remains to be seen."

"Don't sell yourself short," he said. "You said it yourself: it's a process. You're on the road. You'll get there."

"Thanks," she said, then, "Do you still talk to your mother?"

"No," he said, tearing up himself. "She died six months after she was deported. Heart attack. I never heard this definitively, but I am certain that the stress of her situation exacerbated it."

"Oh my God," she said. "That's horrible."

"And I blamed myself," he said. "I mean, my father was blaming me. Part of me knew that it wasn't my fault, but it doesn't matter. My brain can know that, but my *feelings* tell me different. And I can't help it. It affects me. Even to my relationship with Grayson. I handle it worse than I otherwise would because his grumbling reminds me of my dad and sets me off."

"We are the same" Dahlia said. "Screwed over in childhood and left to carry the guilt with us."

Elijah nodded. "I guess we both still have processing to do."

"Yes," she said and then, echoing his words, "but we're getting there. And we can be proud. We did something real here today. Maybe it was our trauma that drove us, my search for answers about my mother and your guilt and questions of self-worth, but we were able to turn that energy towards uncovering what was going on in Mount Hugh."

"You're right about that," he said, musing on how the two of them naturally switched roles, finding strength when the other needed it. Further proof. Although unrelated, they were, in some sense, kin. He leaned in and gave her a hug. Not romantic, but emphatic. Like hugging a sister. He went ahead and said it. "Listen, as far as I'm concerned, we're family, okay? Our own families let us down. But we're in the same boat. We're connected by our past. And what we went through in Mount Hugh. So, we're family to each other, okay?"

"Okay," she said.

"Is that a weird thing to say?" he asked.

"Not at all," she said, hugging harder. "I was thinking the same thing myself."

Out front, a few minutes later, Elijah and Dahlia waited for Grayson to appear. She didn't need to wait, but she felt the need to at least say goodbye, even though the two had never really reconciled.

"Oh, and there she is," Grayson said stepping out of the car, his tone somewhere between joking and insulting. "The thorn in my fucking side."

"Hi there, you old grouch," she said, always able to dish it out.

"So, I guess you're finally done interfering with my investigation."

"Interfering?" he asked. "Do you mean solving your case for you?"

The noise that escaped Grayson was halfway between a laugh and a growl.

"Listen, I want credit on your dissertation," he said. "Don't forget. I was a primary contributor."

"Sure," she said. "But don't hold your breath."

As the car pulled away and Dahlia receded in the distance, Elijah felt some comfort that the case was resolving. Behind the wheel, Grayson boasted about their accomplishment, seeming to forget how fraught the whole affair was when faced with a positive outcome.

"You and me, kid," he said, grinning from ear to ear. "We're going to be famous. Get ready for it. The spotlight. We caught a twisted killer and exposed decades of corruption of two wealthy families. Our names are going to be in national papers. On the radio. They'll be following us around. Celebrity cops."

Elijah couldn't help but be amused. Grayson's gruffness, certainly a point of contention, could be endearing when it wasn't directed at him, and his childlike pleasure at attention was the same. Elijah wondered whether this was what is was all really about for Grayson. He'd been just as driven, in his own way, as Elijah and

Dahlia, but he kept his motivations close to his vest. Sure, it was his job, but there was *something* else behind it. Could it be as shallow as the desire to be famous? Elijah doubted that. In his gut, he wondered if Grayson might be just as damaged as he and Dahlia. Was there some demon from his own childhood he was chasing? In his own way, Grayson also had a strong need for approval. Did he suffer from the same complex as Elijah: a desperation to prove his manhood to the ghost of an unloving father? Musing, he remembered a name: Larry. Whose ghost that *that* been, pursuing Grayson as he scrambled up the hill by the turbine?

"Who is Larry?" Elijah blurted out.

"Larry?" Grayson said. "I don't know. Don't know a Larry."

"You were calling out to one, back by the turbine."

Grayson shrugged. "You're mistaken," he said. "Maybe that was your own hallucination, not mine."

Elijah let the moment pass, but he knew his partner was hiding something. For one thing, based on everything he knew about the effect of the turbine, it dug up psychological ammunition from the past of everyone in earshot. The name "Larry" meant nothing to Elijah, so that couldn't logically be part of a hallucination of his. The other way he knew he was lying was in his eyes. Sure, his mouth had said that it was nothing, but his eyes had told another story. They were haunted.

But that was a mystery for another day.

PREVIEW: THE SOPHOMORE MURDERS

FIVE MONTHS AFTER THE EVENTS OF WHISPERED EULOGY

It was everything he could have hoped for. Everything and more.

Aaron Grayson was a hero and everyone knew it. It had unfolded much as he'd anticipated, with coverage in newspapers, on television and radio. Not just locally either. He'd made national news. He'd heard Dan Rather saying his name on the six o'clock news.

Walking around town, he was recognized. Strangers recognized him, expressing their admiration. Journalist after journalist wanted to talk to him. To interview him, to make profiles. The official story was that it was Aaron Grayson's rebellious ways that had solved the case. His bulldog tenacity that had torn the case wide open and revealed decades of murder and corruption to daylight and scrutiny. Without his well-honed instincts and capacity for action, the whole messy business would still remain uncovered. Journalists called him a role model for other police officers as an example.

Although Elijah shared the spotlight to a certain degree, he was relegated more to Grayson's shadow. It seemed to suit both men. Grayson liked being the spokesperson and although Elijah wasn't denied credit, he didn't have to deal with the press to any great degree. When Grayson asked him about it, Elijah said he was glad to not have to worry about the press ambushing him outside his house. Grayson supposed that made sense for a family man, but to him, any appearance of a reporter or paparazzi thrilled him.

He was finally getting the credit he deserved.

He'd been moved into a bigger office. Had been given a promotion to something they were calling the "special homicide task force." As he walked through the station, his fellow officers sought his favor. Younger officers, rightfully convinced of his status as a role model, curried favor. They asked for his opinion of their cases. They'd ask him, "what does your gut tell you?" echoing a phrase he'd used in more than one interview. Some even called him "Sherlock," mimicking the moniker of "American Sherlock" that had been memorably applied to him in a national weekly newsmagazine.

It was the end of the day and Grayson reclined in his office hair. Nicest one he'd ever had. High back, wheels that than smoothly, comfortably upholstered. The day shift was leaving, and the night shift was coming on. For his part, he liked to stick around until after the shift change. He told himself that it gave him a chance to get to know all of his fellow officers, but if he was being completely honest, perhaps he'd admit it supplied him with a whole other group of admirers, providing him attention to bask in.

Grayson turned on the small tv he kept in the corner of the office. He liked to flip channels while the shift change was happening, enjoying an isolated half hour cool down before emerging to the thrilled greetings of his co-workers. He'd flip looking for press coverage. His name still came up regularly and he loved to see it. Sometimes he'd follow recent celebrity scandals, or unsolved murders at the national level. Not his jurisdiction specifically, but since he was now a national celebrity, it all felt somehow relevant. On this day, he happened across Dahlia being interviews on some academic show on public television about her studies, her PhD which she had received on the basis of her dissertation, her background, and of course the murders.

He laughed at the site of his old rival. "There she goes," he said with a mix of annoyance and mild affection. "Running her mouth as usual."

She got publicity as well, but not all of it was positive. Some viewed her as a clout chaser, trying to publicize her involvement and her upcoming book, an expansion on her dissertation. Others demonized her as an oversexualized adulterer, latching onto her sexual preferences as an excuse to attack her. Although Grayson was old fashioned himself about such matters, he couldn't help but feel annoyed by this. What business of anyone's was that anyway?

They went further, tying her sexuality, her "promiscuous" nature, to the status of her mother as a "fallen" woman, framing her involvement as the child of a woman of low character who had inherited her mother's flaws. Grayson was annoyed to find himself feeling almost protective of her. He hadn't spoke to her since the case resolved but knew that Elijah and she were surprisingly close. As long as it didn't interfere with their work, it was of no concern.

For his part, Elijah had been promoted too, Grayson's closest lieutenant in his new unit. Grayson had met his family and had to admit, it fulfilled something previously missing in his life. Riley's wife was a hell of a woman and that little girl of his was a total sweetheart. She seemed to naturally gravitate towards him. Her smiles warmed his heart, and he decided that little Dora was the one person he could completely drop the grumpy act around.

The middle-aged male interviewer launched into one of those scandal-seeking questions, seeking some connection between his mother's promiscuity and Dahlia's promiscuous lifestyle. Dahlia didn't let it phase her at all, at least as far as you could see. He'd seen her interviewed a number of times. They were hard on her, but she never let them see her sweat. The girl was good in front of the camera.

"Listen," she said. "I'm not sure what you're talking about. I've been with the same person for seven years. Completely faithful."

"Yes, but your relationship…"

"And didn't I read somewhere," she said, cutting off the interviewer's attempt as a tawdry redirect. "That you recently divorced your wife of two decades to start a relationship with a twenty-year-old?"

"Hah!" Grayson blurted out in the office. "That shut him up. Let 'em have it kid." He had to admire her: Dahlia had always been quick with the comebacks. Maybe he *was* warming up to her a little, but he'd never admit it to her face.

There was a quick knock on his door, and it opened without waiting for an answer. It was Elijah.

"Hey Riley," Grayson said. "Thought you'd be done for the day."

"Had a little paperwork."

"How is my girl Dora?" Grayson said. "She keeping you in line?"

"Oh yeah," Elijah said. "She relentless. She asked about you, by the way."

"Oh, did she?" Grayson said, trying for gruff but not pulling it off.

"Yeah. She calls you Gray. She might think you're one of her grandfathers."

"I see," Grayson said. "You don't have to correct her on that if you don't want."

Elijah smiled.

"So, what do you need, kid?" Grayson asked.

"We've got a Dean of Dent University here. He asked for you specifically."

"Dent, huh? Let's see what he wants." Dent was a well-known university in the area. Well-funded and well regarded. Aaron took some satisfaction in the phrase "he asked for you, specifically." He'd heard it a few times in the past few months: a sign that his reputation as the American Sherlock was spreading.

The Dean entered. He was a tall graying man, dressed formally in an expensive looking suit.

"Hello," he said. "I am Dean Crutchfield of Dent University."

"Pleasure to meet you," Grayson said, grabbing the man's hand and giving it a vigorous shake.

"Your reputation precedes you, detective," he said and then, casting a nervous glance over his shoulder at Elijah, said, "is it okay if we speak privately."

"Well, Riley is my right-hand man," he said. "If you can say it to me, you can say it to him."

"I'm sorry," said Crutchfield. "But I really must insist."

For a moment, Grayson considered putting his foot down, but he caught Elijah's eyes. Elijah nodded as if to say, "no worries." He'd brief him later, in any case.

"Fine," Grayson said. "Riley, you can head out."

Once they were alone, Grayson asked, "So, why are you here? And why the secrecy?"

"We've had a murder," said Crutchfield. "This morning. And I wanted you on the case, working to solve it, before the media catches wind of it and tarnishes Dent's reputation."

Although there was a certain appeal – the case sounded high-stakes and high-profile - he couldn't help but ask, "Why me? Why did you insist on talking to me?"

"The victim was the captain of our basketball team," said the Dean. "And his father is one of our primary doners. We have a wing of the library named after him."

"I see. I can understand why it's a sensitive case. Where was the body found?"

"Well, that's part of the reason I think you might be well suited. The body was found at the half-court line of the basketball court. It was a spectacle, almost ritualistic. He way splayed out on the center circle, arms and legs outstretched, almost as if in imitation of DaVinci's Virtuvian man." The Dean handed Grayson a photo. "A note was found at the scene. This photo of it was taken by the forensics team this morning."

The photo pictured a crinkled piece of paper, across it two lines of printed text reading:

In the shadow of Thriller genre,

the Jock exists only to be lost,

a fleeting presence before the real horror takes hold

What the hell? The words meant very little to Grayson.

It was a threat. It implied more to come, that this was merely an opening volley. That it would get far worse. It was bizarre. Inexplicable.

And it was intriguing.

Grayson studied the photo for a moment, then said.

"We're on the case."